"In *Zahara and the Lost Books of Light*, Joyce Yarrow takes her protagonist Alienor Crespo on a dazzling voyage through time, moving between a fictional past and an autobiographical present in a seamless fashion. Yarrow's account of personal loss, search for the self, and her remarkable determination to rescue the past (or what Alienor hopes could be a better past) provide a wonderful and insightful journey into Alienor's own life and into a vividly depicted and long-distant era. It is not only the "lost books" that are recovered in this engaging book, but we come face to face with the many possibilities available to all of us, as we seek to understand the world. These are the possibilities of cooperation between diverse religious and intellectual traditions. These are the possibilities created by mutual understanding, when meaning can be found in both past and present. These are the possibilities that result from the embracing of the intellectual legacies and knowledge of those who came before us. A delightful and thoughtful book."

Teofilo F Ruiz,
Distinguished Research Professor Emeritus of History
and of Spanish and Portuguese
Awarded the National Humanities Medal
by President Barack Obama

"A compelling tale about a woman on a quest about her identity, ancestry, and forbidden past. Ms. Yarrow represents a whole range of historical and contemporary issues in a very engaging style."

Sweta Vikram,
best-selling author of *Louisiana Catch*

"*Zahara and the Lost Books of Light* is an extraordinary entry into another world, compelling, mysterious, and magical. The story is located in today's Spain but the strong echoes of Al-Andalus during the period of the Alpujarras Uprising and the Spanish Civil War bring a reality and a vividness to the narrative that strikes me as very authentic."

Stephan Roman,
former Director of the British Council's cultural programmes in Europe, North America and South Asia and the author of *The Development of Islamic Library Collections in Europe and North America*

"Alienor Crespo, the brave protagonist of Zahara and the Lost Books of Light, is an American journalist with roots in Spain who travels there to explore her origins and finds a treasure, hundreds of volumes saved from the fires of the Inquisition. Thanks to her clairvoyant consciousness Allie learns from her female ancestors how they saved these precious books, living proof of a glorious past when Jews, Muslims, and Christians lived in harmony and their best thinkers produced works vital to our developing civilization. It was the time of the Convivencia (Coexistence) and Joyce Yarrow pays homage to it in this fascinating novel. In the twenty-first century, Allie confronts the enemies of Zahara in the same way her predecessors, Muslims and Sephardic Jews, faced extreme fanaticism during the Middle Ages when the Inquisition shattered the Convivencia, and again during Franco's terror. Ms. Yarrow has created a fiction anchored in historical reality with a fascinating appeal, especially in today's political polarization and ideological fanaticism. *Zahara and the Lost Books of Light* is a page turner that readers will find hard to put down."

Rita Sturam Wirkala,
author of *The Encounter* and *Tales for the Dreamer*

"The best of art is that which brings us into close proximity with our deepest innermost selves, where the Divine One is at its most dear, funny, vulnerable, compassionate, tender, courageous, authentic, sincere. Thank you for taking us there, Joyce Yarrow."

Sura Charlier,
Founder and Director of the
Sufi Universalist Kalyan Center

"Joyce Yarrow has solved the conundrum of time travel with a simple, elegant and entirely believable bit of artifice. Alienor is gifted with *vijitas*, where she is whisked back in time, experiencing key moments in the lives of her female forebears. More often than not, it's a moment of crisis, escaping from the Nazis, inquisitors, or Franco's Guardia. There is also a glimpse of a Golden Age, *La Convivencia*, "the Co-existence", where prior to 1492, Jews, Muslims and Christians lived in harmony. Ms. Yarrow has clearly done her homework, and the details which color the narrative add to the realism of Alienor's *vijitas*. An exciting tale, weaving the past and present on an adventurous journey of discovery."

Jim Metzner,
Author of *Sacred Mounds*

# ZAHARA AND THE
# LOST BOOKS OF LIGHT

# Zahara and the Lost Books of Light

A novel

by

**JOYCE YARROW**

Adelaide Books
New York / Lisbon
2020

ZAHARA AND THE LOST BOOKS OF LIGHT
A novel
By Joyce Yarrow

Published by Adelaide Books, New York / Lisbon
adelaidebooks.org
Editor-in-Chief
Stevan V. Nikolic

For any information, please address Adelaide Books
at info@adelaidebooks.org
or write to:
Adelaide Books
244 Fifth Ave. Suite D27
New York, NY, 10001

ISBN: 978-1-953510-18-1

Printed in the United States of America

# Characters

**Abraham Abulafia** (1240-1291)—founder of the school of Prophetic Kabbalah

**Alienor Crespo**—Seattle journalist

**Carlos Martín Pérez**—Alienor's second cousin

**Celia Martín Pérez Crespo**—Alienor's second cousin

**Eduardo Martín Sanchez**—Celia and Carlos's father, politician

**Hasdai the Seer**—16th century mystic who designs Zahara

**Ibn al-Arabī**—12th century visionary Sufi philosopher

**Idris al-Wasim**—16th century silk-dyer

**Ja'far ibn Siddiqui** (aka Mateo Pérez) Luzia Crespo's guide on the Freedom Trail during WW II

**Jariya al-Qasam** – 16th Century bandit

**Judge Patricia Rubio de Martínez**

**The Librarians of Zahara:**

Celia Martín Crespo – *Tif'eret and Jamal Library of Poetry*

Saleema al-Garnati – *Library of Khalud (Prophecy) Muslim Holy Books*

Malik al-Bakr – *Library of Islamic Sciences*

Reinaldo Luz – *Eternal Library of Babel*

Sufi Rabbi Reb Hakim – *Library of Hokhmah - Mysticism and Wisdom of All Faiths*

Abram Capeluto – *Library of Netsah, Jewish Holy Books*

Suneetha bint Hasan – *Library of Philosophy and the Arts*

Rushd al-Wasim – *Library of Crafts and Animal Husbandry*


**Luis Alcábez**, Alienor's attorney

**Luzia Crespo Laredo** – Alienor's great aunt who marries Ja'far Siddiqui and stays in Spain after World War II ends.

**Mico Rosales**, Alienor's notary

**'Nona' Benveniste Crespo** – Alienor's paternal grandmother and teacher about all things Ladino

**Pilar Pérez Crespo** – Luzia and Ja'far's daughter and Alienor's second cousin

**Razin Siddiqui** – Jariya's companion in arms and eventual husband

**Rodrigo Amado** – Eduardo's colleague

**Stephan Roman** – UNESCO representative

**Todd Lassiter** – Alienor's editor at the Seattle Times

# Prologue

## Granada, Spain—October, 1499

The windows overlooking the Plaza de Bib-Arrambla have been tightly shuttered against the moonlight. Pavestones suffocate under a deluge of books, codices with wooden covers, as well as loose pages heartlessly ripped from their bindings. Hand-written in Arabic, Aramaic, and Hebrew, many of these works are illuminated with gold leaf or inscribed with exquisite calligraphy, only to be thrown together like corpses in a heap. Thousands of tomes lie strewn about the square, stacked as high as the shelves they once occupied in the libraries of Al-Andalus. The poetry of Mohammed Ibn Hani, works of philosophy by Moses Maimonides and commentaries on Aristotle by Ibn Rushd, scientific treatises by Abu Nasr al-Farabi, Muslim and Jewish holy books, all judged as heretical and in equal peril. The smell of incipient violence taints the air.

The forbidden works are to be burned in public view for the purpose of instilling fear. *If you insist on practicing your religion and fail to convert, you will share the same fate.*

Two ethereal forms float under the Arc of the Ears leading into the square. Above them, a dozen severed earlobes caked in blood hang from the keystone, trophies from the day's

---

executions. Ibn al-Arabī, the visionary Sufi philosopher, is clad in a russet brown robe. His piercing eyes are those of a devout skeptic. Beside him glides the Jewish Kabbalist, Rabbi Abraham Abulafia, draped in a flowing white gown with wide sleeves resembling wings. Bearded and wearing tightly-wound turbans, the figures hover above the ground in a diaphanous mist, incorporeal and invisible to the untrained eye. They converse in Arabic, although words are not strictly necessary for teleporting mystics tarrying in a world more than three hundred years beyond their own time.

"Tomorrow, when the sun sets, a million tomes will be set to the torch," laments Ibn al-Arabī. "Countless copies of the Qur'an, immortal love songs and poetry, and works written by Jewish and Muslim scholars on the subjects of philosophy, medicine, religion, history, botany, astronomy, mathematics and geography will soon surrender their wisdom to the fire. I fear *Light of the Intellect* will be among them."

Abulafia surveys the chaos in the square, as if searching for his masterpiece. "So kind of you to worry about my work when your own may well be fated to go up in flames as well."

Ibn al-Arabī gestures at the workmen erecting the wooden ramparts upon which the words of their brethren will soon perish. "Tell me, Abraham, is there no way we can save these treasures from the Inquisition? Must we stand idly by and watch the blaze of the *Devil's Tribunal* incinerate the last remnants of a glorious age?"

Abulafia bows his head. "Carrying them to safety is sadly beyond us. Yet I have no doubt we were summoned to this place for a purpose." He gazes into the pre-dawn light beyond the spire of the nearby Cathedral, searching for a sign. When none reveals itself, the rabbi bows his head. "Perhaps we have failed in our mission."

"Wait," says al-Arabī, taking notice of a worker approaching them. Shirtless and wearing torn, baggy pants, the young man nonetheless carries himself with nobility. From the way he squints, their forms are only vaguely visible to him.

He kneels before speaking. "My name is Tahir and I prayed the Jinn would come to help us."

"We are neither spirits nor earthbound humans, young man, and we need *your* help." Ibn al-Arabī salvages a stiff sheet of sheepskin parchment from the scattered remains of a codex and, using a finely pointed metal pen, draws a detailed map on the back.

"Tahir, sweet boy, you will be our hands. Gather as many books as you are able, in the short time left until daybreak. I will conceal them beneath a cloak of invisibility and tomorrow, upon your return, you may transport your charges to a safe location."

"This, I will do." Tahir takes the map and hides it carefully beneath his shirt.

"Hey! You! Get back to work!" A guard, who sees only a Muslim slave talking to himself, walks toward the threesome. Abulafia quickly whispers a spell and Tahir and the pile of books vanish from the soldier's sight.

"Holy Mother of God, what was that?" The sentry vigorously rubs his eyes before shrugging and resuming his rounds.

With the way clear, Tahir gets back to his labors. Feverishly, he collects the condemned books and manuscripts, securing them in a far corner of the Plaza. He notices al-Arabī cradling a thick tome bound in leather and wood. "Shall I take that one too?"

"Only after our departure." The Sufi sage runs his hand lovingly over the word *Zahara*, ornately engraved on the weighty cover. He opens the book to reveal thick pages written in Aramaic and another older language even he does not recognize.

There is the sound of rushing water and as Tahir watches in disbelief, the illuminated text blurs into waves of gold. The entire page has disappeared, replaced by a dark rectangle, mysterious and beckoning.

"We must be gone," Abulafia whispers urgently. "The sun is rising."

He intones some unintelligible words and the Visitors transform into two steady streams of light, flowing through the portal with a faint whoosh. The cover slams shut, and Tahir reverently deposits the book atop a stack in his care.

The sages continue conversing in the ether, traveling back in time at a deliberate pace. "There is still much to be done if the books are to survive. We will need more help," al-Arabī observes.

"Don't worry, my friend," Rabbi Abulafia replies. "I have found the perfect instrument. If all goes to plan, she will reach us in due course and play her part."

# Chapter One

**February 2019**

It was just another working day, or so I thought. I was out on assignment at the University of Washington, updating a story I'd written about Judith Talavera, the first Sephardic woman from Seattle to apply for Spanish citizenship. I thought it would be simple, just the facts about Spain's new law, presented by an attorney from Granada. This was before the elderly man seated next to me in Kane Hall fingered the dark blue yarmulke pinned to his head and murmured, "How come they want us back *now*?"

A woman from the row behind me responded. "Why does it matter? Nothing their government can offer will compensate us for being tortured and expelled."

I swiveled in my seat to meet her obsidian eyes and wondered how many others in the lecture hall she spoke for. Surely not everyone, since more than a hundred people occupied the tiered seats. Although a few had brought their teenage children, there was a scarcity of the banter and laughter customary at Sephardi gatherings. Something valuable was in the offing. There would be takers and for them the clock was ticking. In eight months, Spain would stop accepting new applicants.

A few friends of my family were present, good souls from whom I'd chosen to keep my distance. I did this not to hurt their feelings but to prevent our shared history from creeping up on me. How could I explain that at any moment I might be wrenched into the past while still living in the present, compelled to share the minds of those who came before us? This altered state, deemed a 'gift' by my grandmother *Nona*, felt more like a plague continually stalking me. Convinced I would never be accepted, I had hidden my affliction and then banished myself entirely from the welcoming, intimate circle of this community. If any of them had been offended by my absence, there was no way of knowing.

I shunted aside my regrets and, along with three generations of Sephardim, listened raptly to Luis Alcábez. The attorney's enthusiasm was mesmerizing as, tightly wound and impeccable in a gray, three-piece suit, he clicked through the slides in his presentation. He explained how an "unprecedented right of return" was being offered to the Jews, who after living for centuries in a country they lovingly named *Sepharad*, had been brutally banished by King Ferdinand and Queen Isabel in 1492.

"You will need to pass a language test and provide some proof of your Sephardic heritage. After that, the only requirement is a trip to Spain, where a notary public will determine if you meet the requirements and help you submit your formal application."

When he reached the last slide, Señor Alcábez opened the floor to questions and a woman with large turquoise beads circling her neck like a duck's collar asked, "Can we pass Spanish citizenship on to our children?"

"Yes. With their passports they'll be able to travel and work anywhere within the European Union."

"What if someone is only half Jewish?"

"What if I speak Ladino and not pure Spanish?"

"Can I hire my own attorney?"

The questions multiplied, cascading down to the stage, and Alcábez answered each one with the patience of someone who had heard them all.

After the flood had passed, I raised my hand. "Was it a struggle to get the law passed by the Spanish government?"

"For the past decade there's been a general feeling that the wrong committed by expelling the Jews should be righted. The Federation of Jewish Communities, which I represent, began advocating for the law in 2012. It was passed three years later."

I was curious to find out more and there was something else: the tug of my cloudy family history, topped off by the pleasant anticipation of a bigger story. At the end of the evening I waited in line to make an appointment for a consultation.

After I introduced myself, Alcábez repeated my name aloud, twice. "Alienor Crespo. It sounds familiar but I can't place it." He asked me to call him Luis and I liked his genuine warmth.

We met the next day at Judith Talavera's home near Seward Park. Judith worked as a realtor but her unruly gray curls and quirky smile seemed at odds with the knit skirt, cardigan sweater and string of pearls. The embroidered family tree in her living room testified to her strong sense of Sephardic identity.

When I interviewed her last year, she wasn't so sure about mine. "Crespo's an unusual name."

"My father's people lived in Belgium until the middle of World War II," I'd replied.

"Ah, that explains it. Most Sephardim came to the Pacific Northwest from Turkey or the Island of Rhodes."

"I know. My mother's family emigrated from Rhodes in the 1930's."

She had responded to this information with a warm embrace. "Then you *are* descended from *Rhodeslis*."

That morning, Judith greeted Luis Alcábez and me like old friends and treated us to fresh orange juice and blueberry muffins. She said she'd recently flown to Spain to complete her paperwork and was expecting approval of her application soon.

When Luis congratulated her, Judith did not look as happy as I expected. "It took longer than I'd ever imagined and they made me jump through endless hoops. But it was worth it. I'll soon be a full-fledged citizen."

"Will you be moving to Spain?" I asked.

She shook her head. "What's important is claiming what's owed to me and my family."

Alcábez took another sip of orange juice. "Alienor, have you considered there might be relatives of yours living in Spain? I can look into it. Who knows, something special may await you."

Taking steps to become a Spanish citizen had not occurred to me. I felt like a screenwriter who'd been asked to play a role in her latest script. Before I could voice my misgivings, Alcábez continued his sales pitch.

"Once you have your passport, you'll be eligible for employment anywhere in the EU. An exciting prospect, I'd imagine."

He was right. This was a real opportunity, even if thousands of miles outside my comfort zone. When the *Post-Intelligencer* surrendered to the blogosphere and shut down its print operation, Seattle journalists became an endangered species. Sure, I was blessed to work as a stringer for the *Seattle Courier*, the only surviving daily. But it wasn't enough to make ends meet. Especially in a town where rents had rocketed up faster than the numbers of techies arriving from California with key cards dangling from their necks. I wondered what it would be like to work for multiple news outlets in Europe. My Spanish was a little rusty, but I'd been fluent when I worked for the Honey Bee Project in Peru. Maybe it was time for a change.

Before we parted, Alcábez offered to connect me with a notary in Spain. "Mico Rosales will help you to formally submit your papers when the time comes. Let me know when you're ready." He made it sound like a done deal.

Outside Judith Talavera's house, the winter wind on Andrews Bay was busy kicking up whitecaps guaranteed to roll a kayak if you were foolhardy enough to paddle in this weather. What had I gotten myself into?

I drove downtown to the *Courier* building, catching Todd Lassiter in his office, his phone lighting up as he juggled multiple writers working on dozens of stories. The window behind him opened to a peekaboo view of the ever-changing skyline he rarely had time to contemplate. Todd scribbled some notes on a blue Post-it and waved me to a seat.

"What can I do for you, Allie?" Todd dilated his gray-blue eyes, lifting his bushy eyebrows. His ruddy complexion didn't come from drinking, as some suspected. It was the result of weeks at sea on a wooden sailboat he'd built himself. In a field increasingly dominated by super-bloggers who boiled everything down to two-hundred-fifty words or less, the metro editor's genuine interest in relevant, in-depth coverage had gained him my respect.

Visits with Todd had a way of strengthening my commitment to what we journalists do best, the portrayal of complexity without judgment. We give equal time to the salmon and the hydroelectric dam, the wolf and the rancher, the cop and the criminal. You might sympathize with one or the other, as long as you don't change the facts to please yourself. And if your publisher pressures you to see things differently you can always stick to freelancing, as I did.

Three years ago, on the day Todd hired me, I'd joined him for lunch at the 13 Coins, now slated for demolition to make way for more cookie cutter condos. We sat at the solid oak counter, side-by-side in our swiveling padded chairs and he asked me what I liked most about being a journalist.

"Job security," I'd quipped, eliciting a snort from my prospective employer. Hints of the deluge of layoffs to come were already making the rounds. Todd lifted his water glass. "Here's to the Fourth Estate holding on to what's left of the life raft."

He had appreciated my honesty then and I hoped he would approve of my plans now. "Remember Judith Talavera, the woman from Seward Park we featured a while back?"

"Sure. Weren't you planning to write a follow-up?"

"I'll go you one better. I've decided to follow in Judith's footsteps and go through the process of becoming a Spanish citizen myself."

"Allie, you've always been a writer who gets up close to her subject but isn't this a bit extreme?"

"Why? How am I so different from Ms. Talavera? You said last year you wished we had the resources to send someone to cover her trip to Spain. I'm offering to go and develop my own story at a fraction of the price you'd pay a staff writer to fly over there."

"Okay, okay," Todd grumbled. "You've made your point and I'm sorry we don't pay expenses for stringers. That said, it's the kind of odyssey readers might go for, the search for identity and all it implies. And in view of the quality of your past work…" He paused, never one to dish out compliments and risk encouraging a freelancer to ask for a raise.

"I'm sorry I won't be available for any assignments before I leave, Todd. I'll send you the Mario Flores story tonight. Maybe there will be enough of a public outcry to convince the Army to protect his family from deportation while he's overseas. I also need to brush up on my Spanish and get in touch with a Rabbi who can vouch for my ancestry."

"Leave it to you to come up with something like this."

I looked at him in alarm. Had Todd finally guessed my well-kept secret? I'd never confided in him how writing the news was all that stood between me and the inner turmoil that threatened to pull me under. But Lassiter was already on the phone with another writer, talking deadlines as he waved goodbye.

Since childhood, I'd fought against a shadowy side of my psyche that played faster and looser with space and time than Stephan Hawking's wormholes. I had no idea where this *gift* had come from, or why. At times I blamed it on the simple fact of never having seen my mother dance. At least not while she was alive.

# Chapter Two

As I left the *Courier* building and walked down the steep grade of Denny Way to the streetcar stop on Westlake, I could hear Mom humming a song in Ladino, the language of Spain's exiled Jews, as clearly as if she'd come back to life and was slipping into the form-fitting, black velvet dress she always wore to her Andalusian dance class. It had been my job to stand on tiptoe and pull the zipper all the way up, careful to avoid getting it tangled in her luxuriant hair. She would then fasten the straps on her red dancing shoes with the thick heels, gather her long black tresses into a bun on top of her head, and throw me a kiss on her way out the door. Staying awake well past my nine o'clock bedtime, I'd listen for the sound of her key in the lock of the downstairs door before allowing myself to fall asleep. Even now it troubles me. On the one night I couldn't keep my eyes open and failed to keep vigil, my mother failed me as well. In the morning, Dad called on his courage and told me there'd been a fatal traffic accident on the Ballard Bridge. My beautiful mother was gone.

Mom had always showered me with affection, encouraging every little curiosity I had. If we were walking downtown and I asked, "Why do they put all the tallest buildings here?" she'd say, "One day you'll make a great architect." When she took me roller-skating around Greenlake and I spotted an eagle perched on a tall Cedar, she called me "a born naturalist." Once, she'd let me stay up late and help her sew a new dance costume. At times she looked sad and when I asked why, she confided her desire, held secret from my workaday father, to travel the world and play her castanets in a Spanish café. Her absence sucked the music out of my soul and the hope from my heart.

For seven days following the funeral, relatives and close friends came by to mourn and sit Shiva with us. In their torn garments they looked more like refugees than neighbors. Seated on cushions on the floor, they spoke about my mother's loving nature and read aloud from a mystical book called *The Zohar*. These Eastern Sephardim from my mother's side out-numbered the Europeans from my dad's, and had immigrated to Seattle from the Island of Rhodes in the 1920's. A few of Mom's older friends brought *sheshos*, pebbles taken from the island's beaches, for us to place with a prayer every time we visited her gravestone.

My bereft father, usually so resourceful, was at a loss in the face of his daughter's overwhelming grief. An English pro-fessor who sought solace in books, Elias often said he thought of me as an "old soul," not realizing I would take this intended compliment as a rebuke highlighting my failure to be a child. If my mother was a thundercloud whose torrential rains both alarmed and nourished me, my father was the snow, quiet and deep. After she died, he suggested I try to picture Mom as dancing in heaven. Hard as I tried, all I could conjure were the remnants of the velvet dress she'd worn on the night she died—torn, bloody, and scattered over the bridge deck.

When Dad returned to work at Seattle University, Grandma Bella, known affectionately as *Nona*, came to stay with us. In spite of my depression, she insisted I go back to school. "Dawn breaks when it's the darkest," was her favorite saying. I knew resistance was useless.

That first day, walking home from John Hay Elementary, the fun of tricking the second grade substitute into letting us out for recess an hour early dissolved into an aching loss. I stopped to wipe my eyes and adjust my backpack. The next moment Mom was there, lightly tripping down the steps to the beach at the bottom of a cliff in Discovery Park. And her young self wasn't alone.

A youthful version of Dad gripped Mom's hand in his as they carelessly abandoned their shoes on a log and broke into a run. The surf crashed over their bare feet pounding in unison on the packed sand. Mom's face glowed in the sunlight, as did her bright, pink lipstick. I felt my entire being reach out to her. My hands tingled with longing. And in the same way that she had coaxed me into the body of an enchanted fish swimming through her bedtime stories, my own thoughts and feelings impossibly merged with hers and I *became* my mother.

Looking south across Magnolia Bay, I admire the reflection of a gleaming, downtown office tower rippling beneath the water, untouched by the salt breeze caressing my cheek. "Eleanora, let's go for a swim!" Elias cries. Not waiting for an answer, he pulls me out to knee-deep depth. My toes turn instantly blue.

"You're crazy! We'll both get hypothermia and die on the day before our wedding. Think of all the disappointed guests and wasted presents."

"Killjoy." He pretends to be angry and sweeps me up, carrying me back to dry land.

Someone has left some half-burned pieces of driftwood in a fire pit and we build a small blaze, enough to warm our freezing legs without attracting attention. "I'm not as boring as you think I am," Elias teases me. Shaking with cold, I take his arm and pull it around my waist. "You are my man of the sea, with unfathomable depth."

This is our moment. No one else's.

I try a few dance steps on the sand, awkward at first until the pulsating gypsy style music in my head grows louder and takes control of my limbs. Then there's no stopping me.

I was ecstatic to have finally seen Mom dance. It was only later that my adult-self cringed at the thought of taking my mother's place during a romantic interlude. Perhaps she had wanted me to see Dad's more demonstrative side.

How innocent I was, with my long, straight hair curled by imaginary seawater, skipping along Taylor Avenue in a bout of euphoria, catching quick glimpses of the rounded top of the Space Needle peeking over the rooftops like a UFO.

I'd almost reached home when my grief returned twofold, sharp as windshield glass crashing through the nightmares that followed Mom's death. I stood zombie-like outside our two-story, family bungalow, a captive forced to play a cruel game in which I lost my mother over and over again, each time more painful than the last. Another round would be more than I could bear.

I resolved right there to shut down the part of my brain playing tricks on me. I would do this by uttering the magic words Mom had gifted me, when I'd been scared to death of a huge raccoon lurking in our driveway, convinced he would carry me off. "I belong to me, I belong to me," I'd recited, as she watched me cross the spot on the blacktop where I'd seen the monster.

That afternoon, I stood in the same place in the driveway and chanted the four powerful words again.

When two weeks passed with no sign of Mom returning to haunt me, my relief was so intense I felt compelled to atone for it by kissing her photo every night at bedtime. From then on, she kept her distance and I tried to get back to being a kid again.

Regrettably, the *Vijita* I experienced that day was the first of many I endured, some dragging me into frightening realms. I soon learned the words "I belong to me" had no power to stop these Crazy Visits, as I chose to call them, from disrupting my life. *Vijitas Lokas* stole my identity and were the exact opposite of *Visitas de Alhad*, the sweet Sunday Visits my family paid to our relatives, bringing dried apricots and sugary delights to share.

One Friday evening, a half hour before sunset, Grandma Nona let me place the Shabbat candles in their holders before she lit them. "Did you know our ancestors in Spain hid their Shabbat candles inside clay pots?" she asked.

Having heard the question many times, I knew the answer. "They were afraid a neighbor might report them as false Christians to be dealt with by the authorities."

"That's right, Alienor. They were persecuted but never gave up their faith."

Dad reached for a stuffed artichoke and Nona's voice faded into the background, replaced by a tingling sensation vibrating up and down my spine.

I'm hiding under the bed.

"Ana, stay here," my sister Raquel hisses. My heart beats furiously in her absence. A moment later she places little Chaim on the floor and he crawls toward me. My brother and I cling to each other like branches atremble with fear of being wrenched off a tree. The mob breaks in and we catch glimpses of legs in leather boots, worn down sandals, dirty bare feet, all angrily stomping. The owners of these menacing limbs call my older sister terrible names I don't understand. "Blasphemer! Apostate! Dirty Converso! Your neighbor saw you light candles and say prayers on Friday night. You pretend to eat ham but lamb is what you serve on your table!"

Some legs disappear and others stay behind. The bed above us starts to shake. I put my hands over Chaim's ears, not daring to visualize what my clenched gut knows is happening. Afterward there's a terrible silence before footsteps return. Rough hands tip the bed over on its side and seize my brother and me. I squirm, trying to fight my way free, desperately holding onto Chaim's hand as everything goes black.

It took a few moments to convince myself I was back in the present, at home with Dad and Nona in our Queen Anne house eating dinner. I focused on steadying my hands as Dad, serene as ever, passed me a platter of roasted vegetables. *Was this what it was like to be crazy? To have the thoughts of other people running wild in your head? To feel the same hot and cold that their fingers feel, to see through the eyes of a perfect stranger or a lost family member, experiencing their deepest emotions?* I was caught between my desire to know who these people were and my resentment at being forced to meet them.

From then on, I worked hard at pretending my *Vijitas* were no more than vivid daydreams and vowed to banish any hint of the supernatural from my life. I labeled as pure fancy anything that facts could not fully explain. My friends were required to exhibit an equal amount of cynicism or face banishment. "Why pretend your life has any meaning when there's no proof it does?" I reproached one of my more sensitive classmates, driving her to tears.

I developed a stutter and was bullied at school. It didn't help that my speech tended toward the archaic and I preferred *cease thy prattle* to saying a simple *shut your mouth*. However, my flowery language, which I worked hard to simplify when I became a journalist, did not make me a sissy. In fifth grade, when Kenny Spader finished one of my painfully incomplete sentences with "dum da dum dum," I slapped him without hesitation. My lack of impulse control didn't bother Dad, who took my side, saying a good slap from a girl could save a guy years of growing up. He sent me to self-defense classes, something I thank him for to this day.

When I could no longer stand keeping my disorder to myself, I took a chance and told Nona about my *Vijitas Lokas*. She reproached herself for having exposed me to too many fabulist tales, stories starring wild-haired psychics who commandeered flying carpets or collaborated with biblical prophets to manipulate the weather.

"There is no evil eye. These yarns are filled with psychological symbols and archetypes you'll understand when you're older." Steeped as she was in the fantastical, Nona drew the line at truly believing in it. So what if her granddaughter imagined she could share the awareness of an ancestor or two? "That's what comes from burying your face in books instead of enjoying life with friends," she insisted.

Nona had no inkling my *sometime else* journeys were as tangible to me as the pinches she loved to bestow on my cheeks. The only way I could convince her was to show her my diary, in which I'd recorded full descriptions of my out-of-body experiences. In the early entries, I'd misspelt a few words and my printing had a terrible slant. Nona's shocked face told me that she understood every word and afterwards, she spoke to me differently.

"Some of the women in our family have been gifted with second sight and sometimes it's the opposite of a blessing. I know your visions are frightening and inconvenient. Try to see them as a burden to be borne until the reason behind them is revealed."

To help me clear my head, Nona taught me a dozen lilting, Ladino songs she'd learned as a child growing up on the Island of Rhodes before World War II. Syllable by syllable I painstakingly learned the lyrics. The notes were easier. Sliding up and down the microtones, I glided from one bead to another on a closely knit string, with no danger of falling into gaps of silence like those that tormented me when I tried to speak. This accomplishment provided some relief, some confidence even. Still, I was unable to shake the feeling I'd always be a freak of nature, living in two worlds at once.

No wonder I chose journalism as my refuge. Covering the stories of others yanked me out of myself. Every day I met and interviewed people who were a thousand times worse off than me: parents who lost their offspring to the God of Addiction, soldiers whose post-war confusion proved more fatal than gunshots and bombs, wives who cared for and trusted their husbands until they woke up in fear for their lives. Some might think someone with my temperament would make a lousy member of the fourth estate. They'd be wrong. There is so much more to life than cold facts. When they sensed my receptivity, people were willing, sometimes eager, to open up and share their stories.

After completing my degree in journalism at the University of Washington, I'd moved out of the family house and rented a studio in South Seattle's Columbia City neighborhood, staying away from family gatherings for the most part. I never did tell Dad about my *Vijitas Lokas*. I was afraid he'd think I was having some sort of breakdown. Wasn't losing his wife and having to raise me on his own enough stress for a lifetime?

With some trepidation I drove over to Dad's to tell him about my decision to go to Spain. I found him grading papers in the attic bedroom he'd converted to a study. The oval window above his desk overlooked a view of the steep hills leading down to the west side of Lake Union and I could see some boats bobbing in the marina.

At sixty-eight, my father's thick brown hair betrayed few signs of grey. He welcomed me with a hug and a "so glad you came by." This made it easier for me to relax and before long we were laughing about some unforgivable mistakes in his students' English 102 papers.

"So you're going to be a world traveling journalist with an EU passport," he said upon hearing of my plans. "Ain't that somethin' special." Fixated on correct grammar, he only used the vernacular when he was happy. I let out a sigh of relief.

# Chapter Three

When Dad made his heartbreaking choice to send Nona to the Kline Galland Home, I'd promised myself I would visit her regularly. It wasn't easy witnessing her withdrawal from the world and bouts with dementia, and at eighty-five her condition was worsening. When someone you've known and loved all your life looks straight at you and draws a blank, you feel terrible, and not only for them. You grieve for parts of yourself known only to that person, dreading the day when everything you've shared will disappear.

In her lucid days, Nona had laughed when I complained about *real* journalists becoming obsolete. "*Mas vale poco ke nada*," was her comeback in Ladino. *Better a little than nothing*. And soon there would be nothing. Because in the end Dad was forced to acknowledge the truth. His sensible, sharp-witted mother's speech now held more gibberish than sense. She would soon leave for the land of the unknowing, guided by those who knew from experience how to see people off to this destination.

Staying away from Nona gave me permission to dread, rather than accept, the inevitable. I visualized her room at the Home as a coffin with cheap furniture, looking out on a sheer cliff that, as a result of my visits, would give way to the power of combined loss in a fatal landslide. So, I kept my distance.

And then I couldn't anymore. It was late April when I drove through the wrought iron gate, my guilt as dense as the giant laurel hedges lining the roadway. Nona had been there for me always and I hadn't seen her for six months.

The palatial mansion, with its fireplace in the lobby and picture windows providing an expansive view of Lake Washington, was not what I'd imagined. Maybe all my apprehensions about bad smells and worse sounds in the Alzheimer's wing had been for naught.

With the help of Anita, a pink-uniformed aide with a soft Guatemalan accent, I found my grandmother on the terrace, wrapped in a colorful blanket amidst a sea of fallen cherry blossoms. Her wrinkled eyelids were closed, soaking in the rays. Anita lifted a paper-thin hand off the chair arm and gently squeezed it.

"One of your admirers is here to see you, dear."

Nona's penetrating, chestnut eyes had faded to a vague brown. Her face, framed by a signature cloud of rebellious white hair, was pale and indistinct.

"Nona, it's me, Allie."

"Alienor, darling child. You came."

*Could this be?* In our family, only Nona used my full name. If she was clear-headed, what a gift it would be. I leaned forward, phrasing some questions I hoped to ask. I started with an easy one.

"How are you?"

"It took you long enough. I need your help. You've got to get me out of here. There are men here who do bad things."

I tried not to recoil, remembering what Dad had said. "Don't listen if she goes paranoid on you. The employees there are great but she gets confused and accuses them of all sorts of things. If she goes in that direction, change the subject." It shouldn't be hard, I thought. Not with the news I'd brought with me.

"Nona, I'm leaving for Spain on Friday. I completed my application and passed the Spanish language test at the Cervantes Institute —"

Her confused look caused me to stop right there, much as I wanted to tell her how impressed they'd been with my fluency. There was also no point in mentioning that I would meet with a notary in Granada to sign an affidavit in person.

"All you need to know is I'll be in Spain for a few weeks and when I get back I'll come and see you."

Her cloudy eyes cleared slightly and shifted into focus. "You know, he saw her one last time."

Decades could pass in minutes for my grandmother, both backwards and forwards. "Saw whom, Nona?"

"Your grandfather told me he saw her one last time in the Albaicín, right after the war."

Grandpa Aharon had died fifteen years ago. I'd always suspected there was something missing from my family history, perhaps a secret that Grandpa shared with Nona, now trapped in her erratic memory. I prompted her again. "Who did Grandpa meet?"

"His sister, Luzia. They were separated during the war. Their uncle Emile brought them together at a café in the old Muslim quarter in Granada. Luzia asked Aharon to convince their father to accept her marriage to a Muslim… and the baby."

Nona had been speaking slowly and now she shut her eyes. Afraid she'd fall asleep in the middle of these revelations, I gently touched her arm. When she returned to her tale, she'd switched to Ladino. The words flew so fast I had trouble deciphering all the Greek and Turkish interlaced with Hebrew and Spanish. I took some notes and was able to piece together how Grandpa Aharon's sister Luzia was by some miracle spared the suffering inflicted on her brother and their parents—Miriam and Jaco—during their internment at Auschwitz. Miriam did not survive.

All this narration was a great effort. Nona slumped in her chair and pulled her shawl tight. I felt like a monster for making her relive these harrowing memories but before I could change the subject, she mustered the strength to continue, thankfully in English.

"After what they went through in the camp and Miriam's death, Jaco could not accept his daughter marrying a Gentile. He disowned Luzia and forbade Aharon to mention his sister's name. They took a ship to America and Aharon told me his father didn't speak again until they reached New York. Later, they traveled by train to Seattle where your grandfather and I met."

"So no one knows what happened to Luzia?"

"For years she sent cards and letters. But Aharon wanted to put the war behind him. He couldn't bring himself to read his sister's letters. After he died, I found them unopened. How terrible for Luzia to think he didn't care."

Something here failed to compute. "Dad told me his Great Uncle Emile survived the war and reached New York. But he said his Aunt Luzia died over there at the age of eighteen. Surely he believes this himself."

Nona smiled sadly. "*La mentira no tiene cavo.*" There's no limit to a lie.

An aide walked by, matching his pace with a frail woman who inched her metal walker down the path. Nona clutched my hand. "Save me, Alienor."

"You're safe here, I promise."

She waved my reassurances away with both arms, showing surprising strength of limb. "Listen to me *hija*. You must use your gift carefully, especially while you're in Spain. Your second sight will grow stronger and put you in danger. You must be strong for your friends and family."

"What do you mean? Is there something about my *Vijitas Lokas* you haven't told me?"

"Tell your father he must let me come home. There are people here who want our beds empty so they can replace us with their relatives." Nona was confusing my problems with her own. I was afraid to press further and risk destroying her already weak hold on reality.

"Please don't worry, Nona. I'll see you again soon." I kissed her on the forehead and went to find Anita. "Is she always so... fearful?"

"It comes and goes. She was glad to see you. The rest is... well...not in our hands."

When Dad asked me, "How did it go with Nona?" I told him most of it, leaving out the bit about danger awaiting me. Rationalist though he was, he'd spent a lifetime watching his mother's predictions come true and I didn't want to worry him.

"Papa, did you ever discuss Aunt Luzia with your father?"

"Your Grandpa Aharon, bless his soul, never spoke about his sister – not once. He hated talking about the past. If I asked questions, all he'd say was, '*Aboltar cazal, aboltar mazal.*' A change of scene, a change of fortune. I assumed my Aunt Luzia died in the Holocaust."

"Nona mentioned some letters coming from Spain."

"Letters from the dead. Sounds like Nona," Dad said with a sigh. "You can look for yourself. Everything's where she left it."

I climbed the stairs to Nona's old room. Her bed was neatly made and on the end table was a copy of *Ladino Reveries*. I would ask Dad to take her the book next time he visited the Home, though the chances of her taking up reading again were minimal.

I looked through the dresser drawers. No correspondence but I did find a photo. A young, light-haired woman cradled a baby in an armless rocking chair, her beatific smile undimmed by the sepia tones. A dark-haired man, presumably the one who caused Luzia's father to disown her, leaned over the pair, his eyes stained with the sadness of someone wishing for the impossible. They were in a garden or an orchard, flowering trees of some kind directly behind them and in the distance, a range of snow-capped mountains.

Downstairs, I crept into Dad's study and located the copy of *The Zohar* he kept close at hand. I opened it and examined the family tree drawn in India ink on the inside cover. There were copious notes under the names and it took several tries and lots of erasures before I was satisfied with the copy I sketched on a blank sheet of paper. "So glad to have met you," I whispered, before adding my Great Aunt Luzia, her lover Ja'far, and the nameless baby in the photo to the family record along with some notes on who married whom and when.

The next morning, I stapled this work-in-progress into my notebook before taking a taxi to the airport.

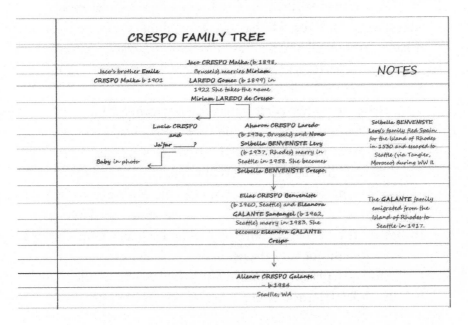

### CRESPO FAMILY TREE

Jaco CRESPO Malka (b 1898, Brussels) marries Miriam LAREDO Gomez (b 1899) in 1922. She takes the name Miriam LAREDO de Crespo

Jaco's brother Emile CRESPO Malka b 1901

NOTES

Luzia CRESPO and Ja'far _____?

Aharon CRESPO Laredo (b 1936, Brussels) and Nona Solbella BENVENISTE Levy (b 1937, Rhodes) marry in Seattle in 1958. She becomes Solbella BENVENISTE Crespo.

Baby in photo

Solbella BENVENISTE Levy's family fled Spain for the island of Rhodes in 1530 and escaped to Seattle (via Tangier, Morocco) during WW II.

Elias CRESPO Benveniste (b 1960, Seattle) and Eleanora GALANTE Sanfungel (b 1962, Seattle) marry in 1983. She becomes Eleanora GALANTE Crespo

The GALANTE family emigrated from the Island of Rhodes to Seattle in 1917.

Alienor CRESPO Galante - b 1984 Seattle, WA

How pleased my mother would be if she knew I'd gotten up the courage to visit Nona before my departure. Brighter than any LED strip, the memory of Mom's smile illuminated the aisle by my seat. I was aboard the Delta Flight from Seattle to Paris with a connection to Málaga, flying to the country she'd longed for but never visited. During take-off, I felt my pulse accelerate, one moment from anticipation and the next from dread at the prospect of what might be waiting for me upon arrival.

*You must be strong for your friends and family.* Nona's parting words echoed through my thoughts. Whatever might happen, I was committed.

The woman chewing gum in the seat next to me dug into her red alligator bag for another piece. "It'll help your ears pop." Her English was lightly peppered with Spanish inflections.

"I'm good, thanks," I said, fearful of starting a nine-hour conversation.

I noted her cashmere sweater and jeans. *Was she a school-teacher on vacation? An actress? Or, far less likely, a journalist like me hoping to prosper in other climes?* She smiled and closed her eyes.

# Chapter Four

A few hours after departure, the flight attendant reached row sixteen with her cart. Like the titanium wings of the aircraft, her calm exterior was engineered for maximum efficiency, her smile adept at softening the reality of being trapped with hundreds of strangers inside a fabricated tube. "Something to drink?" she offered.

My seatmate stirred and pulled down her food tray. "Vodka and tonic for me." She turned and asked, "What's your poison?"

I had a long list. *Editors who cut the last sentence in an article to save space. Friends who posted videos of leopards adopting stray kittens. Any government agent dedicated to deporting a soldier's entire family while he was away risking his life for his new country.* "I'll have a bloody Mary."

I flipped through the pages of my notebook and retrieved the photo I'd found in Nona's room. No matter whom she'd married, my Great Aunt Luzia didn't deserve to be disowned by her father.

Long airplane flights tend to lull my body into full-blown stasis, leaving space for my mind to careen between vivid memories, cryptic dreams and waking fantasies. As I sipped my drink and ran my index finger over what little remained of the photo's glossy finish, the hum of conversation and the drone of jet engines faded into the background. I saw Luzia walking through the darkened streets of a European town, past brown stucco houses, their shutters closed in compliance with the blackout. She looked a few years younger than in the picture, her finely etched features and wartime pageboy cut providing a hint of how Nona, her eventual sister-in-law, might have looked in her prime. Crossing the narrow alley, I reached out to take Luzia's battered suitcase. In a moment, I had taken her place as well.

I'm peering through the rain-smeared windows of a deserted café. It's well after closing time and the barman, still wearing his leather apron, cracks the door and hurriedly scans the sidewalk prior to letting me in. No introductions are necessary. Everything has been arranged in advance. He points to a table across from the bar and asks, "*Avez-vous faim?*"

I nod even though I've got no appetite, and he brings me bread and soup along with a glass of ale. "This should set you right." I reach into the pocket of my cracked leather jacket for some change, causing him to shake his balding head vigorously. "Save what you have. You'll need it."

The barman goes upstairs and soon returns, trailed by a young man who walks toward me confidently. I was given his name to memorize, but no description. In his coarse linen shirt and corduroy pants he could easily be mistaken for a French peasant. Until a close-up view shows a dusky complexion, set off by black curls under his cap that suggest North Africa.

He seats himself at the table. "Are you a fan of traveling?" His intensely brown eyes make a perfect match for the amber ale in my glass.

"Yes, especially in the company of friends." I utter these code words in faltering French, so different from the Dutch I grew up speaking in the Flemish area of Belgium. "I'm Luzia Crespo Laredo. You must be Ja'far."

He winces at my use of our real names and cocks his head toward the garçon, a gesture that clearly asks, *what kind of greenhorn have you brought me?* The sight of a scar on his neck makes me shudder. He ignores my sympathetic look and sticks to his businesslike tone, asking, this time in Spanish, "Do you have papers?"

"Yes, of course," I respond, grateful my parents insisted I learn more than a smattering of their ancestral tongue.

From the inner pocket of my jacket I remove some crumpled papers for Ja'far to examine, first with approval, then apprehension.

"Don't show your documents to anyone. You could be killed and robbed for a lot less," he says.

"How much to take me over the mountains into Spain?"

"Only two thousand francs, since you are by yourself. How old are you?"

"Nineteen."

"Where is your family?"

Despite knowing that Ja'far needs his customers to be self-possessed, my lower lip begins to tremble. I take a long sip of ale and wait until it's possible to speak. "My parents and younger brother Aharon were arrested. He's only seven."

I tell Ja'far how, after the Nazi invasion of Brussels in 1940, my family was forced to abandon our home in the centuries-old Sephardic quarter. How they woke me and my brother and we fled to France in the middle of the night with only the clothes on our backs. How we were forced into hiding when the Germans took Paris, and then mercifully taken in by Uncle Emile, who had lived in the 4th arrondissement for decades.

"Father had made arrangements to smuggle us to Montauban in the Free Zone. On the morning we were to leave, he sent me to the marché to buy supplies for the journey. I was not gone long. When I returned, the apartment was empty. I thought I had misunderstood and was meant to meet my family at the train station. But the luggage they left behind suggested a different story, one I dared not consider."

Ja'far makes no response, other than to lean forward attentively. He waits patiently for me to collect myself and continue.

"I hid in the back room all day, too frightened to come out, even for a drink of water. When Uncle Emile finally came to find me, he told me the truth. 'Your father, mother and brother are being held at the Compiègne detention camp and will be deported to Germany within the week. I have no more friends who can pull strings. You'd better go while you can.' He gave me some money and put me in a car with a friend who was going south."

Ja'far orders a beer from the barman, downing it in a few swift gulps. Doubtless he's heard more stories like mine than a priest on a battlefield. To my astonishment his eyes grow moist. "After our mother died from cholera, my two brothers and I were raised by our father in Spanish Morocco. In 1936, General Franco and the Nationalists staged a coup and took control of the Protectorate. They executed 200 officers who were Loyalists and, with Mussolini's help, airlifted the remaining soldiers to fight on the side of the rebels back home. My father did not want his sons shipped to Spain to fight for the fascists so he moved us from Tetuan to the French-controlled area of Marrakesh."

"How did you end up in France?"

He shrugged like someone asked to explain the obvious. "With no land to farm, we were starving. I went to Paris to find work and when the Germans invaded I was trapped. I was lucky enough to find a way to survive – first as a black marketeer and now as a smuggler of people like you across the Pyrenees and into Spain."

"You're lucky to be fluent in both Spanish and French. Invaluable in a guide."

Ja'far scrapes his chair a few inches back from the table. It seems I've reminded him that I'm a client to whom he's providing a service. "We go tomorrow morning at five, after the curfew ends."

He gives me directions to the meeting place on the other side of St. Girons, where Le Chemin de la Liberté – The Freedom Trail – begins its climb over the mountains.

"I hope you're fit enough to make the journey."

"I came this far on my own. No need to worry your head about me."

Ja'far gives me a dubious look and I'm happy to be let off with a curt nod.

As I came out of the *Vijita Loka*, the airplane hit a pocket of turbulence and I instinctively gripped the armrests, taking a deep breath. It seemed Luzia Crespo had more courage than I ever would.

The flight leveled off and I fell to wondering. *Why did my Vijitas choose to begin or end at certain points in time? Did they finish when my subconscious determined enough was enough? Or was I a mad storyteller captivated by my own fiction, an illusionist who periodically ran out of steam?*

During the 3-hour layover at Charles de Gaulle, a cup of espresso reconnected me with the pleasures of real life. I enjoyed stretching my legs amidst the gleaming storefronts and fast-walking travelers. Preferring paper to Google's electronic offerings, I bought folded maps of both France and Spain at a gift shop. It was easy to locate St. Girons in the foothills of the Pyrenees, close to the Spanish border. I traced the route that Luzia and her guide Ja'far had taken along the Freedom Trail. In no time at all, I was thinking her thoughts and walking in her sturdy shoes.

A family of four has joined us on this unusually clear morning. Muriel and Ernesto Pardo are traveling on a forged exit visa that Ja'far says will have to do. As we get underway, the trail runs flat for a while and Muriel talks softly, out of earshot of their two children. "My Ernesto managed to bribe our way out of Rivesaltes. We had to get out of there fast, since they ship Jews to Germany on a regular basis."

With a rush of hope, I envision a similar way out for my parents and little brother, Aharon. I see myself reaching out to touch my mother's hand and imagine her calling out as she rushes toward me, "Luzia!"

Sadly, it's Ja'far's voice that has broken into my fantasy, reminding me to be careful. The pipedream melts away before it can infect me with further, misguided optimism.

The pathway steepens and we stop often to allow the frail refugees to catch their breath. At first the Pardos try to carry their offspring, but the devoted parents are simply too malnourished from their incarceration. I scoop up the little girl and carry her, while Ja'far pulls the boy along by the hand.

The heavily forested track passes directly above several hamlets, the smoke from their invisible chimneys arriving on the stiff breeze. Damp air can carry sounds for miles and our party of six stays especially quiet on this leg of the trail, hyper-aware of how easy it would be for a shepherd, or worse yet a German patrol, to hear our footsteps.

Strange how, regardless of the tension and the physical strain, I feel exhilarated by the crisp air of the climb and the prospect of arriving in Spain. As we make our way toward freedom, I'm puzzled by how this war-torn country—ruled by a dictator who strictly forbids Jews and Muslims to openly practice their religion—now provides a safe haven, or at least a safe route out of Europe. My Jewish ancestors and Ja'far's Muslim forefathers would have traveled through a mountain pass similar to this one, refugees in reverse, expelled from their homeland centuries ago. *Is irony an emotion?*

After long hours spent tackling increasingly steep hills, we stop for the night at a hut buried so deeply in the forest that without the pieces of red ribbon Ja'far had tied to the tree branches, we'd surely have lost our way. The one-room cabin has only three walls to support its sagging, moss-grown roof.

While the Pardos and their children are settling them-selves on the dirt floor under thin blankets, our guide keeps watch outside. I join him, declining the offer of a cigarette. "I've got plenty," he insists. "I can see how much you want one."

I'm content to smoke silently beside him on a fallen log, listening for danger in the dark.

Ja'far breaks off a piece of precious chocolate to share, and as he hands it over, a rustling of leaves startles the forest floor. Animal or human, impossible to tell. Quickly snuffing our smokes, we wait for a tense five minutes. "False alarm?" I dare whisper. "Hope so," he murmurs.

We move closer together, mainly for body warmth. Some-thing else is at work too. I fall asleep and wake to find my head resting on his shoulder. Embarrassed, I slide a few inches away. "How long did I sleep?"

"With no moon it's hard to tell."

"Don't most smugglers have partners so they can take turns keeping guard?"

Ja'far grunts. "I have good eyes and ears and have lost no one yet. Who told you this?"

"Cristelle. The woman my uncle hired to drive me to St. Girons. She criticized me for taking his money. She said, 'We need people to stay and fight. Why not you?'"

"Each to their own. Today you carried a child up a mountain." Ja'far's gruff voice is laced with kindness and I feel a sudden urge to cry.

Although there's plenty of water to be had from nearby streams, our supply of smoked sausages and bread is barely adequate. By the second night I catch Ja'far cutting down on his own share to make our rations last. His ways are an odd mixture of spontaneous generosity and self-serving watchfulness. As he bluntly puts it, "I'm not, as you say, altruistic. But if money were my only motivation, I'd be better off as an informer. Everyone knows the Nazis pay well."

I could ask if he's acquired this knowledge through personal experience. It doesn't matter. These days he's risking his life for complete strangers.

The third night is the worst. All are exhausted and dizzy from trudging up steep inclines followed by endless, zigzagging descents. Well before dawn, a friend of Ja'far's, a fellow guide, exchanges bird calls with him prior to showing up on the trail to report heavy patrols in the area. We're forced to take a detour away from the shelter. This means enduring a heavy downpour while trying to sleep under the trees. Luckily for us, the sun comes out on the fourth day and we cross the border to reach the outskirts of our destination, *Esterri d'Aneu.*

My joy at our success is muted by sleep deprivation. "Don't worry. You have sufficient papers," Ja'far says, perhaps mistaking my weariness for fear of being deported back to France. "Go with the Pardos to the village police station and tell them you're a Jew. They will call The Joint, and from there you'll be well taken care of, even if you're not Baron von Rothschild."

According to Ja'far, the American Jewish Joint Distribution Committee, better known as The Joint, is known for plucking refugees out of Spanish prisons with or without the state's permission. Hard to believe, yet he assures me it's so.

The Pardos say their goodbyes and as they head toward town Muriel looks back, motioning for me to hurry up and join them.

"You'd better get going. Unless, you'd rather take your chances working with me." Ja'far laughs to cover his discomfort, since we both know his offer is one I should refuse.

I recall my journey south with Cristelle and her cynical appraisal of me. Here is a chance to prove her wrong. And who knew? With luck, my Uncle Emile might one day appear on the Freedom Trail as promised.

"I understand," Ja'far says with a downcast look. "No need to say anything. How selfish of me to ask."

I'm still searching for the right words and have found none that fully express how I feel. "The rainy season is here and I'll need boots and a waterproof coat."

He grabs my hand and holds it to his heart.

I came back to reality more gently this time, having bonded so closely with Luzia that limitations of time and space were irrelevant. It was an uplifting thought, until flattened by an unavoidable fact. If Luzia had been eighteen when she met Ja'far in 1942, she would be ninety-six today, almost certainly turned to dust. I felt a deep sense of loss. Not only was my life-long connection with Nona destroyed by Alzheimers, I would never be able to hug my courageous Great Aunt from Belgium. In a daze, I went to join the line at Passport Control before boarding the Málaga flight.

As we flew over southern France, through thin clouds at low altitude, the red-roofed farmhouses and green hillsides brought Northern California to mind. The closer we drew to Spain, the more the Pyrenees took shape. The same dark recesses and sunlit peaks that Luzia and Ja'far crisscrossed were calling me home.

In Seattle, my *Vijitas Lokas* subverted my efforts to achieve normalcy. Here in Europe, where the past lived much closer to the surface, there was a chance these episodes would begin to make sense. Maybe I could drop the *Loka* and keep the *Vijita*.

# Chapter Five

On the approach to Málaga, we dropped through a cloudbank and emerged into bright sunlight over a turquoise bay. Hi-rise hotels and condominiums encircled the shoreline, barricading the city's heart from view. I called Dad from the airport to let him know I'd arrived safely, then took a taxi and checked into my hotel near the Plaza de la Merced. It was early evening and the temperature was holding in the eighties. I changed into a tank top and shorts and went for a stroll through the Old Town district.

In contrast to the wide boulevards and newly constructed skyscrapers I'd seen from the air, the streets were narrow and pedestrian friendly, many of the lanes closed to traffic. It was a charming and unassuming district where Picasso lived as a child and I promised myself that on my way back to Seattle I'd visit the *Museo Picasso* and buy some prints. As Dad had commented while visiting my starkly functional apartment, "If your walls were children they'd be crying for attention."

I followed the signs to Malagueta Beach, where the aqua-green Mediterranean beckoned me to shed my running shoes and let my toes wiggle with pleasure in the cool water. Afterwards, I sat cross-legged on the sand and ran the fine grains through my fingers, watching streaks of red color the mist in preparation for sunset. My gaze skimmed the water in the direction of North Africa, conjuring up hundreds of ships filled to capacity with Jews who were banished from their homeland at the end of the fifteenth century. I pictured Ja'far's Muslim ancestors, exiled *en masse* more than a hundred years later. How extraordinary that he would meet and fall in love with my Great Aunt Luzia in *World War II* France. How strange that she would choose *me* to relive her memories. Once again I feel my sense of self shifting.

I'm unpacking my things in Ja'far's room above the café. He says that by posing as a couple we'll attract less attention. We both know there's more to it than that.

I find a space in the bookcase he's fashioned out of scraps of wood. The shelves are already crammed with volumes left by refugees unable to carry their weight a step further.

"You have a copy of *The Silence of the Sea*! I read it in Uncle Emile's library in Paris. He told me the *Resistance* is publishing its own books. How miraculous."

"What's miraculous is that you and I met, Luzia."

"I feel the same way and if we're to live together, you'll have to tell me your surname," I tease.

"I'm so sorry." Ja'far sounds genuinely mortified. "You never asked and after a while I assumed you knew. Then again how could you? We're so careful about those things." He pauses, I expect because his tongue, accustomed to keeping secrets, is reluctant to obey.

"Siddiqui."

"I like the way it sounds. Does it have a particular meaning?

Ja'far hoists my empty suitcase up to the top shelf of the closet. "Siddiqui means truthfulness. Not always easy to live up to, but I try."

Tonight is one of our rare nights off during a busy summer and the mutual attraction we feel is strong. Despite my willingness, Ja'far, who is five years older than me, suggests we wait. "There's not much room for romance in a heart consumed by grief. Let's give it time," he says, planting a kiss on my cheek.

I'm not so sure. *What if something happens to one of us? What regrets then?* Ja'far offers to sleep on a small cot he keeps in the closet, and I agree but only if we take turns.

We stay up late, talking about the good—or somewhat better—times before the war. I take a sip of weak tea made from our dwindling stock. "If you've never tasted Belgian coffee your life is incomplete."

"Look at you. Socializing at bistros with friends, innocent and carefree." Ja'far puts on a jealous air. "Lots of male admirers, I'd suspect."

"I was too young to notice… until now," I retort. "What about your days in the City of Light? I'll bet the young ladies swooned."

Ja'far stiffens and I regret my words. He doesn't like talking about his time in Paris. He says there are too many memories of his friends in the Army of Africa who died fighting the Battle of France.

I force him to make eye contact. "You're doing your bit here."

"No comparison."

Like most of our conversations, this one has turned serious. "Luzia, I think we should make one more trip over the Pyrenees, and after that remain on the Spanish side of the border. The Germans have occupied all of Vichy, including St.

Girons. They've posted frontier guards along the whole length of the mountain chain and the level of danger has increased a thousand-fold. Many escape networks have been infiltrated and dozens of guides are being sent to die in concentration camps. I'm afraid our luck will run out."

I slide my empty suitcase under the bed. "There are more refugees than ever. How can we desert them? Despite the 'forbidden zone,' many are finding their way to St. Girons. Without us they'll never make it across."

So far we've guided a half-dozen downed British, American, Polish and Free French aircrews trying to reach Gibraltar, Jewish refugees from all over Europe, and a flood of young Frenchmen attempting to avoid being deported to work as forced laborers for the Nazis. Our life is a blur of hasty encounters and dangerous excursions. Maybe Ja'far is right and we should consider our options.

I'm pouring more tea when a knock vibrates on the thin door and a familiar voice echoes from the hallway. "There's someone here who says he must see you right away."

"We'll be right down, Phillipe," Ja'far calls out to the generous barkeep who has kept us going all this time.

Downstairs the new arrival waits in the café. Klaus, as he calls himself, carries a briefcase and wears civilian clothes. It's the military style backpack that gives him away. Blond and blue-eyed, his is the face of the enemy, impossibly here and asking for our help. Unlike the couple forced to take in the German soldier in *The Silence of the Sea,* Ja'far and I have a choice to make.

"I can pay extra if you take only me. Please," the young man begs. He's only a year or two older than me and plainly terrified.

I understand why Klaus wants to avoid company. There are many Frenchmen who would be happy to stick a knife in him. And if he *is* a deserter, as he claims, the Germans will execute him on the spot.

I take Ja'far aside. "How do we know this man is not an informer who will betray us?"

"If that were so, you and I would have been arrested by his buddies as soon as I accepted payment. I'll keep a close eye on him, I promise."

He looks at his watch. "The sun will be up in an hour."

The three of us leave separately, five minutes apart, taking different routes through town to meet up at the trail.

The weather is passable and we make good progress on the climb, stopping for the night at the usual place. Klaus sleeps with his attaché case gripped in his arms. "If he stole whatever is in that briefcase from his bosses, they may have followed him," I whisper to Ja'far.

"All of our refugees have secrets."

"Until now, none have been Nazis soldiers."

"He's paid us in gold, which means we can buy more supplies to keep our operation going. Don't worry. I won't let him out of my sight. Try to catch some sleep."

My total immersion in World War II France was broken by the feel of a hand with a strong grip cupping my elbow. I jumped up from the sand, reflexes clicking into gear, ready to run across the beach to the safety of the nearby boulevard packed with early evening strollers.

"Alienor, please, I mean you no harm." I risked a quick glance at this man who stood a full shoulder above me and knew my name. In black pants and t-shirt, he looked to be in his mid-forties, solidly built, a narrow bearded face topped by blueish-black curls with a few streaks of silver.

"Please allow my apology to be accepted for frightening you."

"You have five seconds to explain yourself before I yell for help."

"*Aro.*" His shortening of the word *claro,* which means *of course,* confirmed my suspicion that the accent tinting his oddly phrased English was Andalusian. He seemed to presume I spoke little Spanish and that could work to my advantage.

"I hear you are consulting tomorrow with a lawyer called Luis Alcábez."

*How did he know this?* I flinched involuntarily. A slight upturn on the left side of his mouth betrayed my accoster's pleasure at hitting the mark.

"It is not safe. You must go home." He pointed in the direction of the airport for emphasis.

For the first time since arriving in Spain I felt the cold touch of strangeness. "Why?"

"I will explain everything if you are having coffee with me."

We were in full view of people walking the promenade and I found this reassuring. After rinsing my feet under a spigot near the public washroom and putting on my shoes, I followed him into *La Chancia,* a small café overlooking the water. He ordered some pastries and two *cortados con poca leche* at the counter, not bothering to consult me, and when I pulled my credit card out of my purse, he waved it away.

I chose a table by the window and he held the chair as I sat down, with an old-fashioned politeness I would not have expected. The espresso was strong, the milk almost invisible. I felt secure enough, surrounded by people leisurely sipping drinks, to stay and hear him out.

"I'm sorry I cannot tell you my name. I work for an organization that I also have no liberty to identify. I *can* tell you we devote ourselves to the good of the public. I have important advice that I strongly suggest you follow. You must go home. There is nothing waiting for you here. Take the first flight out of Málaga tonight."

In my experience, those who say they're working for the public good are usually doing the opposite. "Forgo my citizenship application? Why?"

"There are many people who do not want your kind returning to Spain. Some of them may even belong to your own family. There are forces at work you know nothing about and it's better for you if it stays that way."

His English had mysteriously improved. He'd also blindsided me, counting on the expectation of rejection and intolerance that runs strong among the Chosen People. He would be hoping for my flight response to kick in and yes, my pulse was racing. But it was with anger, not fear. I focused on keeping my voice level. "I've been told that, unlike you, there are many Spaniards who welcome the return of the Sephardim. Without support from the population, the new law would not have been passed in the first place. I won't be intimidated if that's what you're after."

He pushed back his chair. "You have mistaken my intentions."

"Have I?"

"If you cannot recognize a friend in his own clothes, how will you know your enemy in disguise?"

That gave me pause and for a moment I doubted my swift judgment of him. As he turned to leave, I grabbed my phone and snapped a quick shot, catching his profile in the frame. He kept walking, giving no indication he'd noticed.

Walking back to my hotel from the café I realized how foolish I'd been. If this man knew I'd taken his picture, there was a good chance he'd try to get it back. Or maybe he didn't care. It would be my word against his and what harm could there be in a public conversation?

Secure in my room, I uploaded the photo to iCloud for safekeeping. It was close to 9pm and I tried calling Luis Alcábez. I presumed he worked late at the office like many Spaniards did, after taking long afternoon breaks. When his voicemail answered, I left a message. "This is Alienor Crespo calling from Málaga. Something strange has happened. I guess we'll talk about it tomorrow when I see you. I'll do my best to arrive by eleven so we can keep our appointment with the notary at noon."

It was noon in Seattle and Dad picked up the phone after two rings. "Your second call in one day, you must be missing me. What's it like over there?"

"Now I know why people drop everything to go to the Mediterranean. It's enchanting." I wasn't about to tell him I felt scared and alone and had called just to hear his voice. "How's Nona?"

"I spoke with her on the phone last night and she asked me to give you a message. Of course it makes little sense."

"Try me."

"She said, 'Tell Alienor that a good battle brings a good peace.'"

Nona's words triggered anxiety about what might be in store for me here. Yet wasn't that the point? To shake up my life and start over? It was only natural there would be twinges of doubt, even dread. Like the premonition I'd felt the first time I tried to take a backflip off the side of the Rainier Beach pool. I'd come within an inch of smashing my head on the concrete. *The important thing is that you survived.*

"Dad, I'd better let you go. I'm starving and need to eat before I go to bed. Take care. I'll call again soon."

Downstairs, I ordered an omelet in the hotel's 24-hour restaurant. Despite the bland décor, the eggs were delicious and so was the Sangria. The waitress served me with an understanding smile, another customer dining in two time zones at once.

Back in my room, I took another look at the picture of Luzia, Ja'far and their baby. Knowing her so intimately through our shared *Vijitas* gave Luzia's image a luminescent quality, reminiscent of an image seen through a 3D viewer. After I notarized my application in Granada, I would try to identify where the photo had been taken. Perhaps in the shadow of the Pyrenees or maybe farther south? Instead of shrinking away from my gift, I would invite it to provide me with some answers. Having made this decision, it was easy to slip out of myself and into my great aunt's skin.

It's nearing nightfall on the second evening of our trip with Klaus, when the woods explode with shouts in indistinct German, ricocheting off the steep slopes, making it tricky to tell how far away or from which direction the sound is coming.

With no hesitation, Klaus heaves his briefcase as far as he can into the brush and breaks into a run. We stay calm, as we've trained ourselves to do. We wait to be sure the source of the noise is ahead of us before turning back to take a narrow, barely visible path that will eventually circle back to Saint Girons.

A minute into our brisk walk, gunshots resound from the vicinity of Klaus's flight. Ja'far signals me to a stop. "Whatever is in that suitcase must be extremely valuable or incriminating – or both."

"I forbid you to go back," I say, knowing he'll do as he pleases.

"Go on ahead. I'll only be a few minutes."

Back in our room, my imagination is cruel and there is no wine to drown my fear of losing the man I've come to love.

After endless waiting, I hear the welcome sound of Ja'far's footsteps on the stairs. Empty-handed and contrite, he begins to apologize and stops short when he sees me sitting on the bed in my camisole, arms extended to receive him.

Our coupling seems the only natural thing left in the world, which makes it doubly painful that in its aftermath, I'm unable to control the sobs that rack my body.

"It feels selfish to be happy in the midst of so much suffering and not knowing the situation of my family."

Ja'far strokes my hair and murmurs, "I'm your family now."

Returning to my lonely hotel room was bittersweet. I'd never let myself be as raw and vulnerable as Luzia was with Ja'far. During the two years I lived with my boyfriend Joel, who could reverse-engineer any computer code known to man, I'd managed to keep my gift of second sight hidden. I didn't realize until it was too late how much my secretiveness poisoned our relationship. Each time he rejected my hints about alternative states of consciousness and accused me of being unscientific and irrational, there was a slow leak of hope on my part. If I ever fell in love again it would have to be with someone capable of accepting my 'eccentricities.' This was hard to imagine, given all the trouble I still had making peace with them myself.

As for the man who sought me out on the beach, if his purpose was to discourage me from unearthing secrets from the past he was in for a disappointment. My mother had coached me in using my head when threatened with violence in the schoolyard. "Remember, you're smarter than them. That's why they fear and bully you. You can use words to take control of the situation. If you must defend yourself, use the moves you've learned in your martial arts class. And remember—there's no shame in using the legs God gave you to run."

Exhausted from traveling in both realms, I slept.

# Chapter Six

Next morning, preparing to check out, I searched the room for any stray items prior to zipping up my suitcase. I counted the Euros in my purse and returned my wallet to the compartment it shared with my travel documents. It was then that I noticed my passport was missing. Taking a deep breath, I conducted a thorough search of all my belongings. No luck. *How could I have been so careless? Or had I?* I remembered how my unusually polite companion had stood behind me and held my chair.

Losing your passport while traveling is right up there with walking naked down the street in a dream. Except I was wide awake and in spite of being a seasoned traveler felt angry and violated. It was a good thing that while traveling in South America I'd learned a trick or two when it came to safeguarding documents. Prior to leaving Seattle I'd scanned the first two pages of my booklet and emailed the file to myself. If I did not find the passport at the café or in the taxi I took back to the hotel, I would take a printout to the American consulate in Málaga and apply for a replacement.

Both the café and the US Consular Agency opened at 10am, which meant I wouldn't make the 9am bus to Granada. This didn't bother me so much. It was a minor inconvenience.

What rattled me was the thought of why someone would first warn me to leave the country and then steal my passport.

When I walked into *La Chancia* the next morning, the rotund man working behind the counter recognized me immediately. "Yes! We have your passport Ms. Crespo. I was going to take it to the consulate myself this afternoon if you failed to claim it."

"Where did you find it?"

"In the Ladies Room, sitting on the sink. Our cleaning person found it late last night after we closed."

This made no sense, since I had not used the café's bathroom. *Why was the passport taken only to be promptly returned? Did the thief, who had already warned me to go home, resort to this tactic in order to delay my trip to Granada?* If so, he knew far more about my plans than made me comfortable. I mulled over these uneasy speculations as I thanked the manager profusely and accepted with gratitude the coffee and pastry he insisted I take without charge.

Fortunately buses from Málaga to Granada run frequently. In the taxi on the way to the bus station, I left another phone message for Alcábez, telling him I'd arrive around 2pm. I was anxious to reconnect with my attorney and get his take on what had happened before we went ahead and had my application for citizenship notarized.

Alcábez had been retained by the Jewish Communities of Spain to travel around the world, smoothing the way for Sephardi who wished to apply for their passports. Six months ago, when we'd met in Seattle, I asked him how he liked his job and was treated to a broad smile. "These are my brethren. I work pro bono and it's my honor to seek them out in their places of exile, from Turkey to Amsterdam, Venezuela to Brazil,

New York to Los Angeles, and now Seattle. All around the globe I've connected with people who share my roots. Granted there's a lot of paperwork, but he who eats the meat must gnaw the bone."

Today, I found him in his office, leaning on the edge of his desk in front of a window looking out on the prestigious Calle Recogidas. "So sorry I was delayed, Señor Alcábez."

"No problem. And you must call me Luis. I'm glad you had a safe trip."

We shook hands and he served me a cup of ginger tea. "It's all I drink now. Coffee agitates me, almost as much as troubling phone messages. Tell me. What happened?"

I described how I'd been accosted on the beach and showed him the blurry photo I'd taken. "The man walking toward the door, that's him."

"The nerve of this *imbécil!* That he was able to obtain your name and your whereabouts is very troubling."

"He may have stolen my passport too. But, if so, he left it at the restaurant for me to find."

Luis took a sip of tea and motioned for me not to neglect my own. "If he has your passport number, there's not much harm he can do as long as you have the original document in your possession. Still – it's unnerving."

"I agree. Is it possible he belongs to some anti-Semitic group that opposes Jews returning to Spain?"

Luis grimaced at this unsavory idea. "Mico Rosales, the notary who will certify your papers, belongs to a group called *Stop the Hate*. He'll know precisely who to call. We'll make the report as soon as we get to his office, which is right down the street."

Luis tapped a few numbers on his cell, waited a bit, and then frowned. "No answer. Mico's probably gone home for the afternoon and won't be back now until six. If you had been on time…" He caught himself. "Pardon. Your first time in Spain and here I am scolding you for being unavoidably late, when I should be extending an invitation to take you home for lunch with my family. It's not far from here. We'll take the tram from the Plaza. Don't even think of saying no."

All this was said in rapid-fire Spanish, a good test of my fluency. Thanks to my recent refresher course I barely missed a word. Alcábez, taking charge of my carry-all, motioned me toward the door.

On our way out, he tried Rosales again and left a message. "Hola, Luis here. I'm calling to apologize. Ms. Crespo was delayed and did not arrive until just now. I hope the inconvenience is not a bother. We will come this evening when you return to the office. Also, more applicants are headed your way – there's one from Morocco, who is close to your age and I hear is a real beauty."

He grinned at me mischievously. "Mico recently turned sixty-three and he often jokes about having 'one last fling.'"

Outside, the afternoon heat was reaching its peak. The shuttered shops would have to wait for customers to return in the cool of the evening. We walked through the cramped, down-at-heel streets connecting the wide, elegant boulevards, and boarded a bus. Luis used the travel time to jot down some notes on a case he said was pending in Granada's Provincial Court, while I engaged in people-watching, equally fascinated by the cheerful chatter of schoolkids, the preoccupied manner of the *burguesía* in their business attire, and the wizened faces of the oldsters who rode the SN1 line.

We stopped off at a mercado near Luis's house. The way he spoke of how the "gossip of the grandmothers" led him to the best purchases, charmed me. He picked out a nice chicken and some fresh tomatoes. "I'm going to prepare *pollo paprika*, my son Diego's favorite." He said this with palpable pride. "One good thing that came from two years of estrangement from Felicia is that I learned how to cook."

Wheeling his already overflowing shopping basket up and down the well-stocked aisles, Luis continued to confide in me. "Three years ago, when Diego was nine, my wife and I were living separate lives and close to divorcing. When Felicia wasn't attending one more international conference, she was chasing down medieval manuscripts at auctions all over Europe and purchasing them for the University of Granada's library. Meanwhile, I was busy helping to push through the enactment of Spain's new citizenship law. Poor Diego spent so much time with his grandparents that he began to call my father *papito*. Then our son was diagnosed with leukemia."

"You must have been devastated."

Luis tested the firmness of the eggplant he held in his hand, its glossy surface no doubt reflecting painful memories.

"Felicia took an indefinite sabbatical and I cut back drastically on my hours. We practically lived at the hospital – sleeping side by side in chairs by his bedside while he hung on by a thread. We fell in love all over again." I found his openness and sensitivity as refreshing as I had in Seattle, and in total contrast to the stereotype of the Spanish *machismo* male.

Luis smiled as he picked out a ripe papaya, giving me hope for a happy ending to his tale. "No sign of cancer and Felicia has been talking about giving Diego a sibling. All is well. At least for now."

The Alcábez family lived in a pale yellow, brick apartment building on Calle el Calar, across from the Genil River. We took the elevator to the fifth floor and walked along a narrow veranda decorated with brightly colored flowerpots. From behind the iron railing, I looked out at the terraces stacked in rows above the inner courtyard, a modern version of centuries-old Moorish architecture. The balconies held everything from laundry baskets to bicycles to barbeques.

The lawyer's two-bedroom flat had an old-fashioned feel, with its high ceilings and double windows overlooking a sea of tiled rooftops. He settled me in the living room with a glass of wine and got to work in the small, well-equipped kitchen. By the time an energetic woman with tightly curled blond hair barged through the door, accompanied by a narrow-faced boy with determined eyes, the aromas of paprika, cayenne and garlic were there to greet them.

"*Estupendo*! You made my chicken!" Diego called out, swinging his backpack in the air on the way to his room.

"So you're the American woman! How did it go today?" Felicia was anything but shy. She made me that second cup of espresso I'd been craving all day, and the four of us sat down to a late lunch served on fine china. I was in awe of the white lace tablecloth and took care not to spill anything.

Watching the affectionate glances exchanged over Diego's head while he dug into his food, I felt a pang of regret that Joel and I had never taken the plunge. I sent a silent prayer for Diego's continued health to whomever might be listening and hurriedly took a bite of chicken to cover my confusion. It was a long time since I'd attempted to invoke a higher power on someone else's behalf.

Over an insanely rich tiramisu, Felicia continued her stream of chatter. "Someone wants me to expand my thesis and publish it as a book. Isn't that crazy? Who would want to read an anthology of early medieval Arabic and Hebrew literature? Besides, few people believe in the *Convivencia* anymore."

"I do."

"How so?"

"My grandmother sang songs in a mix of Hebrew, Arabic and Spanish, melodies she said were composed in medieval times, when Muslim and Jewish poets competed for recognition. Is that what you mean by *Convivencia?*"

Felicia's look of intrigued surprise darted across the table. "That's it, exactly."

"Is this your main area of research?"

Her smile gave way to a frown. "I try. But with all the sectarian violence these days, it's become fashionable to deny that the three Abrahamic faiths were ever at peace. It's controversial even for university teachers to discuss the *Convivencia* in class and many of the professors are old Falangists."

"Really? Does Franco continue to have followers in Spain?" As soon as I asked the question I realized how naive I sounded. "I'd love to read your book, Felicia."

"I'm afraid I'm not much of a writer."

Luis butted in. "Don't be so modest. You could make a court docket sound like a poem."

A touch of pink dotted Felicia's cheeks as she hurriedly whisked the plates off the table. We adjourned to the parlor where conversation stilled and helped along by jet lag I was soon fast asleep on the couch. I awoke briefly, self-conscious until I caught my companions napping too. How sweet of them to treat me as one of the family.

Mico Rosales' office was in an upscale, brownstone building straddling the border between Granada's historical district—where the River Darro flows below the castles and gardens of the Alhambra—and the shiny modern business district that touts a more modern flavor. As we waited for the elevator, it was clear Luis was troubled that Rosales had failed to return his calls.

On the third floor, at the end of a long, lushly carpeted hallway, the door marked Notary Services stood open. Inside, a voice on the radio blared. Neither of us heard a word. Our senses were trained on the man spread-eagle on the floor, a bright red bloodstain streaked like a Rorschach test across his shoulder and the right side of his shirt.

"Mico!" With an anguished cry Alcábez crouched beside his friend, touching his neck to check for a pulse. "Hang on, hang on," he muttered, taking off his jacket and pressing the cloth firmly down on the notary's shoulder to staunch the blood with one hand, while tapping the emergency code on his cell phone with the other.

"This is attorney Luis Alcábez calling from Mico Rosale's office at 47 Gran Via de Colón. He's been shot and seriously wounded. Send an ambulance. Yes, he's alive, barely. You'd better hurry. We're on the third floor."

I knelt down, reaching for Mico's hand, and in that instant he became more to me than a stranger. His eyes flickered, unable to stay open long enough to focus. "Thank goodness he's alive," I said to Luis. Then we waited.

It was only after the medics arrived that I stood up and saw the red paint scrawled on the wall – *No More Jews Allowed!* My body went numb with cold and I felt a heavy pounding in my chest. A sense of dread bolted my feet to the floor for several minutes, until the journalist asserted herself and began taking inventory.

It looked like every scrap of paper in the office had been hastily examined and flung into the air. File cabinets were tipped over and emptied, their contents scattered over the floor. Pictures had been yanked off the walls, including Mico Rosale's

*Civil Law Notary Certificate*, which dangled from the top of a bookcase, a web of shattered glass inside its gold-leafed frame.

For a moment I was sitting in the passenger seat of my mother's car, helplessly watching a rain of sharp windshield fragments flying toward her face. I pushed this nightmarish vision away as the medics placed Mico on a stretcher with an oxygen mask covering his face and a life-giving IV connected to his arm.

Two men in black uniforms and white shirts showed up. One introduced himself as Inspector Fernández of the Granada National Police. Slim and with a restless, edgy manner that made him seem permanently poised for action, he looked young for his rank until his experienced eyes met mine. "I'm sorry you had to see this," he said, and I could tell he meant it.

"Are you the one who called?" the inspector asked Alcábez.

Luis nodded glumly. "Mico Rosales is a colleague and good friend of mine. I'm a lawyer and we've worked together for many years." He then explained why we'd come to see the notary.

"Do you have any idea who might have done this?"

Luis looked toward the door through which they were wheeling his critically wounded friend. "Mico tried to keep his head down but he was not one to be cowed by threats."

"What kind of threats?" Fernández's pen was poised over a small pad.

"He notarizes citizenship applications for many Sephardic Jews. As a consequence, he became active in an anti-hate group. If I were you, I'd start by checking with the Federation of Jewish Communities to see if any files they sent over are missing. All of the applicants should be notified if their personal information has been stolen by these Nazis."

Fernández looked grim. "Judging by the graffiti and from what you've said, this meets the criteria for a hate crime and must be reported to the Provincial Prosecutor."

He used his phone to scan my passport and Luis's identification, asking for our contact information and, in my case, someone in the States who could vouch for me. Not wanting to alarm my dad, I gave the officer Todd Lassiter's number at the *Seattle Courier.*

I then showed Fernández the photo I'd captured in Málaga, telling him about the man who probably stole my passport. The Inspector provided his cell number and asked me to send him a text with the picture I'd taken, which I did.

"We have plans to add facial recognition to our database in a few years. In lieu of that, I may ask you to visit our headquarters and look through some printed headshots. If you think of anything else, please get in touch," he added, giving each of us a business card.

Then he addressed me directly. "Ours is a free and liberal society that respects the rights of all. I want you to know that we'll do everything in our power to bring this criminal to justice and to protect you."

In a shared haze, Luis and I left the building and walked side-by-side down the street in silent agreement that we both needed some fresh air.

"I'm so sorry about your friend."

Alcábez briefly put his hand on my shoulder, as if I were the one in need of comfort. "Mico was eager to meet you. He thought you might be related to a woman he knew years ago."

"Really? Did he provide any details?"

"Not many. He did say she was the daughter of someone who escaped to Spain during the Second World War. He was deep into researching that period of history."

*Were my dual realities on a collision course?* What if Mico Rosales had planned to put me in touch with my Great Aunt Luzia's descendants? If he survived, I would be able ask him. Another reason—albeit a selfish one—for hoping he'd live.

"Let's not write him off just yet," Luis said, as if picking up on my thoughts. "Mico's a tough bird."

Alcábez guided me across a busy intersection to the bus stop. "Felicia will be terribly upset. She adores Mico. He's been so generous in authenticating her medieval manuscripts and has done some translating for her too. It's a hobby and he never charges a cent."

We boarded the crowded tram and I found a pole to hang on to. I pictured the notary being carried from an ambulance into the hospital, fighting for his life while I rode through the city, unharmed. People like Mico, who tracked extremist groups, were always in jeopardy. Had I inadvertently added to his? I pushed this disturbing idea aside for a moment and considered the other, professional side of the equation.

If Granada's press corps followed police scanners like we did at home, they were sure to be all over this story. Especially when word got out that a hate crime had been committed. It wasn't what I'd hoped to write about but the story deserved coverage. And as Todd might have said, I already knew more about it than was probably good for my health.

# Chapter Seven

As soon as we entered the apartment, Luis took Felicia into their bedroom. I could hear her sobbing as he broke the news. She came out, eyes red and moist. "Are you okay? How terrible for you to see him… that way."

"Yes, it was." I was moved by her concern for my welfare.

"Of course you've seen this kind of thing before. Maybe you're used to it… oh no, that's not what I meant to say."

"That's okay, Felicia. Lots of people think American journalists have Teflon hides, living in a country as awash in guns as ours."

Luis ended his phone call with the hospital. "They've taken him for surgery. The nurse promised to call me when there's news, either way."

The Alcábezes insisted that I stay overnight. No need to say why. It was obvious that Luis and I were potential targets of Mico's attacker.

Felicia led me by the hand to her son's room. "Diego will stay on the couch. Don't worry – he'll love being near the TV." She gently pushed me toward the bed, insisting I take some rest.

Emotionally and physically exhausted, I nestled under Diego's Batman and Robin quilt. It was oddly comforting to be surrounded by posters of his musical idols, who included

David Bustamante, Natalia and unpredictably, Pink Floyd. I drifted, not toward sleep but into Luzia's troubled world.

It's the height of winter and we've been forced to take time off, bowing to the inevitable hazards of frostbite and snow blindness. Wisdom also dictates that we quit our dangerous calling rather than push our luck too far. There's too much to lose with a baby on the way in less than five months.

Our meager belongings are already packed in Ja'far's duffel bag, along with a thick medieval manuscript filled with exquisite illustrations depicting an unearthly world. The text of the codex is written in Latin and the embossed leather cover is decorated with filigreed metal clasps. Ja'far has admitted to recovering this Christian holy book from Klaus's briefcase and hiding it in the cellar on the night the poor soldier died. I can hardly be angry with him. Perhaps we will sell this treasure and use the money to start a new life.

We head downstairs to say goodbye to Phillipe. Voices float up from the café and we stop on the landing to listen.

"Well is Luzia here or not?"

"What's it to you?" Phillipe is using the irritable voice he reserves for inquisitive strangers.

I creep further down the stairway so I can see the visitor. A tall, thin man with a greying beard and a profoundly weary air stands with his back to the bar. He scratches at the sparse hair on his head, gazing up at the hefty crossbeams, polished with age, eyeing the billiard table and the watercolors of village life that decorate the rough-hewn walls.

It takes a few more moments for me to recognize him, what with all the weight he's lost and the unfamiliar beard. I trip down the steps and race over, throwing my arms around his neck. "Uncle Emile!"

We hold each other so tight I can feel his lungs taking in deep draughts of relief that he has found me. His thin frame trembles with emotion. "My dear Luzia, why are you still here? Cristelle told me she dropped you off safely in St. Girons. I thought you would be in Barcelona by now. I gave up the apartment in Paris as soon as you left. It was too dangerous."

The next logical question is one I ask with my eyes alone, afraid that saying my parents' and brother's names aloud will break the spell that has kept them alive in my heart.

"Little treasure, my *Shatje*, I'm afraid I've lost track of them."

Our eyes meet in a pact of sadness. Someday there will be time to let the tears flow.

"We can only pray," says Uncle Emile. "Meanwhile, you and I must find our way to the United States."

Ja'far quietly walks over, reaching for my hand. Seeing us side by side, Uncle Emile looks confused. Then he notices the bulge under my dress and offers a smile of sad acceptance.

"We're going to get married in Spain," Ja'far says in reply to the obvious question. "We'll have a safe place to live with our baby. I'm the first from my family to return since the Moors were exiled by decree in the seventeenth century. Those who stayed behind passed our house and land down through the generations."

Ja'far fails to mention that to avoid exile, many of his ancestors were forced to take on Christian identities, at great cost to their true natures and with no guarantee of success.

Watching Uncle Emile withdraw into himself, I imagine him thinking. *She's abandoning us, leaving her Jewish faith after all we've suffered. If my brother is alive, how will he survive losing his daughter too?*

It's decided that when the weather clears, we'll escort my uncle over the Pyrenees, accompanying him as far as the turnoff for Barcelona. After that, Ja'far and I will continue south in search of the relatives he's told me live in La Alpujarra, outside a tiny village called Almendrales.

Ja'far insists that Emile take one of the gold pieces Klaus paid us, pressing it into my uncle's hand. "I know you wish us well and we want you to stay safe."

So many unspoken words. I try to read Uncle Emile's face. There is a gentle resolution there. *Let them be happy. So few chances are left.*

I came to myself in Diego's room, filled with joy at the realization that Luzia Crespo's baby, born in the 1940's, might well be living in the foothills of the Sierra Nevada. La Alpujarra was only an hour or two by car from Granada. My delight was short-lived however, obliterated by visions of the crime scene and Mico Rosale's battered body. Staring into space, my brain abuzz with questions about both past and present, I knew I needed rest. I counted each breath, going backwards from thirty to zero, blocking the traffic noise outside the bedroom window. I felt a falling sensation and the next thing I knew, it was morning and Felicia was looking down at me, a smile in her eyes.

"You were sleeping so soundly, we decided not to wake you. There's an article in the morning paper. Luis wants to talk with you."

I unzipped my carry-all, found a clean blouse, and went to freshen up.

Luis was waiting in the dining room. A copy of the *Ideal*, Granada's daily newspaper, was spread out on the table. *Notary*

*Victim of Hate Crime!* blazed across the front page. Although the story did not mention me or Luis Alcábez by name, it implied that Mico Rosales was attacked because of his association with the Sephardi who were returning to Spain. *If whoever had marked him had my file…*

"I think you should go home to Seattle," Felicia said. "That's what I would do. There's no shame in protecting oneself."

With a shock, I remembered my promise to call Dad. I couldn't risk him hearing about the shooting on the TV news and having an anxiety attack. He was already taking medication to lower his blood pressure.

I stepped out on the balcony for some privacy. "Hi, it's me. There's something I have to tell you."

As soon as I broke the news, Dad repeated essentially what Felicia had said, with a caveat. "I know how much effort you've put into this Spanish identity quest and how much it would have meant to your mother. You can wait in Seattle until they've caught this maniac and return to Spain when it's safe to get your citizenship. Doesn't that make sense?"

"It does. I'll look at all the angles and call you tomorrow, okay?"

This was not entirely honest. I was leaning toward staying in Spain. If there was any chance I could help the police, I owed that much to Mico Rosales, who was fighting for his life as a direct result of helping people like me. I had also landed smack in the middle of what promised to be a complex story involving issues I cared about. Someone had to write it. *Why not me?*

The flip side was that although I knew the Spanish language well, I wasn't accustomed to the culture. Even in a familiar environment, a story could backfire and precipitate unintended consequences. *What made me think I could deal with a situation in a foreign country where my own life might be in jeopardy?*

I decided I would call on my Great Aunt Luzia's courage and hope that I'd inherited a fraction of her spunk. She'd refused to abandon Ja'far and partnered with him as an equal in their struggle against the Nazis. Scared as I might be, I wasn't going to retreat in the face of some cowardly person who shot through windows.

Felicia called me back inside. "I hope you like toast with ham and cheese for breakfast." My eyes widened in anticipation and she laughed.

"Any word from the hospital?" She asked Luis as he poured freshly made coffee while she served the sandwiches.

"They've removed the bullet from Mico's shoulder but the shock put him into a coma. No visitors allowed except close family and I'm not sure he has any in Granada."

After breakfast, Luis got a call and went into the living room to take it. When he returned, he told us the police had found a possible match with the photo I'd taken in the Málaga café. "Inspector Fernández wants you at the station. I have an early court appearance, so if you can wait for me…"

"Not a problem, Felicia said. "I'll take her."

The police station was located in the *Barrio Realejo* district, a twenty minute bus ride from Calle el Calar. On the front steps, a woman wearing a wide-brimmed black hat yelled at a cringing teenage girl. "How could you have gotten into so much trouble?"

Fernández was waiting for us on the other side of the security checkpoint. He had a visitor's pass ready for me and found one for Felicia when I introduced her.

No dull green metal or overflowing ashtrays from noir novels cheapened the Inspector's office. His gleaming desk resembled a nineteenth-century replica, as did the chairs he offered. He turned his computer monitor, giving us a view of two faces shown in profile. "What do you think?"

At first glance, the men in the photos did not resemble each other. The shot from the café showed a tall man with longish curly hair and a beard, wearing casual clothes. The subject of the mug shot sported a buzz cut and suit jacket. Still, the wide-set eyes seemed similar. I visualized my accoster minus his beard and the faces came together as one.

"That's him," I said.

"His name is Carlos Martín Pérez."

I got out my phone and tapped the camera icon. "Is it okay if I shoot off your screen?"

Fernandez nodded. "Of course. Perhaps you can help us locate Martín for questioning. He's listed on an ultra-right-wing watch list and although he has no criminal record or connection with Mico Rosales that we know of, he may in some way be connected to the attack. Carlos comes from a prominent family, which complicates things. Something else that concerns us is the timing of the shooting. It took place at noon."

This confirmed what I already suspected. "It's the same time Rosales originally set for our appointment."

"That's not good." Felicia commented.

"It depends on how you look at it," Fernández responded. "If Ms. Crespo had not been delayed coming from Málaga, chances are she would not be sitting here talking with us right now."

The Inspector turned to me. "This Carlos did you a favor. Whether he acted as he did in order to protect you is something we'll try to find out. As things stand, I'm afraid we cannot guarantee your safety in Spain. This is a dangerous person who is potentially tracking your movements. I think it would be best if you returned home."

"Obviously, you don't know this woman," Felicia said under her breath.

I stood up to leave. "I appreciate your concern, Inspector. As it is, I feel an obligation to stay the course. I came here to complete the process of becoming a Spanish citizen and that's what I intend to do."

With a resigned smile, Inspector Fernández gave me his cell phone number to use in an emergency and wished me luck.

When we got to the street, Felicia patted me on the back. "I like your spirit, Alienor. Luis's grandfather was imprisoned in a camp in Cadiz for opposing Franco. His wife waited three years for her betrothed to come home. Many of her friends told her to give up and marry someone else, someone 'safer' they said. She would have none of it."

Perhaps Felicia guessed things about me that I would be the last to discover. For years I'd felt like a fragment, an insignificant part of a narrative largely unknown to me, good reason to choose journalism as a profession and fill the void by chronicling the travails and accomplishments of others. It was my turn now, an opportunity to fulfill a long-held desire to live my *own* story.

I would rent a car for my excursion to La Alpujarra. If there were any traces of my ancestors, I'd find them. These beings were already alive within me. I would let them guide the way. I did not yet understand the purpose of my *Vijitas* but I was done with letting them make me feel like a misfit. On the contrary, I suspected they connected me to a long line of women who'd made the most of what they'd been given. Why should I be any different?

Felicia kissed me on both cheeks, giving my plans her full approval. "I hope you find your relatives. It would be a life-changing experience." She promised to call me as soon as there was any news of Mico's condition.

# Chapter Eight

As I drove the rented Hyundai south, leaving Granada behind, my thoughts circled like the blades of the wind turbines dotting the dry, moon-like landscape. Although they might be as invisible as Don Quixote's enemies, mine were not imaginary. I kept coming back to Mico Rosales, lying in a hospital bed because of a chain reaction I'd unwittingly started. *Or did the attack on him stem from something completely unrelated?* The graffiti on his office walls broadcasting anti-Semitism was so blatant it could easily be a smokescreen.

I took one blind curve after another, relying on the GPS to guide me, eventually turning east to enter Orgiva. The town was listed in the guidebook as one of the most popular of the *pueblos blancos*, 'white towns' that spill down the Alpujarra hillsides with no sense of gravity. A half-dozen backpackers lounged around a bus stop near the grocery store where I stopped to buy a KAS orange soda.

The terrain grew steeper and I zigzagged my way north through the narrow *callejones* of Pampaneira, Bubión and Capileira. An hour later, squinting against the glare of the afternoon sun, I made out the sign for Almendrales, where I'd reserved a room at an Airbnb. I turned onto a road bordered by cultivated terraces carved into the hillsides. So this was where Ja'far brought my Great Aunt Luzia after the war.

I parked my car on the outskirts and as I walked into the village, the cobblestones sent a welcoming vibration through the soles of my feet. It was nice to feel wanted, even by a bunch of oversized pebbles. I reached for my camera, but then resisted the temptation. Some moments refuse to be caught and framed in a box. If my hunch was correct, I was about to close a gap in my family that had existed for more than seventy-five years.

In the outdoor market, two women hovered over a rickety stand overflowing with grapes and persimmons. The younger one met my eyes with an aggressive warmth that attracted me as much as the sight of the ripened fruit. I picked up a bunch of grapes. "¿Cuánto son las uvas?" I asked. She held up two fingers and I dug into my purse.

She watched me closely as I tasted my prize. "*Delicioso, no?*"

"Yes, very. Do you by chance know if a family named Crespo lives nearby?"

The fruit vendor shook her head no, then pointed up the street, at a red and black building several doors past the small church. "Try the Registro Civil in the Town Hall." As I made a move in that direction, she reached out to stop me. "You must wait for the Town Hall to open, after la siesta, at five o'clock."

My audible groan of disappointment provoked a sympathetic smile. "You can ask María, the almond seller. She knows everyone."

I found the elderly María—a blur of activity in her faded blue denim skirt, embroidered white blouse, and thick, rubber-soled sandals. She was closing up for the day, loading her remaining sacks of almonds onto a cart along with a few silk wall hangings she carefully folded. María declined my offer of help and when she was done, peered at me expectantly. I asked her if she knew any Crespos who lived nearby.

"Yes. I remember them. They used to raise silkworms way out in the countryside. Their house is in a small hamlet not big enough to have a name. Who knows what's become of them."

"Can you tell me where the house is?"

"What do you want with them?"

"My name is Alienor Crespo and they may be my relatives. I want to meet them."

She looked me up and down, assessing my hardiness and perhaps something else. "It's a long walk and if you drive you'll need a Jeep or a Rover."

On a slip of paper, María sketched a map, drawn with astonishing precision by her weathered left hand. I thanked her and bought two bags of shelled almonds, throwing them into my pack along with a bottle of water and the grapes. Although I was due to check in at the Airbnb, possibilities awaited in the hills and I was eager to check them out.

The rutted road ran parallel to a ravine, so narrow that I had no idea what I'd do if a car came from another direction. About ten miles out I reached the junction María had marked on the map with a small cross. I pulled over, continuing on foot along a dirt track. The more I walked the more the dry heat leached the moisture from my bones, causing me to frequently sip from my water bottle until it was empty. I stuck to the route religiously, although at one point I took a shortcut that forced me to scramble over a splintered wooden fence. Fortunately, only a cow and a small band of sheep bore witness to this graceless trespassing.

It was late afternoon when I crested a hill and a stone house popped into view. It looked a good half mile away. I took off my sandals and waded across a narrow stream, appreciative of the water cooling my scorched feet. The air carried a pungent blend of anise and sage, giving rise to a daydream of living here next to a gurgling brook, the trees alive with birdsong to keep me company. This fantasy faded as I trudged up the narrow, bramble-lined trail. I was winded, covered with scratches, and empathized with the two barrows I found abandoned near the top of the path, their wheels turned upside down in supplication to the sky.

I passed a small, well-tended vegetable garden bursting with an abundance of chives, red bell peppers, and sweet basil. A good sign that someone was living in the house – my guess would be Luzia and Ja'far's offspring—a son, daughter or even a grandchild who would now be close to my age.

I was feeling light-headed from the change in altitude, I supposed. Maybe that's why I floated so easily from one reality into another.

A priest walks toward me, his belly protruding from under a flowing, black cassock, his gait sure and measured along the stone floor of the church. "Ah! Luzia Pérez Crespo, the mother of the bride. Your daughter Pilar comes here often but I have missed your presence in the back pews. Church isn't your favorite place, is it?"

Father Guillermo smiles at me, marshalling his multiple chins in an attempt to disarm the cutting words that have already hit home. If he discovers that I'm a Jew married to a Muslim, this could have terrible consequences. "I'm sorry, Padre. I'll try to come more regularly. Pilar said you wanted to see me?"

"Yes. She said her father won't be giving her away. Can you tell me why?"

I should have come better prepared to lie. "Some things are hard to explain, Padre. Mateo is a complex man." *Is this the best I can do? Evidently so.*

Father Guillermo makes the sign of the Cross as we walk toward the chapel, deeper into his territory. "Luzia, my dear, I understand more than you think. I knew Father Anselmo. Did you know that he passed?"

"I'm sorry to hear that, Padre. He was a good man."

We are discussing more than the death of a mutual acquaintance. If it were not for Father Anselmo, Ja'far and I would never have married. In 1946, the brave village priest changed Ja'far's name to Mateo Pérez and married us in a Christian ceremony. He risked his life. To this day our marriage remains technically illegal.

The Padre takes a seat near the aisle and invites me to join him. "There's no need for you to worry, Luzia. I don't care if you have posed as Christians for all these years. There are more family secrets buried in Spain than a thousand earthquakes can dislodge."

My legs feel weak at the thought of Father Guillermo being aware of our situation but I will have to make the best of it. At least there is a trace of compassion in his eyes.

"If you're wondering what I *do* care about, it's Pilar. The nuns at the church school have told me she's very devout. For her own good, and in view of the Martín family's pride in their pure ancestry, I need to ask—does Pilar know her true lineage?"

"No. We've deceived her for her own good. You must know the reason. It's been painful, especially for Ja'far. He wanted to raise her in his own faith, to teach her the precepts of Islam."

This is the first time I've called Ja'far by his real name or referred to him as a Muslim in front of anyone since our arrival in Almendrales, more than twenty years ago. It feels like a betrayal and I fear I've made a huge mistake in confiding in this man.

The Padre glances upwards, apparently checking in with God. "Many people continue to search for their dead family members buried in fields or at the side of the road. Republicans or Nationalists, Christians, Muslims, Jews—it makes no difference – they are all God's children. I have seen too much suffering to be responsible for making more. If you agree to tell Pilar everything, I will go ahead with the marriage. She must learn who she is or she will never be content. It will then be up to her to decide whether or not to inform her husband, preferably before they marry."

It should not astonish me that this priest knows his psychology. He may be hoping my daughter will bow out of marrying Eduardo, once she learns how ill fit she is to join the Martín family, with their business empire in Málaga and "pure and untainted bloodline." In light of Ja'far's opposition to the match and his refusal to give our daughter away at the wedding, this might not be a bad result.

"Fair enough, Father Guillermo. I'll tell Pilar. You have my word." It won't be easy. What the Padre has asked of me will be as difficult as convincing a leopard that its spots are not real.

Standing on the steps of the ancient church, the Padre and I chat about the wedding arrangements, pretending nothing is out of place. We part with an air of conspiracy I would never have thought possible between people like us.

These trips through time were becoming almost normal events, taking place in a room within my mind that I walked in and out of at will. But that didn't mean I returned to the present feeling enlightened. I often came back more confused and ig-norant than before. For instance, I'd studied enough history to know that Franco's stranglehold on Spain did not let up, even in the late 60's. Only one religion, Christianity, was recognized when Luzia's daughter opted to get married. So why would Pilar choose to marry one of the dreaded Falangists who sup-ported El Caudillo's repressive regime? I could only hope that the mother's planned revelations caused the daughter to wise up and change her mind about the wedding.

I knew what it was like to marry the wrong person and end up telling lies of omission about oneself. I wished I could tell Pilar about this in person but in spite of these intense *Vi-jitas* I remained marooned in my own time.

Lost in thought, I'd covered the remaining distance to what I believed to be the Crespo house. The ancient stone walls were at odds with the modern, vinyl windows and gleaming, tiled roof. I used the metal door knocker to rap twice on the burnished wood door. Quick footsteps responded from the other side.

"Who is it?" a low-pitched voice asked.

"My name is Alienor Crespo. It's possible your grand-mother was my great aunt, my Grandpa Aharon's sister."

A tall woman with closely cropped black hair opened the door. She adjusted the straps of her bib overalls, showing off bare arms that were tanned and muscular. Her light blue eyes glowed with transparency in contrast to her olive skin. She appraised *my* features with a long look.

"You do resemble Grandma Luzia, especially around the mouth. You have dimples just like hers."

Her remark threw me into confusion and my eyes blurred. "What a lovely thing to say. Does your mother Pilar live here too?"

"How strange that you would know her name. She died when I was a teenager."

I held myself back, not wanting to scare her with a hug. "I'm so sorry."

"Thank you, Alienor."

"I lost my own mother at a young age too. Please, call me Allie. And you are...?"

"Celia Martín Pérez Crespo. I prefer Pérez since it comes from my grandfather. Come in, come in."

I hung back for a moment. I knew exactly how Celia had come by the name of Pérez—used as a cover by her maternal grandparents—but now it came home to me that my second cousin was also a Martín and possibly related to the Carlos Martín who tried to frighten me off in Málaga and was wanted by the police in connection with the attack on Mico Rosales. What had I stumbled into?

Sensing I'd failed to follow her inside, Celia turned around. "Are you waiting for a red carpet?"

She looked honestly befuddled and I liked her sense of humor. I resolved not to ruin our first minutes together with uncomfortable questions and followed her inside.

The interior was clean, the floor well swept. Among the books stacked on a table near a brown leather reading chair, Lorca's *A Poet in New York* stood out. One stucco wall was dominated by a reproduction of Picasso's *Guernica* and beside it, provoking a jolt of recognition, hung a photo of Ja'far wearing a taqiyah. The subtle defiance in his smile suggested the picture had been taken during an era when wearing Muslim head garb in Spain would have been life threatening. And here I was, sitting on the couch with his granddaughter, explaining why I'd come to Spain.

"All my life I've dreamed of going to America, where my great-grandfather, Jaco Crespo, fled with his son Aharon after the war. And now you've come here." Celia's speech was husky with emotion. She had also opened the door to an unpleasant episode in our family history, so I swallowed my reluctance and asked, "Did you know that Jaco Crespo disowned your grandmother Luzia because she was pregnant with your mother and was about to marry a Muslim?"

Waiting for her answer to this loaded question, I watched Celia's face closely for signs of anger. To my relief, she brushed my hand with her own and said, "Don't look so worried. Grandma Luzia never mentioned it but I had my suspicions. Marrying outside one's faith often causes trouble. My grandmother never talked about our American relatives."

"One thing you can be sure of, Celia, is that my father, Elias, would be overjoyed to meet you."

She disappeared into the kitchen, ostensibly to bring out some wine, cheese, and olives but I suspected to collect her emotions as well.

The floor in the alcove where Celia served our snacks was inlaid with ceramic tiles, painted with the same bright geometric patterns used by Islamic artists on the walls of castles and mosques. My cousin picked up on my interest. "Grandpa Ja'far made these tiles himself when my mother and I moved in. It was his way of welcoming us back to the ancestral home, after Pilar's marriage to my father Eduardo fell apart."

"From what I understand, Ja'far refused to give Pilar away at her wedding because she married into a prominent Catholic family."

"How could you possibly know that?"

Ten minutes in and I'd stumbled already. *Why hadn't I prepared for this?* I gulped down my wine as if it held the answer. "Your grandmother mailed letters across the ocean to her brother." It was somewhat true. Luzia had written to Aharon. And I had the photo in my purse to prove it.

Celia cradled the faded picture in her hands, gazing fixedly at her grandmother, who held baby Pilar in her arms.

"I've never before seen my mother as an infant." She pulled a tissue out of her hip pocket and dabbed at her eyes.

With her finger, Celia touched Papa Ja'far's proud face in the slightly wrinkled photo. Her voice, when she found it, came in a reverent whisper. "My *abuelo* Ja'far had a soft heart. He sheltered Republican comrades from Franco's revenge in the 1960s, deemed by his enemies to be a heinous crime that guaranteed him a death sentence twenty years later. My mother told me Grandma Luzia wasn't home when they came for the love of her life. She searched for his grave but he was one of the disappeared whose bodies were never found. From that day forward, Grandma faded like a flower uprooted from the soil. She died in 1992."

My sadness swelled into a wave of loss. "Your grandparents should have been celebrated as heroes."

"Those were the words my mom used. She told me stories about their adventures in the Pyrenees during the war. She was extremely proud of them. She even continued to praise my grandfather, in spite of his refusing to speak to her from the day she married my father."

"Tell me about your brother Carlos."

Celia frowned. "There's not much to tell. Because our father loved only one of us, we were siblings in name only. After our parents separated, Eduardo raised Carlos as a Martín, living in the ancestral villa in Málaga they built with proceeds from the slave trade in the 1600s. He was taught to despise anyone who doesn't have *pure blood* running through their veins. They poisoned my brother's mind."

Carlos Martín, identified by the police from a photo I'd taken three days ago and now confirmed to be my second cousin. I could feel him gripping my elbow at the beach.

"Celia, you should know that I ran into Carlos in Málaga. Actually he sought me out. He pressured me to return to

America. He knew my lawyer's name and said my life was in danger from those who do not want Jews to return to Spain."

Celia squeezed her eyes shut in reaction to this news. "It's painful for me to tell you that my brother may have been sent by Eduardo. Our father would not see your arrival in Spain in a happy light. He is in denial of my mother's mixed ancestry and would not want a new family member digging around in our history. Especially during an election year."

"I'm afraid he may be guilty of more than denial. Mico Rosales, the notary who was to certify my papers, was shot and badly wounded. He's in a coma, fighting for his life."

Celia palmed her forehead. "That this would happen precisely when you arrived in Spain is no coincidence. Eduardo is connected with some unsavory people. He hates Mico for having been a friend and protector of my mother.

What should have been a joyful reunion had turned into a discussion of possible complicity of family members in attempted murder. "I'm listening," I said, slipping a notebook and pen from my purse.

"You may have gathered by now that Mico Rosales is no ordinary notary. He's been a friend of the family since I was a child. True, I haven't seen him for many years and—" Celia stopped in mid-sentence, turning to face me with skepticism writ large on her face. "Why are you taking notes? How do I know you're truly a relative and not some reporter on the trail of a scandalous story?"

*Ouch.* She was a sharp one. I put away my notebook and showed her my passport to prove I was a Crespo. Then I told her I was an off-and-on-again working journalist from Seattle. "And yes, I seem to have landed in something big. But please believe me when I say that my respect for the privacy of my family, which includes you, comes first."

Celia took a visibly deep breath. "I'm sorry. It's a shock, meeting you so suddenly."

"It's my fault for being so insensitive. I turned our first encounter into an interrogation." *The very thing I tried so hard to avoid.*

"No, no, Alienor. It's understandable that you'd have a million questions."

"I'm sure you do too."

We went on this way for a while, like two drivers at a stop sign deferring to each other—*you first, no it's your turn.* She was the first to acknowledge how ridiculous this was by bursting into laughter. She stood up from the couch and affectionately brushed my hair before stepping away. "We need more wine from the cellar."

As we polished off the second bottle of red, we both relaxed.

"What else would you like to know," my cousin asked.

"Well, one thing I'm curious about is whether or not your father knew about your mother Pilar's mixed ancestry before they married."

Celia's sigh conveyed a touch of exasperation. "My mother may have thought she could get away from the angry whispers in the village by marrying a pure-blood Spaniard like Eduardo. But she was not good at keeping secrets. She told Eduardo about her father's real identity after I was born. Maybe she thought becoming a father would soften his heart. On the contrary, he made her life hell. Despite her being a practicing Catholic, he threatened to denounce her to the authorities for tricking him into an illegal, interfaith marriage. She hung on as long as she could but in 1982, when I was ten, she took me to live here, with my grandparents. Eduardo forced her to leave Carlos behind. He was only eight."

"Is Pilar living here with you?"

Her shoulders sank with the weight of sad memories. "I was studying computer science at the Polytechnic University of Madrid when Mom disappeared. I came home to look for her but after a few months I accepted she was…gone for good." Either my cousin could not bring herself to say the word 'dead' or there was more to it.

"That's when I decided to move back here permanently and take over what was left of my grandfather's silk production business. Those little worms have been our salvation." Before she could tell me more, Celia's cell phone rang. "Sorry, Allie. I'm afraid I'll have to take this call."

I took the opportunity to step outside and clear my head while giving her some privacy. Across the valley, the setting sun splashed rays of tinted light over the distant peaks of the Sierra Nevada while, nearby, the almond and apricot trees displayed a bounty of ready-to-ripen fruit. A small statue of the Virgin was tucked inside a bower in the front yard, protected from the wind and whatever rain fell here in winter. The Madonna's presence did little to quell the uneasiness I felt after hearing Celia's narrative.

Suddenly Luzia becomes visible, along with her daughter Pilar, who is dressed in her Catholic School uniform. The girl's brow is furrowed in concentration and her hazel eyes are lovingly trained on the image of Mother Mary. Taking my place behind Luzia's eyes, I join them. My first thought is, *may the wisdom that inspired my lies give me strength to tell you the truth.*

# Chapter Nine

"There's something we have to discuss before you marry Eduardo."

Pilar looks faintly alarmed, then falls back on that beatific smile of hers, the one that says she'll never stopped believing in her favorite Bible story, the one about how God sent a rainbow to Noah as a promise that he would never flood the world again. This gives her hope that when bad things happen, they won't repeat themselves. When she was ten and her favorite goat died, her philosophical side spilled out as generously as her tears. "Mama, all lives must end and it's fortunate that Lady Dulcinea had such a long one." This resilience is what I'm counting on today.

"Have you ever wondered where your father disappears to several times a day – even when the silkworms are hatching and need his constant attention?"

"You mean the hidden room beneath our house where he goes to pray?

"What else do you know?"

"Don't look so shocked, Mamá. You may have sent me to Catholic School but that doesn't mean I'm blind to other faiths. I've seen the books hidden down there, and Papito's prayer rug, the one with symbols he would never dare ask his Christian weavers to produce. And then there's the alcove where you keep the prayer book printed in Hebrew that you brought to Spain during the War. Papito told me it was a gift from your Uncle Emile. He showed me the silver candles and explained why you light them on Friday nights, when you think I'm busy elsewhere."

"He told you this?" I ask. Of course he did. It's so like Ja'far to try and bolster Pilar's self-confidence by entrusting our secrets to her care, leaving me to play the role of overanxious parent.

Pilar blushes. Possibly a sign of regret for betraying her father's secret. I push for more. "Did your papito tell you his real name?"

"Yes, Mamá, he did, which is more than I can say for you."

The iciness in her tone causes me to take a few steps back, readying myself for the onslaught of truth. "Papá is Ja'far Majid ibn Siddiqui and his Muslim relatives once occupied our house. He also told me that the priest who married you rechristened him as Mateo Pérez, a clever way to avoid the ban on interfaith marriages. After the wedding, you became Luzia Crespo de Pérez and when I was born you named me Pilar Pérez Crespo. Sadly, my given name and Papá's surname are both shams. At least you let me keep Crespo."

*I knew this day would come but not how much her angry words would crush me.* "How can you disrespect a name we chose out of love, praying it would give you protection?"

Pilar remains unmoved. "How can *you* not know that in secret Papito calls me Jariya, after his Moroccan great-grandmother many times removed. Jariya al-Qasam was a fearless Morisca bandit who lived here in Andalusia a long time ago. She married Razin al-Siddiqui and the names of all their children are engraved inside the cover of Papa's Qur'an."

I should have known Ja'far would not be able to resist the inquisitive mind of our daughter. She holds out her wrist for my inspection. "Papito gave me this silver bracelet with *Jariya* engraved on the side that touches my skin. He said my name will always be with me, even if I never say it aloud. That there's a lot of power in that which is left unsaid. He is sure that someday it will be safe for the truth to come out. And until then, 'A sleeping lion should not be awakened.'"

My sensitive daughter has heard enough slurs and threats of violence directed by her classmates at both Muslims and Jews to understand Ja'far's warning. Even so, I should have prepared myself better for this moment. All I can do is hope for divine guidance in my choice of words. "Franco decreed early in his rule that all children in Spain were to be named as Christians. So we called you Pilar, like the pillar holding up the church, hoping that you too would be strong. It has turned out to be a name we love very much."

"Why bring all of this up now, Mamá? There is no sense in telling her about the baby boy I lost a month after Ja'far and I safely reached Spain. She may see me as an overprotective hen but I prefer her anger to her pity. On the day before my wedding."

"Because you're marrying into an historic and wealthy family, the Martíns, builders of ships that have sailed out of Málaga Bay for centuries. They are obsessed with their pure Spanish blood. Are you sure you can handle this? What will happen if you tell your intended the truth about your background?"

"What should I say to him? That although I'm a true Christian, like every Spaniard I have ancestors from more faiths than I can count? Or that my Jewish and Muslim forebears are a little closer to me in time than his family would like? It's none of their concern. Please Mamá. I understand why you and Papito lied to me. I respect your decision to protect me. Please respect my choice too. You raised me as a Catholic and that's the world I know best. Eduardo and I love each other. It will all work out. You'll see."

Pilar crosses herself in front of the Virgin and returns to the house. She has always relished having the last word.

"There you are. I thought I'd lost you." Celia's voice jarred me out of the *Vijita*. I found myself standing on the same spot and staring at the distant silhouette of a steeple touching the sky, surprised not to have noticed it before.

"That belongs to the church inside the monastery," my cousin said. The Carthusians call their cloistered community a charterhouse. No visitors allowed, although they do permit some of the nuns to work at crafts within the confines of the walls. Once in a while, I deliver some silken thread."

Just when I was about to ask if any of her mother's friends from Catholic school had joined the Carthusian order, I was startled by the crack of two gunshots fired in quick succession. The pops sounded like they came from a distance, which is why I was so astonished when Celia grabbed my arm and hauled me into the house. I pulled the door shut behind us and was trying to figure out how the lock worked when she stopped me. "I'm sorry I scared you. No harm in playing it safe but there's also no need to panic. They hunt only wild boars and goats, not people. At least not anymore."

She was avoiding my eyes, her hands shoved deep into the pockets of her coveralls. "I'd invite you to spend the night but it gets cold and there are no extra blankets. My friend Jack has a Land Rover. He'll drive you back to Almendrales."

I was hurt by her dismissal. The excuse she offered was thin as the mountain air. If the sound of distant gunfire could upset her so much, there had to be a reason. It didn't look like I'd be weaseling it out of her soon.

"Let's exchange numbers," Celia said. "Tell me where you're staying and I'll come by for you in the morning."

Jack showed up, a lanky outdoorsman with unruly grey hair. He walked me to the Land Rover he'd parked in a clearing about a quarter mile from the house, next to a yellow Jeep I assumed belonged to Celia. As we bounced down the dirt track leading to town, Jack chatted me up non-stop, babbling on about how, twelve years ago, he emigrated from England, bought a sheep ranch, and convinced his neighbors he was an alright guy.

"Your cousin Celia's a brave one, living out here on her own and keeping the family silk business going. She mostly keeps to herself but there are rumors."

"Such as?"

"For one thing, she uses the name Crespo but gossip in the village has it that her father is Eduardo Martín, the far right StandUp Party's candidate for the Chamber of Deputies. He's not popular hereabouts."

Jack's take on Eduardo was consistent with what Celia had told me. When combined with the unsavory episode in Granada, it added an intriguing political angle to the more personal story I'd been planning to submit to the *Courier*.

"Are gunshots a frequent occurrence in these parts?"

"Not really. Most of the hunting takes place at higher elevations, where the goats live."

"Celia was jumpy, a bit anxious. Maybe we should go back and check on her," I suggested, including him in the decision so I wouldn't come off as an alarmist.

Jack found a widened place on the track and swung into a U-turn. When we were close enough to the house to see but not be seen, I asked him to stop behind a stand of trees. "Don't want to invade her privacy unnecessarily," I said, another partial truth that seemed prudent.

Through gaps in the foliage I caught sight of two people sitting on the steps of the front porch. One of them was Celia and the other sat with his head dangling down as though listening intently, a rifle balanced between his knees. When he turned his face to the light, I recognized Carlos Martín, recently described by Inspector Fernández as "a potentially dangerous person."

Was this why Celia had sent me away? Were the gunshots a signal that she should clear the house of any visitors before her brother came to visit?

Even from a distance, their body language bespoke an argument.

"Maybe she was anxious for you to leave so she could spend time alone with her boyfriend," Jack remarked in his live-and-let-live way. "It's a pity they don't seem happy about it."

"I feel like a fool for having made you drive all this way."

"No worries. I like your company."

I might have flirted back if I hadn't been so furious with myself for being conned into worrying about my cousin's welfare. *What an actress you are, Celia Crespo. If I could see through your eyes for one moment maybe I'd understand why you've gone to so much trouble to keep me away from your brother.* Angrily, I tried to evoke *sometime else*, to bring on a *Vijita* and connect my mind with Celia's, thereby exposing her betrayal of our newfound family connection. Nothing happened.

Jack was looking at me strangely.

"Please don't tell Celia we came back," I pleaded. "She might take it the wrong way."

"Okay. I won't tell her she has a paranoid cousin from America."

"Second cousin," I corrected him.

In between bumps on the way back to town, Jack told me some colorful stories about the local customs that failed to register. I was too busy puzzling over why it was so easy to *visit* my Great Aunt Luzia Crespo yet impossible to penetrate the thoughts of her daughter Pilar or her granddaughter Celia.

Jack dropped me off at my rental car at the junction outside Almendrales where I'd picked up the foot trail to Celia's house. I stopped at the market for some groceries before driving to the Airbnb. My host turned out to be a young, long-haired Dutchman named Jeroen. He showed me to my room on the ground floor. "You have full use of the whole first floor. Feel free to make coffee and consume anything you find in the refrigerator."

His unassuming, hospitable manner put me at ease and in touch with how hungry I was. I unpacked the supplies I'd bought and cooked a cheese omelet, devouring it along with toast and marmalade. When I called Dad, he was excited to hear I'd tracked down his grandniece. I neglected to share my conviction that Celia was an accomplished liar. This character trait, which I admittedly shared with her, would not interfere with my plans to add my cousin to our family tree—along with the marriage of her mother Pilar to Eduardo Martín and the birth of her brother Carlos.

I *guestimated* Pilar's date of birth as 1950, based on my knowledge that Luzia and Ja'far had talked a priest into marrying them in 1946. After Luzia's earlier miscarriage, how delighted they must have been to have a healthy baby girl. Then I added nineteen years to calculate Pilar's wedding date and a few more to get to 1972, a likely year for Celia's birth and one that made her twelve years older than me. Carlos was her younger brother, born a few years later. I decided to wait until I learned more about Ja'far's family history before adding his distant ancestor, the brave Jariya, to the tree.

97

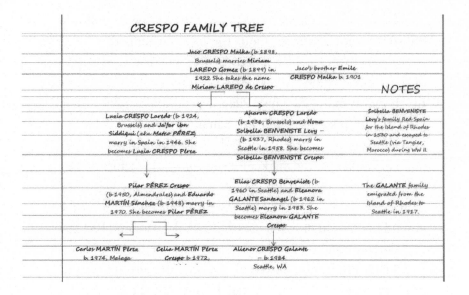

## CRESPO FAMILY TREE

Jaco CRESPO Malka (b 1898, Brussels) marries Miriam LAREDO Gomez (b 1899) in 1922. She takes the name Miriam LAREDO de Crespo

Jaco's brother Emile CRESPO Malka b. 1901

**NOTES**

Luzia CRESPO Laredo (b 1924, Brussels) and Ja'far ibn Siddiqui (aka Mateo PÉREZ) marry in Spain in 1946. She becomes Luzia CRESPO Pérez

Aharon CRESPO Laredo (b 1936, Brussels) and Nona Solbella BENVENISTE Levy (b 1937, Rhodes) marry in Seattle in 1958. She becomes Solbella BENVENISTE Crespo.

Solbella BENVENISTE Levy's family fled Spain for the Island of Rhodes in 1530 and escaped to Seattle (via Tangier, Morocco) during WW II.

Pilar PÉREZ Crespo (b 1950, Almendrales) and Eduardo MARTÍN Sánchez (b 1948) marry in 1970. She becomes Pilar PÉREZ

Elias CRESPO Benveniste (b 1960 in Seattle) and Eleanora GALANTE Santangel (b 1962 in Seattle) marry in 1983. She becomes Eleanora GALANTE Crespo

The GALANTE family emigrated from the Island of Rhodes to Seattle in 1917.

Carlos MARTÍN Pérez b. 1974, Malaga

Celia MARTÍN Pérez Crespo b 1972,

Alienor CRESPO Galante – b 1984 Seattle, WA

---

The bathroom at the Airbnb was spacious, with house plants dangling from a wide beam running across the ceiling, and shelves above the tub stocked with enough towels for a swim party in the moonlit pool outside. As the hot water relaxed my tense muscles, the events of the day – those that took place in the present and in *sometime else* – receded into a forgetful haze. I tilted my head back to wet my hair and felt a wave of gratitude for the peace and quiet. Not for long.

At first, I'm terrified to recognize my great-grandmother Miriam from Belgium, whose death throes in a concentration camp I experienced in a *Vijita* when I was a teenager. It had taken me months to recover. This time, the mood could not be more different.

I'm strolling through the Plaza Bib-Rambla in Granada, dressed in a sleeveless, straight-cut chemise held at the waist

by a tasseled girdle typical of the 1920s. The thin knit fabric of Miriam's dress clings to my thighs as closely as her mind adheres to my own.

I'm a long way from Brussels. The outdoor cafés overflow with overdressed tourists mixing with the less formal locals. I pause in front of four grotesque stone figures, their hunched shoulders supporting a baroque fountain crowned by a statue of Neptune, the god of the sea. A Model T is parked nearby.

I'm almost an hour late. Has he come and gone already?

"Are you Miriam?" The questioner is a young man, dressed in baggy pants, leggings, and a cloak, suggesting either a theatrical costume or real clothes from another age.

"Yes, I'm Miriam. And you are?"

"Shakir. The Founders sent me. We must not talk or call attention to ourselves. I'll lead and you will follow. Come!"

Before I can react he sets off, looking back every now and then to make sure I'm close behind. As our pace picks up, I check to make sure the letter tucked into my waistband is secure. Although I've memorized every word, it would be a disaster to lose the only evidence I have to convince my darling Jaco that his wife is not insane but here for a reason.

Two lines from Shakir's letter come to me as I hurry through the narrow streets, barely keeping pace with him. *Sometimes a window is better than a door… Have faith in what the future holds even if you cannot see it…*

We enter a noisy restaurant, the air dense with the odors of seafood cooking in butter and saffron. My stomach growls, but before the *maître de* can waylay us, Shakir and I are out the side door and descending the stone steps leading to the basement.

The cellar is dimly lit and stacked from floor to ceiling with paper mâché figures of the Saints, taking their rest between dutiful marches in the street, I presume.

Shakir points to the back wall, painted with a colorful mural of characters from the Spanish *Comedia*. Wearing sequined masks, they're costumed like Columbine and Harlequin, with an Andalusian touch. He motions me to come closer. "Relax your eyes."

I do as he says and the figures in the mural gently fade into the background, to be replaced by a large window, its ancient leaded panes clouded with mist. *What could feasibly be visible from this underground room? The innards of a cave? An ancient aqueduct?* The view is dim and blurry, a thick fog gathered on the other side.

Bit by bit the glass clears and a scene comes into focus. A medieval town nestles against a hillock. Three prominent buildings stand close together, each with a symbol raised on the roof – a Cross, a six-pointed star, and an illuminated minaret. I can make out figures walking through the streets, dressed in medieval garb. Jewish men in long black robes and pointy hats, accompanied by women in long skirts, stroll alongside Muslims in pleated baggy pants and leggings, like those worn by Shakir. The peaceful *Convivencia* of my distant ancestors, impossibly come to life. I imagine what it would be like to feel secure in one's skin, in one's faith, with no fear of persecution. To erase the pogroms and the devastation of the Great War from memory and start again.

"It seems so close, a short walk away. I want to see more. I must see more. How can we enter? Is there a doorway?"

Shakir's compassionate eyes are trained on my face. His long-suffering smile belongs to someone much older than his appearance would suggest. "Miriam, what you see is not real. It's a mural painted on the walls of a room inside Zahara, a place which has existed for centuries but remains in isolation. The world is not ready for Zahara or what it represents. It may never be."

A chill of regret settles near my heart. "So you've provided a brief glimpse of heaven and now take it away?"

Shakir sighs. "We share this information with a select few, people like you whom we hope will join us. Maybe your descendants will, in the future…"

I feel driven to ask, "Why me?" But Shakir shakes his head, discouraging more questions. "It's time to go. You're not safe here and should return to Belgium as soon as possible. Have a safe journey home, Miriam. May you live a long and happy life."

Drying my hair and toweling off after my bath at the Airbnb, it came to me how brave and adventurous my great-grandmother Miriam had been in her youth. If Shakir had prescient powers, he would have known her life was to be brutally cut short by the Nazis. Perhaps, as she guessed, he'd been sent to give her a taste of heaven, since there was no way to save her from hell. *Had he known I was there, seeing through Miriam's eyes? That I'd caught sight of the place he called Zahara?* What was it he'd said to her—*Perhaps your descendants will, in the future…*

I shook my head to eject this foolish notion while, at the same time, beginning to harbor some hope that my *Vijitas* were not totally random. As a journalist, I had great respect for cause and effect. Intuition had its place too. I would figure this out eventually.

# Chapter Ten

Celia showed up at the Airbnb at noon, her sturdy work clothes exchanged for a flowery sundress. "I've brought you a present, made with raw silk from the cocoons of our own silkworms. Next time you visit the house, I'll show you how we harvest the threads."

She kissed me on both cheeks just as Felicia had done and I returned the gesture. *Had she warmed to me in my absence?* In time, I hoped she would trust me with her reasons for concealing her meeting with Carlos.

The scarf was beautiful but so stiff that when I draped it around my neck, it crinkled into odd shapes and hung there like a modernist sculpture. Celia laughed at my dismay and said not to worry.

"The fabric will soften after you boil it to remove the sericin. That's the gummy substance, like bees wax, that holds the cocoon together. All these years I've been throwing sericin away as a useless byproduct. Now it seems they use it in bandages for people with sensitive skin and even add it to sunscreen. This high-flying executive from a biomedical firm is coming from Madrid to meet with me today. Dr. Amado says his company has developed something called sericin hydrogel to use in tissue regenerative medicine. Not sure precisely what that is but I'm beginning to think there's an actual market for the sticky stuff."

"Is your operation that big? How much sericin would you have to sell to make any real money?"

Celia eyed me, as if detecting some intelligence she'd assumed was lacking. "China's the main source for sericin and they keep the price low. Which is why it's so odd for a big-time pharma guy to be interested in my small-time setup. Dr. Amado has offered to purchase all the sericin I can provide. He may have something unusual in mind because he asked me if I'd been taught by my mother or grandmother to use this protein in traditional remedies. I told him I know a thing or two but I'm no healer or medicine woman."

A familiar area lit up in my brain. "This sounds like something worth writing about. Is it okay with you if I sit in on the meeting?"

When Celia hesitated, I pressed my case. "There are dozens of bio-tech firms and medical researchers in Seattle. A well-placed magazine article could increase your business."

"Okay, okay. I have some errands to do. I'll come by and pick you up at three and we can drive out to the house. But only if you promise to stay in the background. If the doctor's planning to make an offer, I don't want him distracted by awkward questions."

My cousin returned at four and apologized for running late. On our way out of town, she waved from the yellow Jeep to a few friends in front of the grocery store. Her manner was more outgoing and optimistic than the day before, and she kept up a stream of chatter while driving the erratic roads with the abandon of someone who knew every inch by heart.

In the clearing where Jack had parked his Rover the day before, Celia pulled in next to a gleaming, copper-colored

SUV. "I'll bet he has fun driving people off the road with that thing," I said, as we walked toward her house through the trees.

A puff of smoke reached my nose before I saw the visitor, waiting with a cigarette in hand. In defiance of the heat, he wore dark green polyester pants and a white shirt that strained to cover his overbuilt chest. His walnut-colored hair was combed straight back from his forehead, accentuating sharp cheekbones and glittering eyes, polished and opaque as black glass. To me, he looked more like a salesman or a real estate dealer than a biochemist.

"Dr. Rodrigo Amado, this is my cousin Alienor Crespo from America. I hope you don't mind her joining us."

"Pleased to meet you, Ms. Crespo." The greeting was luke-warm.

"Before we go into the house, let's say hi to the little workers." Celia walked us over to an ancient-looking out-building, the size of a large greenhouse. To step inside was to enter a mini-biosphere vibrating from the whir of fans cir-culating moist air. I'd seen pictures of silk-making but they didn't come close to the real thing. The ceiling-high shelves overflowed with dark green mulberry leaves, rustling madly as hordes of squirming silkworms feverishly feasted on them. Near the far wall, dozens of fuzzy white forms clung to a struc-ture made of coarse straw.

Celia carefully retrieved an errant worm from the floor and placed it back amongst its fellows. "Soon the others will pupate and it will be *our* turn to labor. Each cocoon consists of a single continuous thread about one kilometer in length. We unwind the threads of seven or eight cocoons to make one solitary strand of raw silk yarn."

"We? Who are your helpers?"

Celia looked unhappy with my question so I changed course and asked Dr. Amado, "What percentage of the cocoon is made of sericin?"

He fidgeted uncomfortably. "I'm not totally clear on that. My assistants take care of the details."

"The yield of sericin is roughly twenty-five percent per cocoon," my cousin said, aiming a quizzical look at the doctor. His ignorance struck me as odd too. Dr. Amado had made the journey from Madrid to close a deal to purchase Celia's stock of sericin. So why was the "yield per cocoon" not at his fingertips?

Celia prepared some refreshments and Amado smiled ingratiatingly over tea and an assortment of tapas that my cousin heated up and served us in the main house. I felt something was off. He was halfhearted when discussing sericin extraction yet could hardly contain his enthusiasm when probing her for information about the "esoteric knowledge hidden in La Alpujarra."

She answered him in a sweet tone, tinged with vinegar. "Are you referring to the Moriscos who took refuge here in the sixteenth century, the Christians settlers sent to replace them *after* their expulsion, or the hippies who arrived in the 1980s?"

Amado took Celia's chiding in stride. But when I asked if I could interview him for an article I planned to write, he flatly refused.

"I'm sorry, Ms. Crespo. Our research is strictly confidential. Frankly, I wasn't expecting anyone other than Celia to meet with me, since we have financials to negotiate."

Celia pushed her glasses up her nose, avoiding my glance.

"Sorry, Allie. He has a point."

Dr. Amado reminded me of a Seattle landlord whose misdeeds I'd covered a few years ago. This two-faced citizen donated money to homeless shelters while turning off his tenants' water, forcing them out so he could remodel and jack up the rent. But perhaps I was being unkind.

"Alright. I'll go for a walk while you two talk business."

"Take the path leading up to the orange grove. It starts at the kitchen door. By the time you get back, we'll be done." I took this as a signal that Celia didn't want to be left alone with Amado for long.

The scent of oranges lured me up the trail and I followed. A black and white butterfly with red spots fluttered across the path, entrancing me so that I barely noticed my transition to a *Vijita* with Ja'far's distant ancestor, Jariya.

I'm wrapped from head-to-toe in a lightly woven, brown shawl, a gift from my mother before the Reconquista took everything. Seated at a small table near an octagonal fountain tiled in blue and gold, I pour a stream of hot Arabic coffee from a copper dallah into a ceramic cup. While even the narrowest streets outside are baking in the afternoon sun, here in the centuries-old courtyard lined with small trees, the air is pleasant and cool. How Idris al-Wasim has retained ownership of this well-appointed house in the Albaicin section of Gharnata is a mystery. When the Castilians crushed our rebellion, they replaced the entire population with Christian settlers, or so they thought.

The silk-dyer emerges through an arched doorway, smiling like the young prince he once was, his eyes shining with welcome below his round white cap. Last week, in anticipation of my long-delayed arrival, Idris sent me a poem:

*I was but another river*
*Staying the course*
*When the special light from your eyes*
*Sent a wave of such force*
*It flooded my banks*
*Watering the flowers*
*Leaving me behind to count the hours*
*Until your return*

How sweet of Idris, and how typical of him.

"Jariya, what a pleasure."

The red-and-gold robe is clearly a design of his own making, delicately embroidered with lilies and fuchsias. It touches me, how he's donned this silken garment – illegal for Moriscos to fabricate or wear – in honor of my visit. What a peacock he is.

"Idris, you're a great example of how male birds are more colorful than females."

He feigns annoyance but I can see he allows the joke. I'm one of very few who have glimpsed the exceptional courage hidden beneath his flamboyance. "I've waited all day for the pleasure of your company, Jariya. If you like this robe so much, I'll have one made for you and dye the silk myself. Alas, it may be my last creation."

"I appreciate the gesture but it's not worth the risk."

"If, in order to please you, I must defy the king's ban on Muslim silk, it's well worth the risk."

I knew for a fact that Idris would rather be thrown into a dungeon than refrain from extending his hospitality. Toward the end of the first War of the Alpujarras, he sheltered my family from King Phillip's soldiers, chancing his own life and limb. We needed his help because after the Kingdom of Castile conquered Gharnata and broke its promise to respect Islamic dress and worship, my father— Abd al-Aziz, Servant of the Strong —joined the uprising in the mountains.

Retaliation for not cooperating with the Crown was swift. Our family home was burned and we were lucky to escape with our lives. We stayed with Idris al-Wasim for six months, during which time my mother gave birth to my baby sister. When the call to arms came again, my father ignored Idris's advice to emigrate to Morocco and rejoined the insurgence led by Aben Humeya, in one more hopeless attempt to defeat the forces of the powerful imperial state. Only this time, Abd al-Aziz took me with him to fight alongside a hundred men in the mountains.

By sad fortune, the arms, munitions and food we expected any day from Algiers, never arrived. As far as I know, I was one of only ten survivors, my father not included. My mother and sister escaped on a ship to Morocco with Idris's help. They are expecting me to join them. But something holds me here in Al-Andalus. The feeling one gets when work has been left undone.

"What would you say Idris, if I told you there's a way to save your business? A way to continue fabricating brocade garments worthy of a caliph, with no bribes to pay or fear of exposure for breaking the two-faced King's edict?"

Idris bestows one of his sly, knowing looks. "Woman, I'd say you're a fierce Morisca bandit with a hefty price on your head, not a magician."

"Consider then, that a silkworm, having lost its home, can always lay its eggs elsewhere."

"I'm no caterpillar and I will stay right here, thank you. Stick with what you know best, dear Jariya, relieving unsuspecting travelers of their wealth."

I dismiss the temptation to draw my dagger and take a poke at him. "You're too well known, Idris. They would love to make an example of you. Why not start over where you will have a fighting chance?"

"Purely for the sake of asking, if I were to accompany you, where would we go?"

"To a hidden location in the high country, in the mountains far above La Alpujarra. You can take as many of your supplies as can be carried by six mules."

"Have you lost your mind? The uprising was defeated and our people flushed from their caves and slaughtered. Christian soldiers are rounding up the surviving women and children and putting them in chains for deportation or worse. If they find us…" Idris's mouth gapes, as he searches for words to describe the terrible possibilities.

"They won't find us. It will be more the other way 'round. Trust me."

"How can I, when your plan sounds only slightly better than being burned at the stake for practicing the only trade I know?"

"You're right. I can't guarantee your safety. But I can promise we will make Abd al-Aziz proud and save some remnants of the Islamic Golden Age."

Bringing my father into it is an unfair tactic that works exactly as planned. Idris reluctantly gives his assent with a nod of his bearded chin.

I follow my longtime friend and protector into his workshop, well stocked with dyes and orderly as a proud cook's kitchen.

"What colors shall I bring? So many vials and only a few animals on which to pack them." Painstakingly, like a father forced to choose between his children, he gathers up the indigos, yellows, and greens, along with some skeins of silk.

"Once in the mountains, I can use insects and plants to mix the shades of red my clients prefer. Assuming I have any clients left."

"You will. It's all been arranged. I have faith in you, Idris. As does one of your more eccentric business partners with a gift for seeing into the future. He's here, waiting outside."

"Not Hasdai the Seer? He's been missing from the Jewish Quarter for over a year. I thought he was dead." Idris drops what he's doing and runs outside.

Very much alive, Hasdai stands at the head of a caravan comprised of many more mules than I'd anticipated. To hide his true identity, the Jew often goes by the name Antonio Suarez, exporter of textiles. Idris, still shaking his head in astonishment at the sight of the old man, embraces him.

Hasdai accepts this familiarity with a tolerant smile. "I've brought some special garments for us to wear during the journey. If you dislike them, as I am sure you will, remember that a wise man in disguise fares better than an uncovered fool."

Idris half-heartedly accepts Hasdai's offering, rubbing the coarse brown cloth between his fingers with obvious distaste. "Isn't it bad enough we must give up our silk? Must we now don the robes of the monks who persecute us?"

Disregarding his friend's protestations, the Seer calls, "Hasan, come and help!" to the young muleteer guarding the rear of the caravan. We get to work loading Idris's silk-dying supplies into the leather satchels dangling from the backs of six stoic-looking donkeys. When we're done, the silk-dyer regards the twenty remaining animals and their overstuffed bags.

"What goods are they carrying that are so much more important than my life's work?"

Hasdai takes Idris's arm and explains. "They carry invaluable manuscripts and books saved from the fires of the Inquisition in Plaza de Bib-Arrambla more than seventy years ago. The great libraries of Granada may have gone up in smoke and most Jews and Muslims expelled from Spain, but as long as we have books written in the language of our ancestors, we will continue to know who we are. The books are living proof that Cardinal Cisneros failed in his quest to wipe the earth of all signs of us. This is one of many trips we will make into the mountains until these precious pages are safely stored away."

Idris's sharp guffaw startles the animals. "Hasdai, why would you, a Jew, risk his life to save the holy books of Muslims?"

The Seer shakes his head. "As usual you are as blunt as the spine of a knife, my friend. Why would I not love all knowledge equally? Was not my ancestor Hasdai ibn Shaprut a scholar and the physician to the Caliph of Cordoba? Did he not translate Greek scientific texts into Arabic while at the same time supporting the Jewish scholars he gathered around him?"

Idris looks skeptical, so I add my voice to Hasdai's. "Over the decades, these books have been moved from one temporary hiding place to another and now Hasdai has created a permanent home for them. He calls it *Zahara*, which as you know is the word for light in both Arabic and Hebrew."

Idris relents with a sigh. "Jariya, how can I refuse two friends who've already performed the impossible? On one condition. If we're captured, slay me quickly with no delay."

Hasdai pokes Idris in the ribs. "If you keep slowing us down with questions, that may happen sooner than you think."

I came back to myself, no time having passed. The butterfly that had caught my attention continued its journey as if nothing had happened. What might a physicist say? Had I traveled through a multiverse portal? All I could be sure of was that I was still in one piece.

# Chapter Eleven

On the walk from the orange grove back to Celia's house, I stumbled over a tree root and came close to tumbling down the hillside. Thinking about all these people from the Muslim side of my family was making me dizzy. Had the aging structure where Celia raised her silkworms been built by Idris the silk-dyer in the sixteenth century? I could hardly wait to talk with her.

The first thing out of my mouth when I found her waiting on the porch was "Did your mother Pilar ever tell you she had a secret name?"

"Why ask questions when you seem to know the answers already? It's uncanny."

"Haven't you ever made a guess solely based on intuition?"

"Your intuition is suspiciously well-informed, dear cousin. It strikes me you may possess what Grandma Luzia called a *maggid*, the ability to see beyond one's own time." Celia spoke as matter-of-factly of second sight as *Nona* did. *Had I agonized over nothing? Was my only mistake being born in the wrong country?*

Seemingly oblivious to the effect of her pointed remark, Celia tapped her forehead with her finger. "I do recall hearing Grandpa Ja'far address my mother as Jariya. But only when it was safe to do so. No one else knew about his Muslim background. Especially not my father, with his proud, Castilian heritage."

"Couldn't Eduardo have guessed his Pilar came from a mixed family, what with her dad's dark complexion... in the photo... you know what I mean... " I trailed off, already having over-explained.

Celia was unperturbed. "Eduardo's side of the family never met my grandfather," she said, kicking the dust off her boots before we entered the house. In the kitchen, bulbs of fresh garlic cluttered the windowsill along with jars filled with spices. Her distracted air, as we washed the dishes from lunch, suggested something weighed on her mind.

"Dr. Amado made me an interesting proposition."

I pulled my hands out of the water and she handed me a towel. "How so?"

"The offer he made was not for the sericin. It was for the house and land. He said his company was looking for a place where they can experiment with silk-making and harvesting the byproducts. They're willing to pay top dollar. I'm almost ashamed to tell you how much."

I glanced around the kitchen, committing to memory the simple white tiles splashed with red flowers, the old-fashioned walk-in pantry stocked with bags of rice and flour. One would have thought that *I* was the one about to lose them. I tried to picture Celia living in an impersonal city. It just didn't fit.

"Don't look so glum. I turned him down. I'm not sure Dr. Amado is who he claims to be. You saw for yourself how little he knows about silk-making. Also, I promised my mother I'd never let go of this house and land. I'll have to talk it over with her but I'm sure she still feels the same way."

"Didn't you say that Pilar died several years ago."

"I meant that when I have important decisions to make I go to the cemetery and consult her. That's all."

"I understand, Cousin. I lost my mother when I was a little girl and I envy your strong connection with your own, even beyond the grave." These conciliatory words did not prevent my doubts from crowding in. So far my *Vijitas* had paired me only with deceased, female ancestors and Pilar was not one of them. *Did this mean she was still alive?*

I kept these ruminations to myself. I could hardly say I suspected Celia's mother of being among the living because my out-of-body *Vijitas* were limited to contacts with the dead. My cousin would either conclude I was crazy or accuse me of mistaking her for a superstitious country bumpkin, which she certainly was not.

"Allie, I'm sorry I was rude to you yesterday. It's difficult for me to trust new people. But if you'd like to stay, I've cleared out the guestroom. There's only one thing I ask in return."

"And that would be…?"

"You must explain how you've discovered so many family secrets."

"Only if *you* explain why there are so many riddles to solve."

The spark of challenging humor in her eyes was brief but unmistakable. She had the same Spanish fire as my mother. And definitely the same ability to watch her tongue. Well, if as a child, I'd figured out how to weasel one more folktale out of Nona, it stood to reason I'd find a way to get Celia to trust her secrets with me. And if she did, I saw no reason not to reciprocate. I was about to accept her hospitality when my phone buzzed.

It was Luis Alcábez. "I have some good news. Mico's out of danger. The bullet did not damage any major organs and he regained consciousness this morning. When I saw him at the hospital, the first thing out of his mouth was that he wished to talk with you in person."

The cloud of anxiety that had been following me floated away, taking with it my fear that the notary would die and I'd forever hold myself at fault.

"I'm relieved and thankful," I told Luis. "And if seeing me is important enough for him to issue a summons from his hospital bed, I'll drive over first thing in the morning."

When I shared the good news with Celia, she volunteered to drive me back to the Airbnb so I could use my own car for the trip to Granada the next day. I wanted to celebrate Mico's recovery by taking us both out to dinner in Almendrales but my cousin declined. "Thanks, but some other time. I have business to attend to."

Relief can do wonders for the appetite. I consumed a small, frozen pizza and spinach salad in Jeroen's kitchen and, over a glass of wine, speculated on how much progress Jariya and her friends were making on their mission to transport the contraband books. With a shiver of anticipation, I felt the Morisca's now-familiar aura join with mine.

We three trudge uphill, the path winding through brown hills and past burnt-out orchards, deserted villages and farms, the blistering sun beating down like the flat blade of a broadsword.

Rounding the next bend, Idris points out the dying mulberry trees, their thirst deliberately decreed by order of the Crown. "It breaks my heart, Jariya. No longer will these bountiful trees shade the mountain slopes with their foliage or nourish the silkworms that provide us with our livelihood."

Hasdai the Seer caresses a trunk covered with dried bark. Would that his healing touch could make a difference. "Why punish these plants when, unlike humans, they've committed no crime?"

We all know the answer. The women of La Alpujarra are being cut off from the cycle that ends with the gathering of silken threads and weaving of cloth. Throughout Al-Andalus, deserted farms and looted villages await the Old Christian settlers, recruited to settle here and take possession of all our ancestors have built. I would exile every one of them in our stead if I could.

Always one to sense somber thoughts in need of disruption, Idris playfully punches Hasdai's arm. The beast tethered behind the Seer brays in protest as Idris berates his friend, accusing Hasdai of secretly plying him with alchemical potions. The Seer, accustomed to being teased by the boisterous silk-dyer, ignores him and picks up his pace.

"No need for offense," Idris calls out. "Who cares if you cause me to fall in love with a horse I've mistaken for a woman?"

Hasdai snorts derisively and pushes on ahead. His friendly tormentor follows, eager to savor the tartness of the alchemist's tongue. After the trials they've endured, so many of their friends slain and their own lives shattered, friendship and banter are perchance all they have left.

"Idris, if my powers are such as you describe, why would I waste them on the trivial? Surely I'd add wings to our sweltering robes and fly us to our destination."

The Seer is talking about the cowls that make us sweat profusely while obscuring our too-well-known heads. At the sight of these russet-colored Dominican Friar robes, the few farmers and shepherds we've passed on the trail are bound to think of us as powerful representatives of the Inquisition, traveling on official business. How relieved they must be to see the back of us.

Idris places his arm around the old man's waist, helping him to cross the slippery, moss-covered stones to the other side of a swiftly moving stream. This sweet tasting water flows into the channels of the stone acequias designed by our forefathers to irrigate the land. For them, and for us, an abundance of water is the ultimate blessing.

Suddenly, the path begins to vibrate and the rumble of approaching hooves foretells that the believability of our costumes will soon be tested.

The first soldier, a scout, reaches us quickly. His torso is encased in dull metal armor engraved with the King's seal. In contrast, his legs—covered by thin cotton leggings—make a tempting target.

I step forward and, deepening my voice, address the man's unspoken question in the most gruff, unfeminine tone I can manage. "We are sent by the Inquisitor General to inspect whatever prisoners you hold to find among them any Mohammedans wanted for trial by the Holy Inquisition."

The Crown's warrior stiffens in his saddle and the hand holding the reins of his horse shakes slightly before he regains control. Perhaps his blood is not as pure as he's led his superiors to believe. Even a drop of suspicion can poison an entire lake.

"Father, you may conduct your business with my Commander. His convoy will be here shortly."

If the soldier has any doubts about our identities, he keeps them as carefully concealed as the forbidden capes and pleated tunics hidden beneath our Dominican robes. Better to question him before he decides to interrogate us.

"How many prisoners are you transporting?" I ask.

"We have fifty souls but most are women and children." His smile is one of satisfaction. King Philip has proclaimed a war of fire and blood and given free rein to the soldiers to take whatever plunder they want. Humans, cattle, and property are all fair game.

Unprompted, the solder continues to brag. "With God's blessing, most of the Moors who fought in the rebellion are dead. Their women will be put to work in respectable Christian homes. You'd think they would be grateful. Instead they offer nothing but resistance."

"In truth, the women are the worst," Hasdai the Seer breaks in, perhaps afraid I will lose my temper or my voice will give my gender away. "Moriscas are well known to perpetuate deception in the privacy of their homes, hiding prayer rugs and other paraphernalia used in the practice of their evil religion."

The soldier nods in agreement. "They fight alongside their menfolk and none are more ferocious, armed as they are with sticks and stones. I have the scars to prove it." He points to the back of his head, and I inwardly praise the woman brave enough to inflict such a wound.

The scout's regiment comes into view, a procession of at least twenty men on horseback, guarding a line of fifty or so prisoners, roped together, barefoot and dressed in rags. Their commander remains astride his mount, avoiding close contact with the Brotherhood to which he believes we belong. Happily for us, he remains in control of his troops. Unchecked, they would murder us all in a heartbeat if they suspected duplicity. I picture them ripping off our robes and tearing open the leather bags carried by our mules, emptying satchels of flour to find the precious silk tapestries and books hidden within—a prelude to dumping our bodies into deep ravines where our remains would be lost forever.

As things are, among these men few eyes meet mine and those that do wear cowed looks of abject obedience brought on by the sight of our Church attire. Even in this isolated place, no one is immune from the Inquisition's reach. Having lived much of my life hiding my true faith and identity, today I'm tasting for the first time how it feels to wield power, how one might bend the will of a man without word or deed but rather through the force of misguided perception.

"Raise your hand when I call your name," I command the prisoners, bypassing their guards entirely. I am counting on the soldiers' ingrained deference and fear of the Church to overcome their resistance to sharing their spoils.

Pointing at Hasdai, I say, "Friar Anselmo will take the following miscreants into custody. Raise your hand when you hear your name. If you fail to comply, you will be dealt with swiftly."

I unwind a scroll inscribed with a long poem, and in quick succession shout out some names, making them up as I go. Of course, no hands go up, but Hasdai pretends some have and in the confusion is able to free five of the more emaciated children from their bonds, along with one woman and a tall, bearded man defiantly wearing a taqiyah. Hasdai roughly pushes the seven chosen ones toward me and orders them to sit on the ground. The captives think they've been selected by us Brothers of the Church to endure more horrors and fear haunts their eyes.

One woman wails inconsolably at the loss of her daughter. Hasdai whispers something in her ear to quiet her outburst, while Idris hastily locates the girl and brings her back to her mother. The ten-year-old's beauty shines from beneath much grime, and Idris puts on a smirk as he adds her to our group. A few soldiers grin, picturing the inevitable deflowering, a vision bound to be enhanced by the girl's future defiler being a Brother of the Church. Oh what a joy it would be to expose myself as a woman and, before they realize what's happening, slaughter them right there. I'd make sure to spare a few, so they might spread the word that Moriscas cannot be trifled with.

Idris, so as to further impress the weight of our authority, reads formal charges against our prisoners. "You are accused of apostasy and illegal observance of Muslim rites, including non-Christian prayers, dietary restrictions and frequent ablutions." The soldiers nod in agreement and a few call out, "death to the infidels!" impatient to deliver the sentence.

"All in good time," Idris counters.

When one among the ranks blusters, "Why wait?! Let's send them to hell right now," I fear our rescued brethren are about to be gruesomely slain.

The silk-dyer, accustomed to putting business clients in their place, locks eyes with the interloper. "Each will generously receive a chance to renounce their blasphemy and return to the true faith before any are punished. First we must bring them to trial in Granada. Any who would interfere with the Tribunal will also reap the consequences."

We have liberated eight Moriscos – six children and two adults – more than the soldiers would have expected us to cull from their herd of captives yet not enough to cause suspicion. No one need ask why such young children are of interest to the Inquisition. They know the little ones will either be placed in good Catholic homes to be re-educated, kept as slaves in our monastery, or as is the custom, sold to the highest bidder.

I avert my eyes from those of our people we are compelled to leave behind as the Commander, with a curt nod of farewell, leads his slightly reduced column of misery down the trail in the direction from which we've come.

What a forceful woman Jariya was and how shrewd of Ja'far to invoke the power of her name, engraving it on a bracelet that secretly protected Pilar. What better amulet for a mixed-race daughter forced to grow up in Franco's Spain?

# Chapter Twelve

On my way to visit Mico Rosales at the hospital in Granada, I drove through the outskirts of Lanjarón and pulled over near the ruins of the Moorish fortress that dominated the view of the valley. Jariya, Idris al-Wasim, and Hasdai the Seer might have taken refuge in this very spot, along with the donkeys carrying their priceless cargo of rescued children, silk-dyes, and forbidden books. The tingling in my chest signaled an oncoming *Vijita*. Curiously I felt a hint of control, like a diver bouncing on the end of a board, timing my entry into Jariya's world.

Hasdai the Seer walks beside me. We're a bit ahead of the car-avan, with Idris following behind with the children and two adults we've liberated. As we approach the deserted fortress, the Seer asks, "Why are you crying?"

"This is where my father sacrificed his life so others might escape, including me. Can we stop awhile? If I could have a few moments..."

"Of course, *chica preciosa*." This is Hasdai's favorite nick-name for me, meaning precious child in Judeo Spanish. He briefly touches my hand and I feel a wave of comfort wash over me.

I wish Hasdai had known my father, whose presence I feel now. When I was little, Abd al-Aziz carried me on his shoulders and later I stood beside him in the war against the Reconquista. At home and in the battlefield, he never treated me as less of a person because I was a woman. If any dared challenge this, he would say, "The fierceness in her blood is what counts." Faced with any calamity, he stood by his belief that *We belong to Allah and to Him we will return.* I will never live up to his high moral standards or possess his reservoir of patience.

Climbing the stairs inside the tower, I reach the turret and wait for the Seer, who is a little out of breath and suffering from the heat. I dab his forehead with a cloth dipped in the rose water I carry in a little bottle. To my relief, Hasdai revives.

"Thank you, Jariya, for all you've done to save the works of those who came before us."

"Books are all that we have left to protect, now that the earth has been pulled out from beneath us."

The Seer runs his deeply veined hand over the weathered stone of the parapet. "I think you'll like the design of the archives. The symbols for each library came to me in a dream. Even the familiar cyphers acted strangely, crosses changing shape to blend in with stars and crescents, like constellations remaking themselves. Zahara will consist of much more than hallways and doors. It will be built in accordance with sacred geometry and in equal measure house the drunken ecstasy of the poet and the parable of the sage."

"Will you miss living in the Realejo?"

"Yes. There is no bathhouse or synagogue at our destination. Not yet, anyway."

"We Moriscos place great value on cleanliness too, in case you didn't know, and our bathing gets us into terrible trouble. Did Idris tell you his cousin Nizar was burned for refusing to denounce his wife for 'washing herself as a Muslim?'"

Hasdai invokes a blessing in Arabic for my father and for Nizar's soul. His face is infused with sadness as he continues to pray, this time in the hard-edged language I've come to recognize as Hebrew. Watching him talk with his God, I understand we are much the same.

I would like to stay here longer to honor the last hours of my father's life but as Hasdai gently reminds me, "We have to find a place to camp before nightfall that will accommodate our young guests." I take a moment to compose myself before we descend to join Idris and the others.

A blaring horn pulled me back into the present. Driving on automatic pilot, I'd already passed through the outer suburbs of Granada. Soon the Alamo Car Rental sign came into view.

Fifteen minutes later, I'd dropped off the Hyundai compact and was at the wheel of a Subaru Outback. If I was going to hang out with my cousin in the backcountry, I'd better be able to get there on my own.

Most hospitals radiate an aura of enforced tranquility under stress and the waiting room off the lobby of the Hospital General Virgen de las Nieves was no exception. An older woman steadied her hands by knitting, while a young man sitting next to her rapidly tapped out texts on her cell.

After presenting the required ID at the front desk, I called Mico Rosales's room to give him some advance notice and stopped in the gift shop to pick out some flowers.

I found him waiting for me in a private room on the fourth floor, perched on a medical chair like a bird longing for flight, his knees barely covered by a white hospital gown with blue stripes. To believe Alcábez, Mico was about the same age as my dad. But even with the grey stubble on his chin, he seemed much younger. Actually, for someone freshly out of critical care, he looked pretty damn good. He even attempted to stand up to greet me, before thinking better of it.

"Thanks for coming such a long way, Alienor."

"Please, call me Allie. I got in to see you so easily. Why no police protection?"

"They're here but not in uniform. To be sure, your arrival was noted. And of course you may address me as Mico." I liked the pleasant formality of his tone. We could have been meeting in his office and not a hospital room.

Mico gestured toward the visitor's chair and we sat facing each other. His face was broad, almost Slavic, with brown eyes and a Roman nose adding a touch of distinction. His slow speech was the only outward sign of trauma. That and the IV tube attached to his left arm.

"Luis told me that when he met you in Seattle he felt the hand of destiny, some fated coincidence."

"He did hint that something special might be waiting for me here. Nothing specific."

"That's Luis for you. Never one to leap to conclusions. But your last name did give us a clue. It wasn't until Carlos Martín sought you out that we knew for sure you were related to him and Celia through their mother, Pilar Crespo."

It made sense now, how enthusiastic Alcábez had been about my application.

"My father and Pilar are... I mean *were* first cousins. You knew her?"

"Pilar and I became friends in college. I was so excited that you and I would meet in person and I might find out more about what happened to her. It never occurred to me that someone would…" He looked down at his chest, the bandage bulging through the thin fabric of the nightshirt.

"So you didn't see your attacker?"

"All I know is that he's tall. How else could he have he shot me while standing on a cleaning platform situated well below the window? The police said he hoisted himself up to the roof to make his escape. The security camera caught a glimpse of him, nothing conclusive."

"What did he take?"

"As soon as they let me out of this place, I'll complete an inventory of the office. I hate to think what might have happened if you'd been on time for your appointment. I apologize for putting you in danger."

"Wasn't it *me* who put *you* in jeopardy by applying for citizenship in the first place?"

His chuckle was accompanied by a wince of pain. "You and Pilar have a lot in common. She never balked at taking responsibility."

"Sounds like she made a big impression on you."

Mico's stare shifted inward. "We met at the University of Granada in the late 60s. She was five years older than me and majoring in Comparative Literature. She had an air of mystery about her and wasn't afraid to associate with a Jew, in spite of her Catholic upbringing. Eventually I discovered that her religious instruction was a subterfuge calculated to protect her from the stigma of her parents' mixed marriage. I'm not sure they foresaw she'd become such a devout Catholic."

"Luzia and Ja'far made a big sacrifice," I said without thinking. Noticing his skeptical glance, I added, "Celia told me all about her grandparents." Fibbing to Mico, who I in-stinctively liked, made me uneasy, although I'd grown accus-tomed to improvising cover stories to account for information gleaned from my *Vijitas*.

"Tell me more about Pilar. She sounds like a complex person."

He paused, like someone taking time to make sense of his memories. "I think her fearlessness came from struggling to find her own identity. When I asked Pilar about her up-bringing she said, 'My parents raised me to be myself, as long as I didn't reveal who I was.' To be honest, I was half in love with her."

"Sometimes I feel like an outcast myself," I blurted, irra-tionally jealous of how this woman I'd never met continued to fascinate a man I barely knew. Mico's openness, however, encouraged me to dig deeper.

"It would have been hard on you when Pilar married Edu-ardo Martín."

"I was inconsolable. She was a small town girl – *de pueblo*, as we say—who expanded this city boy's view of life so effortlessly that I thought it was my own idea. We had much in common, having gone through hardships as children and then spurning material wealth in favor of academics. That made it doubly dif-ficult to accept her being swept away by a *misógino* who liked his women tame. Pilar said he told her that majoring in com-parative literature was useless, that she'd be better off doing nee-dlepoint and supervising the maids. She thought he was joking. By the time she wised up, it was too late. She did manage to finish her degree, although I doubt she ever used it for much."

"What a waste," I said.

He nodded. "I didn't see her again for many years and by that time she was in such a disturbed state, I barely recognized her."

Mico squirmed in his chair, pulling his gown a bit tighter around his legs. "These people sure know how to humiliate a man. Isn't having to beg for pain killers bad enough?" He reached to push a red button on the wall.

Seeing his exhaustion, I held back on further questions. In a minute or two, a male nurse wearing a hospital mask rushed into the room. He immediately helped Mico back into bed and closed the privacy curtains, brusquely telling me to wait outside. I was halfway out the door when I overheard Mico ask, "Why a syringe? I'm already getting drugs through my IV. Won't this be too much? All I need is another Vicodin." Then, a second later, he yelled, "Stop!"

I turned and ran to open the curtain. The uniformed attendant was holding down Mico's resisting arm, trying to find a vein. I poked him on the back, none too gently. "Didn't you hear him say he doesn't want an injection?"

Offering no explanation, the nurse released Mico's arm and pivoted to face me, holding the syringe cocked and ready, awfully close to my face. I grabbed his wrist, pulling him off balance while twisting as hard as I could. Suddenly his grip gave way. The needle dropped to the floor and with an exasperated cry, he fled from the room. Apparently he'd decided the fight wasn't worth the risk of exposure.

How this fiend had managed to impersonate a nurse and why the missing guards had failed to stop him from entering Mico's room were questions I'd have to put on hold until the notary and I were safely away. By now Mico had liberated his street clothes from the narrow closet and let me help him get dressed.

"I can't believe you did that."

"Neither can I." My voice shook almost as badly as the rest of me. I may have taken Judo lessons as a child but none of my opponents had been armed.

Mico pointed to the syringe on the floor. "Evidence." Using a towel to retrieve the needle, I wrapped it up tightly before stowing it in my purse.

I peeked across the hall. There was no sign of the security Mico had referred to, uniformed or otherwise. We had to leave and the sooner the better.

Two wheelchairs and a stretcher were lined up along the wall. Guiding Mico carefully into a chair, I wheeled him toward the elevator at what felt like a snail's pace but was the only way to avoid suspicion. The nurse on duty looked at us curiously. "I'm taking him out for a smoke," I said.

"Not permitted anywhere on our grounds. You'll have to go out to the street." Then, under her breath, "Why bother coming to a hospital if your goal is to kill yourself?"

The elevator was empty, giving us time and space to regroup on the way down.

"These people badly want to get rid of you."

"Fortunately for me, their chosen assassin is either a rank amateur or dumb as a rabbit mistaking his own foot for a lucky charm."

Mico's unruffled humor was a bit infuriating. "Don't you realize how close you came?"

"Yes, of course I do. You saved my life and I'm forever in your debt."

I wheeled Mico through the underground garage to where the Outback waited behind the elevator bank on the far side. A family of four drove in and I gave thanks for their presence. If someone was following us, they would be wary of witnesses. I carefully loaded my charge into the passenger seat and folded the wheelchair before loading it into the trunk. Then I called Jeroen at the Airbnb in Almendrales and told him I had a huge favor to ask.

Still quaking with the aftershocks of the hospital room confrontation, I steered through rush hour traffic. Mico was already biting his lip from the oncoming pain, so I allowed myself to use the GPS to guide us out of the city. I would turn location services off as soon as I could. Right now I had to focus on getting us to a safe haven before my passenger blacked out.

# Chapter Thirteen

I don't know exactly what Jeroen told Doctor Cristóbal to convince him to come over to the Airbnb and tend to a gunshot victim, all without notifying the local police. He was one of the youngest docs I'd ever seen. A Black Sabbath t-shirt was visible beneath the unbuttoned white coat he wore over his jeans. Impressively efficient, Cristóbal changed Mico's bandages and mercifully gave him a bottle of hydrocodone tablets. "Call me if there's any sign of fever," he said on his way out the door. "And please keep this visit confidential."

I joined him on the walk to his car. "I have another favor to ask. Do you think you could find out what's inside this syringe?"

I presented him with the rolled up towel, feeling queasy at the thought of what it might contain. "It may be poison. Someone tried to forcefully inject Mico at the hospital."

Cristóbal hesitated. He and his stethoscope were already skirting the law. But how could he say no? "I'll send it to the lab and if what you say is true, we'll have to contact the police."

"Of course. Tell them to call Inspector Fernández in Granada."

I gave the doctor the inspector's number and with extreme caution, he placed the towel in his medical bag.

In the morning, when I thanked Jeroen for all his help, he shrugged it off. "You can recommend this place to your friends. Mind you, only the healthy ones."

I couldn't help laughing. "You can bet on it. Can you find me a fresh towel? I'd like to go for a swim."

Each lap in the sun-heated water carried me further from the stress of the day. I dried off in the poolside hammock, swinging gently and inhaling the fragrance of lemons while looking up through the tree branches into the azure blue sky. This didn't change the fact that what had begun as a simple trip to legalize some papers and learn more about my distant family members, had landed me in the middle of a small war. Both attacks on Mico had taken place when I was nearby. So whoever wanted him dead was keeping tabs on us both. Aside from Luis Alcábez, the only person I'd told about my trip to the hospital was Celia. Of course, she might have mentioned the trip to Carlos...

An hour later, Mico was feeling a bit better and I brought him some orange juice in bed. Jeroen had put his unexpected guest in a small room at the back of the house, near his own quarters.

"Take a seat," Mico said, pointing to the foot of the bed. "There are some things you've earned the right to hear. What do you know about the Atocha Massacre?"

This was not what I expected. "You mean the train bombings in Madrid?"

"That's certainly the first thing people think of when they hear the word 'Atocha.' In 2004, it was one of four train stations where bombs planted inside the commuter trains exploded. One hundred and ninety-two people died. It was a horrific day that scarred our country."

"Wasn't the bombing largely a consequence of Spain's surrender to international pressure to join the coalition during the Gulf War?"

"I'd say yes. And it's a terrible coincidence that another massacre happened more than thirty years ago, in the same area."

"You mean the slaughter of the labor lawyers in their offices on Atocha Street, I believe in the late seventies."

"I'm astounded you would know that."

"I read about the massacre in a book called *Ghosts of Spain*."

Mico shot me an appreciative glance. "It was 1977 and five lawyers were assassinated. Franco was two years dead and the massacre was part of a last ditch effort to continue the terror of his regime. Some of the conspirators were arrested but most fled the country."

"And this is important to us now...?"

"Because Pilar told me she believed her husband Eduardo was one of the assassins. She said he'd lost his father to the anti-Franco Maquis guerillas and his hatred ran deep."

I was taking notes, trying to piece together a chronology. Mico continued, his voice a little stronger than before.

"A few days before the lawyers were gunned down, Pilar overheard Eduardo talking on the phone about 'stomping out the vermin.' After he left their house in Málaga on a supposed business trip to Madrid, she discovered some of the machine guns he stored in the cellar were missing. He came home two days after the bloodbath and when she questioned him, he accused her of no longer trusting him. He even made up a grisly joke about how the wife of a friend of his had her nose cut off for butting into her husband's business. If Eduardo's intention was to frighten Pilar, he succeeded. Although she waited another five years, until Celia was ten and Carlos was eight, to come and see me."

"That she would trust you after all that time was a real tribute to your friendship."

Mico's pale complexion gained some color and I was glad I'd spoken up. "How did you advise her?"

"Given her fear of Eduardo and some sad details she shared about their estrangement, I suggested she inform him that her parents needed her and she was going to take the children with her to Almendrales, to live with them. We agreed she would call me when she was safe. But it didn't work out as planned. Eduardo refused to let go of Carlos. He was callous enough to use the son as insurance against the mother betraying his secrets. His tactic worked. Pilar gave up her teaching position at the University and she and Celia left the Martín house, but without the boy."

This was consistent with what Celia had said. "Did you stay in touch with them?"

"I saw Pilar only once after that, in 1987. Celia would have been about fifteen. The girl was very shy with me when I visited their ancestral home outside Almendrales. I think Pilar was afraid that my visit would provoke Eduardo's wrath.

"It was at this time that Pilar gave me a parcel containing an old book. It was heavy for its size and I could feel the cover was made of wood. She would not let me unwrap it. Nor would she say where it came from, only that it was not safe in the most secure of libraries and the world was not yet ready for its message.

"I offered to store the book in my safe deposit box but she insisted I take it home, saying that no one would think to look for it in my apartment. She gave me explicit instructions on how to take care of the fragile pages and protect the ink by regulating the humidity in my closet. And before she left, she asked me to notarize a document and store it in my office safe in case she ever needed it."

"What kind of document?"

"That's the thing. She insisted I notarize the papers without reading a word, refusing to say why. I was also working as a court investigator at that time and it pains me to think I could have helped her more than I did. Eduardo Martín should have been held accountable for his behavior."

"What happened to Pilar?"

Mico refilled the glass of water on his bedside table and took a deep drink. "Three years after our last meeting, I was horrified to find a story about her death in the Granada edition of *Ideal*. The writer hinted that she committed suicide since her purse was found at the side of a steep ravine. Her body was never recovered. That was twenty-eight years ago. Pilar was only forty years old. If she'd lived, she'd now be sixty-eight."

"Did you ever read the text she had you notarize?"

Regret filled his eyes. "I wish I had. But I made her a promise that death made even more binding. Until recently, I had no reason to believe that possessing the document might be unsafe. This morning I called Luis Alcábez and asked him to check with the police about the contents of my safe. I haven't heard from him yet."

"You know, when Celia told me her mom had died, I felt she was hiding something."

"You Americans love conspiracy theories, don't you?"

"That's funny coming from a man being pursued by unknown assailants. And you must admit it's strange, that on the day we met, Celia went to such pains to hide her meeting with Carlos from me. It's hard to see anything these siblings might have in common other than blood."

"For some people blood is everything. I don't know why the Martín family ever agreed to the marriage. Even if they believed Pilar was a true Christian, she came from a family of silk-makers, a class they looked down on from the heights of their ship-building empire. And that bracelet she wore, engraved with her Muslim name. If someone in that family were to have found it…"

Mico abruptly dozed off, leaving me fully awake to imagine the horrified faces of Eduardo's parents discovering that their daughter-in-law shared a name with a sixteenth-century Morisca bandit. The last time I'd seen Jariya, she and her companions had successfully freed some of their brethren from the Inquisitor General's soldiers. What happened next on their hazardous journey into the Alpujarras? Overcome with curiosity, I made my first try at consciously propelling myself into a *Vijita*. I entered Jariya's world, her blood flowing through my veins, her labored breaths filling my lungs as she hiked up a mountain path.

Having climbed through the thinning trees and past the last of the villages in the foothills, my companions and I now feel secure from pursuit. The angle of our ascent has steepened, deep gorges yawning on either side, making each step more treacherous than the last. Even more challenging is our new-found responsibility for the six young children who climb like mountain ibexes but are in danger of losing their footing when their short legs give out.

As evening falls, we camp near a small spring from which all of us drink deeply, including the mules. When we remove our monastic garb, the children laugh and clap their hands at the sight of Idris and me in our pantaloons with ribbed leggings, and Hasdai in his black robe and pointed hat. It's then that I notice the tall bearded man is missing from our group. Did our clerical disguises convince him we were frauds who would betray his people to the Devil's Tribunal? If so, he made a terrible mistake and risks being netted by one of the renegade bands of soldiers, roaming La Alpujarra in search of easy pickings.

We prepare to sleep in the open, relinquishing our tents to the children. It's a clear night and since smoke can travel for miles, it would be suicide to build a cooking fire. Instead, we share our supplies of flatbread and dried fruits with our fellow travelers.

The Morisca we liberated the previous day crouches near the tent's door, guarding the lives within, including that of her own daughter. So many in Al-Andalus maintain double, if not triple, identities. Determining who is who can be nigh impossible. From bitter experience, these women know better than to trust strangers.

"If she convinces herself we are duplicitous, she might decide to murder us in our sleep," Idris broods. "Jariya, why don't you speak with her and see if you can dispel her fears?"

"I'll say we're going to a place where she and the children will be safe and can live freely."

"And where might that be, other than heaven?"

"My dear friend, you will know everything when the time comes. Better to stretch your trust like a bow. I promise you the arrow will fly true."

Before Idris can question me further, I approach the Morisca, moving slowly so as not to startle her.

"My name is Jariya al-Qasam and I'm glad you're with us."

Her dark eyes seek mine as the moonlight exposes a bruised face beneath the headscarf. "My husband vowed to protect us and ran off like a coward when the time came. Why should I believe what you, a total stranger, say?"

"I have more than words to offer." I untie a swatch of green silk from around my neck. "Let the favorite color of the

Prophet Mohammed, peace be upon him, speak for me. Wear it for protection. All I ask in return is to hear you say your name."

She holds the scarf in her hands, tugging on it to test for strength, her forehead smoothing the slightest bit. "My name is Fatima and I'm from Juviles. All was taken and there is nothing to live for save my daughter."

"I'm your sister in sorrow, Fatima. Two years ago I lost my father in battle and my mother and brother to exile." Not being one to freely share my story, I'm unnerved at how the words tumble out.

She takes my hand. "I wish you peace and I thank Allah that I still have my child."

Her simple gratitude knocks against my heart, gently prodding me to go on with my story. "A friend asked me to join the rebels. My job was to keep watch on their encampment. I saw later that this was our leader, Razin al-Siddiqui's way of provisioning me with a task to take my mind away from grief. Razin taught me how to fight and I recently recruited him and his men to conduct raids on our tormentors and free as many children as we can. We'll meet up with him soon. If you wish, you can join us, or we can arrange a journey with your daughter to Morocco. Think about it. You're amongst friends now. Take some rest and we'll talk tomorrow."

Reassured to see Fatima abandon her vigil and join the children inside the tent, I take my own turn at sleep.

I awake between the break of dawn and the rise of the sun, in time to perform my ablutions and prayers facing east, my bones stiff as I kneel on the cold ground. Idris softly snores nearby, huddled under a pile of blankets, and I gently wake him to do the same.

I then seek out Hasdai and wait for him to finish his own observance in Hebrew before asking, "Why not inform Idris of our plans? He has trusted us with his life."

The Seer frowns. "As well you know, Jariya, peace is often more valuable than truth. Let our friend enjoy his blessed ignorance a while longer."

On our third day of travel, we reach Capiliera and head north into the mountains on a little known track. Our destination is ten leagues away. The higher elevation brings a chill to the air and yet again we don our Dominican garb, this time for warmth. The children are clothed in makeshift ponchos made of blankets, each responsible for the care and feeding of two mules.

At long last we walk through a meadow peppered with the same pale blue petals I remember from last year, growing alongside the small shrubs and hardy white snow stars close to the ground. It's Hasdai who discovers the almost invisible trail meandering through the tall grass. Our little band follows along, until the rushing sound of raging water announces our arrival at a steep drop-off overlooking a narrow gorge.

"We're here," the Seer announces.

"Where?" Idris asks.

"The Poqueira Ravine," I tell him.

Idris gasps. "How are we going to cross? Even if we survive the descent and forge the river without drowning, we'll be faced with an impossible climb on the other side. With all our burdens, human and animal, it would be pure insanity to try."

Hasdai claps his friend on the back. "Idris, have you not heard of the tunnels carved deep inside the Cave of Zahara?"

Idris exhales irritably. "Some kind of myth for children I presume. I don't see how that matters, in our present predicament."

The Seer chortles. "You will."

Squatting on the ground a few feet from the edge of the cliff, Hasdai reaches into a small leather bag strapped to his waist, pulling out a fistful of multi-colored pebbles, and arranging them in a circle that he divides into four quarters. With a stick, he scratches symbols and characters in the earth to complete each quadrant.

"He's drawn a Seal of Solomon to protect us," Idris whispers, his skepticism swiftly traded for reverence. As a devout Muslim he also respects the Jews for their devout love of ritual. One of the many reasons I invited him to join us.

Hasdai the Seer places a prayer shawl over his head and sings softly to the stones, the melody wavering in the way of a familiar Arabic song yet sung in a strange tongue. As he chants, the wind sweeps away the notes.

At Hasdai's signal, I reach under a gorse bush and pull aside the dead branches we added as an extra precaution during our previous visit. I'm relieved to see the large metal stake protruding from the ground, grown rusty but still firmly attached to a thick rope of braided wire that the Seer grabs and flings over the rock face.

"Jariya, I know how much you enjoy this mode of transportation. I suggest you go first."

"How can you tease me at a time like this?" I gulp a deep draught of air.

"Make sure to go down in a straight line so you don't miss the entrance," he advises unnecessarily. This is no easy maneuver and if I fail there will be no one to catch me.

Grasping the chain, I lower myself, hand-by-hand, alternating between bouncing my feet off crevices and swinging wildly in the air. My sole thought is to control my balance and steady my descent, in spite of the heady combination of dizziness and panic threatening to engulf me. No matter that I've survived this trial before. Forcing myself to relax and breathe deeply, I remind myself of my purpose. I will not disappoint those who have entrusted me with so much.

After a few interminable minutes, my left foot encounters the ledge and I inch sideways, relieved to see the yawn of the opening exactly where I expect it to be. I swing back to add momentum and throw myself forward, landing inside the cave. My bruised hands slowly loosen their tight grip on the metal rope. As soon as I release it, the chain, pulled by unseen hands, slithers out of the opening into thin air.

# Chapter Fourteen

The silence is complete, unbroken by the sound of dripping water or the whisper of batwings. I know that if I raise my arms they will scrape the ceiling of the narrow, three-meter-wide burrow. I will never be at ease in this eerie, confining space.

Hasdai is the first to follow, barely out of breath from the rigors of the cliffside descent, despite his advanced age. Could he have imbibed one of the magic potions Idris accuses him of dispensing? He lets go of the metal snake and it falls to the tunnel floor with a clatter, lying motionless for a moment before being summoned back to life when pulled from above.

Idris is the next to climb down. I watch him work his way down the cliff face, clutching the chain for support each time he changes his foothold. Everything progresses well until he comes level with the entryway and hangs there, only a few feet away, unable to move close enough to touch the solid rock. His arms seem strong yet I worry he will let go and fall to his death on the giant boulders below.

I cup my hands and yell, "Use your momentum!"

Idris responds, bending his knees and using the chain to swing himself backwards and forwards. He swings to the highest point the chain will allow and dangles in the air like an undecided bird. Then, Allah be praised, gravity takes charge and the silk-dyer sails into the tunnel, sliding vertically across the slick stones until forced to a quick stop by the tautness of the chain.

He lies motionless. Either the breath or the life has been knocked out of him, I dare not think which. Finally, with a grunt he rolls over and struggles to a sitting position, more indignant than injured. "You were right to keep me in the dark, Jariya. One hint at the madness of this venture and I'd never have agreed to come."

Declining my help, Idris struggles to his feet. "So tell me. Are the children joining us too? How can you plant them in harm's way after what they've been through?"

His distrust of my judgment rankles and I'm tempted to ask if he thinks I should have left the little ones with the soldiers to be sold as slaves. But his concern for the children is understandable.

"There's no cause for worry. We'll have plenty of help bringing everyone down safely, the books and your silk dyes too. All but the donkeys. They'd die of fright."

Hasdai's laugh bounces against the walls of the narrow shaft as the three of us wend our way deeper into the tunnel. We pass through a wide archway that serves as the entrance to the cave proper.

"The air is so fresh. Is there some ventilation at work?" Idris asks. I'm counting on his curiosity about all things mechanical to increase his commitment to our cause. But before I can enlighten him about the air shafts, a dozen torches flicker to life.

Voices dart at us from all directions, causing us to spin around in confusion. A moment later we're encircled by a group of men, some with pistols drawn, others armed with more primitive weapons, including harquebuses mounted on their shoulders. I hunt among them for a familiar face and, when I fail to find it, fear flutters within me like a small bird sensing the presence of a hawk.

We have all heard the gruesome stories of renegade bandits robbing and then proceeding to drink the blood, not only of Christians but of their own brethren who pray to the East. Men who, having lost everything, live only for looting and taking revenge. All I can do is pray that these men surrounding us serve a cause greater than plunder. And if this be true, they should welcome us with shouts of joy.

The first shout is far from friendly. "Look what we've caught! Three unholy fathers up to no good!"

The warm Dominican robes we've worn to frighten our enemies into submission are having the opposite effect.

Throwing off my cowl, I step into a pool of light in the middle of the cavern. A spot of blue sky floats far above me, where the air shaft collects its life-sustaining gift.

"It's Jariya!" someone cries.

Miraculously I recognize Razin al-Siddiqui, my childhood friend and comrade in many a mountain battle. Razin is the tallest of the bunch and the only one carrying a flintlock musket. The last time we met, he told me he intended to ask my father for my hand in marriage. The sight of him fills me with more joy than I thought myself capable of after *baba's* death.

Razin comes to stand beside me. I want to throw my arms around him but it would be unseemly. He addresses me warmly. "*Salaam 'alaykum.* We expected you sooner, Jariya. How many souls have you brought?"

"Six children and a woman to look after them. Also a Seer and a silk-dyer. The little ones will need your help climbing down. And the saddlebags contain many fragile items and perishables, so take special care with them."

"We're always careful. My men will take care of everything before we secure the entrance. Rumors are circulating that the enemy has intensified their search for you."

Hasdai comes over to greet Razin and give instructions. "The children must be taken immediately to the Port of Almeria."

Razin loses no time in collecting the young ones and preparing them for the journey we all hope will bring them to safety. Rumor has it there is a *New Orgiva* on the western side of Marrakech, a haven for Moriscos with fertile fields and running channels of water, much like here. They say a new Granadan kingdom is being created there and with Allah's blessing, someday we'll reconquer the old one.

Before he leaves, Razin pulls me aside. "There is something I've wanted to do for a very long time."

Gently, he brushed his lips on my cheek, forbidden unless we were engaged. Enough for me to know I will pine for him the entire time he's away.

By the time Mico joined me in Jeroen's kitchen, I had returned to the present. It looked like I could control where my *Vijitas* began but not where they ended or what happened in between. Although no time had passed while I was 'gone,' the separation from Jariya was more painful than before. And I was worried about her safety. Her risks on behalf of others were admirable and inevitably destined to multiply. How illogical, my fierce desire to preserve the life of someone who had died centuries ago.

Mico's phone rang and Luiz Alcábez's voice was slightly distorted by the tiny speaker. "Rosales! How are you?"

"Much better. Thanks to your client, Alienor Crespo. She broke me out of the hospital just in time."

"In time for what?"

"Someone tried to stab me with a syringe. We don't know what was in it – not yet."

"*Que bárbaro!* On top of everything else you've endured.*"

"I'm okay, Luis, but I'm concerned about the state of my office."

"It remains taped off as a crime scene. Inspector Fernández told me the safe is emptied of everything, save for a few rare and valuable coins. Strange behavior for a burglar."

"And my files?"

"You'll have to examine them yourself to see what was taken. For now, all we know is that Alienor's papers are missing. Where are you? Is she with you?"

"Yes, she's okay. Thanks for calling to check on me."

"Of course, Mico. I'll be in touch if I learn anything more."

Mico ended the call and poured me a cup of coffee. He was definitely more energetic and alert than last night. Over a light breakfast, provided by the ever-attentive Jeroen, he advised me to go home to Seattle. "Much as I would profoundly miss you, I'd be pleased to know you were safe."

*Profoundly.* I checked his face to see if he was joking. His earnestness both alarmed and attracted me. Our age difference spanned more than twenty years, a gap I realized he was determined to cross when he leaned over and kissed me lightly on the lips. *Was it a coincidence that moments—or was it centuries ago—Jariya had received a chaste peck on the cheek from Razin?*

I felt pleasantly bashful. As Luis had said, Mico was someone who wouldn't mind a casual liaison. It was a relaxed invitation, offered in a spirit that left room for both acceptance and refusal. That he chose to test the wind, rather than sail straight into it, made it much more likely he'd reach his goal.

Mico leaned in again and this time we shared a full on, lingering kiss.

Gently, I broke away, aware that Jeroen might walk in at any moment. I took Mico's hand and turned up his palm. "I see that with some patience you may get lucky."

He laughed. "Let's hope it comes to more than that."

There it was again, the easygoing emotional honesty that disarmed me. Why did I feel such a strong urge to reciprocate, when we'd only known each other for a few days, the majority of which he'd spent in a coma? Had our shared trauma created some kind of bond? I needed to think this through. Or did I? Why tangle myself up in the same overthinking and distrust that got me in trouble with Joel? On impulse, I reached for Mico's hand and said, "There's something about me you should know."

Mico ignored my offer and stood up to look out the window. "Who's that out front standing next to your car?"

I raced outside in time to see a boy walking swiftly away from the Outback. "Hey! Stop!" My words had the opposite effect and he sped up his pace to a run, disappearing down a slope in the road.

I jumped into the car, ready to drive off in pursuit. But when I tried to close the driver-side door, Mico was there, holding it open. "Maybe we should read the note the kid left for us." He pulled a thin sheet of blue-lined paper from under the windshield wiper.

Dear Cousin Alienor,

I spoke with my sister and I've changed my view of certain things. We need to meet. Please come to Celia's house as soon as you receive this. Come alone. Do not bring Mico Rosales with you. There are things you need to know that only I can tell you.

Carlos

I showed the note to Mico and he looked it over carefully. "How did he know you'd be with me? Something's not right." He disappeared briefly and came back with a flattened cardboard box that he tossed on the ground and used to slide himself under the car. Half a minute later, his muffled voice cried, "Got it!"

He handed me the silver gadget he'd detached from the undercarriage. It was the size of a cigarette pack, with a miniature display screen and a universal wireless symbol. A strong magnet had been used to hold it in place. "Carlos is tracking us."

"There's more than one candidate," I said. "Let's leave this thing in place and see who turns up."

"Do you think that's wise?"

"I passed wise when I kissed you."

"You'd better let me come with you, Alienor. It might not be safe."

"Carlos asked me to come alone."

"All the more reason for you to suspect his motives. Besides, I haven't seen Celia since she was in high school. I was never able to offer her my condolences on her mother's death."

How could I refuse?

We drove toward the Crespo homestead, the sun still high enough for the clouds to set shadows adrift over the rolling hills. The silence between us was charged with what had happened between us in Jeroen's kitchen, so I concentrated on dodging the potholes.

Near the fence I'd climbed on my first expedition, I turned off the paved road to drive cross-country, putting the Outback's shocks to the test as we bounced over the rough terrain. When we reached the clearing near Celia's house, I narrowly missed hitting a blurry figure darting across the dirt track. Male or female it was impossible to tell.

"Who was that? I'd better check on Celia," Mico exclaimed as he jumped out, setting off at a run down the dirt path and leaving me to park the Subaru next to Celia's Jeep. As I reached to turn off the ignition, my cell phone rang. I badly wanted to ignore it but how could I when I saw the caller ID?

Anxious to join Mico, I accepted the call while walking down the path toward Celia's house. Dad's firm voice came on the line. "How are you sweetie? I hope you're keeping safe. The last time we spoke, you said you'd tracked down your cousin. What's she like? Are you staying at her house?"

"Celia invited me but I haven't moved in yet. She's an accomplished silk maker and we're getting to know each other. It takes time. How is Nona doing?"

"About the same." He sounded disappointed that I wasn't more forthcoming. How could I tell him there'd been a second attack on Mico's life when he didn't even know about the first?

"Everything's okay. I'm on my way to Celia's right now. Maybe we can talk more later. I'll call you soon."

The door to the house stood open. Mico stood frozen in place inside the mudroom, surrounded by Celia's gardening tools. His riveted gaze led me down to something that at first my brain refused to process, an inert form sprawled on the floor, arms and legs akimbo in a pose that can only be achieved by a lifeless body. Carlos's body.

Mico's knuckles strained as he tightened his grip on the handle of a flat shovel. He saw me staring at the dark red stain on the blade's cutting edge and shook his head emphatically. "Allie. It's not what you think."

Anyone who does crosswords is familiar with the sensation of letters rearranging themselves into words. Except this was no harmless game and the word taking shape in my mind was *revenge*. Celia told me on the day we met how Eduardo resented Mico's longstanding friendship with Pilar. "It's possible my father convinced Carlos that Mico was responsible for our mother's death," were her exact words.

"If Carlos attacked you because he blamed you for his mother's death, then you acted in self-defense."

Mico opened his mouth wide, miming incredulity. "Carlos may have wrongly believed I broke up his parent's marriage but this... Allie, believe me, I had nothing to do with." He gestured downward at the body without looking at it, the picture of genuine distress.

My training was in ferreting out the truth. I had to consider whether or not Mico had lied when he said all he'd done was to give Pilar some advice. Had they been lovers and if so, had they quarreled? *There are some things you need to know that only I can tell you,* were Carlos's last written words. *Had Mico insisted on accompanying me to Celia's in order to silence her brother? What other deceptions might he have practiced?* The sharp point of doubt cut through the trust that had grown between us.

Mico took a step forward. I reacted instinctively, maneuvering behind him in the cluttered space and shoving him out the front door with all my strength before latching it shut.

# Chapter Fifteen

"Allie, please!" Mico called from outside.

With shaking fingers, I fastened the lock to the mudroom's inner door and forced myself to step around Carlos's lifeless body. As I ran into the living room, I remembered seeing Pilar confront Luzia about the secret room under their house, where so much of her parents' lives had been hidden. The house now belonged to Celia and the entrance to that underground haven could be almost anywhere. If I failed to find refuge before Mico burst through an open window or broke down the front door... I pushed away my rising panic and carefully examined the walls for any signs of a concealed entryway.

Mico continued his assault on the front door, yelling for me to let him in. Then quiet. He was sure to be searching for another entrance. I sprinted through the hallway to the back of the house. In Celia's bedroom, I blindly ran my hands over the walls, searching for a gap. My frantic movements were leading nowhere. I tripped over a throw-rug and tumbled to the floor, grazing my elbow. My eye was caught by a flash of color and I sprang to my feet to investigate.

In the walk-in closet, a dozen, colorful tiles formed a hexagon on the floor. Geometrical designs covered most of them, but the central, larger tile was inscribed with two words, one in Arabic, the other in Hebrew. I massaged my sore arm as I sounded out *Tif'eret*, a term I vaguely recognized. Why was this highly decorative art hidden from view in a closet? It made no sense.

I looked more closely. The tiles were raised a full inch above floor level. Either a craftsperson had been careless or... I curled my fingers around one side of the border and pulled. The trapdoor swung open on hidden hinges to reveal a large opening in the floor.

Perched on the edge of the cavity, I aimed my cell's flashlight into the emptiness, looking for a ladder of some kind. My dangling legs made contact with the first rung and I lowered myself, groping with my hands until they found a handrail to grip and I could step down into the tunnel. My eyes adjusted as the darkness dissipated, replaced by the glow of a rose-colored light with no visible source. The walls were smooth as sheetrock and the floor paved with textured concrete, definitely not the primitive burrow I'd anticipated. The air contained a hint of jasmine, Celia's perfume, but I had no way of knowing if she was there, somewhere ahead of me, or if the fragrance had drifted down from above. I checked my phone. There was no reception, no way to call the police. To return to the surface, where Mico might be stalking the house, was too risky. A cord dangled nearby and, summoning my courage, I pulled on the rope to shut the trapdoor and seal myself in.

The only way now was forward. Proceeding cautiously through the dimness I looked straight ahead using my side vision to scan the wall murals painted on either side. Horseshoe-shaped, black and red arches were cleverly rendered, extending into infinity and creating the illusion of walking through a much larger space.

A faint, whirring sound played in the air, my guess would be from an electrical generator nearby. Directly above,

I glimpsed a square of blue sky confirming my suspicion. The underground habitat beneath the Crespo home was constructed with air shafts in the same way as the labyrinth that Idris and Jariya roamed in the sixteenth century. It might even be the same one.

Rounding a corner, I detected what appeared to be a wall blocking further progress. Was I to be trapped in this small space, waiting for Celia to find me if she was still alive? An image of an enraged Mico standing above her with the shovel raised above his head flashed across my mind's eye like a frame from a horror movie. I banished this worst case scenario by focusing on the obstacle, which on closer inspection I found to be an ancient, sturdy-looking door constructed of rosewood and engraved with letters identical to those I'd seen on the tiles concealing the trapdoor. Oddly, no doorknob or lock was visible.

"How am I supposed to get in?" I asked, voicing my frustration.

To my surprise, the carved letters slid sideways, revealing a camera lens and an intercom speaker.

"Place your thumb on the pad," a female voice commanded.

*Had the door responded to my voice? And how could my thumbprint be of any use?* I put these troublesome questions aside and obeyed the instruction. The door swung open on silent hinges. Feeling part burglar, part invited guest, I entered a room softly illuminated from above, much like Jariya had stepped into a circle of light in an underground chamber to make herself visible to her fellow bandits.

Although common sense told me I would never meet my distant ancestor in the physical realm, I felt Jariya's presence growing stronger. It was not the right time for a *Vijita*. Not with Carlo's lifeless body upstairs and his possible killer on the loose. But Jariya's thoughts were determined to possess me and stopping them was beyond my control.

I'm seated next to Fatima on a boulder situated near the entrance to the cavern. Her eyes are clearer and her face more relaxed than on the night we met outside the children's tent she'd guarded so ferociously during our travels.

"Thank you, Jariya, for reaching out to Mahja."

"Your daughter eats whatever food I give her yet refuses to let me comb her hair."

"Don't take it personally. She's afraid to let anyone get too close. Mahja's bracelet of remembrance barely has enough beads to honor all the family members she has lost."

"What will you do once you get to Morocco? Do you have any relatives there?"

"Not a one. Will you come with us?"

"Not yet. There's too much to be done here."

Fatima's narrow face flushes with anger. "I live here too. Why should I run away and leave you to fight? What kind of example will that set for my daughter? I know your plans don't include me. Maybe it's time you reconsidered."

Her outburst douses me like a waterfall. This woman deserves my trust. "Come with me. There's something I want to show you."

Lighting a torch, I guide Fatima through an unmarked entryway behind a spur jutting out from the solid rock wall that marks the beginning of the salt mine. We enter an area excavated to form a maze that only a select few can pass through safely. Hasdai has forbidden the use of maps and written records, so I carefully follow the route I've memorized, turning right three times, then left, then right again. After twenty minutes we reach a site where great chunks of earth and minerals have been scooped out of the walls.

"What's happening here?" Fatima asks.

"These cavities will one day be libraries, the future homes of the books that were liberated from the Devil's Tribunal more than a hundred years ago. The atmosphere in the salt mine is ideal for preserving paper and these written treasures have been brought from all over Spain to be kept safe and out of the hands of those who would still burn them if they could."

"Fatima places the palm of her hand on the roughness of a newly created support wall. "I want to be a part of this."

"There's much to do. It's our responsibility to guard these treasures and pass them down through the generations. Some have already died defending this place and once you join us there's no going back. If you decide to go to Almeria with Razin and sail to Morocco, I won't hold it against you."

"I would hold it against myself. If it were not for your kindness, Jariya, my Mahja and I would have been separated and sold as slaves."

"Kindness means nothing without justice. And speaking of Mahja, maybe she will grow up to be one of our Librarians. We'd better go back before she misses you."

We've scarcely turned around when a dark figure appears and floats toward us like an apparition. Fatima and I have no time to run and I say a prayer to Allah under my breath.

"Have no fear, my children. How could you believe a Sister of our Order would hurt you?" The nun comes closer and recognizes me. "Jariya, what a blessing to see you well and unharmed."

It was Sister Adoración. I had last seen her when Hasdai took me to the underground cells below the monastery that once housed mystical nuns hiding from the disapproval of the Church. With the Sister's permission, their secret hiding place has been connected to the far end of Zahara's main tunnel. "It's our great fortune to receive the protection of the Sisters of the Carthusian Order," Hasdai had said when introducing us.

Today, the Sister is a little out of breath. "I've been sent by the Prioress to tell you we're undergoing our yearly inspection by the Brothers. For the upcoming three days, it will not be safe for you to contact us. But don't worry. The codexes you stored with us are safely hidden away."

"Thank you for coming to warn us, Sister Adoración. I'll tell Hasdai and the others."

"Bless you, my child. Walk in God's grace," she says with a conspiratorial smile.

"*Assalamu alaykum,*" I reply in Arabic. *Peace be upon you.*

I understood why this *Vijita* had been thrust upon me. Because in spite of the terrible circumstances under which I'd made the discovery, I knew for certain that here, below Celia's house, I could finally explore for myself the modern version of the labyrinth of cultural treasures hidden away by her sixteenth-century ancestors. Ancestors who belonged to me, too. It was even possible the library I'd just entered was built on the primitive site that Jariya and Fatima visited.

There were hundreds of volumes occupying the metal shelves, spines facing outward, alongside stacks of unbound manuscripts and folios filled with loose parchment pages. Incredibly, not a speck of dust liberated itself as I carefully opened a volume with a cover of soft vellum, probably calfskin. Although I'm no linguist, I surmised from the line breaks that I was looking at collections of verse, written in Arabic or possibly Aramaic. I also found poetry books penned in Hebrew. *How many of such treasures had Jariya and her bandits transported on their donkeys, day after day, up into the mountains and into the cliffside opening of the cave?* How extraordinary that thousands – perhaps millions of pages had been saved from the wrathful bonfires of the Inquisition and taken here to be protected from the outside world.

Everything in this library spoke of age, yet there was no sign of decay. *How had these delicate tomes survived without becoming mildewed or showing other signs of decrepitude?* If this underground lair was originally a mine operated by the Romans, there might be a preservative in the atmosphere, as Jariya had said. I'd heard of books being stored in salt mines during times of war or when a library was being remodeled.

A door opened at the far end of the room and there was Celia. In place of her usual coveralls, she wore a flared white skirt and pink blouse. "I see you've found our poetry collection. It's called the *Library of Tif'eret and Jamal,* which means compassion and beauty in both Hebrew and Arabic. We have original manuscripts of poems by Mohammed Ibn Hani, Solomon Ibn Gabirol, Ibn Arabī, Judah Halevi, and Ibn Abulafia. Enough for a lifetime of reading."

"You left the trapdoor ajar," I said, lacking the courage to come right out and tell her what awaited upstairs.

"I know it wasn't a good idea. I thought I'd be absent for only a few minutes." She was running her eyes over the shelves and, inspection complete, swiveled her gaze to lock with mine. "Some books are out of order."

Under my cousin's wary observation, I returned the volumes I'd examined to their rightful places. "We try not to disturb them," she said. "Some are so brittle, even a touch could turn them to dust."

*To dust.* Like Carlos, whose lifeless body lay upstairs on the blood-soaked floor. "I'm so sorry," I began.

"It's alright. You have no way of knowing how fragile these books are. My intention was to introduce you to Zahara properly. It was difficult but I got permission to add your voice and your thumbprint to our security system in advance. It was going to be a surprise. Obviously you figured it out on your own."

So far Celia had seemed sane enough to me. But who in their right mind would think there'd be no problem about recording a guest's voice or lifting her fingerprints from a wineglass *or whatever* without permission? Under ordinary circumstances I'd have confronted her. But the bad news in my charge was claiming front and center and would keep no longer.

"It's about your brother. I barely know how to say it."

# Chapter Sixteen

Celia clenched her fists, grief and anger at war. I wanted to offer comfort but her rigid posture said *keep your distance*. I could see she was fighting to contain her emotions, forcing herself to think, to make sense of what I had told her.

"I have to see him."

She tapped out numbers on a keypad to reset the electronic lock and I followed her out of the *Library of Tif'eret and Jamal* and through the tunnel, until we reached the overhead entrance I'd used on my way in. After we climbed the ladder, she pulled it up behind us, firmly shutting the tiled trapdoor so it was flush with the floor of the bedroom closet. It was odd, having entered her house from below, like two children in a fantasy novel. Unfortunately, the dead body we had come to view was painfully real.

"Where is he?"

I took my cousin's hand. As we approached the mudroom, I had this crazy notion we would find it empty—that I'd been fooled by my already questionable senses.

Everything was as I'd left it, the bleak scene now magnified by Celia's presence. Collapsing to the floor, she pulled her brother's head onto her lap, stroking his face, her own body trembling as she held his. She began to rock him back and forth and that's when I saw his hands were tied behind his back.

"Should I call the police?"

She nodded, so I hunted for Inspector Fernández's card in my wallet and got him on the line. "Inspector, this is Alienor Crespo. You may recall showing me a picture of Carlos Martín in your office in Granada. He's dead. Someone killed him. His body is here, at his sister Celia's house outside the village of Almendrales in La Alpujarra."

"Stay right where you are. I'll contact the local authorities and be there myself within the hour."

"We're in mountainous country."

"Don't worry. I already have your location on my phone. Are you alone?"

"I'm with Celia."

"Lock the doors and windows and stay inside. I'll see you soon."

The police would want the crime scene preserved, so as gently as I could, I pried Celia away from her brother's body. I settled her on the couch in the living room and left her for a moment to pour two glasses from a bottle of DYC whiskey I found stowed in a kitchen cabinet.

"I'm so sorry, Celia. In the note, Carlos asked me not to bring Mico. If I had known what would happen..."

She downed her drink. "How could you have known? It's not your fault, Alienor. This was not Carlos's first visit. He came to see me on the day you and I first met and insisted on a prearranged signal so he could be sure I was alone. He was agitated, claiming that our father told him that Mico Rosales not only caused our mother's death but was also actively working to discredit the StandUp Party. I tried to help Carlos see that Eduardo puts politics first and has manipulated him with terrible lies that only a loyal son would believe. I told him I hadn't seen Mico since I was fifteen and I was sure he and our mother were never more than friends—that all Mico did was to help her escape Eduardo's rage. My stubborn brother refused to believe me. He was working himself into a rage. So I broke a promise I made to my mother years ago. I told Carlos that Pilar is alive and well, living as a nun in the Carthusian Charterhouse nearby."

*Alive.* My hurt at having been kept in the dark by Celia competed with my joy at hearing her mother had survived. The news also confirmed my instincts about why I'd failed to make contact with Pilar. My *Vijitas* were limited to deceased, female relatives. Something good to know, even if at the moment I was better off focusing on the activities of the living.

"How did Carlos react when you told him your mother was alive?"

"It was a lot to take in and he was skeptical. I promised to take him to the Charterhouse to see her."

"Is that why he came here today?"

"Probably. I didn't even know he was in the house until you told me he was..." Her voice broke on the unspoken word.

I showed her the note that had been left on the windshield of the Outback, asking me to come to her house without Mico and signed by Carlos.

"I'm not sure, but I don't think it's my brother's handwriting."

"Do you think that Mico...?" A painful question to ask a grieving sister but what choice did I have?

"Listen to me, Allie. One thing I'm certain of is that Mico did not kill Carlos. Mother once described him as the most gentle man she knew. In spite of having made the mistake of marrying my father, she's an excellent judge of character."

"Does Mico know about Zahara? He told me Pilar was dead and I'm sure he believes it. What kind of cruel deception *is* this?"

"My mother insisted Mico be kept in the dark about all of it. She said he'd already risked enough helping her to escape Eduardo. And although she's never admitted it, I can read the love for him she holds in her eyes. As for her becoming a nun… well let's put it this way. Temptation out of sight is out of mind."

"You might both see Mico differently if you heard him ranting and raving like he did when I locked him out of the house. He showed his real face—*Ech`o la fiel.*" This was one of Grandma Nona's favorite Ladino phrases. It brought a very slight smile to Celia's lips.

"Grandma Luzia liked that expression too. I'm grateful she isn't here to see another member of our family murdered."

Celia's mention of Luzia carries me into her presence. She looks much older than I remember, curly white hair lending her face a cherubic quality. I don't know why, in the midst of these harrowing events, I've been gifted with another chance to share her consciousness. I *do* know that I welcome a chance to find out.

I'm gazing out the window of a small cottage, built in the humble style of a hermitage. Pilar walks toward me down a tree-lined path, enfolded in an aura of serenity fitting for someone wearing the white robe and black cowl of a nun. Although not the last thing we would have expected of our headstrong daughter, Pilar's transformation has been difficult to accept, especially for Ja'far. How sad that they will never have an opportunity to reconcile.

Pilar enters the hut and my chest tightens with the burden I've come to share. She sits down beside me on the hard stone bench, caressing a string of prayer beads.

"Mama, I didn't expect to see you until your first yearly visitation. They're exceedingly strict about this." The rustic cabin holds no comforts that might tempt a nun's family to stay longer than the allotted few days.

"In my case the Prioress made an exception."

"Why?"

"So I could come in person to tell you something."

"Whatever it is, you must not be afraid to say it, Mama."

"They've murdered your father. His old enemies came for him just when we thought we were at peace."

Pilar closes her eyes, going to that place where she takes refuge when she prays. At times like these I wish I could share her faith.

"Tell me everything," she says.

I had not planned to relate the more painful details but like Ja'far, Pilar has always preferred her truth unvarnished. "Do you remember when you were small, how Papa would bring strangers to our house in the middle of the night?"

"I remember waking up and hearing voices whispering in the kitchen. I thought they were ghosts and hid my head under the pillow."

I stroke Pilar's cheek, my hand coming away moist.

"Tell me more," she says, gripping my wrist.

"Those night-visitors were friends of Ja'far's who needed a place to hide."

"You mean Republicans?"

"Who else? Your father saw it as his duty to help the hunted. He allowed dozens of them to hide in the tunnels below our home. They would leave by way of the passage that to this day connects our house with the monastery. We never suspected you would one day choose the Charterhouse as your home. Thank goodness the nuns continue to be our friends."

Pilar pins me with one of her *you never tell me anything* looks.

"I'm sorry. Only yesterday we talked about showing you all of Zahara and telling you more of our history. But now your papa is gone."

"He will never be gone, Mama. And you of all people will keep his light shining."

As always, Pilar is right and I regret that we kept so many secrets from her. I wish now that I had told her the truth about the caretaking responsibilities Ja'far and I took on after the war. Responsibilities that tied us to our house and the tunnels below. It was difficult to tread the line between protecting our child and telling her what she was entitled to know.

"In those days your father would lead our guests in reading the forbidden books. He would bring them food and water and join in their endless discussions about how someday they would take the country back from fascism. As time passed, fewer came to us for help and eventually we thought all the unpleasantness was over. But franquistas have long and unforgiving memories."

My throat goes dry, rebelling against the unsayable. Pilar pours me a glass of water and waits for me to continue.

"Last week, while I was away visiting a friend in Málaga, they came for Ja'far. They called him a red dog and then took him out behind the house and shot him in the head. Our neighbors saw everything but all they could do was watch as the thugs threw his body on a cart and wheeled him away." For Pilar's sake I keep my voice steady. Ja'far, the love of my life, lies in ditch somewhere under the cruel sky. I try to banish the image of his lifeless eyes staring up at me.

"They made your father pay for his good deeds with his life. Not one of them was tall enough to reach his ankles, much less his knees."

Pilar pushes aside her veil, throwing her arms around me and our anguish echoes off the stone walls of the little hermitage.

I broke free from the *Vijita* and Luzia's tormented psyche only to have our shared sorrow follow me. Ja'far's death and Carlos's murder took place decades apart yet I'd experienced them both within minutes, a traveler trapped in a negative vortex.

Celia was seated in the same position on the couch she'd occupied before my undetected absence. At the sight of my tear-streaked face, she asked, "Why so much grief? You and Carlos were at odds and barely knew each other."

"I witnessed your mother Pilar's breakdown when she learned your grandfather had been slain by the franquistas."

"How is that possible? It happened years ago."

I was done hiding my abilities from my cousin. "It's not easy to describe. I experience what I call *Vijitas*. People from the distant past to whom I'm related inhabit me, or I inhabit them, it's hard to tell. I always return to the exact moment of my departure. Sounds crazy, I know."

"I wouldn't say so, Alienor. There's more to this world than what appears on the surface. Like I already told you, I suspect you have a *maggid*. If you were a Muslim, Grandpa Ja'far would have said you have *al-hibat ar-ru'eeya*, the gift of seeing. Since our ancestors are of mixed origins, you're doubly blessed. You can be sure there's a reason behind these gifts, a higher purpose."

"I never thought of it that way. Maybe I should have fully confided in you sooner."

"Secrecy is a habit harder to break than truth-telling."

A knock sounded at the door. Celia put her finger to her lips and whispered, "Please, not a word about the libraries."

In his uniform, Inspector Fernández looked taller than I remembered. He ducked under the archway into the living room, accompanied by a colleague he introduced as a member of the *Policia Local.* Behind them in the mudroom, a technician in a white jumpsuit leaned over Carlos.

"This is most strange," Fernández remarked. "Only today we cleared Carlos Martín of the attempted murder of Mico Rosales, and now he turns up dead. If you would be so kind as to tell me who found him and under what circumstances." The Inspector spoke to me in English, perhaps his way of stressing my tenuous connection to his country and the expectation of my full honesty were I to remain here.

"Celia invited me to lunch and I arrived early. She was out shopping. As soon as I saw Carlos, I knew he was dead. That's when I called you."

I'd done my best to give the falsehood some credibility but I doubted Celia and I would be able to keep track of all the half-truths and falsehoods we were about to tell. It was a necessary evil given how much was on the table. We were protecting a bond of trust that had held strong for more than three hundred years, as well as tons of invaluable paper and ink people had dedicated their lives to saving.

"Did your brother come to see you often?"

"No, we were estranged for many years," Celia said. "Recently he started to reach out. He was letting go of old grudges. A privilege that comes with age. He was forty-three."

Her observation must have touched a nerve because Fernández took a quick glance at his own image reflected in the mirror over the couch. I guessed him to be about the same age as Carlos. "Any particular grudge I should know about?"

"Only that Carlos was angry with our mother and me for leaving him and our father in Málaga. After she died, for many illogical reasons, Carlos held our family friend Mico Rosales responsible for her death."

The Inspector turned to me. "Are you sure there was no one else here when you found the body?"

I delayed answering, torn between wanting to tell the truth and the negative consequences for Mico if I did. The inspector waited me out.

"Mico was here. He was terribly upset and he left."

Fernández pounced on my response. "Did Rosales believe it was Carlos Martín who shot him in his office?"

I felt my face overheating as I remembered that one brief kiss and how my affection for Mico was so swiftly replaced by panic when I saw him standing over Carlos. "It's possible he did. And as you know, there was another attempt on Mico's life yesterday, at the hospital."

The inspector nodded grimly. "This morning I received a lab report from Doctor Cristóbal about a syringe filled with enough morphine to kill ten people. Did you witness the attack at the hospital?"

"Yes. The assailant wore a medical facemask. If I hadn't intervened, Mico would be dead."

Fernández maintained his impassive expression, as policemen do, but not before I saw a glint of new respect in his eyes. We were interrupted by a ghost in antiseptic slippers, the police technician. He and the Inspector left the room to discuss whatever had come up.

When Fernández returned from the murder scene he was rubbing his forehead, as if something beyond his understanding had occurred. He spoke gently to Celia. "I'm very sorry for your loss, Ms. Pérez, and I hate to ask this question. Is there any reason you can think of for the killer to cut off your brother's right thumb?"

My cousin reacted by running to the bathroom, where we could hear her retching. As we waited in mutual discomfort for Celia to return, all I could think of was that Mico, even if he did think Carlos had tried to kill him, would never in a million years have mutilated his body. The murderer was someone else and by disclosing Mico's presence at the scene, I'd implicated an innocent man. I cursed the double-edged sword that is truth.

Inspector Fernández took the opportunity to ask. "Do you know where Mico Rosales is, Ms. Crespo? He may have some explaining to do."

"I'm sorry," I stammered. "I have no clue."

"You may be in shock. I'd advise you to get some rest." Fernández's sympathy was unexpected and contradicted my assumption that he lacked depth simply because he practiced the surface protocols of his profession.

"We'll talk again," he said. "And if you remember anything, please contact me."

Celia rejoined us, her eyes bloodshot. "Whoever did this is bound to have left some incriminating evidence." Her rigid self-control in the face of losing her brother floored me. I admired her for channeling her sorrow and rage into helping to catch his killer.

Fernández must have noticed too. He took a step back and bowed his head slightly. "You're right and that's why we'll be quarantining this house to preserve the scene. Is there another place you can stay, Ms. Pérez?" he asked Celia.

"At the Airbnb with me," I said.

Although my offer was sincere, I was sure we'd return to the house after the police left. I was also sure that each time we used our thumbprints to gain entrance to the underground tunnels, we'd be forced to relive the horror that possessed us now.

# Chapter Seventeen

True to my prediction, on the day after Carlos's murder, Celia and I snuck into the quarantined house. From outside the closet, I watched her press her thumb down on a Hebrew letter in the center of the geometrical design. As the trapdoor sprung open, she turned to me. "Grandpa Ja'far painted and laid these tiles himself. It was painful to destroy their perfect symmetry when I installed the biometric lock. It was a welcome change from the old days when only a miracle prevented our enemies from discovering the tunnel entrances and prying them open."

As Jariya, I had seen Hasdai the Seer invoke a spell of invisibility at the mouth of the cave leading to Zahara. Perhaps his magic had lasted longer than anyone knew.

My cousin reached through the floor to release the ladder and I followed her down into the dimness, where she moved with the instinctive ease of a mole navigating its underground home. Each time we entered a turnoff, the color of the ambient lighting changed – starting with purple and changing from pink to orange to red. From above, natural light flowed through the air shafts to illuminate the motifs and symmetrical patterns of the stained glass windows. The effect was enchanting. Recessed doors appeared at regular intervals, all of them engraved with words in Hebrew and Arabic and symbols like the ones I'd seen the day before.

"Does each entryway lead to a library like the one under your house?"

"Good guess. The caretakers of Zahara are called Librarians. Some live in houses above the archives while others spend much of their time below and submerge themselves in antiquity. At one time there were twenty. Today, only eight maintain the tradition. Grandpa Ja'far was born in Morocco and was a descendant of one of Zahara's founders, Jariya al-Qasam, who left Spain after she and her band of Moriscos transported thousands of books to La Alpujarra. They packed these treasures onto mule trains and brought them up to this old, deserted salt mine. The dryness is perfect for preserving brittle pages."

I longed to tell Celia how Jariya and her friends rescued so much more than books. She deserved to know more about my *Vijitas* and someday soon I would share more.

"Why do you call this place Zahara?"

"If only I could show you *The Book of Zahara*, Alienor. It was authored by Hasdai the Seer, who documented the construction of Zahara in great detail, as well as the metaphysical framework he used to organize the libraries. The book has been missing since the 1980's. Some say the parchment itself has magical powers. Not that I believe all that."

If this was the book Pilar entrusted to Mico, she must have had a good reason not to reveal its whereabouts to her closest living relative. I decided to trust her judgment and say nothing.

We continued our walk through the tunnels.

"It's hard on the senses to spend so much time underground, so we swapped out the fluorescent lamps for something more friendly," Celia explained.

"There must have been many changes over the years."

"There's so much to tell." Celia's voice lifted, her enthusiasm eclipsing her grief for the moment. "I'll start with the basics. Hasdai modeled Zahara on the Tree of Life – the Sefirot – a symbol of spiritual evolution shared by Muslims, Jews and Christians alike. He located the libraries within the Tree and named each one after an attribute of the Divine Presence – known as *Shekhinah* in the Kabbalah and *Sakinat* in Sufism. The libraries have both Hebrew and Arabic names for Wisdom, Understanding, Mercy, Prophecy and so on.

"So in addition to the books, people of all faiths are welcome to work here?"

"Absolutely. That's why an underground synagogue and mosque were once connected to our Common Area, so the Librarians could attend services. Now that these places of worship exist legally in Spain, we no longer maintain them here."

The lighting took on the pale green shade of a Reineta apple and Celia used her voice to open a door that was camouflaged to blend into the jungle painted around it. We stepped inside and a dozen monitors blinked.

"This is our Control Room. I installed most of the equipment myself, using money from the silk business and my teaching job at the technical college."

"How many people know about this place?"

"Only the Librarians and a handful on the outside, like you. Without trustworthy friends, Zahara would've been discovered and destroyed almost as soon as it was built."

"A precarious arrangement."

"Everyone takes a vow of secrecy, something we will absolutely require of you. There's a myth that when a Librarian is sworn in, the two powerful mystics who arranged for our books to be rescued from the Inquisitors in the late fifteenth century are in attendance—the Sufi master, Ibn al Arabī and the Jewish rabbi, Abraham Abulafia. There are times when I have sensed their presence. Reb Hakim, the Sufi Rabbi who looks after the *Library of Mysticism and Wisdom*, has had the same experience, strange as that may sound to you."

"It's not strange at all, given the history of this place. What does seem hard to believe is that over the centuries no one has betrayed your whereabouts."

"Not that we know of. First, fear of the Inquisition and then the ferocity of Franco's wrath were reason enough for everyone to keep their vows. Nowadays, the books have gained in value, some of them worth millions, making us feel less secure. A few Librarians would prefer to have the state protect us. Not me."

Celia lowered herself into a plush executive chair in front of the console, patting the seat of a second chair to invite me to join her. She punched some buttons to queue up recorded views of different sections of the tunnels, each screen marked with time-code showing when the video had been logged.

"We monitor everything that happens in the tunnels from this room and any unauthorized thumbprint or entry triggers the cameras. See that yellow light? It indicates movement was detected since I was last here. Sometimes it's an animal, a dog or a cat, even a rabbit that has found its way in. This time we're looking for a human. If Carlos's killer succeeded in using my brother's thumbprint and a recording of his voice to gain entry to Zahara, then he is somewhere on these tapes and we will find him. Her voice wobbled slightly when she pronounced her brother's name but she made it to the end of the sentence.

"What makes it worse is that I only recently added Carlos's thumbprint and voice sample to our database, along with yours, Allie. I planned to take him on a tour of Zahara before we visited Pilar at the Charterhouse. He was ready to reconcile with our side of the family and from what he said, willing to share some important information. Now someone has made sure that will never happen."

She stood up and backed away from the switches and monitors as if they'd become radioactive. "The system we spent years designing has been hijacked by a murderer. We were mistaken to put all our trust in technology. Computers have no loyalty and can change sides at the flip of a switch."

"From what I've seen, you've done an excellent job. No system is perfect," I ventured.

"I know you mean well, cousin, but we've already wasted valuable time." Celia reclaimed her seat in the leather chair.

It took us roughly a hundred minutes to view twelve hours of high-speed playback. "Nothing but empty corridors," I remarked.

"That's because the Librarians rarely venture into the tunnels unless there's an important meeting in our Common Area. The collections are housed beneath their living quarters and can be easily accessed. What we're looking for is any unusual activity."

On the verge of falling asleep, I perked up when Celia stopped the tape. A tall, slender woman wearing a rose-colored hijab filled the frame. My cousin pressed play to return to normal playback speed. Our subject's confident stride held a touch of grace as she balanced plates and cups on a tray.

"Nothing out of the ordinary here. That's Saleema al-Garnati making her deliveries. She's a talented potter who spins most of our tableware on her wheel. For generations, Saleema's family has watched over the *Library of Khalud*, meaning Prophecy in Arabic. Their collection includes hundreds of copies of the Quran that were saved from the fire, as well as works penned by famous Sufis and other mystics."

Almost as clearly as they'd appeared during my *Vijitas*, I saw a team of stalwart donkeys burdened with saddlebags of books and led by a determined Jariya al-Qasam. A pity Jariya would never meet Saleema and Celia, who were equally brave in their own way. I was sure she'd have felt a strong kinship with them.

Celia tinkered with some switches on the control board and the images on the screen changed to show a door engraved with Hebrew lettering. "You're probably wondering where the Jewish holy books are kept," she said. "This is the *Library of Netsah*, meaning Eternity in Hebrew, cared for by Abram Capeluto, a direct descendent of Hasdai the Seer. When things calm down, I'll arrange for you to meet him."

I held my peace about my firsthand knowledge of Hasdai. When the time was right, it would make for a very interesting conversation.

As Celia and I continued to scan the security tapes, we were joined in the Control Room by a slim man with an acne-scarred face and a neatly wrapped turban. His jeans, burgundy shirt, and expensive-looking gray vest, conveyed a businesslike air.

"Alienor, this is Talvir Singh, recently recruited from the Punjab by Saleema. He's an IT expert and is working with us to make sure our security isn't further compromised. Talvir's name means 'beautiful gift to the world,' a fortunate coincidence, since we badly need his services.

"Talvir, this is my cousin Alienor from Seattle. You can trust her. Allie's the one who found my brother Carlos." She averted her head, blinking away tears.

"This is beyond terrible. I am truly sorry for your loss." Talvir reached down and took Celia's hand in both of his. "May he find peace."

"Thank you," Celia said, wiping her eyes. They shared a quiet moment before getting back to work.

I wanted to ask Talvir why he'd come all the way from India to guard the literary treasures of a bygone age. A pity there was no time for casual conversation.

He and Celia spent an hour switching between monitors, making sure we hadn't missed anything. My job was to listen for any out-of-the-ordinary sounds on the audio track. Except for Saleema's footsteps, all was quiet.

Before we left the Control Room, I asked Celia if Carlos's thumbprint would be erased from the database as a security precaution. She paled at the inference and Talvir answered for her. "It wouldn't be wise to do that. The only chance we have of catching this fellow is by waiting until he tries to use that thumbprint and triggers the alarm."

Celia pushed back her chair and took a deep breath. "If you can hear me, Carlos, I swear on our Grandmother Luzia's grave, whoever did this will not go unpunished."

She left Talvir in charge with instructions to call her at the first sign of a break-in and we returned to the house, via ladder and trapdoor. "I was planning to take you to meet my mother but today is not the day. She'll be distraught over Carlos and also angry at me for not bringing him to see her sooner. Never mind that she was the one who swore me to secrecy about her new life as a nun in the first place."

"That seems harsh. Pilar has to know what a difficult situation – "

"You don't know my mom. She's got in the habit of rewriting family history. She's never forgiven her *own* mother for allowing her to marry Eduardo. As if Grandma Luzia or anyone else on earth could have stopped her. The day she married my father, my mother put Zahara in jeopardy. And the day she left Eduardo and we moved back to my grandparent's house, she made things even worse. That's why she ended up in a nunnery and I was forced to fend for myself."

I saw Celia's outburst as her way of processing grief, at least until the next step in the process, whatever that might be. Her anguish at losing Carlos on the verge of their reconciliation was mixed with anger and frustration. Feelings I experienced in my own way when I chose to give up my *Vijitas* with Mom. Using what Celia referred to as my *maggid*, I could have shared Mom's awareness but she would never have been conscious of my presence or been able to hear me say the words *I love you*. It was a one-way street I refused to drive down.

On the way back to the Airbnb, I felt a surge of expectation. The light in my room would be on, Mico waiting there to explain everything. In his place I found Jeroen, reading a book by firelight in the living room. The warm, terra cotta walls and indigo blue rug were soothing to the eye. I felt the band around my chest loosen up a notch or two.

"I hope you weren't waiting up for me."

"Of course not... well, maybe a little. The roads through the foothills can be treacherous." He sounded sincerely concerned and although I had no intention of burdening him with my problems, there was something about the artlessness of this Dutchman that disarmed me.

"I'm okay. Although it's been a day of extremes," I admitted.

"You look like you could use something to eat. I'll make you an omelet. It'll be but a minute."

It was a mite longer but well worth the wait. I wolfed down the goat cheese, tomato, and eggs spiced with oregano, and my energy returned. "What a lifesaver you are."

Jeroen offered me a glass of cognac. "It may take more than eggs to fortify you. The police came by this evening. I told them I didn't know where you were. After that, your friend Mico arrived, in a big hurry to pick up his things. He asked me for pen and paper, so I suppose he's written you a letter. Whatever you've stepped into, Ms. Crespo, I respect your privacy and you're welcome to stay here as long as you like."

The way Jeroen instinctively took my side meant a lot. It also brought home how little I knew about whatever it was that I'd "stepped into." I thanked him and went to my room.

On the dresser an envelope with my name on it radiated reproach. Like the writer, the handwriting was straightforward.

Dear Allie,

Late this morning, while you and I were driving to Celia's place, Carlos left a voice message on my cell that I failed to hear until it was too late. He warned me that Celia and her friends were in danger. He said we should stay away from her house. The fear in his voice was unmistakable.

*I notified Inspector Fernández that I'll be back in my office by tomorrow morning and available for questioning. Our mutual friend, Luis Alcábez will represent me. It's only natural the police would suspect me but you, Alienor - how could you go to all the trouble of rescuing me and then turn around and judge me capable of such a terrible crime? I feel gratitude for how you took care of me, which is why I'm giving you some time to readjust your thinking.*

*Respectfully, Mico*

I read the note twice, looking for clues to help me decide where I stood. I was miffed at Mico's high-handedness. He assumed I'd be willing to ignore what I'd seen with my own eyes and question my own judgment. The trained-to-be-skeptical journalist saw the letter as an attempt to control me while pretending to be magnanimous. If that were true, I'd have to tell Mico where to get off. My intuitive, emotional side rejected these cold thoughts, pushing them aside to make room for the warmth of attraction and a tendency to believe Celia when she vouched for him. Perhaps if and when I saw him again…

Too many confusing thoughts. I stretched out on the bed and buried my head in a soft pillow lightly scented with lavender. Jeroen thought of everything.

# Chapter Eighteen

Half a night's restless sleep left me craving more. I tried keeping my eyes closed but this only encouraged the rush of images—Mico lying on the floor of his office, the nurse threatening me with a syringe, Carlos's bent and broken body. I could leave Spain and formalize my application for citizenship some other time. I'd never considered myself an especially brave person. So far my most dangerous assignment as a journalist had been a helicopter ride with a swiftwater rescue team working a flood in western Washington.

Weighing on the other side was Celia, caught up in a murder investigation on top of losing her brother, with no time to breathe much less grieve. She needed my help and I had a hunch that if no one followed up on whatever Carlos had discovered, more people might die. And what of Zahara? How could I leave without exploring that wondrously mysterious place?

I sat up in bed and texted a pitch to Todd Lassiter: *What would you say to an in-depth piece about the politics of Andalusia? There's a tie-in with the resurgence of right wing politics in the States that I think will interest your readers. I've already developed a contact. Awaiting your green light. Best, Alienor.*

It was late afternoon in Seattle and Todd's reply flew back within the hour: *That police inspector called me from Granada and I told him you'd make a model prisoner. Let's talk.*

On top of his weird sense of humor Lassiter had uncanny intuition. He picked up my incoming call on the first ring, possibly for the first time ever.

"If it's not Alienor Crespo, stirring up more trouble to write about."

This was a dirty dig. He knew I'd literally punched my fist into the wall when my first feature in the *Courier* resulted in the subject's brother being arrested and threatened with deportation to El Salvador. A hotshot in ICE had used my vague references to Private Mario Flores's family history to track down his undocumented relatives. Ironically, my story about the Army's failure to protect Flores earned me an award from the Journalism Society of Western Washington.

"I made a huge mistake, Todd, and one I'm sure you'll never let me forget. But I did find the family a lawyer and we set things right. After that, I promised myself to be more careful."

"Inspector Fernández thinks being careful means you'll be taking the next flight to Seattle."

*To me it means selling you a story I can write in good conscience without breaking my promise to Celia.* "What if I told you that one of my distant Spanish relatives is a right wing politician? There's a lot going on here that mirrors the divide in the States. I can give you a story that will resonate with readers on a national level."

His response was awhile in coming. "You do know how to wear a person down. Okay, Alienor. You've got the green light. Just remember to play it safe. You're not a war correspondent risking her life in Syria."

Todd's comparison, combined with my sleepless night, put me on edge. I went to brush my teeth and in the round mirror over the sink saw a person guilty of deceiving both herself and her editor. Although I'd pitched an angle that was real enough, my true intention was to investigate Carlos's murder. To do this behind Inspector Fernández's back might be asking for trouble. And even if I did find a motive for the crime, I'd be unable to write about it without shining an unwelcome light on Zahara's existence.

Just after I dressed and applied sunscreen to my reddened arms, cursing myself for having worn short sleeves the day before, Celia called. "Are you still in Almendrales? If you're already en-route to the airport, I'll understand."

"How could I leave you in a situation like this? Have the police removed the crime tape around your house?"

"Soon. They took Carlos to the morgue in an ambulance and will finish their forensic work this afternoon. We'll be holding a memorial service later. Why don't you move in as we originally planned? Unless you feel uncomfortable staying in a place where—"

"Of course not. I appreciate your having me. Anyway, Mico sent me some news that's better not discussed on the phone."

"We'll talk when you get here. After that, my mother wants to meet you."

I was floored by the prospect of meeting Pilar in the flesh after having shared her intimate interactions with her mother, Luzia. *Was it possible she would recognize me?* Exactly how my *Vijitas* worked remained a mystery I was afraid I'd never fathom.

I went to find Jeroen and pay some of the extras on my bill. No more midnight omelets or comforting small talk.

The front door to Celia's place was open. In the mud room where Carlos had died, I felt a hint of his ghost rising to meet me. For a moment I dreaded being swept into his consciousness and forced to relive his violent end. True, it might be a quick way to identify the killer. But then again, what was I thinking? The family members I accessed in my *Vijitas* belonged to a women-only club.

Celia met me at the threshold of the inner door. She wore a simple black dress with short sleeves and her eyes were hollow from weeping. "You need something more appropriate to wear to the memorial service. I might have something that will fit you. Let's go see."

I'd brought only casual, late fall clothes with me to Spain, a sweater or two just in case, no premonition I'd need anything else. I set down my suitcase and accepted the dark blue skirt and matching blouse my cousin offered. With some hesitation, I gave her Mico's note, concerned about how she might react to it in her vulnerable state.

I changed in the bathroom and came out to find Celia holding Mico's letter pressed to her heart. It looked like she was trying to absorb the ink on the paper containing her brother's last recorded words. "Carlos was trying to warn us. If only Mico had listened to his voicemail, my brother might still be alive. How terrible when someone you love is destroyed by the consequences of something you wish you'd had the power to change. What good is knowledge if it only brings more suffering?" It was hard to tell if she was talking to herself or to me, so I stayed silent.

Celia picked up a bouquet of forget-me-nots from the table near the door. "My mother is expecting us. We'd better get going."

This time, at the bottom of the ladder leading down to the tunnel from her bedroom, we turned a different way. My sense of direction told me we were headed for the Charterhouse and I knew from my most recent *Vijita* that the nunnery had been connected to Zahara centuries ago. "Isn't it unusual that Catholics would befriend your cause?" I asked Celia.

"These nuns are Carthusians, mystics who commune with God directly. They've been our allies for hundreds of years, an unbroken chain of friendship."

We reached a junction where the smooth surfaces and softly colored lights of the hi-tech passageways were replaced by earthy smells, gouged dirt walls, and low ceilings supported by rough-hewn, wooden beams. Celia slowed down. "Watch your step – sometimes there's a dead bird or squirrel. How they get in, no one knows and they're impossible to catch."

We walked for less than a mile, the flashlights from our phones luckily illuminating no animal corpses. Celia stopped in front of a massive metal door and pressed an old fashioned buzzer mounted on the wall.

"Why can't we enter through the front gate of the monastery?"

"They're officially open to visitors only once or twice a year. To change that custom would arouse suspicion, so we use the tunnels instead."

The door creaked open to reveal a nun, her face haloed by a dark cowl contrasting with the pristine white of her robe. "Who comes to speak to those who have chosen silence?"

"*Shalom. Asalaam Alaykum.* God be with you, Sister," Celia answered. Hearing these greetings spoken in three languages, the Sister stepped aside to let us enter.

Celia nudged me. "When you come back you must remember to say those exact words and in the same order. Otherwise, you'll be politely but firmly turned away." She swung her flashlight from wall to wall, revealing deserted cubicles on both sides.

"In the 1930's these old cells were occupied by refugees from our 'Little World War.' The nuns took in anyone, no matter what their religion, ethnicity, or politics. My grandparents brought people to hide here but they were so secretive I doubt my mother knew about it until she came to live here in the monastery."

At the end of the block of cells, Celia guided me up a winding staircase leading to an outside door. We emerged at the edge of a small lawn bordered with flowering trees. After the claustrophobic, underground trek, it was good to relax in the open air. I recognized the spire soaring above us as the one visible from my cousin's front yard. "The nuns live in secluded housing on the other side of the church," she said. "They spend most of their time alone, withdrawing into silence to escape the temptations of the world."

Pilar received us at the door of the same vine-covered visiting lodge where I had last seen her embrace Luzia after learning of her grandfather Ja'far's death. Although she was much older now, the pain in her luminous eyes had remained constant. She accepted the flowers from Celia before greeting me. "My daughter tells me you've come all the way from America to rejoin our family. It's so sad you would come to us at this time. Yet there must be a reason."

"Thank you for allowing me to attend the memorial service and share your sorrow. There is no greater loss than that of a child."

She reached out to hug me. "No matter what higher power we call on for comfort, grief visits us all. Will you pray with me?" I was touched by her warm acceptance of someone she barely knew.

Carefully, Pilar lowered herself onto the bench, suggesting physical frailty daily overcome by spiritual strength. We joined her and bowed our heads, sharing a deep silence broken only by the occasional chirp of a bird outside the small, octagonal window. Celia was the first to speak. "Mama, there are some questions that have come up."

"Ask away."

"You've often said my father is obsessive in his beliefs. How fanatical *is* he?"

"I can tell you that Eduardo loved Franco and has continued to hate the Reds. I'm sure he knew about the plan to massacre the left-wing labor lawyers in 1977. But I doubt he would have perpetrated any violence himself. Still, there were times…"

Celia locked eyes with her mother. "Were you afraid of him?"

Pilar grimaced. "It was Eduardo who was afraid of *me*. I overheard him giving information to the Falangists about the attorneys on the day before the murders. If this ever came to light his political prospects would be butchered too." She raised and lowered her hands as if balancing platforms on a scale. "In the end we made a bargain. He let me leave Málaga in return for my silence. I was able to keep you but I should have fought harder for custody of Carlos. I failed to shelter him and now he's dead."

"Mama, you had no choice."

"Everyone has a choice, my child." Retreating into herself, Pilar rocked from side to side, her voice subdued. "God's truth is I failed your brother by leaving him to be raised in a poisonous environment. Eduardo embraced Hitler's crazy theories about race superiority and I'm sure he hasn't changed in spite of his new, more moderate veneer. I may live a cloistered life but that doesn't mean I'm ignorant of the new threats facing our country. Your father and those like him want to rid

Spain of the *undesirables*: Gypsies, Jews, Muslims, immigrants – anyone who by their standards is of impure blood."

"You haven't seen Papa for more than thirty years. Perhaps he's learned a thing or two."

Pilar pulled herself together and sat up straight, incredulous at her daughter's words. "Don't believe him, Celia. If Eduardo's watered down his message, it's because people will never vote him into the House of Deputies if they know what he really stands for. He calls it the StandUp party… pity there's no one willing to stand up to *him*."

"Carlos *was* beginning to stand up, Mamá. I helped him to see through Papa's lies and unlike most, he was willing to admit he'd been misled. I'm sure those first eight years of his life, the ones he spent with you, had a lot to do with shaping his character."

"I wish that were so. After our separation, Eduardo never permitted me to see Carlos, although for some reason he allowed Luzia to visit her grandson from time to time. The boy deserved so much more than a mother who failed him, a mother who was – and still is – so easily deceived." She tugged her rosary beads in opposite directions, caught up in some inner conflict.

"What is it *Mamaíta*?" Celia asked.

"It might be nothing but there's a priest who comes here every month to take our confessions. I've come to trust him and we even talk about your father sometimes. No matter how much time passes, I can't help wondering if I might have done things differently in those days. Last Sunday I got up the courage to tell Father Gerard about my suspicions about Eduardo's involvement in the Atocha Massacre. Only it wasn't Father Gerard. I had shared my secrets with a stranger. I had no idea until he spoke through the grill in the confessional, and by then it was too late."

"Do you know his name?"

"No, and something inside me said not to ask."

Celia massaged her mother's back. "Even if he was appalled, this priest would never break the sacred confidentiality of the confession." She spoke these comforting words while sneaking a worrisome look at me.

Not for the first time, I wondered why—given all the unfortunate events that had transpired since my arrival—my newfound family members seemed to trust me so completely. I would not let them down. I would do my best to cut through the net I felt encircling us.

"I've got to go to Málaga and fill out some paperwork," I told them. "I can try to talk with Eduardo. I'll tell him I'm researching a book or something. I might find out something useful."

Pilar held up her right hand, palm outward. "Remember that Eduardo thinks I'm dead and all his secrets are safe. If he finds out otherwise, he and his unsavory friends will breach these thick monastery walls and find the tunnels beneath us."

Celia gently lowered her mother's arm. "Normally I'd agree with you, *Mamaíta*. But now we know for certain someone is planning something big, something involving Zahara. Carlos tried to alert us and they killed him. I think we owe it to my brother's memory to do whatever we can to avert disaster."

She'd said *they*, not *he* killed Carlos. I couldn't believe how unfair I'd been to Mico.

Pilar stood, smoothing the tunic of her habit. "We can also show respect for your brother's memory by being on time for the celebration of his life."

# Chapter Nineteen

I had assumed the service would take place in the Charterhouse's church but here we were, retracing our steps through the dingy old tunnel leading from the monastery to Zahara's more streamlined passageways. We were a dozen or so, our faces bathed in the greenish-blue light of a Picasso painting. With his love of Spain's diversity, the artist might have reveled in the sight of us: a veiled nun in mourning walking beside her bareheaded female companions, two men in black suits, one head covered by a yarmulke and the other a taqiyah, a bevy of women wearing somber attire and hijabs, and a pair of elderly gentleman with full beards flowing over the tops of their linen robes. Celia said most were Librarians and the others immediate and trusted family members. I recognized Talvir the computer guy with his turban neatly wrapped.

"So your Prioress has no trouble with you leaving once in a while?" I asked Pilar.

"We have thirty entirely sequestered nuns living at the Charterhouse, as well as people like me, who take refuge from the outside world and are accepted as non-initiates." Her ready answer betrayed no offense taken.

"We Converse Nuns perform most of the chores and physical work and in return we're granted more freedom. Since I'll always put my family first, I'll never be able to take my vows and wear the bands on my cowl. But that doesn't mean I have no real calling or close connection with God."

I noticed a gray metal Cross on a chain encircling her neck. "Do you still have the bracelet your father gave you, the one with *Jariya* engraved inside?"

"Yes, of course." Pilar eyed me curiously. "Celia didn't tell me you had a gift."

Why hadn't I known these women would see through me? After all, it was our shared inheritance.

The procession moved through a series of ever-widening archways welcoming us into a spacious, circular room with a domed ceiling. This was the first chamber I'd seen in Za-hara without a reinforced door. Religious symbols of all kinds adorned the columns and walls.

"Welcome to our Common Area," Celia said. She took my arm and pointed upward, at a life-like mural covering the curved walls all the way up to the ceiling.

It was the same scene my great-grandmother Miriam had mistaken for the real thing during the *Vijita* I shared with her in Granada. Like Miriam, it was easy for me to think I was looking at something that existed in three dimensions. The people had the same life-like animation and the mosque, syn-agogue, and church were backlit to create the illusion of an outdoor view. It was a vision of the future, impossible during the lifetime of its creator and unlikely to come to fruition anytime soon.

The Common Area had been constructed to transcend the cramped feeling of underground life and I supposed it once accommodated far more than the dozen people assembled here now. Wooden benches curled around the circumference. Celia was seated along the circular wall along with everyone else.

When she wanted to speak, she stood and raised her hand, waiting for silence.

"I wish to say a few words about my late brother, Carlos Martín Pérez Crespo. If he had lived he might have traded the name of Pérez for Siddiqui, in honor of our grandfather, Ja'far. My childhood memories of playing hopscotch and dominoes with Carlos were buried by distance and the pain of being torn apart. I had no way of knowing what kind of man he would become, so when some began to judge him by his reputation for spreading hatred, sadly, I believed them. Recently I found out how wrong I was. My brother had the courage to choose truth over the diet of lies on which was raised. His last act was to sacrifice himself to keep his family safe."

My cousin failed to mention the gruesome way in which the murderer had obtained Carlos's thumbprint and the danger this presented to Zahara. Didn't her fellow Librarians deserve to know what they were up against? I assumed she had her reasons.

Saleema al-Garnati, the same woman I had seen on closed-circuit TV the day before, crossed the room and embraced my cousin. "My deepest sympathies for your loss. May God give you strength."

"Thank you, Saleema. I'm sorry Carlos never had a chance to meet you."

Celia went to stand beside Pilar and they accepted condolences, along with bunches of flowers that accumulated on the floor at their feet.

After everyone returned to their seats, she took me aside. "If you want to stay you'll be required to swear an oath of secrecy."

She'd cornered me. I was being asked to place Zahara's security above my own needs as a journalist. I'd done this before when protecting a sensitive source. This time, the stakes were higher.

"No problem," I reassured her. "But in return I get to ask why you have chosen to trust me with secrets that have been closely guarded for centuries?"

"There are two reasons. You've met Talvir, right?"

"You know I have."

"Well, with a little information there's nothing he can't find out about someone."

"And their fingerprints too. Taken without consent, I might add."

My cousin shrugged. "Isn't it enough that we've decided to include you?"

"What's the second reason?"

Celia ignored my question and walked toward the center of the circle, her head high, confident I would follow. She was right. At this point nothing would have stopped me from meeting the occupants of this zealously protected world.

"Everyone, this is my cousin, Alienor Crespo. I hereby vouch for her honesty and integrity. Does anyone object to her being initiated into our community?"

When no one responded, Celia turned me to face the group and asked, "Do you, Alienor Crespo, promise to keep in strictest confidence all knowledge that is shared with you about Zahara and the books we have all sworn to protect?"

"Yes, I promise."

She introduced me to each Librarian by name and I jotted their names down in my notebook:

Celia Martín Crespo – *Tif'eret and Jamal Library of Poetry*
Saleema al-Garnati – *Library of Khalud (Prophecy) Muslim Holy Books*

Malik al-Bakr – *Library of Islamic Sciences*
Reinaldo Luz – *Eternal Library of Babel*
Reb Hakim – *Library of Hokhmah - Mysticism and Wisdom of All Faiths*
Abram Capeluto – *Library of Netsah, Jewish Holy Books*
Suneetha bint Hasan – *Library of Philosophy and the Arts*
Rushd al-Wasim – *Library of Crafts and Animal Husbandry*

That was all there was to it. I returned to my seat and Celia announced, "Reb Hakim has something important to say."

The Sufi Rabbi rose slowly from his seat. It was easy for everyone to see his multicolored robe, kindly face, and brightly embroidered cap. What a clever idea, I thought, to hold meetings in a circular space where each person is always within sight of the other.

As he spoke, Reb Hakim's eyes beamed with a glow that touched each person. His manner was direct, with no excess gravitas. "For the first time in our history a violent crime, a murder, has happened in the house of one of our Librarians. In my view, this has changed everything. We need more protection than our security system alone can provide. This is why I'm asking your permission to speak with Sandra Díaz Ramírez, a member of the Spanish government and trusted friend. My plan is to ask her to nominate Zahara as a World Heritage Site. Due to the exacerbation of the threat this community has lived under for more than four hundred years, this request would be processed by the World Heritage Committee on an emergency basis. Now we must decide whether or not – "

"How can you even think of this?! I refuse to support this reckless idea that would divulge our existence to the entire world." The heated objection came from Saleema, and she did not hold back. "Reb Hakim, you of all people should know that even today, Muslims are forbidden to pray at the Great Mosque of Cordoba. Puffed up politicians, academics and closet fascists are also denying the Semitic contributions to Spanish culture. To them the entire concept of the *Convivencia* is a threat. How do you think they will react if their identity as 'eternal Spaniards from before the time of the Visigoths' proves to be fiction, a complete fraud? They will not accept our existence and what we stand for without a fight."

Abram Capeluto, his short beard striped gray by life's harsh paintbrush, spoke next. "Saleema, I understand your point but times have changed. Do we need to continue with all this secrecy? We may find welcome where before there was only hatred."

"Abram, you are my dear friend but you are also naïve." This came from Celia. "I strongly agree with Saleema. If we go public, the most sacred and inspiring remnants of the *Convivencia* will be divided up and claimed by conflicting groups. What's left of our unity will dissolve."

"She's right you know." It was Malik al-Bakr, from the *Library of Islamic Sciences,* speaking with crisp authority. "The simple existence of the collection is evidence that the *Convivencia* once existed between poets, writers, philosophers and scientists of differing faiths in medieval Al-Andalus. I'm not sure the majority of Spaniards are ready to accept this and, as we learned yesterday, there are some who violently oppose us."

Saleema backed him up. "They want to bury all Arab contributions to Spanish culture. How many school children know that Gibraltar is *Tariq's Mountain*, named after Jabal al Tariq, who led the conquest of the Visigoths? This country is not ready for the truth."

Talvir spoke up. "Even if Saleema is right, the longer we stay hidden, the greater the chance of our being discovered by the wrong people and destroyed. If we came out in the open, they would never dare."

"Like they didn't dare destroy the Republic?" Pilar exclaimed. "How many of you have relatives who died during the Civil War? And look at what happened to those who came out of hiding too soon?"

"The difference is that we will be under the dual protection of UNESCO and the Spanish government," countered Reb Hakim. "And let's face it – after the terrible act that took place in Celia's house, it may be impossible to keep our secret much longer. To go forward with this nomination, we must first permit a member of the World Heritage Committee to inspect the libraries and determine whether or not this site meets their criteria for the World Heritage List. I beg you to give permission for the inspection."

"What if the Inspector decides to give an interview to the press on his own? What then?" asked Celia.

Reb Hakim laced his fingers in a pensive knot, acknowledging the importance of the question. "UNCESCO has promised to guard our privacy and I believe them. And remember, even if the nomination is approved we will hold another vote on whether or not to accept."

I could see both sides. If the Librarians and the books in their custody stayed hidden, they could avoid publicly challenging their potential enemies, like Eduardo's StandUp party and their ilk. On the other hand, if they went public as a Heritage site they'd have the benefit of state support and a chance to share an immense gift with the world. As an added bonus, I'd be freed from my vow of secrecy and be able to write about them.

The discussion continued with no clear decision in the offing. In my *Vijitas* I'd glimpsed some difficult decisions made under duress by the founders of Zahara. Perhaps they were fortunate to have no time to spare for this messy, democratic process. Jariya in particular was a woman of action, a warrior whose sword was tempered by the flames of injustice. I wished I had a fraction of the fire in her blood flowing through my veins.

I'm busy unpacking a saddlebag of books in a secluded area of the mine.

"It's hard to imagine this primitive alcove as anything other than an indentation in a wall of salt," says Razin, who has come to find me. He places his hands around my thickened waist. "You should be resting."

"Hasdai says this room is destined to become a great library."

"And you, Jariya, are destined to become a mother."

Razin and I have lived together as man and wife for a year. Idris al-Wasim gave me away in marriage and recited the beautiful words of the contract: *Praise be to God, unique in perfection, glorious and exalted, perfect in acts and words, who harmonizes the hearts of women and of men.* Afterwards we danced the Zambra to pipes and flutes, a taste of the happy days Moriscos enjoyed before our music was outlawed.

"Dear wife, have you thought about my proposal?"

"I have, and I do not want to leave Zahara."

"Do you not wish for our baby to grow up free from worrying his mother will fail to come home from battle? It's time we left for Morocco, before you're too big to travel."

I resist my longing to give in. "Even if I *were* to agree, you are needed here, Razin. Who best knows the secret routes to the coast and where to meet the southbound ships?"

"I won't let you take this journey by yourself. Too many dangers on land and sea, even if you weren't with child."

I understand why my loving husband feels protective. But why can't he see the affront in this? *Am I not also a seasoned fighter whose reputation strikes fear into those who would enslave us?* The baby kicks, I assume in agreement. *Or is he reminding me of his helplessness and urging me to listen to his father?*

Razin senses I'm relenting. "You know I'm right, Jariya."

"Alright then. Fatima will come with me. After two years of guiding others on the trails, she knows the way well. Once she accompanied a group all the way from La Alpujarra to the Maghreb and made the return trip alone."

Fatima is also a mother and will understand my concerns, a fact I don't mention since it's hard to admit to Razin how much I fear the pain of childbirth.

"Good. It's settled then. I'll join you when I can." Razin forces a smile which I try to return. Lately, he's been reading to me from books that were saved from the fire. My favorite is the one about the customs and famous markets of North Africa where, with Allah's blessing, my baby and I will soon be living. I vow to learn how to decipher words on the page without my husband's help by the time we meet again. If ever we do.

It gave me chills, the idea of Jariya al-Qasam and Razin al-Siddiqui taking time to read the books they risked their lives to bring to Zahara. How pleased they would have been to see their descendant, my Great Uncle Ja'far ibn Siddiqui, return to Spain hundreds of years later. To know how he and many others continued to safeguard not only the written word but the flesh and blood of those who would otherwise be condemned to oblivion.

As I pondered the connections between past and present confirmed by this latest *Vijita*, the community meeting came to an end and the Librarians began leaving the Common Area. Reb Hakim appeared at my elbow.

"There's something I'd like to show you, Alienor, if you'd kindly accompany me."

I searched the room for Celia's face. "Don't worry," said the Reb. "I've already spoken with your keeper and she approves."

In the corridor, I fell in step beside him.

"Celia thinks very highly of you and told me in private that she believes your gifts will play an important role in helping Zahara survive."

*So that was her second reason.* "I appreciative all this confidence in me, Reb Hakim, but what makes you think I'm worthy?"

The Sufi Rabbi chuckled, like someone who knew a lot about my inner life without asking. "I don't see you running away from the challenge and that's what matters."

We stopped at a plain, wooden door with no inscriptions or markings of any kind, unusual for Zahara. "Mystics have never gone in for ornamentation," Reb Hakim said, unlocking the primitive padlock. "What glory they experience comes from their contact with the Source."

The shelves inside the *Library of Mysticism and Wisdom of All Faiths* were unpolished, the grain of their untreated wood suggesting the humility common to the authors of the books they supported. In contrast, the Librarian showed off his collection with considerable pride. "We have dozens of books penned by Jewish and Muslim mystics such as Abraham

Abulafia and Ibn al-Arabī. There are even a few Christian works of that nature, including Michael Servetus's *The Restoration of Christianity*, in which he advocates for more tolerance of other religions—a heresy that caused him to be burnt alive, along with his creations. But that's not what I brought you here to see."

Reb Hakim pointed to an open volume displayed on a lectern. "This invaluable codex was delivered to Zahara by Ja'far Siddiqui and Luzia Crespo, Celia's Great Aunt and Uncle and, from what she says, yours too. They told my predecessor they found the manuscript among the possessions of a German soldier who died on the Freedom Trail while trying to cross the Pyrenees. How the book, which was sent to Dresden for safekeeping, ended up in a soldier's briefcase in occupied France is a mystery."

So this was the book Ja'far had taken from Klaus on the night the German soldier was killed. How typical of him and Luzia to resist the temptation to sell it in spite of hard times.

Reb Hakim gently caressed the title page. "You're looking at the original, illuminated version of *Scivias*, written and illustrated by Hildegard von Bingen, a mystical nun who refused to accept the patriarchal hierarchy of the church. In one of her visions she saw the great maternal figure of Ecclesia with a multitude of souls going in and out of her womb. Hildegard was an extraordinary woman who even dared to oppose the Crusades at a time when that would have been deemed heretical."

As a writer often in dire need of inspiration, I was drawn to the portrait of St. Hildegard on the frontispiece, showing her sketching on a wax tablet, tongues of fire licking her forehead to awaken potent dreams. "It's a miracle in itself that the book made its way here. For sure it would have been destroyed when the Allies set fire to Dresden."

Reb Hakim beamed. "How true. Imagine the world receiving the news that a cherished work of genius has been returned to the Wiesbaden State Library."

"To do that, Zahara would need to come out in the open," I said.

"Yes. It's one of the reasons I want us to accept UNESCO'S offer."

"You make a good case but Celia's reasoning against this seems solid too. I hope you can come to an agreement."

"I only hope it doesn't take too long. Our enemies have other plans for us and we can't afford to sit here and wait for them to act."

# Chapter Twenty

When a burglar has the key to your house, it's simply a matter of time before he uses it. Celia and I met with Talvir in the Control Room to discuss the protective measures being taken to prevent further intrusions.

"I've added some code to the database," he said. "If Carlos's thumbprint is used to enter Zahara, security will be alerted and the intruder's every move will be tracked as soon as he enters. We have volunteers on call 24/7 to intercept and detain him."

I wasn't sure I agreed with this strategy. "Wouldn't it be better to give this guy some rope and see what he does when he leaves? I could follow him, find out who he works for."

"Easy to say, Alienor," Celia observed, "but if he detects your surveillance he'll take steps to evade you. He might bring explosives into the tunnels and set them off. We can't afford to take the risk."

She was right. Like Seattle's star speed skater, Apolo Ohno, Celia had used her peripheral vision to avoid a dangerous collision.

Leaving Talvir to fine-tune the surveillance technology, she invited me to walk with her into a section of tunnel lit by a subdued shade of yellow. "Allie, there's someone I'd like you to meet. Reinaldo can better explain what happens when we fail to keep this place locked up tight."

The walls in this sector were painted with abstract expressionist designs that struck me as inappropriate until I saw our destination. Of all the library entrances, this was by far the most colorful. The door panels framed a decoupage of glossy book covers arranged according to genre. Romances were characterized by half-dressed, well-endowed models, mysteries by dark allies drawn in blood-red ink, literary classics by exotic fonts, and science fiction by futuristic scenes of flying cars and monorails.

The door was opened by a distinguished looking man with thick grey hair that tumbled over his high forehead. Celia touched his shoulder and then mine, like a schoolteacher introducing a pair of students she hoped would become friends. "Alienor Crespo, meet Reinaldo Luz, keeper of our most unusual library."

"I've heard a lot about you and am very pleased to show you my humble collection," Reinaldo said. There was nothing humble about his starched pink shirt and maroon tie.

"I need to look after the silkworms," my cousin added. "With everything that's happened I've totally neglected them. I'll leave you two to get acquainted."

I followed Reinaldo into a hexagonal-shaped room, with heavily-laden bookshelves towering floor-to-ceiling on five sides, the sixth wall opening into an area leading into another hexagon, beyond which I thought I glimpsed yet another one. Strategically hung mirrors intensified the impression of endless space. I stood transfixed. "It's Luis Borge's the *Library of Babel* come to life."

In response to my haphazard guess, Reinaldo gifted me with a huge smile. "Borges believed that a library's polished surfaces represented and promised the infinite." He spread his arms wide, embracing the entire collection. "Everything in here was printed in the twentieth century and banned from distribution in Spain.

"Our version of the *Library of Babel* was conceived and built by my grandfather, Horatio Luz. It infuriated him that modern books were as much endangered by Franco's repression as those hunted by the Inquisition. Nearly five hundred thousand books were published under *el Caudillo's* rule and all of them had to pass the judgment of the censors. Being a big fan of Luis Borges' work, my grandfather asked permission from the Zahara community to redesign these rooms to match Luis Borges' description."

"He sounds like quite a character."

"You have no idea. Horatio loved books and it infuriated him to see them castrated, as he inelegantly but aptly phrased it. He traveled all over Spain in search of banned books, many of which had been imported from other countries and translated into Spanish. We have copies of DH Lawrence's *Lady Chatterley's Lover*, Ray Bradbury's *Fahrenheit 451*, and Georges Simenon's *Lock 14*.

"Regrettably, Grandfather was not as discreet as his predecessors and his efforts did not go unnoticed. In nineteen-sixty-five, our house was raided. Fortunately, the secret police thought the library beneath our residence was the only one here. Instead of burning my *abuelo's* books, they tore off the covers and ripped up the pages. They also arrested him and he served three years in prison. If it weren't for his family connections, they would have killed him."

I looked up at the camera mounted over the door. "Zahara has much better security now."

"True. In Horatio's day we had no fancy locks on the trapdoors in our houses. Years after the disaster, my father and

I reassembled the collection and we used the torn-off book covers to create the montage you see on the door. We even have the 'unpurified' translations of the original James Bond series, with all the saucy words preserved."

Reinaldo pulled a slim, pink volume off a nearby shelf. "This journal is a favorite of mine, the *Iberian Ruedo Notebooks*, published in the 1960s by Spanish exiles in Paris who opposed the Franco regime. Print copies are rare but I hear that a compilation of all sixty-six issues has been published in Valencia. Times are improving, in spite of the censorship that still exists. To this day, translations of many world classics and even works of Spanish literature are being reprinted using expurgated texts approved by the dictator's censors."

"Was this library included in Hasdai the Seer's original design?"

"When it comes to the future, even the best of clairvoyants can be neglectful of details." Reinaldo came off as wickedly smart as his shirt.

"Do you agree with Celia that Zahara should stay hidden from the outside world?" I asked.

The eccentric Librarian scowled. "Ten years ago I was more optimistic about the future. But now that the right wing is regrouping all over Europe, and after what happened to Celia's brother, it looks like we may need outside protection."

I was trying to think of something hopeful to say and coming up empty when Celia came to get me.

"Stop by anytime, Alienor," Reinaldo said, bowing with a semi-comical, patrician air. "The *Eternal Library of Babel* will be waiting."

It was late afternoon and I'd barely had time to unpack the clothing I'd brought to Celia's place from the Airbnb. The smell of simmered oregano and fresh garlic wafted down the hall, as my cousin puttered in the kitchen, humming to herself.

We ate outside, devouring grilled vegetables and slices of bread topped by Serrano ham that would have horrified our ancestors on both the Jewish and Muslim sides. We washed it all down with a bottle of *tinto*. When the red wine made us sleepy, Celia brewed up some Belgian coffee, a Crespo tradition I'd first heard about from my Great Aunt Luzia, during a *Vijita* in Southern France.

I showed her the family tree I'd recently updated in my notebook. "It's still hard for me to believe I traveled with Luzia and Ja'far on the Freedom Trail."

Celia's eyes lit up. "Grandma used to talk about those days but never in such detail. You really do have a talent, Alienor."

"Not by choice. I consider myself a logical person mistakenly connected to the inexplicable."

"This kind of gift is never an accident, Allie. I sensed you were special as soon as I met you. So did my mother. You have direct experience of things about which we can only guess. I believe you were sent to us for a reason."

Every day, the protective gear wrapped around my psyche became more like a Kevlar vest made obsolete by an invasion of disarming friends. It would take some time to let it all in. Time I didn't have right now because Zahara was under threat.

"Celia, I'm sorry to bring this up but I've been wondering how the killer knew about the biometric lock? How did he know Carlos's thumbprint would be recorded in the database?"

My cousin winced. "I've been asking myself the same questions. Every new Librarian swears an oath of secrecy in a ceremony similar to the one you were part of today. Theirs is not a vocation that can be inherited. It's a commitment of the heart and soul, which is why we recruit most Librarians from outside the community. They must be willing to retire from their professional lives and live in relative isolation. Since all we have is each other, we're very close knit."

"Has a Librarian ever left Zahara and moved elsewhere?"

"I know what you're thinking, Allie, and it's impossible. For Zaharans, the well of loyalty never runs dry."

I soldiered on. "Painful as it is to consider, *someone* out there knows more than they should. In all these years, you can't tell me there hasn't been one case where –"

Celia had the look of a cat being dragged by the scruff of its neck toward some food it detested. "There's probably nothing to it, but Roberto Díaz left our community a few years ago. He moved in with his daughter Carmen in Madrid, where he was being treated for testicular cancer. Roberto oversaw what used to be the *Christian Mystical Library*. It is now combined with Reb Hakim's *Library of Mysticism and Wisdom of all Faiths*."

"Whom did you recruit to replace Díaz?"

"No one. We kept expecting him to get well and return. Díaz was the first Librarian to leave a house empty since the founding of Zahara. Their place was sealed off from the tunnels and sits there, empty. Sad, really."

"I think I'll take a look."

"Why not? It's nearby but you'll have to go on your own. I've got a delivery of raw silk to make to the Charterhouse. It's a tradition with us. The Converse nuns, including my mother, are excellent spinners. They market their wares through a *vendedor* at the outdoor market in Almendrales."

"Is this vendor by any chance named María?" I still had the map the almond-seller had provided.

"Cousin, you know far too much for your own good. We'll have to keep you here, permanently."

After savoring a dessert of homemade flan that Celia miraculously found time to make, I exchanged the dress shoes I'd borrowed from her for my well-worn trainers and walked through the orchard toward the house where Carmen Díaz and her parents once lived. Although the hour was getting late, there was plenty of light left.

The house looked deserted, with the exception of some overgrown herbs and stubborn wild flowers in the kitchen garden. The wide windowsills set into heavily worn stone were reminiscent of the sturdy Amish farmhouses I'd seen in Pennsylvania when I visited Joel's family.

"Those Amish are stuck in the past," his father had said derisively as he drove us through the countryside.

"Better to live in the past than waste the present." My wisecrack earned me a disapproving look from Joel. I'd let it go and we were already married when I kicked myself for not heeding this warning that he wasn't the right partner for someone like me.

Cautiously, I mounted the decaying porch steps of the structure that had prodded my memory. I twisted the round knob on the front door and it opened easily. Had some hippies wandered up from the lowlands to squat in this remote location? In that case I'd assume bedsheets would be covering the windows instead of plywood.

The atmosphere inside the house was musky with neglect, so I left the door ajar. I was breathing in the scent of lavender from the garden when, mid-breath, my air supply was cut off by a brutal chokehold. Unable to turn my head, I couldn't see my attacker's face. A sharp object pressed against my side made escape impossible.

Applying pressure to my Adam's apple, he pulled me outside and marched me downhill, away from the abandoned house and through the lengthening shadows of the trees. Each labored breath felt like it might be my last. I pictured Dad's distraught face when he heard of my death and wished I had listened to his warning.

We stopped in front of an equally derelict but smaller outbuilding, surrounded by a wide veranda cluttered with upside down barrels.

"Stay still," he said in English, running his warm, sweaty hands over my ice-cold limbs. I was still wearing the thin, dark skirt and tailored blouse Celia had loaned me for Carlos's memorial. "No cellphone, huh?" His whisper was hoarse, a movie gangster's rasp.

"Close your eyes and keep them that way." He spun me around to face him while he completed his search. I kept my eyes shut, imagining the knife gripped in his hand at the ready. When he was satisfied that I was clean of devices, he kicked the heavy wooden door open and gave me a shove that sent me soaring backwards into the darkness. There was no time to shield the back of my head before a searing pain threw me out of my body.

# Chapter Twenty-one

"We said we wouldn't interfere."

"What choice do we have? So much depends on the survival of this brave young woman."

Once again Abraham Abulafia, founder of the school of Prophetic Kabbalah, has undertaken a mission with Ibn al Arabī, the Sufi sage known as the Great Teacher. Coming together from worlds apart, they are here to deal with an emergency. Neither one is happy.

Al Arabī gazes toward the mountains, where the late evening clouds hide the last of the sun under a cloak of darkening velvet. He turns to Abulafia and states his case. "Why not leave these humans to solve their own problems? Would it be so terrible if this fledgling mortal were to continue her dance between body and soul in another dimension?"

Abulafia stares at his friend unbelievingly. "Have you forgotten how her ancestors, Jariya al-Qasam and Hasdai the Seer, devoted themselves to fulfilling our purpose? Without them, the books that the slave Tahir liberated—written in more languages than the zodiac has signs – would have no home and be scattered to the moon. This is our chance to pay our debt to them."

Al Arabī's sharp exhalation brings his physical form into focus. "All right. Let's hope she is able to stand the touch of light without going blind."

The mystics materialize inside the olive mill, accompanied by a young physician carrying a medical bag. He has no idea how he got there, why there is an inert body on the floor, or to whom the voices inside his head belong.

*She will be fine if you listen closely and do as we say.*

The doctor takes a close look at the patient. Alarmed by her ashen face and shallow breathing, he examines a wound on the back of her head. He wipes the blood from his hands and is about to apply a bandage when his fingers begin to glow so brightly he has to turn his head away.

"Put your hands over her eyes and we'll do the rest."

The doctor, sure by now that he is dreaming and will soon wake up in bed next to his wife, obeys.

I awoke to blackness broken only by a thin shaft of light flowing through a slit in the wall. My head rested on a rock that should have crushed my skull when I fell but for some reason had not. I felt no pain and when I fingered the back of my scalp, where the wound from my fall should have been, a smooth scar met my touch. Strange.

There was no sign of my attacker. Squinting through the dimness, all I could make out were the outlines of two conical millstones mounted on a round metal plate. I was imprisoned in an olive mill.

In the distance, I heard Celia calling my name. I answered with a yell for help and got up as quickly as I could, amazed to find no bruises or broken bones. The door held fast when I gave it a shove. Loudly calling Celia's name, I put my shoulder to the hard wood with the same negative result.

I explored the floor and found what felt like a coil of unconnected piping. Thinking fast, I stripped off my blouse, unfastened my bra, and tied the straps to the rubber tubing. Standing on tiptoe, I stretched my arms as far as they would go and pushed my makeshift white flag through the narrow opening in the wall. Then I called out again as loudly as I could, hoping that Celia would either hear me or see my makeshift distress signal.

Within a few minutes, I heard noises on the other side of the door. A moment later, Celia stood before me, the heavy-duty wire she'd untangled from the hook-latch dangling from her closed fist. "Are you okay? We've been looking for you for hours. Maybe we should post your bra on YouTube as recommended equipment for travel safety kits."

Her amusement faded when I told her the details of the attack. Awkwardly, she encircled my shoulders with her arm in a protective gesture. I knew what it was like, fighting to overcome social inhibitions. I was liking her more and more.

"Your attacker wanted you out of the way. We don't know why and if we're going to find out, we'll need reinforcements." She slid her cell from the back pocket of her jeans and made the call.

"Talvir, something's happened and we need to take a look at the old Díaz place. I'll meet you there. Please bring Reinaldo Luz with you."

While I dressed, my cousin questioned me.

"Did you see his face?"

"No."

"How tall was he?"

211

"Maybe six feet. I came up to his shoulder."

"What was he wearing?"

"All I saw was a mask before he pushed me inside the mill. And there was something shiny on his chest."

"Shiny?"

I searched my memory and came up with a glitter of red on silver. "He was wearing a pin of some kind."

Talvir showed up with Reinaldo, who in his hurriedly misbuttoned shirt might have been a character from one of the new wave novels in his *Eternal Library of Babel.* When Celia filled them in, they both gave me worried looks. Talvir gently parted the hair around the scar on the back of my head. "It's a miracle you survived."

"No doubt about it," I said, blinking back unexpected tears brought on by his concern. A faint picture of kind faces looking down at me as I lay on the olive mill floor floated to the surface of consciousness, only to disappear.

We scaled the hill to the Diaz house. In the front room, the only signs of habitation were light rectangles on the wall where picture frames once hung. The larger of the two bedrooms was empty. In the smaller sleeping chamber, an inflated air mattress pressed up against the wall, next to it a wooden crate was stained with wax drippings from a half-burned candle. I sniffed the air and there it was, the smell of lavender that last night I believed had come from the garden.

We found more evidence of recent occupation in the kitchen. Celia picked up a half-full coffee cup left by the side of a sink filled with dirty dishes. "Whoever squatted here left in a hurry. The big question is, did he find the entryway to the tunnels?"

Talvir was busy examining the floorboards in the pantry. He called Celia over to show her a square of slightly mismatched wood. We watched as he got to work methodically removing the screws. "The damn things are coming up too easily. I know Roberto Diaz would have done a better job closing this up."

Reinaldo crouched down next to Talvir. "It looks like someone pulled out each screw and afterwards carefully re-torqued it. This is a serious breach."

The original flooring, several shades darker, formed the outline of a trapdoor.

My cousin hurriedly left the room. "Tell me when you're ready!" she called from somewhere in the house.

"Okay!" Talvir shouted, and the trapdoor sprang open, controlled – as I later learned – by a lever hidden inside the fireplace. It made sense that each Librarian would create a unique way, known only to them, to enter their underground archive. This opening was larger than the one in Celia's closet and connected to a flight of steep stone steps.

Reinaldo was the first to descend. When I made a move to follow, Celia grabbed me firmly by the sleeve. "You've been through a lot, Allie. We can handle things from here. Go back to my place, take a shower, and lie down. As soon as we know anything, I'll come get you."

Any rejection I felt was offset by how she had come to take my participation in Zaharan affairs as a given.

Back at Celia's house, I cleaned up the remains of the meal we'd shared before my disappearance drove her out into the woods to search for me. As far as I knew, everyone in this branch of my family had at some time either gone missing or been denied access to the others. How cruel of Eduardo to ban Pilar from seeing her own son and then rigidly control Grandma Luzia's access to Carlos after his wife's supposed death.

With no warning, I slipped into a *vijita*, my hands belonging to Luzia, my fingers clutching the ends of a black lace shawl.

Anxiety grows as I walk through the wrought iron gate. The front garden is ablaze with colorful roses and azaleas. *Will I be admitted or turned away with disdain? Only one way to find out.*

A maid in full uniform meets me at the massive front door, pointedly examining my scuffed shoes and wrinkled denim skirt and looking doubtful when I say, "Please tell Mr. Martín I'm here to see my grandson."

I'm told to wait in a library. I doubt much reading is done by the occupiers of these red velvet chairs surrounded by self-important books with gilded letters engraved on their leather spines. It's been five years since I've seen Eduardo, whose light blue suit jacket and pink Polo shirt give him the look of a male model.

"What are you doing here, Luzia? You know my agreement with Pilar was that the boy be left alone. Now that she's gone to her just reward, the rules apply to you as well."

Any thoughts of compromise are vanquished by the onslaught of these cruel words that Eduardo seems to believe will put me, the grieving mother of his supposedly deceased wife, in her proper place. More than ever I rejoice that my daughter is safe and has chosen the anonymous life of a nun over living with this terrible man.

"I've brought Carlos a gift for his birthday. Will you at least permit me to present it in person?"

Eduardo glowers but eventually he gives in, unwilling to be seen as the ogre we both know him to be. Ah, the vanity of men.

We wait in tense silence for the governess, whose black dress with a lace collar suggests an allergy to 1980s fashion, to bring my grandson into the library. Carlos is wearing a sailor suit and his resemblance to Pilar is striking – the same curly black hair and green-brown eyes, the same intense air of querying the world. When he hesitates at the sight of me, his minder pushes him none too gently in my direction. "Give your grandmother Luzia a hug."

Reluctance tightens every muscle of his twelve-year-old face. Although I understand its source, this cuts me to the quick. I swallow my pain and put on a smile, trying to make eye contact with him. "Your grandma is so happy to see you, *muchacho dulce*."

Carlos compromises by offering his hand and after fulfilling that painful duty, risks a peek at me.

The possessive father has made no move to leave the room.

I hold out the package and Carlos takes it, ripping off the wrapping paper. His eyes light up at the sight of the Secret Wars action figures. "How did you know?"

"Because your mother couldn't stop talking about your love for action figures. She would have been so excited for you to have these."

The boy tightens his hands around the Iceman and looks over at his father. With a dismissive gesture, Eduardo issues a command to his son. "Tell her not to try to buy you with presents."

It's torture to see the joy vanish from the little boy's eyes, replaced by a dull anger I'm certain has been hatched by Eduardo's lies. Carlos thrusts the toy at me and I have no choice but to take it back. If only I could take back my grandson's pain. If only I could find a way to tell him that his mother is alive, without jeopardizing us both.

The governess retrieves her charge and Eduardo walks toward the door, waving for me to follow. "You'd better go before you upset him further. I hope you haven't filled Celia's head with stories about how monstrous I am. My daughter should know it's not my fault that Pilar hid her impure blood from me and ran away with that Jewish notary. Whatever happened to her, Pilar deserved to die. And if I catch Mico Rosales hanging around Celia I'll have him thrown out of the country to join his greedy brethren."

What a nice show he's put on for little Carlos' benefit. If I could, I'd grab the child and take him to his mother. Alas, that's not possible.

Although he thought Pilar was dead, Eduardo had continued to be fiercely jealous of Mico. *Jealous enough to have ordered the notary killed?* This seemed a plausible theory. Proving it was another matter.

How cruel to raise a boy in the belief that his mother deserted him before she died. How unjust that the invisible walls surrounding my *Vijitas* prevented my warning Luzia that her grandson would eventually learn the truth and lose his life attempting to protect his mother and sister. What Carlos thought he was protecting them *from* was the question of the moment.

"We've had an unrecorded breach."

I hadn't heard Celia enter the guest room. Barely acknowledging my presence, she continued to think out loud. "It's my fault for removing the surveillance camera near the Díaz house after we closed the entrance. If this intruder is the same person who killed Carlos, why did he use the only entrance to Zahara without a biometric lock?"

"I'm sorry to be so blunt, but have you considered that he tried to use Carlos's thumb and it didn't work out?" I could find no gentler way of stating this grisly theory.

Celia flinched but she knew as well as I did there was no way to tiptoe around the subject. "After what happened last night, it's more likely we have two different people, both of whom have figured out how to bypass our security system."

A soft knock on the front door interrupted us. Of all the people I might have envisaged, the elderly nun in a white habit and black veil who followed my cousin into the living room was the last. Celia cleared her throat. "Alienor Crespo, meet the Reverend Mother María Teresa, Prioress of the Carthusian Charterhouse."

Even with my limited knowledge of Catholic contemplative orders, I appreciated how unusual it was for the Prioress to visit the outside world.

Our visitor declined to be seated and addressed Celia in a formal manner. "As you know, Carthusians have at times provided sanctuary to the persecuted. During the War, the monks who gave refuge to Jews and partisan fighters in the Tuscany Charterhouse were killed by the Nazis. Here in Almendrales, we've done our best when called upon and your grandparents brought us many seeking shelter from the storm."

"We've never ceased to be grateful for your protection, Mother."

"Maybe so. But today was different, Celia. Today, something outrageous happened that may cause our Charterhouse to be censured by the Church. Eduardo Martín came to the main gate and forced his way into the heart of the monastery where no man has trespassed for centuries. He was beside himself. I could see he was devoured by grief and so I invited him to accompany me to the adjacent Vicarage, where such encounters are permitted. When he calmed down enough to speak, your father claimed that a friend of your family named Mico Rosales had murdered his son Carlos. He then accused your mother, Sister Pilar, of sheltering the murderer within our Charterhouse."

"I'm so sorry," Celia said. "If I had known – "

"Please, let me finish," insisted the Prioress, taking a deep breath. "When I refused to let him see Sister Pilar, or to conduct a search of the monastery, he threatened to denounce our Order as indecent and immoral and to go to Rome if necessary to press charges. I again refused and if the Vicar had not intervened and ejected Señor Martín from the premises, there is no telling what might have transpired."

Celia looked shell-shocked. "Yesterday, when I called my father, the pain in his voice told me he already knew about my brother's death. He called me a traitor and hung up."

The Mother Superior had regained her equanimity and spoke more kindly. "Come and see me when you've resolved this." Watching her exit the house through the mud room where such horrible violence had taken place, I shivered.

Celia shut the door behind the Prioress. "Eduardo knows Pilar is alive. Her concern about the new priest who took her confession was justified."

"That man is no more a priest then I'm a rabbi," I said.

# Chapter Twenty-two

"What did your father mean, calling you a traitor?"

Celia rolled back her shoulders, plainly throwing off the unpleasant word and the weight of anxiety that came with it. "I'll make us some coffee."

The house continued to vibrate with the Prioress's indignation, so we took our cups outside and dropped into a pair of low-slung canvas chairs in the back garden. Celia stretched out her legs and planted her heels on the ground. "Exactly how did my father learn that my mother is alive and what else does he know?" she asked.

It took a moment and then it dawned on me that Celia was turning to *me* for answers.

"This new priest who took Pilar's confession – he could be your dad's informant about what goes on in the Charterhouse. What's equally worrisome is that he might be aware of what's happening in the tunnels below."

Celia white-knuckled her coffee mug. "Zahara is in danger on so many fronts I'm beginning to lose track."

She was understandably frustrated and swimming against the undertow of grief for her brother. Capable as Celia was, if we were going to come up with a plan, the job fell to me. "I'll drive to Málaga and interview Eduardo for the political analysis I pitched to my editor at the *Seattle Courier*. Given your father's ambitions, I think he'll jump at the chance to talk to someone from the American press."

"What if he's the one who sent the man who attacked you? You risk walking into a trap."

"That thug had no way of knowing I'd come snooping around and he gave no indication he knew who I was. I'll take care, Celia. I promise."

My cell phone buzzed and Luis Alcábez's confident voice came through. "Alienor, are you okay?"

"I'm working on it."

"Really?" Alcábez sounded dubious. "Mico called two days ago. It must have been awful for you, walking right into a murder scene. I'm so sorry your first trip to Spain has turned into such a disaster."

"I appreciate your concern, Luis, but I'm okay." I wanted to say more, to tell my attorney I'd been recently assaulted by an unknown party. But why share half a story when it's impossible to tell the rest? Maybe someday Zahara would go public but for now my agreement with Celia made disclosure impossible. A promise was a promise, a vow a vow.

"There's something else," Alcábez went on to say. "I arranged for Mico to meet me at the police station and have a talk with Inspector Fernández to clear himself. He never showed up. Do you have any idea where he might be?"

"No. But if Mico contacts me, I promise I'll let you know."

"I hope you're coming back to Granada soon. Felicia and I are concerned."

"Thanks, Luis. I'll drive over to see you after I've interviewed Eduardo Martín for an article I'm writing."

The attorney was slow to respond. "Alienor, that's a powerful and arrogant family. Martín aims to become one of the first openly extreme, alt-right politicians elected to the Congress of Deputies. Be careful."

"No need to worry. He won't mess with a professional journalist," I said, aware that we both knew better and this was pure wishful thinking.

Alcábez hemmed and hawed and finally let it go. "I'll be away for a few days. If anything comes up you can reach me through Felicia." He wished me well before disconnecting.

I asked Celia how I could contact Eduardo and she gave me the number for the Martín Shipping Office in Malaga. "It will be more credible if you reach out to him through his business."

There was no answer so I left a message. "Good morning. My name is Eleanora Benveniste. I'm a freelance journalist and I'd like to interview Señor Martín for a piece about the new political party that is backing his candidacy and the rejuvenation of the far right in Spanish politics."

In no time at all, Eduardo's secretary called back to schedule an appointment that afternoon. With one sentence, I'd cut through the layers of middlemen inevitably surrounding an aspiring politician. If my mother were alive she'd surely have forgiven my use of her identity as my cover.

As a journalist, I took pride in my objectivity. Yet this family saga I was chasing had me cast as a player committed to changing the outcome of the story.

I reached Málaga in the late afternoon and with some persistence found a parking spot on a rundown street bordering Avenue del Arroyo de Los Ángeles. Proceeding on foot, I scrutinized the flamboyant graffiti, each spray-painted tag shouting 'this is mine!' from the colorless walls and metal grills of permanently boarded-up shops. A good location for a populist party looking to plant its roots in working class soil.

The interior of the StandUp Party office was quieter than the name would suggest. A young woman in a plaid skirt and white blouse came to greet me. "I'm here to pick up the latest campaign materials," I said. "I hear the party has a good shot at landing a seat representing Málaga in the Congress of Deputies."

This fabrication earned me a beaming smile from the most preppie-looking woman I'd met in Spain. "I'm just a volunteer," she said, "but Señor Martín says that for women like me the sky is the limit. We're going to bring back the glory days of Spain."

I'd looked up their chances, which were next to nil, but I went along with the charade. I came away with a rolled up *Make Spain Great Again* poster emblazoned with the flags and swords of the StandUp Party logo. It was destined for the first trash can but I stowed the leaflet version in my purse.

I'd last seen the red brick mansion, with its view of the Mediterranean and garden bursting with color, during a painful *Vijita* that I shared with Luzia. The house was as unchanged as the somber uniform of the maid, whose counterpart in the nineteen-seventies had led Celia's grandmother into Eduardo's library. It was hard to tell if the red velvet chairs were new or the same ones Luzia saw when she braved Eduardo's wrath to visit her grandson. Pilar's husband in name only was now twenty-five years older than when last I'd seen him through his mother-in-law's eyes. The gray hair was a given and the haggardness I took as a sign of grief over losing his son.

"Thank you for seeing me. First, I want to say how sorry I am for your loss."

Eduardo ducked his head, as if sympathy were a blow to be avoided. "I didn't expect to be approached by an American journalist. Your countrymen aren't known for their interest in international politics."

He escorted me to a seat at a glass-covered table with place settings for two and the maid brought us a light lunch. Over fish and shellfish soup, I took advantage of the opening Eduardo's offhand remark had offered. "Your point of view may not prove popular with some Americans, but as you know there's been a shift in the wind. Even the liberal mass media is picking up on the changes in Europe."

Upon hearing me utter this catchphrase about the press, my subject relaxed and nodded his approval. Maybe this would be a more pleasant experience than he'd expected.

"It's true we're experiencing a worldwide shift to the right," I added. "And it's about time."

The pamphlet I removed from my purse was met, as I'd hoped, with a smile of recognition.

"I see you're already familiar with our platform, Ms. Benveniste. We plan to eliminate corruption, curb immigration, criminalize abortion and centralize the Spanish state, which has become a confederation of autonomous fiefdoms with no national identity."

My host's gaze followed mine to a photo mounted on the wall above the fireplace. A stern man stood at a lectern in front of a microphone. "That's Blas Piñar López. Along with my father, he founded New Force, a largely misunderstood effort to establish continuity after Franco's death. StandUp is proud to carry on his legacy."

I stifled my urge to comment that 'establish continuity' sounded like a euphemism for maintaining fascism and asked, "If you oppose immigration, how do you feel about the new law offering citizenship to the descendants of the Jews expelled in 1492?"

"It seems fair," Eduardo said coolly, the question being a soccer ball he knew how to field. "The Sephardim did nothing to deserve the Order of Expulsion. Although I must say, there are Muslims who are also demanding a so-called right of return. We don't need more of them to blow up our trains." He clenched his fist before adding, "Or kill our sons, including my own."

When I failed to respond, he went on. "I assume you're unaware that my son died a hero's death."

We shared an uncomfortable moment, as the maid cleared off the table and served us coffee and biscuits. Eduardo waited for her to leave before continuing his train of thought. "I don't have all the details but one of my colleagues informed me that the murderer of my son is one Mico Rosales, a Jew who secretly converted to Islam and joined a terrorist cell in the Alpujarras. Like my father, who was executed in 1950 by an assassin sent by the Maquis guerillas in exile, my son was martyred for being a good Spaniard."

I set down my coffee cup carefully, lest it rattle in the saucer.

Celia's dad observed me closely. "Yes, I know it's shocking."

"Dreadful," was all I could muster. What he'd said had too many implications to absorb all at once. The man knew a lot more than Celia and I gave him credit for. If he truly believed Zahara was a terrorist cell, then who had manipulated him into swallowing the lie? And if he knew his daughter Celia was a leader of the Zaharan community, did he hold her to blame for her brother's death?

"What are your plans for strengthening the economy?" I asked, shifting to safer ground.

"That's simple. First we eliminate corruption. We drain the swamp and then..."

The double-doors swung open. Eduardo clicked his tongue in annoyance as the maid ushered in a short man in a light grey suit, yellow shirt and tie to match. He walked toward us cautiously, his puffed up chest and exaggerated gait confirming his identity even before he removed his hat. A flicker of surprise in his eyes betrayed that he'd recognized me too. Less than a week had passed since Dr. Amado's tour of Celia's silkworm operation.

"Eduardo, it's good to see you," he said, pointedly ignoring my presence.

The red pin on Amado's lapel looked similar to the one I'd seen under duress the night before. On closer inspection, I saw a Cross turned upside-down to become a raised sword, with the hilt and arms ending in the shape of a fleur-de-lis. The pin might have pointed to the doctor as my assailant at the Díaz house, if Amado's build had not been so slight.

"Eleanora Benveniste, meet Dr. Rodrigo Amado, my right hand man and advisor," Eduardo said. "Please, come join us and have a biscotti."

# Chapter Twenty-three

Despite Dr. Amado's arrival, Eduardo did not cut off the interview. "Fire away, Ms. Benveniste. The doctor may have a thing or two to contribute. So, where were we?"

*Where were we indeed?* This was too opportune a moment to pass up and there was something I wanted to ask Eduardo's friend.

"Was it you who informed Señor Martín that a terrorist killed his son?"

He bridled at my impertinence. "What gives you the right to question me, young lady?" It was almost funny, my being there under a false name and Dr. Amado, the pseudo scientist, pretending not to recognize me. My guess was he had his reasons for keeping Eduardo in the dark about his activities in the Alpujarras, in particular his contact with Celia.

"Ms. Benveniste is a reporter who may be able to help our campaign." Eduardo sent an ingratiating smile my way as he spoke to the doctor. "There's no harm in talking with her."

"Carlos Martín alerted me to some jihadis in La Alpujarra who were planning an attack on a target in Granada. He had infiltrated their mountain hideout. Before I could take action, he was dead." Dr. Amado's concocted story proved him to be as good an improviser as he was an imposter.

"So you've notified the authorities?"

"This isn't America, where accusations are all one needs." His pomposity had increased to meet the challenge. "I'm here to discuss the situation with Señor Martín and make sure we're equipped with enough evidence to make the charges against these terrorists stick."

Amado's unflappable manner implied he had no problem revealing this information to me. *Was it already too late to warn Celia and the others?* For all I knew, the police had already raided Zahara on the basis of the charges the deceitful doctor was talking about.

I looked at the screen of my phone like I was reading a text message "I'm so sorry, Señor Martín. My editor wants me to cover a breaking story. I must leave but I hope to complete our interview soon."

Eduardo rose from the table to shake my hand. "I've enjoyed our interaction," he purred.

"It's been my pleasure as well," said Dr. Amado. For whatever the reason, he'd decided to let my cover as Eleanora Benveniste stand, if only for as long as it took me to pack up my notebook and head for the door. I walked slowly, clutching my pen so hard I was afraid it would break in my hand.

I was driving a bit over the posted speed limit on A-7 East toward Motril, when Celia called. "If you're still in Málaga, stay put. If not, turn around and get as far away from the Alpujarras as you can. Understand?" She cut off before I could answer. It was obvious Celia was in trouble and trying to protect me. I wanted to call Luis and ask for his help but I'd be breaking my confidentiality agreement with my cousin and I couldn't bring myself to do that.

I reached Almendrales having miraculously avoided a flat tire while traversing the unpaved backroads to the Crespo house.

A brown military truck was parked in the clearing and the foliage lining the path to the house had been trampled. I pictured jackbooted men crushing everything in their way. But this did nothing to prepare me for the *Guardia Civil* officers swarming over the house in their dark green uniforms, roughly examining Celia's delicate possessions with a carelessness calibrated to intimidate. I spotted her in the middle of the living room, defiantly eye to eye with a senior officer with three gold stars on his sleeve.

"Captain Suárez, you know this search is illegal and won't stand up in court. Police are required to show a warrant and the judge's clerk must be present the whole time." Her voice had reclaimed its strength from the clutch of sorrow.

The Captain might have held the same stiff posture for decades under Franco. He maintained his ground under Celia's assault with a thousand yard stare, no chance of a blush or a guilty smile replacing the sneer on his lips. "Certain rules are suspended during a terrorist investigation."

The action now moved to the bedroom, and from the quickness with which the invaders located the trapdoor in the closet floor, I gathered someone had told them exactly where to look. Rather than stand by while the lock was forced with a crowbar, Celia opted to open it voluntarily, using her thumbprint. "Let me go down with you. I can guide you. Please, be careful with the books."

Her anguished pleas ignored, Celia's hand sought mine, as the officers disappeared down into the tunnels.

Celia got out her cell. "Talvir, the Guardia is here. They're already in the tunnels. You'd better warn the others."

"Is it alright if I call my attorney, Luis Alcábez?" I asked her. "We need legal advice and I'm sure we can trust him."

"Go ahead, what choice do we have? The whole world will learn about Zahara now and see us in the worst possible light."

Luis's office number went to voicemail and when I tried his home, Felicia answered. "He's out of the country, doing some work for the Jewish Federation in England. In case you don't already know, Mico Rosales has been charged with murder and the police want to question him, and you, as important witnesses."

There was no trace of warmth in her voice, nor should there have been, not after my unfair treatment of Mico, the Alcabez's longtime family friend. Nonetheless, I needed her help. I took a gulp of air. "The Guardia Civil is searching Celia's house and the tunnels right now." The situation felt as unreal as it sounded.

"Guardia? Tunnels? What are you talking about?"

By this time, a pair of officers had climbed the ladder and re-entered the house through the trapdoor. They stomped across the room to report to their superior.

"Felicia, I'll have to call you back," I said, disconnecting in time to hear one of the new arrivals brief Captain Suárez.

The shorter of the two officers had more decorations on his chest and did all the talking. "We found two blocks of Semtex explosive in a room below the house of a Muslim woman, Saleema al-Garnati, who has been on our watch list for some time. There's also a map of the parade route of the Crosses of May festival that may be of interest to the Terrorism Unit and a notebook of instructions written in Arabic. We've taken al-Garnati into custody."

"Nice work apprehending the suspect, Lieutenant Romero," said the Captain.

Celia's voice in my ear trembled with rage. "All this is because when Saleema was in college she had a Pakistani boyfriend. She's the perfect scapegoat."

Captain Suárez summoned his men for an announcement. "The people who live above these tunnels are now classified as witnesses and must be brought in for questioning. We should take the American in too."

Celia slipped something into my hand and whispered, "Go now while you can."

I snuck into the kitchen, closing the door partway to conceal myself while I watched Lieutenant Romero approach my cousin. "Celia Crespo, evidence has been found providing just cause to bring you in for questioning."

She moved to block his view of the kitchen. "If you found explosives in the tunnels, they were planted there by someone from outside our community, in my estimation, the same person who assaulted my cousin and broke in last night."

The lieutenant roughly seized her arm. "You can protest all you want as long as you come with me."

At the front door Celia resisted, holding onto the frame for leverage. "Wait. What about the libraries? How can I be sure your men won't damage the books?"

"Evidence must be taken into custody."

"Some of the books are extremely fragile. You can't move them without professional supervision."

"Right," said the Lieutenant, plainly humoring her. "As of now the contents of the libraries are in quarantine. But we do have the right to impound everything in the tunnels if we decide to do so. In the same way we're empowered to detain you for questioning. Come willingly or not. It's your decision."

Head held high, Celia left with the Romero. Quietly, I backed away from the kitchen door.

Captain Suárez spoke briefly on his cell and scanned the room, doubtless in search of me. There was no guard posted out back and I crept outside, praying my exit would go unnoticed. With no idea which way to run, I instinctively chose a narrow track that wound through the woods and would quickly take me out of sight.

I jogged for half an hour, before stopping to catch my breath and retrieve Celia's gift from my pocket. It was Inspector Fernández's card, on the back of which she'd scrawled, *find out what he knows*. Since there was no cell phone reception, contacting the Inspector would have to wait.

I was desperate to know what was happening underground. For all I knew, the books had been loaded onto a truck and were headed God knows where. I had to get down there to check, but how could I, with all the entrances blocked by disciplined, uniformed men?

I was unprepared for the simple answer that came my way.

Jariya is waiting, backlit by the sky where the meadow abruptly ends. Bluebells and snow stars inhabit the cliff's edge, along with modern descendants of the gorse bush I vividly remember. My bold Morisca ancestor from the Siddiqui side of the family watches intently as I pull aside the branches covering the metal stake and the cable wound around its base. I reach down and grasp one end of the braided wire.

"Can I trust this?"

Her voice sounds softly within my skull. "Why not?"

This is a different kind of *Vijita*. I am *me*, Alienor, acting on my own behalf in my own body and my own time. It is

Jariya who appears to be out of her element, slightly trans-parent yet embodied enough to watch over me from another dimension.

I look down and feel adrenaline coursing through me as fiercely as the river rapids below. I know what I have to do and I'm terrified. Yet perhaps because I've experienced this descent before, having merged with Jariya when she performed the stunt centuries ago, I'm able to take control.

Alternating my hands along the rope, I focus on becoming one with the downward pull of gravity and linger only as long as needed at each foothold before moving on. When I reach the ledge bounding the cave, I bounce lightly off the rock face to generate momentum before swinging in to land gently on solid ground. Whatever relief I feel is tempered by my fear of what's to come.

There were no torches or airshafts to light the way and without my cell phone flashlight, I would have been doomed to im-mobility. I took a step forward, then another, before paralysis set in at the thought that only one tunnel branch led to my destination and I wasn't sure which one.

Methodically, I felt my way around the edges of the main cavern, where I'd once witnessed the dramatic arrival of Jariya, Hasdai and Idris with their saddlebags of books and silk-dying supplies. A jagged outcrop from a boulder bruised the palm of my hand, as if reaching out to tell me something. It was the same ledge shared by Jariya and Fatima when they talked about defending their homeland. And behind it I found the entryway I sought.

The maze was narrow and musty, with low ceilings and numerous dead ends to discourage exploration by Zahara's enemies. I recalled how the Moriscas had walked through a maze-like pattern memorized by Jariya until they reached the site of the first library to be carved into the walls of the salt mine. I did the same now, three rights, a left, another right. The flashlight swept past a door and I slowly brought it back, breathing a sigh of relief when the beam revealed a biometric lock. Leave it to Celia to keep things tidy. I pressed my thumb on the pad and the latch clicked open. On the other side I recognized the section of tunnel that ran below my cousin's house.

For a moment I was pleased to have come full circle, until I saw the Guardia patrol member standing watch outside the *Tif'eret and Jamal Library.*

I was trapped in place and hoped he wasn't pulling a 24-hour shift. Hugging the wall, I willed myself to melt into it. *How could one person's breathing sound so loud? How could ten minutes feel like an eternity?* I was close to accepting my inevitable discovery and capture when a series of rapid, indecipherable instructions squawked from the officer's radio and he set out in the direction of the *Library of Khalud.* This was my chance to zip over and see if the Control Room had been breached. It was a risk I had to take.

# Chapter Twenty-four

As I let myself in, I thanked the person with the foresight to camouflage the entrance to the most important security asset Zahara possessed. The door to the Control Room blended perfectly with the lush green and yellow foliage of the wall mural. The trick worked well, as testified to by the smudges of muddy footprints on the tunnel's concrete floor, prints left by those who had recently walked by without a second glance.

Strapped for time and in danger of being detained by the Guardia at any moment, I tried to recall what I'd learned from watching Talvir and Celia work the control board. The surveillance cameras were up and running but it was hard to figure out how to access the feeds. Some of the buttons were labeled with blue tape and black initials that didn't tell me much. Through trial and error I discovered how to punch up views of the guards stationed in front of each of the libraries, rifles at the ready, maintaining a holding pattern while assumedly waiting for orders. My college training in digital TV news production had finally paid off.

I accessed a feed labeled *Common Area* and there was Dr. Amado, deep in conversation with Captain Suárez, the Guardia officer who had orchestrated Celia's arrest. Hanging in the background was a tall man in dark blue sweatpants and a matching hoodie.

I turned up the audio and Captain Suárez's irritated tones filled the Control Room.

"I understand what needs to be done, Dr. Amado, but my men are not pack mules and will become suspicious when they see the unmistakable value of these books. The illuminated manuscripts alone could be worth millions and I will not assist you in a theft of this magnitude. We are required to log all evidence in situ and leave it in place until it can be examined by our superiors and that's exactly what I plan to do."

The video feed showed Amado's face scrunch into a scowl and turn bright red. "If you couldn't manage the entire job you should not have accepted my generous offer. The Society will take note of your uncooperative attitude."

The Captain stiffened. "We expected to find evidence of terrorism and we did. The main suspect, Saleema al-Garnati, has been arrested and we've rounded up the others for questioning. I'm proud of what we've achieved here today."

He walked toward the door, stopping once to turn and say, "I repeat. Nothing was agreed to regarding the content of the libraries and I advise you not to do anything foolhardy." This mixture of opportunism and professional ethics boggled my mind.

After Captain Suárez left the Common Area, Amado fixed his attention on the tall man, who pushed off his hoodie to expose a headful of long greasy hair.

"Nice work Mauro, I can't wait to see how these kikes and kebab lovers turn on each other after a week rotting in jail. Word will spread about their deadly plans and people will appreciate the StandUp Party's commitment to fighting terrorism."

235

Like his boss, Mauro wore a red sword with a fleur-de-lis hilt pinned above his heart. It was easy to imagine him locking me up in the olive mill while planting Semtex below Saleema's house. "What are we going to do about the books?" he asked.

"For the time being, nothing. We've got to stay on the right side of the Guardia. But don't worry, I have a plan and in the meantime we've got some housecleaning to do. Celia Crespo's American cousin Alienor has slipped through the net.

"Don't worry. I'll find her."

"When you do, hand her over to Captain Suárez and he'll have her deported. After that comes the Díaz girl. We can't risk her changing her mind about cooperating. She lives at 13 Calle Miguel Servet in Madrid. Take care of her."

"In the same way I took care of Carlos Martín?"

Amado flinched at what was no doubt an unpleasant memory. "The traitor would have ruined our plans, and for what? To save his spinster sister and her traitorous friends?"

There it was. Carlos was butchered by his father Eduardo's coldblooded friend for the sake of a treasure trove of priceless books. I knew exactly what they had in store for Carmen Díaz, who Celia had told me moved to Madrid to look after her parents. The ruthless doctor must have blackmailed her into betraying Zahara's location and she was now a loose end to be cleaned up. I noted her address.

The damning evidence on the video feed would be useless unless I could find a way to take the recording with me. Rummaging through a drawer built into the control panel, I found the instruction manual for the digital recorder. I flipped through it until a schematics diagram appeared, and saw with relief that the external flash drive was attached to the unit by a USB connection, easy to remove and store in my bag.

I had what I needed to prove Dr. Amado was a murderer. The recording would also clear Mico of the charges against him and exonerate Saleema Garnati too. Obviously Amado had pointed the Guardia in her direction, although the video did not show him admitting to planting the Semtex. The tape was a goldmine of incrimination. All I needed was a trustworthy person in authority to view it.

With Alcábez unavailable, the one option I had left was to convince Inspector Fernández, who worked for the Granada National Police, to intervene in a Guardia Civil operation.

Fernández picked up right away. Halfway through my account, he interrupted so forcefully I had to pull the phone away from my ear. "You withheld information on the murder of Carlos Martín. You failed to tell me about the tunnels under your cousin's house. You waited until the Guardia Civil raid was fully underway and all over the TV news before calling me. Do you seriously think I'll ride to your rescue?"

"I understand how you feel, Inspector. I know you might be putting your career on the line by investigating another law enforcement agency. But doesn't it infuriate you that this Captain Súarez was either tricked into believing a library caretaker is a terrorist or he knows better and doesn't care? I think Dr. Amado and his people belong to a hidden society with a fascist agenda. Please, I know you believe in justice. You told me so yourself when we first met."

My cell beeped. Inspector Fernández had disconnected. This was upsetting but nothing compared to the horrendous crash made by the Control Room door as it caved in, admitting two Guardia officers, each on one end of a battering ram.

Before the officers could react to my presence, I stood up from behind the control panel and confronted them indignantly. "Why destroy the door when I could easily have let you in? Don't you realize the locking mechanism could provide us with clues about whoever is providing technology to the suspects?"

There was no response, so I continued. "Your intrusion is taking up my valuable time. Captain Súarez asked me to analyze this system and my work here is not yet complete."

The officer closest to me looked like a young recruit in his 20's, easily impressed. He knelt down to examine the lock on the door they'd destroyed. The other Guardia was older and wore his wide-brimmed cap at a jaunty angle. He stared at my legs, then looked up at my face, eyebrows raised. I glanced down and saw the muck splattered on the hems of my slacks by the dirt floor of the old tunnels. Just my luck to have worn a light grey pantsuit to the interview with Eduardo Martín. Thank goodness my pink silk shirt was presentable.

"Who are you?" he demanded. "I've never seen you on assignment with us before."

"I'm an American IT specialist on loan from the US National Guard. As you know, we have an exchange program that started last year. Your Captain called me in because he needed someone on short notice. There was no time to change my clothes and I may have ruined my shoes on the dirt path leading to the suspect's house."

Wary that one of the officers might use his radio to check my story, I played back an old recording of the Librarians tending to their duties and moving around in the tunnels. "I've got lots of footage to go through, since these would-be jihadis were stupid enough to log their own activities."

The older Guardia leaned in for a closer look and I switched off the monitor before he could notice the dated timecode.

"I suggest you two let me get back to work."

"Sorry to have disturbed you," said jaunty-cap on his way out.

I found a filing cabinet left over from the pre-digital age and extracted a folder bulging with papers. Poking my head out of the opening where the door had been, I saw only a few Guardias at their stations. I tucked the folder under my arm and checked my bag to make sure the hard drive I'd confiscated was safely stowed away.

As expected, there was a sentry stationed near the ladder leading up to Celia's trapdoor. I gripped the file folder with both hands to make sure he understood it was an object of importance.

"Do you know where Captain Súarez might be?"

He shook his head. "Would you like me to call him on the radio?"

"Thanks. That won't be necessary. I'll transmit my report as soon as he contacts me."

He acknowledged my departure up the ladder with an almost imperceptible click of his heels.

Celia's house was empty of personnel and I was able to find my suitcase, still packed with clothes I'd brought over from the Airbnb. The Guardia's operation was winding down and I imagined the fury and dismay of the Captain when he discovered the already 'looted' Control Room.

Keeping an eye out for Mauro, who would be hunting for me at his master's behest, I walked up the path to my car.

The gas gauge of the Outback was perilously low and I searched on my phone for a station I could reach on a couple of gallons. Then I remembered the little device Mico had found under the chassis and advised me to leave in place. Amado had likely used the GPS to keep track of Mico when he was with me and that's how he was able to set him up for Carlos's murder. Clearly Dr. Amado's purported PhD was in framing people. What a fool I'd been to fall for his gambit. More than ever I regretted my misinformed statement to Inspector Fernández and wished there was a way to take it back.

The Guardia Civil Land Rover was parked only a few yards away from the Subaru. I scrambled under both vehicles to relocate the tracker from one to the other. I hoped the Rover would take my pursuer on a wild good chase and buy me some time.

# Chapter Twenty-five

Although speeding on a near empty tank is never a good idea, I reached Orgiva in record time. The sun was setting over the mountains, which meant it was past 8pm, and I was lucky to find an open gas station. I filled up and drove the Outback around back and out of sight. I got out my laptop from the carryall and plugged in the flash drive that I'd disconnected from the video recorder in the Control Room. It took only seconds to copy the clip into an obscure folder buried several layers deep within the operating system. As a second backup, I copied the file to the USB memory stick I always carry with me and taped it to the undercarriage above the left front wheel well of the Subaru. At least I wouldn't make it easy for them. I stashed the flash drive under the spare tire in the back, next to the tire iron I planned to use to defend myself if necessary.

At the market near the gas station, I bought some cheese sandwiches, chips and a large soda. I was feeling more like a fugitive than a journalist, living from moment to moment in search of the next jumping off point. I didn't like it. I had my passport on me and considered driving to the American Embassy, the equivalent of American soil, and asking them to shepherd me safely home. What a great idea, if not for the likelihood of Captain Súarez invoking extradition based on charges of aiding and abetting terrorism. *You're a woman without a country, an outlaw forced to sleep in her car.*

At dawn, I drove to Luis and Felicia Alcábez's apartment in Granada and dropped in, uninvited.

It took some time for a sleepy Felicia to answer the door. Her cool, "Hello Alienor," made it plain she was not pleased to see me. How could I blame her? So far I'd brought nothing but danger and uncertainty across her threshold.

"I'm sorry, but it's not a good time." She put her hand on the doorknob, about to shut me out when in the background I heard Diego's shrill voice. "It's the lady from America!" He pushed Felicia aside to take my hand and towed me to his room to show off his latest pop music posters.

When Felicia came to fetch me, she wasn't alone. Mico was with her. Presumably he was hiding out at her house and remained a suspect in Carlos's murder, in large part because of me. I supposed she'd enlisted his help in ejecting me from the apartment.

"I'll go peacefully," I said. "But first I want to apologize to Mico. "I made a huge mistake and misjudged you — "

"It's okay," he interrupted. "You were in a state of shock at the sight of a dead body and there I was, standing over Carlos. If I'd been in your place I might have drawn the same erroneous conclusion. You saved my life in the hospital. I never lost faith I would see you again under better circumstances."

"Generous of you to say, Mico. But you're a suspect in a murder case because of my ill-considered words."

"I'm a suspect because I was set up by whoever murdered Carlos."

"And I know *exactly* who that was. But first, I have to explain some things to you and Felicia. It's quite a story."

Mico grinned. "Ever the journalist." He took my hand, squeezing it lightly as we walked into the dining room, where Felicia had set out some coffee and cinnamon pastries.

There were crumbs on the floor below the chair she offered me and the pristine, white tablecloth I remembered was spotted with enough food stains to make me feel comfortable. "Sorry for the mess. Luis is out of town and I've been busy with deadlines," Felicia said.

Sharing what I knew about Zahara would be a tremendous relief. Celia could hardly disapprove, since all their secrets had been blown to the winds by the Guardia raid. And she had already granted me permission to ask Luis to act as their attorney. *So where to start?*

"I assume you both know about the books that were burned in Bib-Arrambla Plaza in 1499. Well not all of them were incinerated. A few thousand were rescued and transported to an old salt mine in the Sierra Nevada for safekeeping. My cousin Celia lives directly above a maze of tunnels known as Zahara. There are eight underground libraries, archives of sacred and secular books which prove the existence of the *Convivencia* in medieval Spain."

Felicia's forkful of *leche frita* stopped midway to her mouth. "This is like a myth come to life. Unbelievable, yet now that I think of it, why not? I finally understand your confusing phone call. Someone has raided this place?"

"Yes, explosives were planted as false evidence in the tunnels and the Guardia was called in."

I described my meeting with Celia's father Eduardo and Dr. Amado's conspiracy to discredit the Librarians and steal the treasures housed by Zahara. "I'm sorry. I would have called you and Luis and shared all of this sooner but I was sworn to secrecy. Since the raid by the Guardia, Celia and the

Librarians are being held in *detención incomunicada*. No one knows where."

I finished to stunned silence.

"If I ever need someone to keep a secret, it'll be you," said Mico.

"There's also a video you must see." I set my laptop on the dining room table and queued up the clip.

When we reached the sequence where Dr. Amado confessed to having Carlos killed, Felicia and Mico both gasped.

"From what you've told us," Felicia observed, "your cousin has some powerful enemies, perhaps including her own father."

I turned to Mico. "Do you know anything about the Society that Dr. Amado said would 'take note' of the Guardia commander's disobedience? The members wear a pin like the one on his lapel. It's a red Cross turned upside down to make it look like an upraised sword. The hilt and the arms end in a fleur-de-lis."

From across the table, Mico's eyes bored into mine. "What you've described is a variation of the Cross of St. James and it may provide an important clue about who and what we're facing. St. James was known as the "*Muslim slayer*" and in medieval times Christians prayed to him to grant them victory over their Islamic neighbors. Eventually his sword became a symbol of the Military Order of Santiago."

"And that means today?"

He got out his phone. "I'm not exactly sure, but the fact that they've turned the blade of the sword upward signifies they're prone to violence. My fellow members in *Stop the Hate* keep track of these fanatics. I'll call and find out what they know."

Mico went into the kitchen for some privacy. I could hear water running in the hallway bathroom and Felicia brought me a towel and washcloth. "Take your time," she said. "You've been through a lot."

The hot soak released the tension in my muscles and also broke down the defenses that, like Scotch Tape and a tube of old glue, had held me together for the past few days. The stress hormones that I'd relied on to drive me were gone and all I had left was deep breathing and gratitude for having a safe place to land among friends.

When I emerged from the bath, I could hear Mico talking with Felicia in the dining room. "My sources tell me that Eduardo Martín, Celia's father, is deeply involved with the Cisneros Society. They have influence with the government and law enforcement far beyond what we can imagine. I think they're setting things up so Eduardo Martín will be seen by the public as the hero who broke up a jihadi conspiracy. His flailing political party will gain a big advantage and the Society will further its agenda to promote racial purity."

I joined my friends at the table. "We can't sit back and let them destroy five hundred years' worth of history, cooperation and priceless knowledge. If we don't take action, the lives of innocent people will be ruined and fear and hatred will remain unchecked. I'll write an exposé and get Reuters to publish it internationally. My editor at the *Seattle Courier* can help make that happen."

Mico looked doubtful. "Words alone won't get the Librarians released from detention. As the video confirms, the explosives were planted in the tunnels and meant to be found by the Guardia. The strategy of these right wing zealots has successfully brought down the full weight of law enforcement. For the general populace, stopping terrorism is paramount. They will think that justice is being served and won't care about international opinion."

"Then let's find a judge to review the evidence," I said.

Felicia perked up. "When he gets back, Luis can contact the investigating judge they've assigned to this case."

"That's a good start but it's not so simple," Mico said, stroking the five o'clock shadow on his chin. "Allie's video contains no detailed confession of Amado's guilt. Luis will need more proof if he's going to convince the judge not to file charges against the accused. Otherwise, they will be tried at the National Court in Madrid, in the chamber that handles terrorism cases."

"So my hard-won evidence has come up short?"

"Not short, but in need of corroboration. I've been told that the Cisneros Society has their annual meeting tomorrow, at the Valley of the Fallen. Eduardo should be there, with the rest of the faithful. Of course they won't allow the general public to attend, or any journalists who have not proven their loyalty."

"As far as I know, Eduardo believes I'm a sympathetic reporter by the name of Eleanora Benveniste. Maybe I can isolate him long enough to make him face the reality of who killed his son. He could become a powerful ally."

"That's a lot to expect," Mico said.

"Not if he loves his son as much as I think he does," I responded.

Meanwhile Felicia was shaking her head so violently that her blond curls bounced. "As soon as this Dr. Amado sees you, he'll turn you over to his friends in the Guardia."

"Then we won't let that happen," Mico said. "Allie's right. This may be our only chance to confront Eduardo with the truth."

They argued back and forth until Felicia gave in. "I wish I could drive you as far as Madrid."

"I need you to stay here and fill Luis in when he gets home," said Mico.

"Then let me rent a car for you in my name," Felicia pleaded. "I can do this online and you'll have a better chance of avoiding the police."

Before we left, I uploaded the digital recording of Dr. Amado's conversation with Mauro to my YouTube account. I set the access as password protected and emailed the link to Todd Lassiter, asking him to sit on it until he heard from me again. Whatever happened, we'd have insurance.

Although it was mid-afternoon, Mico and I were psychologically and physically drained and spoke little as we took turns driving the non-descript Ibiza. We stopped to grab some food in Jaen and passed through several small cities on our way north. As we neared Madrid, Mico became more talkative, telling me about the controversy surrounding The Valley of the Fallen.

"Many people feel it's a crime for Franco's tomb to share space with the unidentified bodies of those who fought against him. And recently a high court ruled that the government can move his remains elsewhere."

"What about the Cisneros Society's role in all this?"

"They believe in the importance of what they euphemistically call purity of blood and use Franco's monument to promote their distorted view of history. Of course it's ultimately about power."

In the *Las Delicias* neighborhood of Madrid, we checked into a small hotel, also booked in Felicia's name. The *recepcionista* shrugged when I told her I'd forgotten my passport on the train.

Upstairs, our little room was dominated by a floor to ceiling window looking out on a narrow street lined with busy eateries. Of the two full-sized beds, I chose the one closest to the window. I unpacked my sensible nightgown but Mico had no change of clothes and apologized in advance for sleeping in his underwear. His dismay made me laugh so hard he looked concerned for my mental health. "You're facing a trumped up murder charge and this is what bothers you the most?" I sputtered.

Around nine o'clock we went out again. Given Dr. Amado's instructions to Mauro to silence Carmen Díaz, we owed her a warning that her life was in danger. I also hoped to learn how her parents' house came to be the jumping off point for the invasion of Zahara.

We took the Metro and got off at the *Lavapiés* station. The neighborhood hosted a United Nations of shopkeepers including Bangladeshis and Senegalese. *Was the world more ready than I'd thought to adopt Zahara's philosophy of peaceful co-existence?* My optimism ended when we stopped at a newsstand where headlines trumpeted Spain's struggle to stay whole and the worldwide drift to the ultra-right. Although Mico and I might succeed in exposing the Cisneros Society, it would be like flushing out one weasel amongst thousands.

If the address Dr. Amado gave to Mauro was correct, Carmen Díaz lived on *Calle Miguel Servet*. Her residence turned out to be a *Corrala*, a style that Mico told me was named after the open-air corridors typical of these apartments building. It was near dinner time so hopefully the family would be at home. A woman with dyed red hair came to the door. When she saw Mico, she pulled a quilted jacket around her flimsy housedress.

"Are you Carmen Díaz? I'm Alienor Crespo, Celia Crespo's cousin."

Carmen's kohl-lined eyes narrowed and she took a step back. "How did you find us?"

There was no way to directly answer that question without frightening her off. "I've come because we need your help in figuring out something that happened at your old house in the mountains above Almendrales," I said. "A few nights ago, someone ambushed me and used the trapdoor to climb down into the tunnels. Since the entrance to Zahara was well concealed, it's surprising he knew where to find it."

"There's a lot at stake," Mico added. "Otherwise we wouldn't be here."

When a neighbor stepped out on his patio to indulge his curiosity, Carmen grudgingly admitted us and closed the door. We were crowded into the vestibule, surrounded by umbrellas and outdoor clothes. "If I tell you what happened, will you make sure that terrible man goes to jail?"

"That's the plan," said Mico.

"He called himself Doctor Amado and claimed to know everything about my father, whom he accused of treason and subversion. He threatened to have Papa arrested if I didn't tell him how to break into the tunnels. Dad never told me much, but I knew about the libraries underneath our house. After he fell ill and we moved to Madrid, he forbade me to talk about our old way of life. He has only a few years left. I'm not going to let him go to prison to protect a bunch of old books."

"Do you know where the doctor got his information?"

Carmen pressed her lips together firmly. I couldn't blame her for being a protective daughter.

"Please," Mico interjected. "Innocent people will go to jail if you won't talk with us."

She stared at the floor and then up at the ceiling, as if the prospect of what she was about to say haunted her. "I suspect it's Uncle Ramon." This was difficult for her to admit and her voice quivered. "My uncle is a good man, in spite of his politics," she insisted. "He's an Old Falangist and disapproves of my father's liberal views. Ramon and my father were always getting into arguments. I suspect he passed on my father's ravings to someone who knew this evil professor."

*Evil Professor.* Dr. Amado would be pleased with the nomenclature.

The ex-Librarian's daughter had helped us out and it was time to level with her. "Carmen, you should be aware that Amado knows where you live. I overheard him planning to silence you. Unfortunately, we can't call the police because a handful of them are in his pay. The good news is that we have a plan."

"*Now* you finally tell me! After tricking me into revealing everything!" She gripped the edge of the umbrella stand, either for support or to set herself up to grab a parasol and stab me.

"Like Alienor said, we have a plan to take down the professor and have him put away." Mico's calm voice did little to defuse the anger smoldering in her eyes but he kept at it. "I'm sorry this has come as such a shock but all will be well if you stay home with your doors locked until we contact you."

"And if your precious plan fails and I don't hear from you, what then?"

Mico took a business card from his wallet and handed it to Carmen. "If you haven't heard from us in twenty-four hours, call Luiz Alcábez. He's a well-connected attorney and will arrange for police protection you can count on."

Carmen gave Mico her phone number and turned to face me. "I suppose you expect me to thank you for the warning."

"I should have contacted you sooner," I said. "So much has happened, so fast. What I *can* say is that everything you have told us will be put to good use in stopping those who want to hurt not only you, but everyone associated with Zahara."

She pushed us out of the vestibule and closed the door before I could complete my little speech.

# Chapter Twenty-six

Back in the cramped double-room, Mico and I sat on the edges of our beds in semi-darkness, sharing a bottle of wine. The only light came from the floor-length curtains, glowing with the soft pink of the neon *Panadería* sign across the street.

I wanted badly to text Dad and tell him I was okay. Mico put his hand over my phone. "You mustn't underestimate the surveillance capabilities of the Guardia, or the tech savvy neo-fascistas who belong to the Cisneros Society."

To hear him talk, you'd think he dealt with situations like this every day. Maybe he did.

"You shouldn't have to go through this, Alienor."

"I have my brave notary by my side."

He eased over onto my bed, lying down next to me, ankles crossed. I stretched my body out to match his and we both gazed up at the pair of wooden beams crossing the ceiling, three feet apart. "They're like us," Mico said. "Strong on their own but stronger linked together."

Without that second glass of wine, maybe I wouldn't have turned my head so invitingly. And if the kiss hadn't been every bit as sweet as the one in Almendrales, we might have stopped there. But it was and we didn't.

I read somewhere that the libido is stimulated by the presence of danger. And being with an older man *was* different. It was like making love to life itself, savoring the moments we have here on earth without any hurry for one to lead to another.

When our breathing slowed and the time came to share more than the physical, I asked Mico if he'd ever been married.

"I think it was her elegance that initially attracted me to Naomi," he said. "My ex had a way of ruffling her hair so it resembled the feathers of a black woodpecker my mother once photographed in the Pyrenees. You, on the other hand, resemble an inquisitive parrot that never stops talking."

In retaliation for this insult I tickled him under his armpit. Mico reacted by running his hands over my breasts. He was starting to tweak my nipples when I firmly pushed him away. "Tell me more about your marriage to Naomi."

"There's not a lot to tell. We parted because she was more concerned about living inside the lines."

"What lines do you mean?" I was hoping he didn't mean those of fidelity.

"When I joined *Stop the Hate* and started going to meetings Naomi was actively opposed. She didn't understand why I was willing to take risks on behalf of strangers. It's difficult when you have a passion and your mate doesn't share it. And when you have no children… What about you? Did you ever take the plunge?"

"No." Suddenly I wasn't so keen to continue our talk.

"Come on, it's only fair. Tell me."

"Well, I did live with someone for a while, a programmer at Microsoft named Joel. When I had trouble piecing together a living as a freelance reporter he badgered me to sign on for a fulltime job as a tech writer. And there were certain… eccentric episodes on my part that I didn't feel comfortable sharing.

I ended up keeping too much to myself. Not healthy for a relationship."

Mico seemed satisfied and didn't pry. I could see myself divulging a lot more to him, eventually.

We made love a second time, letting our hands and mouths learn the secrets of our bodies. There was a lightness to his touch that slowly but surely set my limbs on fire, first smoldering, then bursting into flame. That night I slept better than I had since arriving in Spain.


Mico stood in front of the window, backlit by the morning light. He was fully dressed and his frown was not a welcome sight after our beautiful night together.

"What's wrong?"

"I was planning to leave for the Valley without you."

I sat up. "Why in the world would you do that?"

"Please, don't get upset. Like I said last night, it's not fair for you to be burdened by this situation. You're not yet a citizen and our problems are not yours to solve. I don't think you realize how treacherous these people can be."

"Really? Who walked in on Carlos's dead body? Who was attacked and imprisoned in an olive mill? And more importantly, who swore an oath to be a caretaker of Zahara and all it represents? No one held my nationality against me then."

"That's exactly why I decided to wait for you, Alienor. You've handled yourself remarkably well. All I want is for you to know what you're up against and when you make your decision, take my feelings into account."

I should never have poured that second glass of wine. Mico was acting like a slumbering knight poked with a stick. His protective instincts were aroused just when I most needed him to have faith in my ability to handle myself.

I looked around for my nightgown, all at once feeling at a disadvantage in my nakedness. Mico found the garment on the floor and handed it over. This gave me time to calm myself before I reacted.

"So, Mico, tell me about this Society you fear will make mincemeat of me, the woman who fought off your assassin in the hospital. Are its members actual followers of Cardinal Cisneros, the zealot who brought the Inquisition to Spain? They couldn't possibly be that old."

His laughter broke the tension between us. "It's worse. They think they're his descendants. Maybe a few of them are."

"It's hard to believe that such people exist in the twenty-first century."

Mico's eyebrows lifted as a comment on my naiveté. Come to think of it, I'd have reacted the same way if some fool questioned the existence of the Ku Klux Klan.

"I'm going to take a shower and I need to know you'll be here when I come out."

"Of course I will. Be quick about it."

That was more like it.

Waiting for the water in the shower to achieve hotness, I thought about how Mico and I had been through lots of ups and downs in a short time. We'd become much more than friends and he deserved my full trust—not some censored version of who I was. The prospect of sharing my true self with him was both exhilarating and frightening.

We decided to leave the Ibiza in Madrid. As Mico put it, "Whoever might be looking for us will assume we're traveling by car. On public transport we can lose ourselves among the schoolchildren and elderly Francoistas on their way to visit the monument."

It was late morning when our bus reached El Escorial and we found a taxi to take us on the twenty minute trip to the Valley of the Fallen. The driver, who looked old enough to have had his own firsthand experience of the Civil War, wasn't shy about expressing himself. "The memorial is not a preferred destination. Tens of thousands are buried there, casualties from both sides. It's a gloomy and sinister place." As we got underway, he continued his unsolicited monologue.

"Like everything else in this country, there is no stability. Every time the Left wins an election, they promise to move Franco's body elsewhere and rename the shrine. Maybe this time the Supreme Court will approve the plan. Unless, as usually happens, the Right returns to power and we start all over again."

The road wound upward and the tallest memorial Cross in the world came into view, piercing the sky from atop a massive grotto covered by stunted trees. The Holy Cross looked almost as high as the 600-foot Space Needle in Seattle but that's where the similarity ended. One was a dark symbol dedicated to the colossal ego of a dictator and his obsession with Catholicism; the other was built for the 1962 World's Fair, a futuristic observation tower celebrating science and space travel.

As we came closer, I glimpsed the four, larger-than-life statues hewn into the base of the giant Cross. "Those are the four Evangelists," Mico said. "Franco was able to build on such a grand scale because he used Republican prisoners of war as his main source of labor. The basilica they constructed below the rocks is almost as large as St. Peter's in Rome. But we're not here to visit the monument. I reserved a room at the Valley Guest House, a former monastery located directly behind the shrine."

He showed me a brochure asking visitors to *Stay with us in the Valley of the Fallen.* I hoped our stop would not be a permanent one.

Through my *Vijitas*, I knew of one fierce opponent of Franco's regime who survived into the 1980s, before losing his life to the Falangists. Ja'far's body had never been found. Whatever it was that my great uncle was up to after the Spanish Civil War officially ended, Luzia had helped him, of that I was sure. She comes to me now. In a dimly lit place, her thoughts become mine.

Ja'far told me he'd bring them tonight. I've set up cots in the passageway leading to the library under our house. I wish we had more light down here. What these young ones have been through has been terrifying enough without adding darkness to their fears. Ja'far says their mothers are all political prisoners. Impossible as it seems, a guard risked his life to warn them their babies would be stolen away in the night. Maybe the sentry was thinking of his own children.

They tell the mothers that they are taking their offspring to be baptized but everyone knows what happens after a child's disappearance – a state-sponsored adoption with a new 'approved' family. Franco claims he's saving the race from the mental illness of communism by correcting the 'racial inferiority' of Republican children. It's like we're rescuing refugees from the Nazis all over again.

Someone knocks on the trapdoor, three soft taps followed by two loud. I loosen the latch and hear Ja'far's soothing voice. He's good with the little ones, including our five-year-old Pilar. Maybe someday, when all this madness is behind us, we'll have a few more children of our own.

There are four of them, quiet mice, not a squeak among them. A little girl in a torn dress, maybe four years old, holds a sleeping baby wrapped in a dirty blanket. I reach out to take the infant in my arms and with trembling lips her sister lets go. The two boys are a bit older and stare at me with wide, alarmed eyes.

As the children ravenously gobble up the cups of goat's milk mixed with cereal that I've prepared, the baby cries with anticipation. Ja'far has somehow found a bottle with a nipple and warmed up the contents, a small miracle. The littlest one gets to work.

We know we can't keep them for long. The roads are muddy this time of year and the Guardia could easily pick up my husband's tire tracks leading here from the main road. I try not to think about what will happen to the mothers when the prison warden discovers the children are gone, or the fate of the guard who had the courage to smuggle them out.

"How long?" I ask.

Before answering, Ja'far wolfs down some cereal himself. "In the morning Paco will take them in his bread truck to a school for the blind in Malaga, where no one will think to look. The mistress keeps a roster of the mothers' names, in case some survive to reclaim their youngsters."

When I bring some oranges down from the kitchen, our tiny visitors cry out in delight. For their sake, I try to feel hopeful.

Leaving our taxi driver to make his escape from the Valley he hated so much, Mico and I walked toward the guesthouse, our path crisscrossing through a checkerboard of manicured lawns. Everything about this place seemed surreal, including the colossal Cross that loomed above us from every line of sight. This was no place for children.

"Of all the babies who were kidnapped by the Francoists during and after the war, were any found and reunited with their parents?" I asked Mico.

"How do you know about that?"

"I've done my research and I'm also a woman who knows that a mother never gives up hope."

"You're right, Allie. They've continued to search for the *niños robados*, but time has destroyed most of the evidence, making DNA testing of little use. As many as thirty thousand parents have died in limbo, not knowing if their children are alive or dead. Maybe that's why people claim to have seen Franco's ghost swirling around this memorial. Can you imagine the guilt?"

Near the entrance to the guesthouse, he stopped to slip a necklace with a delicate gold Cross around my neck. "If anything, you might prefer a Star of David, but in this case appearances are everything."

We checked in as 'married guests,' making a show for the receptionist about what a "privilege" it was to be staying at the sprawling abbey, now run as a hotel by the same Benedictine monks who looked after the Basilica across the way.

Our austere room with two single beds was heated and minimally comfortable – and as romantic as a bed of tacks.

A light knock at the door startled me.

"It's okay. I've asked for a tour," Mico told me. "If they tell us there's a conference room in use today and unavailable for viewing, that may well be our target."

The monk who came to fetch us was clad in a black robe and introduced himself as Brother Benito. His youth and talkative demeanor was more appropriate for a socially adept college student than a solitary acolyte.

After showing us the church, the impressive library, some small classrooms and the well-appointed public dining spaces under the arches, our guide announced the tour was over. On the way back, we passed a set of sturdy, double doors.

"What's in there?" Mico asked Brother Benito.

"That's our largest private meeting room. It's been booked by an organization but after they check out, I'll be delighted to show it."

Mico stroked the door, ostensibly admiring its patina, while I distracted the Brother by peppering him with questions about how the monastery had been converted into a hotel. I admired my partner's sleight of hand as he slipped a small microphone into the recessed corner of a carved panel, hiding it below the tip of an angel's wing.

"We'd better get dressed for dinner," I said, thanking the Brother for his hospitality as we turned to leave.

"Eleanora Benveniste! Is that you?" Eduardo's voice boomed through the corridor. I was forced to stop and respond to what he believed to be my real name. Mico, who was walking a few steps in front, wisely kept going. This was an opportunity I couldn't pass up.

"What a pleasant surprise, Señor Martín. My first visit to this illustrious place and I'm lucky enough to run into a friend."

Behind Eduardo, the members of the Cisneros Society were exiting the meeting room, conversing in the reserved manner of the nobility. Well-tailored, dark blue or gray suits were the norm and in lieu of sinister cowls they wore red pins on their lapels, easy to recognize if you knew what you were looking for – the inverted Cross of St. James, hewn in the shape of an upraised sword.

I was trying to work out how to convince Eduardo to meet with me in private, when he smiled like a man with schemes of his own. "It's lovely to see you, Eleanora. We're taking a half-hour break and I need some air. Would you like to accompany me?"

Either Eduardo wanted to flirt or he was going to ask me to write a feature singing his praises. Either way, I was getting in deep, swimming over a tangle of lies that could easily grab my feet.

# Chapter Twenty-seven

As soon as we exited the guest house, Eduardo Martín began spewing words in abundance and kept up his diatribe throughout our walk across the plaza to the semi-circle of harsh gray stone cradling the entrance to the monument. The exterior walls were free of ornamentation except for a ravenous-looking eagle carved in relief and covered with the symbols of the Falange—the arrow and the yoke.

I'd been wrong about him wanting to flirt. Eduardo didn't come right out and say he was determined to recruit me as the first female member of the Cisneros Society. Instead, he injected a slew of loaded questions into the conversation, such as "Isn't it a shame to see so many countries overrun with immigrants with no respect for their hosts' culture or religion?" and "Don't you think we need tougher leaders, to control the dissent flaring up around the globe?"

I played my part and delivered my lines. When I said, "It may take time, but heads like yours will prevail," I could see he was moved.

"Ms. Benveniste, you must join our afternoon session. We'll discuss how best to support the upcoming campaign of the StandUp Party. Your coverage could make a huge difference in Spain's future."

"I hope Dr. Amado will be there too."

He slowed his stride. "How did you know Dr. Amado belonged to the Cisneros Society?"

"You're wearing the same pin I saw on his lapel when you introduced us."

"Ah, you don't miss much, do you? The good doctor is scheduled to arrive tomorrow. It looks like you'll have to make do with me."

We left the bright sunlight behind and crossed the threshold into the gloom of the underground Basilica. Eduardo hailed the security guard at the gate like an old friend. "Great to see you, Jorge."

Vaulted high above us, the cathedral-like ceiling had been designed to induce awe in some and in others such as me a touch of claustrophobia mixed with dread. As we walked down the vast, black marble floor leading to the faraway altar, reflections from torches on the walls created the impression of flames licking at our feet. Angels carved from stone and armed with swords that said *we mean business* populated the alcoves on either side. And if that wasn't ominous enough, tapestries depicting the apocalypse of St. John dominated the walls. The war between the Church's idea of good and evil was alive and well, and being fought right here. Latin choral singing echoed all around us, amplifying the intensity.

Eduardo took my arm, wrapping it around his. This was his idea of a stroll down a promenade and I half expected him to wave to other visitors. "Thousands of El Caudillo's followers come here to celebrate his birthday," he said proudly. "We should return in December and join them." I marveled at how he'd not only bought my cover story but had convinced himself that we enjoyed a world in common as fans of *El Generalissimo's* brutal regime.

We reached the nave and stood gazing at the crucified Christ above the altar. "A pity we don't have time for me to show you the great leader's tomb," he said.

*What about the thousands of unidentified bodies interred without ceremony beneath the forest floor all around us?* With effort, I reined in the urge to confront him with the question.

It was a relief to head back to the guest house. I had deviated from our plan and my partner-in-crime would be worried. It was impossible to look for him without setting off Eduardo's paranoia alarm. I could only hope Mico's microphone setup worked and he could stay tuned to whatever happened in the conference room.

Eduardo led me to a seat next to the one that had been saved for him at the long, highly polished table. The buzz of conversation among this group of impeccably dressed men gave way to quiet anticipation and my new "friend" introduced me. "Ms. Benveniste has expressed a keen interest in the Cisneros Society and as a journalist of integrity, we can count on her to earnestly convey our message." I controlled the nausea his words brought on and smiled as sweetly as I could.

There was a sameness to the dozen faces assembled, a well-bred look fostered by good living. In spite of Eduardo's cordial introduction, as the youngest person in the room and the only woman I felt a touch of animosity mixed with envy coming from this group of fanatics.

Even the furniture bespoke a different era. The chandelier, woven leather chairs, and oil paintings in gilded frames lent a baroque feel, as did the bronze sword prominently mounted on the wall. The one happy exception was a projector wheeled into the room by a tow-headed young man. I reached into my purse and found the thumb drive. There was no obvious damage from its ride taped to the wheel well of the Outback that only yesterday I'd driven in such haste from Orgiva to Granada.

Eduardo was busy shuffling papers and preparing to deliver a talk I surmised would be augmented by PowerPoint slides. I tapped his shoulder lightly, a buddy asking for a favor, and filled my voice with as much saccharin as it would hold. "I took some photos of your staff when I visited your campaign office. I'd love to share them if you don't mind."

He readily agreed.

I handed the memory stick to the blond projectionist, asking him to plug it into the iPad I'd been so glad to see on the table. "I'm so sorry, ma'am," he said, with what sounded like genuine regret. "There's no USB connection, only a VGA port for the projector."

My hopes had been tied to a sinking stone "I can't believe this," I said, "for want of a tiny adapter, the whole battle is lost."

The technician smiled sympathetically, oblivious to the extent of my frustration. If I was unable to show Eduardo proof that Dr. Amado had murdered his son, there was no way I could win the aspiring politician over to our side.

By this time, the society members were getting restless and mumbling to themselves while staring at the blank screen. Eduardo nervously tapped his forefinger on the table.

"Go ahead with Senor Martín's presentation," I told the young man.

I returned to my seat next to the guest of honor, who whispered in my ear. "This is my first time seeing the complete version. I'm anxious to know what you think."

The lights turned down and the screen filled, but not with PowerPoint slides. It was a video, a slick propaganda piece that opened with martial music and shots of the brave Guardia Civil rounding up a group of terrorists. According to the female narrator, whose voiceover was delivered in the melodramatic tones of a 1950's anti-communist newsreel, the police had received a tip from a vigilant member of the StandUp party and were "rooting out the jihadis and their sympathizers from tunnels hidden beneath innocent looking houses in La Alpujarra."

I recognized Captain Súarez but the faces of the Librarians being arrested were blurred out, possibly for legal reasons. The videographer—who must have surreptitiously shot the footage on his cellphone—wasn't going to jeopardize the chances of a conviction by prematurely broadcasting the identities of the accused. Oddly, an exception was made for one onlooker standing in a doorway inside my cousin's house. The indignant dismay on my face had been captured perfectly. The camera lingered on my face for two seconds before the video cut to a shot of Celia and the others being loaded into a van. It happened so quickly that for a moment I thought Eduardo hadn't recognized me. His firm grip on my arm and the way his fingernails dug into my skin said otherwise.

I broke away from Eduardo's grasp and stood up, dismayed to see Mauro blocking the exit. If the strongman was here, then Dr. Amado was nearby. Eduardo yanked me down so roughly the back of my knees jammed into the edge of my chair. "Don't make things worse for yourself," he hissed.

In the final frames of the video Eduardo appeared in front of an official building with *House of Deputies* engraved on its stone portico. It was hard to tell if they'd used a green screen or he'd traveled to Madrid for the shoot. He spoke with commanding authority, addressing the audience directly: "Use your vote to secure our borders against criminals like these and contribute to the safety of our Patria. Support the StandUp Party and we promise your voice will be heard, not only in Spain but throughout all of God-fearing Europe."

The production credits were brief, with *Cine Superba* listed under *Produced By*.

Acknowledging the applause of his colleagues, Eduardo stood and led them in prayer. I barely heard the discussion of political strategy that followed. My plan to expose Dr. Amado had been shot down by a technological glitch. And my terrible luck was compounded by my being caught on film during the Guardia raid. I was outed as a member of the wrong team and had no backup plan whatsoever.

Dr. Amado took the empty seat that had been saved for him at the head of the table. When he saw me look his way, his lips curled into a satisfied smile. The others sat in shocked silence.

Eduardo stood looming over me. He pulled back his hand to slap me and at the last second dropped his arm. "You're a spy, a fraud and an imposter. You'll get what you deserve."

I looked straight up at him, holding his eyes for as long as I could. "I'm not the one who betrayed you. Your son's murderer is in this very room. Everything I've done has been aimed at exposing him. And I have the evidence right here." I held up the thumb drive for him and the others to see.

Eduardo knocked the memory stick out of my hand and it flew through the air, landing on the floor mat near the door. "You're either a pathological liar or a deluded fool."

He addressed his compatriots around the table. "I'm sorry for exposing you to this infiltrator and for allowing her to manipulate me. The matter will be taken care of."

Mauro came to stand behind me, an ominous presence. I tried to control my breathing and closed my eyes but there was no comfort in the darkness, only fear.

"She's not a liar."

Mico stood in the doorway, my laptop under his arm. He quickly bent to retrieve the USB stick from the rug and connected it to the slim PC. "If this doesn't convince you, nothing will," he said to the room at large, flipping open the thirteen-inch screen and holding it up so everyone could see.

# Chapter Twenty-eight

Dr. Amado's eyes were trained on the laptop's screen as he worked hard to keep the muscles in his face under control. With so many members of the Cisneros Society present, he was obligated to let them see the movie in which he'd starred, courtesy of the security cameras in Zahara. Maybe he'd forgotten how much he'd incriminated himself during the raid, not an unreasonable mistake for a narcissist caught up in the myth of his own infallibility.

When the recording reached the point where the doctor coolly justified having ordered Carlos's death, I glanced at Eduardo's face and saw a father confronting a truth so ugly that being turned to stone might have been a blessing. This was the moment I'd been counting on, yet I couldn't help feeling sorry for him.

Seconds later, Eduardo came to life. He grabbed the sword from its case on the wall and held its point quivering less than an inch from the doctor's throat. Knowing he would be next, Mauro started for the door. Mico stuck his foot out and tripped the hitman, sending him crashing into the wall.

Holding the sword-point steady at Amado's jugular, Eduardo commanded, "Lock the door."

Mico complied.

Dr. Amado found his voice. "Tapes can be doctored. We all know that."

"He's right," I said. "The original is uploaded to YouTube and will be released publicly if anything happens to me or Mico Rosales."

"Why take her word?" Amado's voice reeked of sarcasm even as his throat quivered at the touch of cold metal below his chin. "This woman has already lied about her name, which is in fact Alienor Crespo, and her political affiliation. I'm relying on all of you to give me a fair hearing, in the same way you fairly elected me president of this venerable society." He spoke with cocksureness, like someone confident he'd correctly gauged the mood of his peers.

Eduardo slowly lowered the sword.

"She's had her say. Now it's the doctor's turn to defend himself," someone said, eliciting a general murmur of agreement.

The "Professor" did a good job of hiding the relief he undoubtedly felt. "What I'm about to say is for the Society's ears only. I won't speak in front of this woman or her co-conspirator."

"I'll have them escorted to their room," Eduardo said. He summoned a monk and took him aside to whisper instructions. Our chosen minder looked more like a pro wrestler nicknamed Goliath than a Benedictine holy man. Nothing in this place was as it seemed. It was as if the expansive reality of my *Vijitas* had gone into reverse. I was surrounded by closed minds impossible to penetrate.

"Before you go, give me that laptop," Amado commanded and Mico was forced to relinquish the PC and submit to a humiliating search.

As Goliath hustled us out of the conference room, the Cisneros Society members conspicuously avoided eye contact.

They were here because of their strong beliefs in National Catholicism and a return to authoritarian rule. For that reason alone they would favor their leader's version of events over mine. Worse yet, they would see Zahara—or for that matter any proof that a *Convivencia* once existed between the three faiths living under Muslim rule—as a major threat to their white nationalist creed. So what if a few explosives and a map had been planted as false evidence to discredit their enemies? No citizens were hurt. And if Amado succeeded in confiscating Zahara's most valuable written treasures for his own profit, not one of these men would blame him for reaping the spoils of war.

Goliath insisted on joining us inside our Spartan room, settling his considerable weight into the only chair. His masters must have reasoned that a behemoth stationed in front of our door would have alarmed the other guests. He examined the windows carefully, which seemed a waste of time because they were mortared shut, and kept us in sight at all times.

Mico sat cross-legged on the bed, ear pods connected to his phone, listening intently. Nodding his head up and down for Goliath's benefit, he appeared to be keeping time to the music on his phone while actually monitoring the Society's discussion of our fate down the hall.

All at once he unplugged the device and tossed it over his shoulder. When I queried him with my eyes, he made a sweeping motion that ended with a hard downward slam onto the mattress. They'd swept the conference room and crushed his bug.

There was nothing to do but wait for the Society's verdict. I was not optimistic.

An hour passed in slow motion. It was beginning to look like Mico and I had deftly maneuvered ourselves into a trap of our own making. Was my father about to lose me in the same way he'd lost my mother, she following her dream of dancing and me in the midst of claiming citizenship in the land that gave birth to the music she loved?

Goliath went to answer a knock on the door that sounded like a pre-arranged signal. Eduardo entered and I was baffled to see him kiss the monk on both cheeks. "Thanks for looking after my friends, Brother Dario. I knew no one would dare come after them while they were in your care."

"You're most welcome," said the monk, who I was beginning to see in an entirely new light.

Turning to me, Eduardo looked contrite. "I hope I didn't hurt your arm. If Rosales here had not appeared and shown the damning video, I might have done far worse. Please forgive me, Ms. Crespo. That is your real name, isn't it? According to Amado you are my daughter's second cousin. I've decided to help you."

I was struck speechless but not Mico, who stood up from the bed to address his longtime nemesis. "Is that what the Society decided after we left, to send you to trick us into trusting you so you can lead us more easily to the slaughter?"

Eduardo smiled cynically. "A reasonable scenario, if based solely on my previous actions. But that's not what happened."

"Then tell us what did," Mico demanded.

"I'll tell you but we need to be quick about it. We don't have much time. It was easy for Dr. Amado to make his case. First, he described Ms. Crespo here as 'a Jewish journalist who cooks up evidence.' Then he said we needed to unify for the sake of the party. Amado is smoother than a dish of flan—"

Mico held up his hand to stop Eduardo's flow. "He's telling the truth, Alienor. I was listening and those were Amado's exact words. It was right before they found the bug."

"What happened after that?" I asked Celia's father.

Eduardo curled his hands into fists and jammed them together in frustration. "The doctor convinced them that the jihadis in La Alpujarra killed my son. It was like the incriminating evidence they had seen with their own eyes evaporated on contact. The idiots absolved him of all guilt. But after seeing your video I know better. I should have listened to Carlos when he called last week and tried to warn me about Dr. Amado. I grew angry and shut him down."

Sometimes the truth really does set us free. Gone was the over-confident politician and bullying zealot. In his place stood a father broken down by guilt over the part he'd played in the death of his son. A man who seemed ready to redeem himself by changing sides.

"Brother Dario, it's time!" Eduardo shouted and Goliath emerged from the bathroom with a towel wrapped around his hand. The powerfully built monk motioned for us to stand back as he efficiently smashed a window facing the woods at the back of the guest house. The mortar had either disintegrated or been "window dressing" all along.

Mico cleared away the shards of broken glass and we threw our luggage out before scrambling over the sill ourselves, leaving Eduardo behind. Brother Dario followed, with a little more difficulty because of his size. We crept alongside the building, keeping as low to the ground as possible.

"You can join the crowd out front," the monk said, "and make your way to the bus."

Mico was right behind me as I rounded the corner, with about a hundred feet to go before we reached the public area. The door of a delivery van parked near a side entrance slid open and before I could react, Mauro had pulled me inside and put a gun to my head.

Mico held up his empty hands. "Take me instead."

"Why not both of you?" Mauro countered. "Get in or she dies right now."

Mico moved forward and I heard a loud 'pop!' My eyes forced themselves shut, as if refusing to see my lover killed would make it not so.

"Allie! Let's go!" Mico cried.

I looked down and there was Amado's hitman crumpled in a heap on the metal truck-bed. Looking up, I caught a glimpse of Brother Dario running towards the woods. A revolver, equipped with a silencer, lay abandoned on the ground.

A bus was parked in the distance, near the entrance to the monument. With some fast walking through the swarm of tourists, Mico and I reached the loading zone. The green-lit marquee read *El Escorial*. A line had formed to wait for the driver to open the passenger door. Mico and I blended right in.

Eduardo stepped out of the shadows. "Before you go there's something I need to say to Mico."

"I'm listening," Mico said in a neutral tone.

Eduardo plowed on. "I want you to know it was Dr. Amado, not me, who sent Mauro to kill you in your office and when that failed, to finish the job in the hospital. Not that I'm totally innocent. It was I who told him about the letter Pilar wrote and gave to you for safekeeping, documenting her suspicions that we organized the Atocha Massacre."

"Did you participate in the massacre?" I asked.

"No," Eduardo said. "But Amado did. And when the opportunity came for me to run for public office, well you can see why the doctor wanted Mico out of the way. I've allowed myself to be used by an unscrupulous villain and his blind followers. They recruited me after my father's assassination. I wanted revenge on the leftist Republicans as well as the anarchists and all who supported them. The Cisneros Society pulled me in with their talk of vengeance and rejection of false reconciliation."

"They offered you political power. That must have been terribly appealing."

Eduardo didn't deny it. "They're all-powerful, with tentacles stretching everywhere, even into the justice system. These people are more than capable of adding a charge for Carlos's murder to the indictment of the so-called terrorists in La Alpujarra."

"Including your own daughter."

"Yes, including Celia, who I totally misjudged. For her sake, I need to stay on the Society's good side and keep track of what they'll do next. I made a show of believing Amado when he denied his own words and accused you of manipulating the recording. I forced myself to beg him not to expel me. The hypocrite agreed, saying the StandUp party would suffer without my leadership."

Eduardo pressed something into my hand. It was the Santiago pin he'd removed from his lapel. "Alienor I want you to take this as a token of your courage. I wish I could give you something more substantial in return for what you've done and for your willingness to listen to me after all the harm I've done."

"Eduardo, you should come with us to the National Police – I know an inspector who is more interested in justice than taking sides. Otherwise –"

His face softened. "I appreciate your kind concern. I could not save my son but if I stay here, there's a chance I can help Celia and my ex-wife whom I treated so badly. Please, when you see Pilar, tell her I'm sorry for my behavior at the monastery. When I found out she was alive, I was angry at her for deceiving me for so many years. But taking into account what she thought I had done…"

"Pilar is alive?" Mico looked back and forth between our faces, like we were aliens bringing news from another planet.

"Celia wanted to tell you herself, at the right time," I said.

The bus was loading. At a loss for words, Mico grabbed out suitcases and gave them to the driver, quickly boarding the bus.

Eduardo and I exchanged cell numbers and shook hands. He was one of the most indecipherable people I'd met. I would never have thought he'd choose me as his confidant. I did, however, understand his need to clear his conscience. Although he'd split his family apart with his fierce political convictions and religious zealotry he seemed willing to risk paying a terrible price in order to make amends.

Once onboard, I took a seat across the aisle from Mico, who refused to look at me. I gave him some time to think things over, craning my neck to get a view out the back window, on the alert for signs of pursuit on the road receding behind us.

# Chapter Twenty-nine

We were back in our hotel room in Madrid, recovering from our ordeal. Mico was finally making eye contact after having snubbed me for the entire return trip from the Valley.

"Allie, I'm sorry I reacted so badly. All you did was defer to Celia's wishes and it's clear she and her mother had their reasons for keeping me in the dark. The main thing is that my dear friend Pilar survived."

"She's a nun now, Mico. It can't go beyond that." I was kidding, but the pang of jealousy was real.

Mico blushed at my ill-advised remark and then grabbed me to administer some mock punishment. Our wrestling was rudely interrupted by my cell phone.

It was Luis Alcábez. "I got home last night. So sorry I missed you. How did things go in the Valley of the Fallen?"

"Badly. But we did manage to convince Eduardo Martín that his real enemy is the Cisneros Society. As far as I can tell, he's changed sides."

I put the phone on speaker so Mico could hear my attorney's response. "That's good news. I'll add Senor Martín to the witness list for the judge."

"What judge?"

"Patricia Rubio de Martínez is the investigative judge assigned by the National Court. They handle the most serious criminal cases, including terrorism."

"I thought judges didn't actively get involved in investigations."

"They do in Spain. Yesterday Judge Rubio took the bullet train to Granada. Tomorrow she'll interview Celia and all of the Librarians at the scene of the alleged crime. You should be there too, Alienor."

"So they have all been released from custody? It seems impossible."

"We're not there yet," Alcábez cautioned. Everyone is back home except for Saleema al-Garnati. A complaint of conspiracy to commit an act of terrorism has been issued against her. She'll be formally interviewed in Madrid next week. The prosecutor also notified me that Saleema's fingerprints were found on the Semtex. Based on what else Judge Rubio finds during her investigation, she will either issue instructions to the court to try Saleema's case or declare her innocent and drop the charges."

"I hope we can make it to La Alpujarra in time to talk with the judge," I said.

"There's a high-speed train leaving Madrid at eleven a.m. I'll meet you at the Granada station at three in the afternoon and we can drive the rest of the way together."

"We'll be on time," Mico said.

"Sorry, my friend," the attorney responded with vigor. "If you appear before the judge she's likely to order your arrest and that would cloud the waters of Saleema's case with your own. Until you are cleared, you remain a suspect in a murder case. Remember, they found your fingerprints at the scene. That's consistent with your finding the body but could also be interpreted as an indication of your guilt."

"I understand," said Mico. "When we get to Granada, I'll turn myself in at the police station." He paused before adding, "Only if you'll agree to represent me."

"Of course I will." Luis spoke more calmly, now that this was settled.

Over breakfast at the *Panadería*, I texted Mico the link and password to the video incriminating Dr. Amado. "Luis is right," I said. "You need to clear yourself. Inspector Fernández strikes me as a fair man and when he sees the evidence, let's hope he stops breathing down your neck."

I wished I had total belief in my own words.

Our train left Madrid a few minutes early. Neither of us had slept well the night before and since conversation led to the depressing possibility of Mico going to jail, we kept silent for most of the way. Normally I'd have been glued to the sights we sped past but I was dog-tired and fell asleep, waking when we pulled into the Granada station.

It was time to say goodbye and Mico's assurance that we would see each other soon didn't make it any easier. We held one another, both reluctant to be the first to let go. At last he disentangled himself and said, "Good luck with the judge. You'll make a great witness."

I was too choked up to respond and he left before I could recover. As I stepped off the train, the *Vijita* caught me in the middle of a good cry and I recognized the bright energy of Jariya's spirit turning within me.

I'm walking next to a donkey, holding its lead with one hand and clutching the thick strap of a heavy shoulder bag with the other. Although Fatima is with me and I couldn't wish for better company, it's hard to quell my longing for Razin. I fear that he will miss the birth of our baby.

Like me, Fatima is dressed as a Christian woman, both of us in black. If we meet any of the settlers who now occupy the houses they stole from us, we will claim to be widows traveling to stay with our dead husbands' families in Murcia.

Walking along the riverbank, we pass a waterwheel and come to the abandoned fort where my father died during the rebellion. This time I don't stop. It's too painful to think he might be watching me turn my back on our homeland in exchange for an easier life across the sea.

I was with Baba when he manned the ramparts of the tower, relentlessly firing his harquebus at the enemy. Each time I passed him more ammunition, my heart sank at the sight of the dwindling supply of bullets and black powder stacked on the earthen floor. When it was clear there was no hope, he smuggled me out through a secret passageway leading to the water. He forced me to board a boat he had at the ready, a man waiting at the helm.

"You must go, Jariya. Your mother needs you."

I wanted to remind him how fiercely the women in our village fought against the soldiers. *Hadn't I earned the right to stay and die with him?* But I could see there was no chance my stubborn father would budge.

Today I have my own child to think about. I hope Razin is right and Fatima and I will be picked up in Almería by one of the many ships sent by the Ottoman Sultan and roaming the coast in search of those like myself. If we do reach Morocco, I'll find a place to settle in New Orgiva where my father's favorite flowers and herbs can flourish in a garden of remembrance.

The timing of the *Vijita* troubled me. *Had Jariya's separation from Razin been permanent? Would something similar happen to me and Mico, now that he'd decided to turn himself in?*

I spotted Luis on the platform, self-assured as ever in a dark green suit, his brown hair parted carefully to the side. He took my suitcase and scanned my face. "Your eyes are red. Is something wrong?"

"It was hard, letting Mico go to the police station alone. He should have someone with him."

"He'll be fine. One of my associates will be present at his interview. So far the evidence is purely circumstantial."

I wasn't so sure. Justice was as likely to misfire as hit the mark. DNA testing in the US prison system was proving some innocent.

Luis drove to the old quarter where we stopped for lunch. I sipped my iced tea while he took a healthy swig from his glass of beer. "It's a good sign that Judge Rubio wants to interview all of Saleema's friends and colleagues. If they become flesh and blood to her, she may begin to trust their testimonials and ultimately decide to release Ms. al-Garnati."

On the street outside the restaurant, Alcábez gave me an awkwardly delivered hug. "When this is over we'll get you your citizenship papers. It's usually a simple procedure." He winked and we shared a laugh.

With Luis at the wheel driving south toward La Alpujarra, I was finally able to relax and enjoy the open sky and the cloud formations hovering over the approaching foothills. The countryside, with its Moorish ruins and ancient aqueducts, increasingly felt like my own.

Suddenly, flashing lights from the rear cast a flicker inside our car. I was hoping it was local law enforcement, which might be easier to deal with, but when they exited their vehicle the Guardia insignias on the navy blue uniforms of the two officers were unmistakable.

As Luis pulled over, I saw him tap 112 on his phone, the equivalent of 911 in the US. He leaned over and spoke softly. "They're wearing stolen uniforms. The dark blue is for ceremonies only. We need to stall until the real officers arrive."

He handed the officer his license when requested. "I'm a practicing attorney, registered with the Colegio de Abogados."

"Get out of the car. You're driving a stolen vehicle. We're taking you in on suspicion of theft."

The Guardia impersonators dragged Luis and me out of the Mercedes.

As one of them began to push me into their cruiser, I resisted, standing my ground until the closest car in oncoming traffic was more than a hundred yards away. Then I dropped to the ground, simulating a dead faint that put me over the white line into the path of oncoming death. There seemed no other choice than this potentially deadly and public one.

Brakes screeched as the lead car skidded to a stop, creating an instant jam on the highway. Horns blared and drivers shouted in frustration. Hearing the wail of approaching sirens, our would-be kidnappers backed off and made their exit, tires squealing.

The real police were initially reluctant to believe our story about the fake cops who tried to abduct us. They were on the verge of taking us in for creating a public nuisance, when Luis produced a photo of the men in their stolen uniforms that he'd taken with his phone. "They were after my friend," he said. "She's a famous journalist. Maybe they wanted a ransom from her publisher."

I was too shaken by my narrow escape to embroider on Luis's clever lie but I assumed he knew what he was doing.

The older, heavyset officer arched his eyebrows. "Journalists are rarely targeted for financial gain," he said, pulling out a cloth handkerchief to wipe the sweat from the late afternoon sun off his brow. "I assume a story you're working on has touched some nerves. Try to stay out of trouble and have a nice day."

Luis was shaking with anger as we sat in his unmoving car and waited for our frayed nerves to settle down. "Did you tell anyone about our travel plans?"

"Only Mico." The words came out automatically. The rest of my brain was replaying flashbacks of lying prostrate on the highway, my heart pounding with fear as the ground trembled with onrushing cars.

"Well someone knew exactly where to find us. When we meet with Judge Rubio I'll alert her to the possibility that an employee of the court, someone who knows her schedule, may be working for the Cisneros Society."

I was simply happy to be alive.

# Chapter Thirty

It was late afternoon when Luis and I reached Celia's house. The door to the silkworm shed opened and my cousin emerged, deep in conversation with a tall woman in a business suit accessorized by a necklace of small gems. A leather briefcase dangled from her hand and a tortoise-shell barrette held her upswept auburn hair in place. "I knew the silk industry was reviving in La Alpujarra," she said. "But not how much hard work is involved."

My cousin introduced Judge Patricia Rubio de Martínez, who expressed her pleasure at meeting me and Luis. "Your reputation as an excellent attorney precedes you, Señor Alcábez. And Celia has already told me a lot about you, Alienor." Her warmth was disarming, as I was sure it was meant to be.

"Now that we've met, let's take a look at where the explosives and the map were found." Having broken the ice, the judge was all business.

Celia led us into the house, which looked in good order considering how much damage had been done during the raid.

"Your Honor, I'm glad to see you've worn sensible shoes. You're going to need them."

Although the judge's eyes widened at the sight of the open trapdoor in the bedroom closet, she descended the ladder without hesitation. We followed Celia into the section of tunnel roped off by the police.

"This is where they found the Semtex," Luis said.

Judge Rubio opened the flap of her briefcase and removed an eight-by-ten photograph that she proceeded to compare with her own observations of the scene. "If I were a terrorist, I'm not sure I'd leave incriminating evidence in such an obvious place. Why not hide it?"

"Your Honor, that's an excellent question," Luis observed. "The night before the raid, someone broke into a deserted house connected to the tunnels. My theory is that the evidence was planted at that time, for the express purpose of incriminating Saleema al-Garnati."

"You may entertain all the theories you want, Señor Alcábez. It is the unvarnished truth I'm after. And your client's fingerprints were found on the explosives."

"Something that everyone in Spain knows, thanks to whomever chose to leak this information to the press."

Judge Rubio smiled thinly. "I'm aware of how this case is being exploited in certain circles, Señor Alcábez. You can be assured it will not affect my impartiality."

I was impressed by how directly Luis spoke his mind to the judge and her willingness to listen and respond without pulling rank on him.

Celia opened the door to the *Library of Khalud*, the one cared for by Saleema's family. The shelves were empty.

The judge's brow creased with displeasure. "Were all the libraries emptied by the Guardia?"

"No, your Honor, only this one."

The judge got out her cell phone. "The reception here isn't good but I assure you that as soon as I return to my hotel in Almendrales, I will order the Guardia to return each and every book they confiscated to its proper location within twenty-four hours."

Celia's eyes glowed with gratitude. "We're most obliged, Judge Rubio."

Judge Rubio nodded thoughtfully. "You're a tightly knit community. Do many of you know Saleema al-Garnati well enough to speak to her character?"

"Yes, many of us are eager to speak on her behalf," Celia answered.

"Excellent. I'll return tomorrow at noon and conduct the interviews in the presence of your attorney."

Her Honor toured a few of the libraries and I was surprised at how knowledgeable she was about some of the more ancient texts. She seemed overwhelmed that such a place as Zahara existed. At one point she said, "These books belong not only to Spain but to the entire world." This reinforced my impression that she would, at the very least, be impartial and dismiss the distorted version of our activities spread by the sensationalist press and the allies of the Cisneros Society.

When the time came for the judge to leave, Alcábez seized the chance I knew he'd been waiting for. "Your Honor, please let me accompany you back to your car. There's an urgent matter we need to discuss."

We spent the night at Celia's, me in the spare bedroom and Luis on the couch in the living room. We stayed up late, mainly because he wanted to know what I'd discovered about the Cisneros Society that almost got us killed on the highway. "Desperation in an adversary is a good sign," he commented, "if one survives to tell the tale."

Half asleep at breakfast, I became more awake with each word overheard from my attorney's early morning call with his wife. "I'm feeling hopeful, *querida*. Judge Rubio is conducting a thorough investigation. And when I told her word has leaked out about our meeting with her, she agreed to look into who from her support staff might be responsible."

Alcábez had neatly avoided telling Felicia about the frightening experience on the road from Granada to Almendrales. I wasn't one to criticize, since I'd no intention of sharing certain events with my editor or my dad until I saw them in person.

The judge wasn't due back until noon. Maybe I could use the time to throw some words together. I unzipped my notebook to document the events of the past few days.

An hour later, Celia stuck her head in the doorway. "We're having a meeting in the Common Area to prepare for the interviews with the judge. Why don't you and Luis join us?"

"Sure."

We need your perspective," Celia explained. "Not everyone sees Saleema's role in our situation in the same light. It was devastating to be detained by the police and have our security and privacy compromised."

The three of us migrated down to the tunnels and joined the Librarians in the Common Area, where the atmosphere was thick with anxiety and discussion was already underway.

"I wish she was here to defend herself but it is a fact that during the past year Saleema has grown increasingly upset about what she sees as the persecution of Muslims in Spain and around the world." It shocked me to hear Talvir of all people say this. After all, it was Saleema who had convinced him to come all the way from India to help Zahara's cause.

Reinaldo from the *Library of Babel* was the first to respond to Talvir. "You may be right about Saleema's anger, which in my opinion is justified. But we're talking about an artist who expresses herself in clay, not violence."

"If there's one thing I've learned it's that people are complex," Abram Capeluto said. "Based on Talvir's observations, we need to hope for the best and prepare for the worst."

"That's ridiculous!" Celia protested. "Someone doesn't change overnight from a sweet and caring individual into an unfeeling terrorist."

"We should let logic, not emotion, guide us," Reinaldo insisted.

The back-and-forth continued. Both Talvir and Reinaldo were adamant about refusing to vouch for Saleema to the judge. "How can I defend her when so many questions remain unanswered?" were Talvir's exact words.

Suneetha bint Hasan, the soft-spoken woman who looked after the *Library of Falsafa and Bina*—the terms for philosophy and wisdom in Arabic and Hebrew—spoke of all the kindnesses Saleema had showered on her colleagues, including cooking for those who fell ill and dusting and rebinding books not officially in her care.

Celia thanked Suneetha and went on to say, "This whole thing looks like a setup designed to break us apart. Everyone knows that Saleema is a potter. Someone left the Semtex for her to find, knowing she would mistake it for a block of clay and pick it up. That would explain the fingerprints."

"I hadn't thought of that," Talvir admitted.

At that point, Celia introduced Luis Alcábez. "We're lucky that Alienor's lawyer has come to our aid."

"Your legal situation is perilous but not hopeless," Luis said. "No crime was actually committed and I am hoping we can prove to the judge that the evidence against Saleema was planted."

Reb Hakīm had been patiently awaiting his turn and now spoke with calm authority. "If you do not realize how perilous a situation we're in, after the publicized raid by the Guardia and the fracture of our unity in the face of these terrorism charges, there isn't much I can say. Therefore I'm going to assume this group has come to its senses and once again ask your permission to invite Stephan Roman, a member of the World Heritage Committee, to inspect Zahara."

"And if Saleema is convicted? Will the Committee consider us for Heritage site status then?" Talvir's question was a good one.

"This is our opportunity to emancipate priceless cultural artifacts held under lock and key for too long, and introduce them to the people of Spain and the entire world," the Reb answered. "I believe Saleema's name will be cleared. Regardless of that, now that Zahara's existence is public knowledge and our enemies are still active in trying to discredit or, God forbid, destroy us, the Committee should move quickly to protect all that is in our care."

I understood his logic, even if *regardless of that* was a cold phrase to use when talking about the fate of an innocent woman.

After Talvir threw up his hands in surrender and Reinaldo nodded his assent, Reb Hakim raised his hands to quiet the buzz of discussion. "Those in favor of Mr. Roman's visit, please say aye."

The vote was a unanimous yes and Celia walked over to shake the Reb's hand. "We haven't always seen eye to eye but you've worked tirelessly on behalf of safeguarding what we all value and love. Thank you."

The Common Area filled with murmurs of agreement, including my own. Celia put her hand on her heart to acknowledge the emotion of the moment. "Okay, everyone," she said. "We need to set up a place for the judge to work. If you haven't yet written a statement for her to review, make sure you get it done before your interview."

While we waited for Judge Rubio to convene the proceedings, I passed the time working in my notebook, rendering yet another version of my family, this one as complete as possible. I added as much as I could to the Siddiqui side, starting with Jariya and leading up to the birth of Ja'far around 1920. Most of the Siddiqui's time in Morocco seemed destined to remain a mystery.

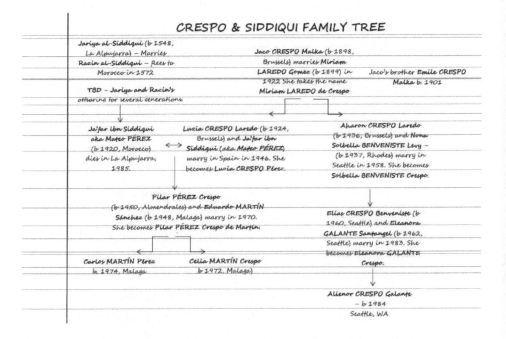

### CRESPO & SIDDIQUI FAMILY TREE

Jariya al-Siddiqui (b 1548, La Alpujarra) – Marries Razin al-Siddiqui – flees to Morocco in 1572

Jaco CRESPO Malka (b 1898, Brussels) marries Miriam LAREDO Gomez (b 1899) in 1922. She takes the name Miriam LAREDO de Crespo

Jaco's brother Emile CRESPO Malka b. 1901

TBD – Jariya and Razin's offspring for several generations.

Ja'far ibn Siddiqui aka Mateo PÉREZ (b 1920, Morocco) dies in La Alpujarra, 1985.

Luzia CRESPO Laredo (b 1924, Brussels) and Ja'far ibn Siddiqui (aka Mateo PÉREZ) marry in Spain in 1946. She becomes Luzia CRESPO Pérez.

Aharon CRESPO Laredo (b 1936, Brussels) and Nona Solbella BENVENISTE Levy – (b 1937, Rhodes) marry in Seattle in 1958. She becomes Solbella BENVENISTE Crespo.

Pilar PÉREZ Crespo (b 1950, Almendrales) and Eduardo MARTÍN Sánchez (b 1948, Malaga) marry in 1970. She becomes Pilar PÉREZ Crespo de Martín.

Elias CRESPO Benveniste (b 1960, Seattle) and Eleanora GALANTE Santangel (b 1962, Seattle) marry in 1983. She becomes Eleanora GALANTE Crespo.

Carlos MARTÍN Pérez b. 1974, Malaga

Celia MARTÍN Crespo b 1972, Malaga)

Alienor CRESPO Galante – b 1984 Seattle, WA

Celia's fingers lightly touched my arm. "It's a beautiful tree, Allie. I only wish the leaves represented more of the living."

I swallowed and said, "You would have loved Eleanora, my mother."

"I'm sure I would have. And my grandparents would have adored you."

After a shared pause of remembrance, Celia asked me to help her with the silk harvest. "We need to keep the business going. Otherwise, there's no electricity and no food on the table."

"I'm game," I said. This would be a welcome diversion from worrying about my upcoming testimony before the judge.

Inside the production shed, Celia showed me three large metal basins, each filled with white cocoons floating in brown liquid. "We'd better get to work before the water cools down. I hope you're not squeamish."

Careful to avoid spillage, we transferred one of the bowls to a metal table next to a contraption my cousin said was a spinning machine.

"We use the ancient Chinese method. First, we boil the cocoons with the pupae inside, so they won't turn into moths and break the continuous strands of silk they produce. The heat also softens the cocoons, allowing us to unwind the threads."

My cousin checked my face for signs of shock and saw enough to prompt an explanation. "The pupae are already in a comatose state so I doubt they feel anything. And if we let them live, they would only have twenty four hours left, since they die shortly after mating."

While reflecting on this sad reality, I watched Celia swirl a three-inch straw brush through the water. When she pulled the brush out, some threads and their cocoons came along for the ride and she held them high above the basin. Firmly grasping the filaments in her fist, she shook the cocoons back into the water and wound the raw silk around her hand.

"Now watch as I feed these into the spinner." She threaded the combined strands into an eyelet attached to a rod on the machine and pushed down on a foot pedal. The machine began turning, unwinding threads from the cocoons in the basin and wrapping them around its reels at a steady pace.

"Who taught you how to do this?"

"You met Rushd al-Wasim, our Librarian of Crafts and Animal Husbandry, in the Common Area on the day we swore you into the clan. His mother Suna, having no daughter of her own, passed her silk-making knowledge down to me before she died."

"Knowledge that originated with Idris al-Wasim?"

"Yes, without Rushd's ancestor Idris and the silk business he moved here from Granada in the sixteenth century, our community would never have survived."

I told Celia about the friendship I'd witnessed between Idris al-Wasim and Hasdai the Seer and how Jariya had joined them in rescuing Morisco children from King Phillip's soldiers. When I mentioned Jariya's marriage to Razin Siddiqui, my cousin laughed with delight. "You have to tell Pilar about all the romance that runs through our veins. She has already decided to forego taking any vows. Who knows? This might draw her back into the world."

I could understand Celia wishing that Pilar would rejoin society. As someone who up until recently felt like an alien stranded here on earth, I knew how attractive withdrawal could be.

I was assigned the job of feeding the machine each time she gathered a new batch of filaments. The rhythm of the task and the coordination of our movements soothed my jangled nerves and slowed down time in a pleasant way.

Suddenly Celia's hands stopped moving. "Do you think I said something to Dr. Amado that hinted at the existence of the tunnels, or did he come here knowing about us already?"

I ran the last of my threads through the machine before answering. "Are you looking for a way to blame yourself, Celia?

That's not a good idea. We know Amado blackmailed the Díaz family and by the time he showed up at your house, his plans were already in motion. You discussed silkworms and sericin with him, that's all."

"I guess you're right. But I can't help feeling guilty about my lack of discretion." She shook her head sadly. "There are times when all we can do is accept what happens and move forward."

After that we steadily worked in tandem, lost in our own thoughts.

# Chapter Thirty-one

"Ms. Crespo, please be seated."

Judge Rubio presided at a plywood table supported by three sawhorses and covered with documents. This improvised bench was positioned in the center of the Common Area, a hub around which the circular space revolved and an apt metaphor for the power wielded by the judge. Her Honor's impressive black robe complemented the dark suit and red tie worn by her stenographer.

I sat next to Luis, both of us facing the magistrate. He smiled. She did not.

"I see you've brought your laptop, Ms. Crespo. Please be aware that our interview is private and confidential and can only be shared with the parties to the proceedings. If you publish any details of this investigation in any form you will open yourself to prosecution for willfully interfering with the process of justice."

Her stern formality was a sudden shift from the judge's initial cordiality. I couched my response carefully. "I understand, your Honor. I have no intention of taking notes during our interview. There is, however, something on my laptop that I think you should see."

Judge Rubio fixed an inquiring gaze on Luis. "Señor Al-cábez, are you aware that I am required to share any new evidence with the public prosecutor, who has the right to be kept informed of the progress of my investigation?"

"Yes, your Honor."

"Then let us proceed."

The judge waited patiently while I tapped some keys and turned the screen to face her. I clicked Play, hoping the video would get a much better reception from her than it had from Dr. Amado's pals at the Valley of the Fallen. This version was longer and contained more damning evidence.

Judge Rubio watched impassively, her hands folded on the table. When Dr. Amado's tirade began, she leaned forward, her eyes glued to his livid face as he ranted: "I can't wait to see how these kikes and kebab lovers turn on each other after a week spent rotting in jail." Throughout the rest of the playback, the judge shook her head rapidly, as if attempting to shake off his vile words. I knew the feeling.

"Ms. Crespo, how did you gain possession of this video?"

"I copied the clip from a much longer recording made by the security cameras here in Zahara, your Honor. The remaining footage is backed up on a server and can be made available to you."

"This is an important piece of evidence regarding the murder of Carlos Martín and I will pass it on to the judge who is assigned to that case. The video also has some bearing on the matter at hand, in that it proves there are some who seek to use the accusations of terrorism against Saleema al-Garnati to advance their agenda."

Encouraged by her remarks, I told Judge Rubio how Dr. Amado had blackmailed Carmen Díaz into giving up Zahara's location.

The judge sat back in her chair and frowned. "Thank you for this new information. I *will* be interviewing Ms. Díaz myself and I will take all evidence under careful consideration when making my judgment on whether the Crown should prosecute Saleema al-Garnati." She rifled through some papers and found what she was looking for.

"Ms. Crespo, I've read the written statement you submitted about your time in Spain and, in particular, your interactions with the Librarians here in this place you call Zahara. Tell me, how well do you know Saleema al-Garnati?"

"Your Honor, I met her once at a memorial service and community meeting. She spoke very sensibly about the need to protect Zahara from outside hostility."

"Have you at any time suspected that she might be planning a terrorist attack?"

"No, your Honor. She is a craftsperson with a highly developed aesthetic sense. A creator of beauty, not a destroyer."

"Have you at any time suspected that a member or members of this community might be engaged in terrorist activity?"

"No, your Honor. Absolutely not. The Librarians have devoted themselves entirely to preserving the breadth of knowledge accumulated during and after the time of the *Convivencia*, an important part of Spanish history that is also of value to the entire world."

"Thank you for your cooperation, Ms. Crespo. That will be all."

I was relieved to be dismissed so quickly. Luis walked me out and gave my hand a warm squeeze before heading over to the *Library of Tif'eret and Jamal*, where the others awaited being summoned to occupy the hot seat.

"Has Talvir Singh been interviewed?" I called after him.

Luis gave me a thumbs up. "Yes. And he wants to see you right away."

The door to the Control Room had been reattached to its hinges and opened easily at the touch of my thumb. Inside, the only signs of the recent ransacking were some broken knobs on the video switcher. Talvir swiveled around in his chair to face me. "You've got an external hard drive that belongs to us," he said. "I also heard that you put it to some good use. Maybe now is the time to – "

He broke off when he saw my alarmed expression. I was picturing the rented Outback being driven around by some sightseers, the metal box I had hidden still neatly tucked beneath the car jack in the trunk.

The IT expert listened to my account of what had happened on the day of the raid, how I'd removed the drive from the video recorder, and the events that followed. "I doubt we'll get the drive back," he said. "But having you here safe and sound is worth a dozen Samsung T3s. Besides, we upload everything to a secure location in the Cloud."

"I wish you'd told me that."

"I'm sorry. We were extremely busy on the day Celia showed you around."

"You told Luis you wanted to see me?"

"Right. I think I know how we can prove Saleema's innocence."

"Then you *do* acknowledge she could have been framed?" Celia had joined us.

"Of course," Talvir said. "It's a strong possibility that so far lacks evidence to back it up. If the Cisneros Society was responsible for planting the Semtex, we need access to their website and other communications in order to be sure."

"Isn't that something the judge can accomplish with a subpoena?" I asked.

"Going through legal channels could take more time than we have, especially if we want to stay ahead of the Society's plans to discredit us."

Celia leaned over Talvir's shoulder to look at his computer screen. "What have you cooked up?"

He indulged a self-satisfied smile. "Since the Cisneros Society's name fails to come up in any search results on the Internet, I'd say they're using a VPN to maintain secrecy."

"Which means?" Celia looked perplexed and so was I.

"It means they have their own hidden Virtual Private Network running parallel to the public one. All their data flows through encrypted tunnels no one else can see."

"Like *our* tunnels were before the Society and their friends in the Guardia broke in."

"Touché, Celia. And if we're going to breach their defenses, first we need to know the physical location of their email server, which is connected to the VPN using a router. Once we've hacked into the router, we can install software that intercepts their traffic. We'll be able to read their messages and better yet, modify them."

"How do we find out where their email server is?" Celia asked.

"That's the tricky part. Isn't your father a member of the Cisneros Society? I heard that he's come over to our side."

"How in the world can we trust him?" Celia's voice rose in distress. "A few days ago, he invaded the Charterhouse, scared the Prioress and accused my mother of harboring my brother's murderer."

"That was before I convinced him that it was Dr. Amado who issued the order to kill Carlos. Eduardo said he's decided to stay with the Society long enough to help you get clear of the bogus terrorism charges. Isn't that proof enough that he's changed?"

Doubts crowded in, contradicting my hastily spoken words. Maybe I was being naïve. Full-blown fascists don't turn on their brethren overnight based on one good deed. Unless Eduardo, who had lost his own father to the left and now his son to right wing zealots, was honestly sick of the cycle of violence. He'd been convincing when he broke down at the bus stop. Was it a temporary conversion? People backtracked from high moral stances all the time.

"What harm can it do to ask him to tell us where the Society keeps its server?" Talvir had a good point.

"Which one of us should make the call?" I asked.

"It's my dad. I'll do it."

After Celia left, taking her cell up to the house to get reception, Talvir asked me, out of the blue, "How about a game of cards?" He was already dealing, so I agreed. It's amazing how a few hands of Shanghai Rummy can take your mind off things. Soon I was losing big-time.

"So Talvir, what brought you here? I'm sure you could be making a bundle in the corporate world."

"So my parents thought." He smiled ruefully. "Their mistake was to bring me up to honor the teachings of a holy book, the *Guru Granth Sahib*, and respect the right of every person to follow their faith. A true Sikh will stand by those who fight for what is rightfully theirs. When Saleema told me about Zahara the die was already cast."

Talvir was in the midst of telling me how his family came to terms with his decision to come to Spain, when Celia reported back, mixed emotions flickering on her face. "It was strange, talking with my dad so openly, after all these years of keeping my mother's whereabouts a secret. But he *does* want to help. He told me the email server is in the back room of *Cine Superba.*"

Film credits rolling on a screen in a conference room replayed in my head. "That's the company that produces propaganda for the Cisneros Society. They do good work, I'm afraid."

"Right. I wish my father could tell us more. Unfortunately, he says he's been locked out of the Society's more sensitive communications since the incident at the Valley of the Fallen."

"My fault and I'm surprised they let him off so lightly," I said. "If the StandUp party weren't so popular with their alt-right supporters, I think the Society would get rid of your dad altogether."

Celia nodded glumly. "I confess to hoping he stays safe. By the way, he said he has a lot of respect for you, Alienor."

I wasn't sure how to react to this compliment, given the ambiguous nature of its source.

Talvir, however, was looking pleased. "I know exactly how we can get to them. But we'll need someone in Granada." He collected our playing cards and shuffled them into a neat stack, like the game was already over and we'd won.

"It sounds risky," I said. "Why can't you hack their server from here?"

"Because I'm not a TV actor pretending to perform miracles on my keyboard." Was that irritation I detected in the tech expert's normally patient voice? "In real life," Talvir continued, "someone has to plug in a device loaded with software that cracks the password on the server and then installs itself. Once that's done, everything can be run remotely."

"My father did say he'll continue to help," Celia said. "Maybe this is a job for him."

Talvir reached for his jacket. "I'll go," he said. "Eduardo's done more than enough and like you said, he's been shut out and is probably under suspicion. I've already had my session with the judge and since I'm not needed here, I'm the logical choice."

# Chapter Thirty-two

I awoke the next morning determined to get serious about the story I'd promised Todd Lassiter. With their decision to go public, Zahara might soon be a household word in Spain. I'd better get on with it if I wanted to publish an exclusive. I already had the first two lines:

Hidden in a salt mine in the high foothills of the Sierra Nevada, a national treasure has survived the turmoil of centuries. If all goes as planned, Zahara will soon be revealed to the world and designated as a World Heritage site.

My cell rang with a call from someone whose ID got my full attention.

"Eduardo, how are you?"

"Excellent, thank you." He sounded a little breathless. "I have some good news but not much time to talk, so listen carefully. Yesterday, Inspector Fernández received an anonymous call. He was told where to find the body of a well-known criminal, Mauro Torres, in the woods surrounding the Valley of the Fallen. It was suggested that he pass this information to the police in El Escorial, along with a request that they fax the corpse's fingerprints to him in Granada. It was also suggested that Fernández compare these fingerprints with any found at the scene of my son's murder.

"Today, the unnamed caller checked back with the Inspector and was thanked profusely for his help. One of Mauro's fingerprints was a perfect match for a print found on the handle of a knife retrieved from a stream a mile from Celia's house. There was no blood but when they tested the blade they found Carlos's DNA. Mico Rosales is in the clear and will soon be released."

Mauro must have taken off his gloves and disposed of them before throwing the knife into the stream. The knife he'd used to cut off Carlos's thumb. Before I could frame a response that would not bring up this horrific image, Eduardo hung up. I was very grateful to him for what he'd done in view of the intense pain and guilt he justifiably felt and the hot water he'd be in if the police identified him as the caller.

I wished I could be there to see the look of relief on Mico's face when Inspector Fernández clapped him on the back and said he was free to go. Suddenly my day was a lot brighter.


Stephan Roman arrived in the afternoon, sent by the World Heritage Committee. It looked like the world was determined to shine its light on Zahara. This impression was strengthened by the sight of the photographic equipment Mr. Roman brought with him, which included a powerful flash attachment.

"I hope you're aware of how light can damage our fragile books and manuscripts," Celia warned him.

"Of course, of course, Ms. Pérez. The flash is only for taking photos in the tunnels."

"As you'll see, we have a perfectly good lighting system," she informed him.

I was tempted to ask if he'd been expecting a primitive burrow teeming with rabbits.

Stephan Roman was British and his thick sweater and sturdy boots defied the warm spring weather. It was easy to picture him hiking over moors and beaches at all times of year.

Talvir had double-checked Roman's credentials and it was time for me and Celia to take the scholar down to the Libraries. Upon entering the tunnels, he paused to admire the murals on the tunnel walls and how cleverly the arches had been painted to stretch into infinity. "One could believe these were real, leading us back in time."

Celia gave him a brief history of Zahara, its founders and design.

"How inspired Hasdai was to shape Zahara in the form of the Tree of Life, its tunnels being the branches leading to knowledge," Roman said. "I'm privileged to be here."

At Roman's request, we started with the *Library of Islamic Sciences*, or *Maktabat Aleulum* as it was called. Malik al-Bakri met us at the door. Malik's slightly hooded eyes gave the impression of shyness, until he raised his gaze and the magnetism of his inquiring nature pulled you in. He and Stephan spoke in Arabic and the excitement in their gestures made it easy to tell when their thoughts synchronized.

Roman was in his element. Instead of taking notes, he kept his hands free by speaking into a lavalier mic attached to his phone. Malik would hand him a book and the UNESCO scholar, who had donned surgical gloves, would examine it carefully before dictating a description in English:

"*Spiritual crafts and natural secrets in the details of geometrical figures*, written in Arabic in the ninth century by Abu Nasr al-Farabi. Born in Turkestan, died in Damascus, Farabi may have been the first to use mathematics to describe the complex geometric patterns created by Islamic artists. He was also the founder of Arab Neo-Platonism."

Celia chimed in. "We shelved Farabi's Arabic translations of Aristotle in another library. But this volume was meant to stay here, with the other scientific works."

Roman agreed. "During the Convivencia the boundaries between disciplines were blurred. It wasn't unusual for a philosopher to also be an accomplished mathematician, inventor, physician or musician – and almost all of them were poets."

As the Heritage Committee's representative continued his examination of the science library, my head spun trying to keep up. One book that Hakim was especially proud of was a treatise on natural plants by Ibn Al-Bautar, a sixteenth-century botanist from Málaga. A double border of red ink surrounded each page and the title was illuminated in blue, red and gold, forming a frame with plant motifs at the top.

"I know of only two other editions of this treatise," Roman said. "One is in Egypt and the other kept in the library of a monastery outside Madrid. Some fourteen hundred medicinal remedies are listed. This work was extremely influential throughout the world in its time."

Abram Capeluto met us at the *Library of Netsah* (Eternity in Hebrew) filled with Jewish holy books. He offered up the pride of his collection, a Hebrew bible with pages illuminated in burnished gold.

"This bible provides strong evidence of the *Convivencia*," he told Roman. "It's an example of how Medieval Jews, Muslims and Christians not only co-existed, they collaborated. The text is inscribed in Hebrew by a single hand, the gilding and floral motifs are Christian in design and the geometric patterns in the later pages are directly influenced by Islamic aesthetics."

Roman cradled the bible tenderly, the picture of an overwhelmed father. "To think that thousands of books and manuscripts such as these were burned. What a terrible loss."

He turned his incisive gaze on Celia. "Do you have any idea of the value of these manuscripts, Ms. Pérez? Last year a similar bible was purchased at auction by the Metropolitan Museum of Art for more than three million dollars."

She smiled knowingly. "They were priceless even before Sotheby's and other auction houses existed to hawk their wares, Mr. Roman."

Abram next produced a book on astrology, penned in Latin by Abraham Ibn Ezra and entitled *De Nativitativus*. Again Roman dictated into his phone's recorder. "Ibn Ezra was the apostle of Hispano-Arabic science among European Jews. The woodcuts in this edition are exquisite, as is the Gothic lettering. There is only one other known copy at the Biblioteca—" He stopped abruptly, looking down at his shoes.

"Water!" he said, in horror.

It was bubbling up through a grate in the concrete floor, sloshing around our ankles.

Celia bent down, checking the depth with her finger. "This is impossible. We've never had any groundwater seep in, not even during the rainy season. The nearest underground spring is almost a mile away. I don't understand."

Outside the Netsah library, water was flowing along the tunnel floor in a steady stream from the direction of the monastery. It was not deep, perhaps an inch or two, but if the flow kept up at its present rate it would rise and drown everything. Celia was already sprinting toward the source.

"I can't believe this!" Stephan exclaimed. "Shouldn't we call emergency services?"

"They'll never get here in time."

"I'll do what I can to move the books on the lower shelves to safety," he said.

"If it rises too fast, make sure you evacuate," I urged him, before running after Celia.

As soon as I reached the primitive tunnel leading to the monastery, I turned on my cell's flashlight and slowed my pace to a jog to avoid falling on the slick, muddy surface turning to liquid beneath my feet. The metal door guarding the entrance to the lower cells was closed and next to it water gushed from a dark green, three-inch diameter hose dangling from the wall.

Celia was already there. "No one's responding to the door buzzer. We'll have to use the main gate."

We backtracked and scrambled up the ladder into Celia's house, running outside and up the path to where the jeep was parked. The drive to the monastery gate took less than five minutes but felt unbearably long. I visualized the power of water sweeping through the tunnels, destroying everything in its path.

"It's an emergency!" Celia yelled in answer to the nun at the Charterhouse gate who calmly inquired about the reason for our visit. We ran through the outer courtyard, past the church, and toward the door concealing the staircase we had descended on the day of Carlos's memorial service.

Celia yanked the door open to reveal the upper length of a hose that ran straight down the wall adjoining the stairs. Together we grabbed hold of the rubber tubing and pulled upward. We met total resistance.

Celia abruptly let go. "We've got to follow the line to the source of the water."

The fat green snake was routed under the hedges surrounding a low, brick building. One of the windows had been raised a few inches, enough to allow the hose to pass through into the kitchen. It was hooked up to the sink.

We ran around and knocked on the thick front door. No answer.

The same nun who had admitted us through the gate appeared, looking alarmed. Celia ran toward her. "Water from the kitchen is flooding the tunnels underneath the monastery. We've got to get inside."

"What tunnels?"

"Please! Open the door and we'll do the rest."

The Sister sorted through a ring of keys attached to her waistband and let us into the kitchen. Never, before or since, has the squeak of a turning faucet sounded so sweet.

# Chapter Thirty-three

A somber group of Librarians congregated on the benches of the Common Area to vote on Stephan Roman's proposal to move Zahara's treasures to a safer place. The scholar had been dreadfully upset by the near disaster.

"Imagine what would have happened if no one had been down here. How long before there's another flood that gets out of control?" Stephan had acted on his own, contacting the University of Granada and eliciting an offer of temporary storage from the School of Library Science.

"It will take UNESCO close to a year to build or remodel a permanent home for the books and officially recognize Zahara as a world heritage site. In the meantime, we can raise funds to build a public entrance to the tunnels that is, let us say, more user friendly."

He got a few laughs on that one. "Maybe we should add a rollercoaster and a cotton candy stand so the Americans will come," Reinaldo Luz said. "No offense, Señor Roman."

"None taken, since I'm British," our distinguished advocate assured the *Library of Babel* custodian.

"Why preserve the original site if there won't be any books left here for people to see?" asked Suneetha bint Hasan, the ever-serious Philosophy Librarian.

Roman put his palms together, a supplicant waiting to receive an answer from a higher power. "Perhaps we can re-purpose the underground libraries to showcase the authors, their accomplishments and life histories. We could commission portraits and sculptured busts, add murals depicting how scientists, philosophers and poets from the three Abrahamic faiths mingled and collaborated during the *Convivencia*."

The next question came from Malik al-Bakr, who had bonded with Roman over the treasures in the Islamic Sciences Library. "Moving our books and manuscripts will be a delicate enterprise. When do you propose we start?"

Roman smiled at this first sign of acceptance. "If the community agrees, I can arrange for packing supplies to be delivered tomorrow."

Reb Hakim held up a cautionary hand. "We have to consider that Zahara was flooded by someone who wants to scare us into moving the collection."

Abram Capeluto, the keeper of Jewish Holy Books, nodded in vigorous agreement. "Judging from what Alienor's told us, the Cisneros Society is embedded everywhere. It would be child's play for them to hijack a few trucks."

A murmur of concern circulated around the room and Roman waited for silence before resuming his pitch. "All of your fears are justified. This is why UNESCO approved my request to use emergency funds to cover security during the transfer. Two off-duty Guardia officers we can trust will ride with each vehicle."

"Guards or no guards, one thing we know for sure is that our adversary is ruthless." I was relieved to see the speaker was Talvir Singh, standing in the doorway, safely returned from his stealthy mission in Granada.

"Does the Society know Zahara has been nominated as a World Heritage site?" I asked.

"Yes, they do," said the IT expert. "I've seen enough of their emails and texts to be certain."

Capeluto ran his fingers through his silver beard, a gnome untangling his thoughts. "You're playing a dangerous game. If the Society catches onto your tricks they could easily feed you a trove of disinformation."

Talvir walked further into the Common Area, taking a seat between Celia and me before answering Abram's comment. "True, my friend. But everyone knows disinformation is a two-way street."

Stephan looked uncomfortable and Celia whispered something in Talvir's ear to shush him. Then, looking at the expectant faces around her, she put the question. "Are we ready to vote on accepting the Committee's nomination as a Heritage Site and their proposal that we move our books to the University of Granada?"

"I second the motion," Suneetha said.

The approval was unanimous, if a little grudging. As Grandma Nona would have phrased it in Ladino, *"better take one than I'll give you two later."* Celia added an extra "aye" on Pilar's behalf.

The meeting was coming to an end when Saleema al-Garnati made a surprise entrance. Her customarily animated eyes drooped in weariness and her face was not nearly as round as I remembered from before her detention by the Guardia. Celia sprang to her feet and ran over to embrace her friend. Others followed and someone started a round of applause.

When she could be heard above the din, Saleema made an announcement. "Judge Rubio has ordered all charges against me dropped. And yesterday, according to Luis Alcábez, arrest warrants were issued for Dr. Rodrigo Amado and Mauro Duarte in connection with the murder of Carlos Martín."

"Finally some justice!" Malik cried.

"Not until we find all the books they stole from my library," insisted Saleema.

While everyone talked at once, congratulating Saleema and telling her the judge had ordered the return of her books, Talvir signaled me he wanted to talk.

I followed him into the Control Room, where the gadgets were now as familiar as the silk-harvesting equipment Celia had trained me to use. I was more mechanically adept than I'd thought.

I must have laughed, because Talvir asked, "What's so funny?"

"Me and my self-imposed limitations."

"Would you rather suffer from overconfidence?" he asked, removing his laptop from its case. "If the Society wasn't so brash as to keep their server in a facility open to the public, I'd never have been able to hack their VPN server. Thanks to Eduardo, we now have full access to their communications, with the exception of their WhatsApp group, which Eduardo is keeping an eye on. The idiots forgot to delete his ID."

"So what are they up to?"

"I've been reading through Dr. Amado's emails. Have a look at this one, sent yesterday."

As I read the words on the screen, I heard them spoken with the fake sincerity typical of the doctor:

Dear and Faithful Comrades!

We will soon show our countrymen what true dedication to Spain's ultimate destiny means. Our message will reach into homes, offices and the halls of the powerful. Our reach will extend far beyond Andalusia. So we must be at our very best. We stand on the shoulders of those with the courage to reconquer our homeland and reclaim our heritage from the Muslim and Jewish invaders. This event will have reverberations around the world and be entered in the history books. Do not fail to join us when the call comes!

In solidarity,

Dr. Rodrigo Amado

"Just what the world needs. Another rabble-rousing despot waving the banner of false patriotism," Talvir muttered. "I found a half dozen messages basically saying the same thing. He's careful not to mention the time or place of the action. That will be broadcast to the WhatsApp group, at the last moment possible, giving us little or no notice beforehand."

"Great. We're no better off than before. How many people do you think have received these emails?"

"They use the blind copy field so there's no way to tell. It could be hundreds, although I doubt they number in the thousands."

"Still, so many more of them than us. Do you think they're planning to attack the trucks?" I asked.

"Let them try," Talvir scoffed. "They'd never dare openly attack the Guardia. As long as the vehicles have an escort, we'll be fine."

"Then what's the *event* Dr. Amado is so excited about?"

Talvir was tapping the down arrow on his keyboard, scrolling through the captured emails. "Good question. If I find more clues, I'll let you know."

"By now Dr. Amado knows Judge Rubio has made him a wanted man. That gives him a good motivation to stay out of the public eye."

"Or a reason to make one last stand," Talvir said. "We must maintain our vigilance."

The next day, Mico showed up without notice. He'd lost some weight and refused to talk about his experience in jail, other than to say he wanted to kiss the judge for freeing him. He was the same affectionate friend, more than willing to share the guest room at Celia's house with me. Evidently my hints about my *Vijitas* when we were together in Madrid had not turned him off.

"Isn't Mico a little long in the tooth for you?" my cousin joked.

"His teeth are fine, exactly the right length for nibbling a person's ear," I'd surprised myself by retorting. But with so much work to be done in such a short time, Mico and I had little time for that sort of thing.

Over the course of the next few days, we worked day and night with the Librarians to pack the books in accordance with Stephan Roman's exacting specifications. Each tome or manuscript was wrapped in clean tissue paper before being encased in bubble-wrap to lie flat in the box. We placed the heavier and larger volumes at the bottom and padded the empty spaces between them with newspaper to center the weight for safe handling.

We labored with a sense of urgency, thankful there had been no water damage. But no one whistled while they worked, far from it. As the shelves grew lighter the general mood became heavier. By the time the vans arrived, one would have thought the bulky boxes were coffins and the trucks hearses sent to carry them on their final journey.

We walked as a group through the tunnels, making sure no precious cargo would be left behind. After that there was nothing left to do but say goodbye.

Right before the UNESCO trucks pulled away, under armed guard as promised, Stephan – who had been acting like a cheerleader urging everyone on – gave a little speech.

"It may take decades for the connection with antiquity, shared hope and wisdom you embody to permeate your new home. But I have every reason to believe it will. Generations to come will benefit from their exposure to you."

I'm not sure the bibliophile was aware he'd addressed the books rather than us.

# Chapter Thirty-four

It was eight o'clock, close to nightfall, with only a few clouds drifting across the cobalt blue sky. The street lights in front of the Library Sciences building at the University of Granada were lit and the plaza was beginning to fill with students and the general public. It was reassuring to see two private security guards milling around. We were there for the opening of the *Convivencia Exposición*, hastily assembled by Stephan Roman and his helpers after the arrival of the books from Zahara. Because it was a gala affair, a few tuxedos and long gowns stood out amidst the more prevalent jeans and tank tops. An occasional headscarf bobbed within the crowd and I wished there were more. It would take a while before word got out that all were welcome here.

Mico and I hadn't seen each other for three weeks. He'd been busy attending to the notary business that paid his bills, while I was at long last writing at Celia's house without fear of interruption. I'd sent off part one of my story to Todd that morning and was sure it wouldn't disappoint. Well maybe a little, depending on what he'd been expecting. Best case scenario, he'd ask for a series of articles, giving me a chance to plug up the holes remaining in my investigation of the Cisneros Society.

For this important night, Mico had opted for black pants and a white shirt with a dark blue turtleneck beneath. He greeted me with mock horror at the high heels and Flamenco style dress I'd borrowed from Celia. If my mother was watching from heaven, then so much the better.

When I noticed he was holding something behind his back, Mico danced away before presenting the bouquet of flowers with a flourish. "In honor of our continued friendship and myriad possibilities for the future. Tomorrow we'll certify your citizenship application. That is, if you still want to."

"Of course I do! How else can I keep tabs on you?"

We joined the line winding its way along velvet ropes toward the entrance to the exhibit. Most of the librarians were already inside, having worked feverishly to make all this happen.

The doors opened and as the line inched forward, I heard voices chanting from somewhere behind us. It sounded like a group of sports fans giving voice to their feelings after an exciting game. The commotion grew louder and Mico and I spun around. A troop of young men in close formation marched toward us, carrying torches over their heads that spewed fire. The words they bellowed came in clearly now: "You will not replace us!"

The demonstrators weren't close enough for me to be sure they wore Cisneros Society pins, but the sight of so many green camouflage shirts sent a jolt of apprehension through my chest. As they drew closer, their bodies and faces became surprisingly *less* distinct, blending together like Stormtroopers marching in old newsreels. They came to a stop parallel to where we stood. That's when I noticed that the carts they wheeled were covered with heavy canvas.

Mico tightened his grip on my hand. "What do you think they've got under those tarps?"

For a terrible instant I envisioned machine guns mowing down the crowd of well-wishers. Seconds later, Mico's question was answered by the torch-wielding marchers, who in unison whipped off the coverings. The carts were loaded with neatly packed books, their spines visible. The spaces between the volumes were packed with crumpled up newsprint. One spark was all it would take.

I looked around for the security guards. They seemed to have gone inside along with most of the crowd.

Dr. Amado held a book up over his head, haranguing his minions in a high nasal voice. "The time has come to set fire to these evil Qur'ans and show the world that Spain cannot be cowed into submission!"

He pointed to a teenager barely taller than the tripod he carried, camera attached. "You! Keep your hand steady! These pictures will instill fear of retribution in Muslims around the world. They must be taught a lesson."

Mico had already called 112 but it was all happening too fast. Angry murmurs circulated yet no one seemed willing to act.

"We have to intervene," I said, taking a deep breath and kicking off my heels in preparation. Mico grabbed me around the waist and wouldn't let go. "They could be armed. Let's wait for the police."

"Stop!" An elderly woman broke out of the waiting line, running in her ankle-high leather boots with surprising speed to confront Amado. "We've suffered enough under fascists like you. I lost two of my children to your heartlessness. You are not going to drag my country down again!" She spit in his face and placed herself in front of one of the carts defiantly.

Others from the crowd quickly followed her example, Mico and I among them. Soon all five carts were surrounded, total strangers having locked arms to protect books that most of them had probably never heard of, much less read.

Our adversaries stood frozen in place, while Amado continued to bellow commands, high-pitched as a screech owl. "Don't just stand there! Defend your posts! Carry out your mission! What are you, a bunch of *cobardes*?!"

With his purple face and distorted mouth Dr. Amado looked like he'd have a stroke any second. He continued to yell commands at his followers, which they ignored until the sound of police sirens startled them to life. Many of them fled the scene and Amado in sheer frustration grabbed a lit torch and ran toward the aging woman who'd led the charge against his men. He viciously pushed her out of the way and tried to thrust the burning stick into the cart. She screamed and the men on either side of her wrestled the torch out of the doctor's clawing hands, pushing him to the ground and pinning him down.

By now the two sides were attacking each other and the altercation blew up into a full-fledged brawl. If someone were to pull out a gun... TV images from the 2017 Charlottesville riot in Virginia invaded my mind as I watched a young man with a Swastika tattooed on his arm punch a middle-aged man in the face.

The Granada National Police arrived swinging their truncheons. They wore armor and helmets and did not hesitate to deliver rough justice to a few neo-Nazis so revved up they may not have realized who they were resisting.

The police handcuffed Dr. Amado and carted him off, along with a dozen of his crew.

I looked for Inspector Fernández and instead found Stephan Roman briefing someone whose nametag read *Inspector González.*

"These fanatics want to antagonize the Muslims of Spain and the entire world by burning their most holy books in public," Roman informed the policeman. "Their goal is to provoke a holy war that no one will win except the fascist politicians who are trying to scare the public into once again bringing a strongman to power."

González sighed. "From what I've seen the public has little interest in supporting crazies like these. We'll lock these up and others will come to take their place. In the meantime, Spain splinters like a dried out husk."

Saleema al-Garnati, came running out of the Library Science building. "Where are my Qur'ans? Are they safe?"

"Yes," said Stephan. "The university staff and students are carrying them into the building right now."

Saleema's eyes flashed. "It's a good thing I wasn't here when that beast of a man tried to burn them. I might have killed him."

"That's exactly the kind of reaction he was hoping for," I said.

She nodded bleakly. "I know. And his strategy would have worked. At the very least, riots would have been sparked in other countries, as happened when *Charlie Hebdo* published those blasphemous cartoons of the Prophet, blessed be his name."

Saleema went to help retrieve the Qur'ans and Mico and I made our way into the exhibit, determined to carry on.

The opening was a one-time event designed to celebrate the 'discovery' of the books. The main exhibit would be curated and presented in full next year. In the meantime, one main attraction had been chosen to occupy the display case in the center of the cavernous lobby. Under glass, a pair of thick

tomes lay open for viewing, one penned in Arabic and the
other in Hebrew. A printed description was mounted on an
easel beside them:

> *The Assemblies of Al Hariri, a Maqāmah written
> in Arabic by Al Hariri of Basra (1054–1122), contains
> fifty anecdotes of humorous social and moral commen-
> tary meant to entertain and educate. Composed in Saj',
> a form of rhymed prose interspersed with verse once
> memorized by scholars, the book is illustrated with min-
> iatures portraying thirteenth-century Muslim life.*
>
> *One hundred years later, Judah Alharizi wrote
> The Book of Tahkemoni (The Book of Wisdom or the
> Heroic) often referred to as the jewel of Hebrew Ma-
> qāmah, following the exploits of Hever the Kenite, a
> roguish trickster who is one moment a teacher and a
> beggar or adventurer the next. Within the text, Alharizi
> pays tribute to his Arab predecessor:*
>
> *Attend, all ye who Wisdom's walls defend. Wher-
> ever truth be run in all that men have said or sung,
> have you seen, heard, read, or tasted sweeter words than
> those of the master of rhymed prose, the Ishmaelite, that
> font of delight, right riddler, teller of tales who never
> fails, al-Hariri?*
>
> *These two exquisite manuscripts representing the
> Maqamat form were protected for centuries in the
> underground libraries of Zahara, and have now been
> united for public display. Together, they provide tan-
> gible evidence of the intensely creative, multicultural
> collaborations marking the period of medieval Spanish
> history known as La Convivencia.*

The chatter of the circulating guests bounced off the walls and high ceilings. Some browsed the photographs on the walls, the only way to view books so fragile they might never see daylight. A few were engrossed in examining a scale model, a fanciful construct in which the rudimentary concrete tunnels and reinforced libraries of Zahara were transformed into pristine hallways and drawing rooms more appropriate for a luxury hotel. I hoped Zahara's brave Librarians would be consulted and changes made before the ground of their new home was broken.

Celia came over with her father in tow. "I heard what happened," Eduardo said. "Thank goodness everyone's safe."

Seeing the two of them reunited gave me hope for other, more challenging and widespread reconciliations in the future.

Across the lobby, I spotted Inspector Fernández . I looked around for Mico and saw him cornered at the refreshment table by someone I assumed to be a client. I was on my way over to rescue him, when a flash of light coming from a doorway near the elevator caught my eye. I walked over to investigate.

"Abraham Abulafia, can you believe this?" said a disembodied voice.

There were two of them and in a matter of seconds they took physical shape in front of my disbelieving eyes. I recognized both men from portraits I'd seen in books kept in Reb Hakim's library. Ibn al-Arabī, the Sufi mystic and Abraham Abulafia, famous for his passion for the magical attributes of the Hebrew alphabet.

"Can I help you?" I asked, feeling foolish at once.

A distinct chuckle sounded inside my head, like a test tone calibrating a piece of equipment. Al-Arabī's intrusion into my psyche might have felt scary if his amusement hadn't been so infectious and made me laugh at myself for having asked so prosaic a question. I was also aware that if someone in the lobby looked over at me, they'd see a woman standing in a doorway talking to herself. I moved into the stairwell and the apparitions followed.

By this time my surprise had been swapped for intense curiosity and a feeling that at last I might learn the origin of my *Vijitas Lokas.*

*You're right, Alienor.* Abulafia's voice seemed deeper than Al-Arabī's, although the resonance came from within my own skull. I opened my mouth to reply and then closed it, sending a thought instead. *Why did you choose me?*

The famous rabbi hesitated and I supposed he was looking for a way to simplify his explanation. *Do you remember when you were a little girl and your mother appeared to you in a vision?*

*Yes. Did you send her?*

*No. Your gift is your own and no one can give or take it away. It was your receptiveness that we noticed. When we discovered the Crespo family's connection to Zahara, certain possibilities presented themselves. It was my friend, Ibn al-Arabī who suggested we enhance your visions – your Vijitas as you call them – to help you on your way. You did the rest.*

*After all this time, you decided to show yourselves. Why now?*

Footsteps announced someone coming down the stairs and one of the security guards appeared, walking smartly despite his overly husky build. Where was he when we needed him during Amado's crazy assault? I leaned against the staircase wall as casually as I could. "I hate crowds, needed a little peace and quiet."

He gave me a searching look and walked out into the lobby.

*He's one of them.* It was Al-Arabī this time. *Be careful.*

I followed the bulky guard out to the lobby. He was making a beeline for the glass case containing the *Maqāmahs* and he carried a holster at his hip that was definitely not empty. There were more security guards on duty than before the incident with Dr. Amado and his gang, but they had no reason to suspect one of their own. Would they listen if I shouted loud enough? All they'd see was one of their fellow officers being hounded by a crazy lady.

Out of the corner of my eye I saw Eduardo Martín talking with Stephan Roman. For the second time that night, I threw off my high heels. I ran over and grabbed Celia's father by the arm, pointing in the direction of the fake guard.

"I know him!" Eduardo said in a loud voice.

The intruder changed course, running toward the outside door.

Eduardo gave chase and by the time I got outside he'd already tackled the intruder on the lawn. As they struggled, the wild-eyed man managed to draw his gun. I ran over and kicked it out of his hand. They tussled until Eduardo finally pinned down his opponent.

"You're insane. He might have killed you." Inspector Fernández had recovered the gun and was rolling his eyes at my recklessness.

Stephan Roman said the only sensible thing to do was to end the celebration early. "We're going to need a better level of security," he said, the choicest understatement I'd heard since my arrival in Spain.

Mico brought me my shoes. "I can't leave you alone for a second."

"I hope you never will." I couldn't tell which one of us was more embarrassed. I didn't care, as long as the kiss we shared lasted a good long time.

Jariya was calling me. Still holding onto Mico, I went into the *Vijita*.

I'm rocking my baby on the porch of a house overlooking fields planted with vegetable seeds from back home. Like Razin said, the crops here in New Orgiva are irrigated by acequias, babbling with the sound of rushing water we delighted in as children, when we held hands and watched the channels of life-sustaining irrigation flow down the hills in La Alpujarra.

I've named my baby Razin Siddiqui, using my husband's surname in the hope this will bring him here to Morocco someday. And perhaps one of our descendants will one day return to Spain and the Siddiqui family will take its rightful place once more.

I took Mico's arm and we walked from the University to his apartment on Cuesta de la Victoria. It was a bit of a hike and on the way, I told him all about my *Vijitas*. When I got to the part about using my mother's magic words to make the visions stop, he laughed. "I knew you were special, just not how much."

That night we held each other in bed. The snuggling was more than enough. And in the morning, when I told him I'd gotten behind in my work, Mico cleared out some space in his home office.

"I need to send at least half the story to Todd this afternoon. And please don't let me forget to call my dad when he wakes up in Seattle, which should be about nine hours from now."

"Happy to oblige, ma'am. As long as you promise to tell him all about me."

Two days later, we paid a visit to the monastery, entering through the front gate with the Prioress's blessing. Mico carried a heavy parcel and we met Pilar at the visitor's lodge. Watching their joyous reunion, I felt relegated to the periphery of the intense memories they shared. I was tempted to turn away and leave them to it. Then I thought about Luzia being cast out of the family and how, because of me, she and Ja'far would now be included in our ancestral tree. It wasn't easy but I tamped down my jealousy and found room in my heart to be happy that their daughter and Mico had rediscovered their link.

When she and Mico were done catching up, Pilar gestured toward the package. "Is that what I think it is?"

Carefully she unwrapped the ancient tome and read the title on the wooden cover aloud, "*The Book of Zahara.*" The letters glowed with a soft light of their own.

"Legend has it the book contains a portal leading to other worlds," Pilar said reverently. "Do you think I should open it?"